CELUS-5
A Silver Ships Novel

S. H. JUCHA

Published by Hannon Books, Inc.
www.scottjucha.com

ISBN: 978-0-9975904-4-9 (e-book)
ISBN: 978-0-9975904-5-6 (softcover)

First Edition: March 2017

Cover Design: Damon Za

Acknowledgments

Celus-5 is the eighth book in *The Silver Ships* series. I wish to extend a special thanks to my independent editor, Joni Wilson, whose efforts enabled the finished product. To my proofreaders, Abiola Streete, Dr. Jan Hamilton, David Melvin, Ron Critchfield, and Pat Bailey, I offer my sincere thanks for their support.

Despite the assistance I've received from others, all errors are mine.

Glossary

A glossary is located at the end of the book.

-1-
Sojourn

"Black space," Teague declared, quoting his father's favorite expletive.

"Ser Racine, you've something specific for our attention," Captain Asu Azasdau said calmly, hiding his smile at the youth's unbridled exclamation.

"Apologies, Captain, we have anomalies," Teague said and shifted his telemetry board's view of the distant planet to the *Sojourn*'s massive holo-vid.

Captain Asu Azasdau and Willem, a self-aware digital entity (SADE) and the exploration mission's co-commander, turned to regard the display.

The *Sojourn*, Haraken's first explorer ship, was tasked with finding a new colony for the home world and had just entered the Celus system, making for the fifth planet outward from the star. This was the *Sojourn*'s maiden voyage. Willem and his fellow scientists selected this planet, over the other nineteen identified warm-water worlds, as having the optimum opportunity to support human life.

Celus-5 was still billions of kilometers away so optical telemetry was limited. But Teague Racine had a keen eye for resolving shapes within soft imagery, probably due to the extensive amount of time he spent underwater with his Swei Swee friends, the six-legged, claw-snapping, whistling aliens that his father, Alex Racine, had rescued.

<Black space,> Asu sent to Willem via his implant, the tiny Méridien comm device planted in his cerebrum.

<I couldn't have said it better,> Willem replied via his comm link, <although I've never used that specific expression.>

The captain and SADE stared intently at the object partially buried in the sands of an ocean shoreline. Despite the fuzziness, there was no mistaking the unique outline of a traveler. Nothing in the universe resembled the elongated seed-pod shape of the fighters used by the alien

Nua'll to devastate planets, as their giant sphere made its way across the galaxy.

"Ser Racine, you said anomalies ... plural," Willem reminded Teague, who might have been the son of the famous Alex Racine, but was still a sixteen-year-old journey crew member on his first expedition.

"Second image on the holo-vid, Willem," Teague replied. "This visual is taken a few kilometers farther south along the coastline. I'm referring to the polar directions in standard assignment of the ecliptic and solar rotation."

In the image, and not 50 meters apart, were the partial outlines of two more travelers, both nearly obscured under encroaching sands.

"I'd say they've been there for decades, at least, Willem," Asu said quietly.

"While I'm not in favor of random estimates," Willem replied, "if this was a prior stop by the Nua'll before the aliens encroached on the Confederation, it seems more likely that we should be considering a century or two, not decades."

"Ser Racine, widespread telemetry on the system, review all signal sources immediately," Asu ordered, suddenly concerned for the presence of danger.

"Anything specific, Captain?"

"Yes, a giant sphere."

Willem tapped into the *Sojourn*'s controller, which was serving Teague's board with telemetry data, so that he could analyze the imagery as well. While his avatar couldn't breathe a sigh of relief when he found no telltale sign of the Nua'll sphere, he was nonetheless greatly relieved.

"Nothing, Captain," Teague replied. "This was my second scan. I ran the original one when we first entered the system. I searched for bodies and ships. The only large round objects found were the star, planets, and moons. No other round objects."

"Good job," Asu acknowledged. He glanced at Willem for confirmation, and the SADE nodded his agreement, which drained the tension from Asu's shoulders.

"Any other anomalies to report, Ser Racine?" Willem asked.

"None at this time, Willem," Teague replied. "But as Dad would say, 'there's always tomorrow.'"

A reminder of the world-shaking events that Alex Racine had encountered and overcome in his brief twenty-year history with the Méridiens and Harakens was no comfort to Asu, Willem, or the rest of the crew stationed around the bridge. Everyone wanted to believe that, in this fashion, Teague was the polar opposite of his father, but the sight of long-buried travelers on the planet of the expedition's intended destination quashed that hope.

* * *

After Teague's shift, he approached a cabin door, one level down from the bridge, and it slid open at his approach, attesting to the fact that Ginny was constantly aware of Teague's position in the ship. It might have been unnerving to Teague, if Ginny hadn't been an integral part of his world since she had first arrived on Haraken, one of ten orphans brought from Sol, the Earth's system, by Julien and Cordelia.

"You're bubbling," Ginny teased Teague.

"No, I'm not. Well, maybe a little. Guess what I found on telemetry?"

"Three travelers buried along the shoreline of our intended target?" Ginny replied nonchalantly.

"What ... how?" Teague sputtered.

"Word gets around fast on this ship, youngling of the Star Hunter First," Ginny replied, calling him by the translation of Teague's Swei Swee name.

"Have the Swei Swee been informed of what we've found?"

"Everyone knows."

Ginny would have moved worlds to be with Teague on this journey, but it wasn't necessary. Not only humans and SADEs were aboard the *Sojourn* but Swei Swee too.

"What did the Swei Swee say?" Teague asked.

"They were extraordinarily silent on the subject. Maybe they'll talk to you."

"Let's go," Teague said and dived out of the cabin with Ginny hot on his heels.

The Swei Swee occupied a section on the third deck. Entry was through a 4-meter chamber enclosed at both ends by double sliding doors. The construction enabled the moistened air in the Swei Swee section to remain inside and not inundate the rest of the ship.

Teague and Ginny quickly passed through the isolation chamber to find the Swei Swee clustered in the common section, enjoying a meal of faux fish, a concoction first invented aboard the city-ship *Freedom* during the voyage from Libre to Haraken. To the delight of the Swei Swee, the high protein mixture could now be produced in varying fauna shapes and sizes from food stocks, much as Haraken meal dispensers served the humans aboard.

"Companions," Teague whistled.

"Teague," the four Swei Swee whistled in return, but when Ginny stepped from behind Teague's substantial stature, true hands dropped their meals on the low table, and the aliens rose on their six legs, bobbing softly.

<Little Singer,> the Swei Swee sent to Ginny.

<So you've heard what we've found,> Teague sent to the Swei Swee, including Ginny in the comm link. After any initial greeting with a whistle or warble, Teague made the effort to switch to comm implant communications so that his companions could continue to practice with their new technology.

Ginny activated the view screen behind Bobs A Lot, who twisted his eyestalks behind him to take in the screen, and downloaded the imagery of the first traveler Teague had shown the captain and Willem.

<Dark traveler,> Sand Flipper sent.

<It would appear so,> Teague sent in reply. <Willem thinks this was a previous stop of the Nua'll sphere.>

<People escape. Search endless waters,> Whistles Keenly added. Of the four Swei Swee, he was having the most difficulty with the implant, because the software wasn't accurately translating his thoughts, which

could be eloquently expressed in subtleties of whistles, warbles, and tweets. Both Teague and Ginny enjoyed his musical style when he spoke in his own language but refrained from tweaking the translation software app. It was beyond their capabilities. Whistles Keenly would have to wait for another session with Mutter, the Swei Swee's beloved Hive Singer.

<It's possible they did,> Teague acknowledged. <The People chose an ideal landing spot to escape their travelers and make it into the waters.>

<Let's hope the sea was welcoming,> Ginny sent.

<Yes, no hunters!> Bobs A Lot sent with urgency, which elicited a snapping of sharply pointed claws from Sand Flipper, Swift Claws, and Whistles Keenly.

<This is the other landing location,> Teague sent, switching the view screen to the image of the second landing site.

Bobs A Lot scuttled to the other side of the table, and sixteen eyeballs extended high on their stalks to stare at the dim outlines of two more half-buried travelers.

<Several hives,> Sand Flipper commented.

<Generations of younglings,> Swift Claws added.

<The images aren't clear, and that made it difficult to distinguish any dwellings on the cliffs,> Teague said. When the eyestalks shrunk halfway back into carapaces, Teague quickly added, <But we're still far away. As we draw closer, the dwellings may become visible.>

<Two or three hives. Many, many seasons of younglings. Cliffs covered with homes,> Whistles Keenly sent.

<What you're saying would be true, if there were no hunters on the land,> Ginny said.

The Swei Swee rose on their walking legs, alarmed by Ginny's thought, and sets of eyestalks swiveled from Ginny to Teague and back again

Teague sought to counter Ginny's statement and calm his friends. <There's no evidence of land hunters, but, again, we're too far away to determine that. It might be that the Swei Swee who escaped couldn't find the materials to build their houses, so they chose another location.>

The eyestalks settled down from their extended position, and legs were lowered to more comfortable positions.

<Nice save,> Ginny sent Teague privately. <I hope it's true, but who knows what the Swei Swee found on this planet.>

* * *

When Teague passed puberty, his interests changed. The sea no longer held his complete attention, and his thoughts were filled with concepts of other worlds and the aliens who might live there. And there were scientists who were engaged in the activities Teague dreamed of doing — Willem and his interstellar exploratory team.

At the same time, Renée de Guirnon, Teague's mother, was concerned by the lack of her son's social development. Teague's time was primarily spent in the company of his Swei Swee friends, and when it came to the question of her son's social skills, it was Renée's opinion that ruled over Alex's.

When Teague professed his interest in interstellar exploration and asked if he could work with Willem, Renée told her son, who already was tall enough to look her in the eyes, "As your father would say, I'll make you a deal. You enroll in one of Espero's schools, and I'll speak to Willem myself about giving you time to observe aboard the telemetry station."

The schools, of which his mother spoke, were primarily dedicated to new immigrants, which didn't endear Teague to the idea. His education could technically have been delivered through his reader and his implant, but rather than object he agreed.

True to her word, Renée set up weeks, when school was in recess, that Teague could visit Willem's observatory. More important, she got what she wanted for her Teague — time in the presence of other children.

What neither Alex nor Renée expected was the uproar that Teague's attendance in school caused among the young Swei Swee, and, in an extraordinary event, Alex and Renée found they had an unusual guest at their home one evening. They were relaxing on a couch when a whistle pierced the open window. The Swei Swee First waited outside, and rather than invite the leader inside, where he would be most uncomfortable, Alex stepped outside.

"The hive is unsettled," the First whistled. "The Star Hunter First's youngling has been absent from the waters for too long."

"Teague is attending school to learn many things, including about the worlds above us," Alex whistled in reply.

The Swei Swee leader kept two eyestalks on Alex, while the other two turned upward to gaze at the night's stars. "Four Swei Swee young want to be with your youngling," the First whistled.

"Where Teague goes, younglings don't whistle. They speak the Star Hunter's language and learn from books written in our words," Alex explained.

"Star Hunters whistle in the Swei Swee language; Swei Swee whistle in the Star Hunter language," the First riposted.

"That isn't going to be easy," Alex said, trying to think of a way to reason with the First.

"Destroying the world traveler wasn't easy. It cost the People many hives. The First asks the Star Hunter leader to make this possible."

When Alex agreed that he would try, the First extended his claws and Alex thumped them, acknowledging his intentions. The First whistled his approval, whirled, and scurried home to his mates.

What ensued was the focus of Terese, Emile, Mickey, and the SADEs to design a manner in which the Swei Swee young could communicate directly with humans, participate in their education, and journey to the stars.

There were fundamental problems to overcome for Swei Swee physiology before they could join a Haraken ship's crew. Their breath ways were in need of frequent moistening, and they whistled and warbled, which not everyone understood, much less were able to imitate to reply.

Fortune for the intrepid Swei Swee came in the guise of Emile Billings, whom Terese Lechaux, the planet's chief medical expert, had brought with her from New Terra, years ago. Emile was a renowned biochemist.

Emile studied the breath ways problem for months, deciding to use a nanites approach. The Méridiens had accomplished incredible feats with nanotechnology, applying what they called nanites to myriad tasks, and the Harakens had taken the technology even farther.

When Emile was ready to apply his solution, Swift Claws, Teague's closest Swei Swee companion, volunteered to be the test subject. The young adult Swei Swee entered a sealed chamber that Emile flooded with a mist of specialized nanites, which selected the cells of the breath ways for attachment. Within the mist, a second type of nanites bonded to those attached to the breath ways tissue and created tiny hollow cylindrical structures. The tubules acted as super-transpiration wicks, sucking molecules of water from the air to keep the breath ways moist.

Swift Claws stayed on land and out of pools for a week to ensure that there was no degradation in his breath ways tissue. Even though the experiment was a success, there was a second hurdle to surmount, which was communications.

This second incredible technological feat was solving the communications problem. In a delicate operation, Terese inserted a tiny implant through a hole in a Swei Swee's tough carapace between the four eyestalks, embedding the device into the brain.

Prior to the operation, it took extensive experiments to determine which part of the alien brain should receive the implant. The devices would probably never be used similar to the manner in which humans employed them with their numerous applications. Instead, the Swei Swee implant was designed primarily for communication and data capture from the aliens' sensory input.

Mutter, Cordelia, and Julien provided the translation software for both Swei Swee and crew, who could now communicate effectively with one another, without regard to converting thoughts into the receiver's language. The sender's bio ID identified the originator's language, and the receiver's implant apps handled translation, if it was necessary.

Again, the test operation went well, this time on Whistles Keenly. However, the next part was a bit trickier. The concept of communicating by thought was more foreign to the Swei Swee than humans could have imagined. It was Ginny who taught Whistles Keenly that she could sing to him in his mind, without a single note passing her lips.

When Whistles Keenly heard Ginny in his mind via his implant, he didn't register how it had gotten there and sought to accompany Ginny by whistling audibly. To stop the Swei Swee, Ginny placed her hands over his mouth parts and continued to sing via her implant. Whistles Keenly, not wishing to be rude, simply sang along with Ginny in his mind.

It was when Ginny played back her recording, via the implants, of the two of them singing together that Whistles Keenly understood what had happened. He bobbed up and down so enthusiastically that he strained some of the muscles in four of his walking legs. Along with Ginny, Whistles Keenly became a teacher of the other three journey crew members — Sand Flipper, Bobs A Lot, and Swift Claws.

During the final design stage of the *Sojourn*, Alex added a wrinkle when he asked the Assembly to consider allowing six journey crew members, Teague, Ginny, and four Swei Swee, to join the expedition. The Assembly's reaction was one of consternation. The thought of adding teenagers and Swei Swee seemed to complicate the mission with unnecessary risks.

"On the contrary," Willem told the Assembly representatives, "Celus-5 is covered in substantial bodies of water. The ocean's vegetative coloring and growth suggest that the seas will support life as we know it. I can't think of a better way to survey the water qualities and organisms than with a team of Swei Swee."

When asked about the teenagers, Willem said, "The Swei Swee's lives would be immensely improved by the presence of a People's Singer. Ginny is imminently qualified to fulfill that role, and, as to the sixth member, I need say no more."

It didn't matter whether the Assembly thought that accepting Ginny meant accepting Teague or that Alex Racine had requested Teague be added to the roster, either way the Swei Swee, Little Singer, and Alex's son were approved to take part in the unprecedented journey of the *Sojourn*.

Nyslara

Queen Nyslara's jaw jittered in anticipation of the steaming delicacy heaped on a tray and placed before her by two servants. The hunt for ceena, the sea creatures, grew more difficult with the passing of seasons. An entire skimmer crew was lost in the effort to bring her this dish, but that was the duty of the soma, the queen's people, to see that she was properly serviced, as was due her penultimate position.

The skimmers' quarry was not only rarer to locate but had become more dangerous when encountered. Stories abounded of the easy hunts generations ago, scooping young off the beaches and netting females in shallow waters. Ceena were plentiful then, and Nyslara's soma feasted on them every day. Now, ceena was the queen's treat, and the hunters returned to the old ways, scouring the grassy plains for small creatures, many of which shared the underground with them.

Black, short-nailed claws picked a ceena shank from the tray. Sharp, needle-like teeth in an elongated snout cracked the tough shell, and the queen sucked the sweet flesh from the leg. She savored the nest's favored meal, hissing her delight as she swallowed chunks of the meat.

The tray held six times more than what Nyslara could consume, but the expanse was the traditional serving to a queen. When satiated, she waved an imperial hand at her servants to remove the tray, selecting two enormous claws from the tray before it was whisked away. Nyslara's feedwa, the queen's dogs, whined in anticipation, and she tossed a claw to each one.

The feedwa, despite echoing many features of the Dischnya, the desert people, were more lizard-like in their build, low to the ground, longer snouts, and prominent canines that were displayed outside closed jaws. In contrast, the Dischnya appeared as a cross between an ancient dog and rat, standing on powerful, hocked, hind legs that ended in 6-centimeter claws. Hard, dark nails tipped the forearm hands, and both hands and feet carried the pads of an old race that existed by digging in the earth.

All Dischnya were furred, except for the rat-like tail, but the fur's color and pattern varied and identified each soma's nest. Small ears, yellow eyes, a pointed snout, with a long tongue, and sharp teeth, especially the incisors, completed the head. The formation of the Dischnya mouth caused their language to be spoken with a slight sibilance.

The noticeable difference between Dischnya males and females was the absence of an adult male's tail. A youth's tail was truncated in a ceremony, as he passed into the ranks of hunter or warrior.

The Dischnya weren't native to Sawa Messa. Their home world was the fourth planet outward from their star and was called Sawa, by the people. But as the millenniums passed, Sawa continued to dry, and the nests spent more and more time underground, congregating around deep reservoirs of water.

The people's primary food supply had always been the plains animals, herds of which roamed the grassy plains, but those were decimated throughout the ages by drying conditions, which withered the grasses, and the insatiable hunger of the ever-expanding nests.

Technology reached a point where the Dischnya could build crude rocket engines and small space worthy shuttles. A ring of small asteroids surrounded Sawa. It was suspected that they were the remains of a massive impact on one of the many small moons that orbited the home world.

The Dischnya long admired the green of Sawa Messa, the fifth planet outward from their star, which they observed as their home world eclipsed the fecund-appearing planet when their orbits aligned. More than a hundred years ago, the first nest, led by their queen, took the one-way trip to Sawa Messa.

The soma were housed deep in a chunk of space rock, as chemical rocket engines shoved the asteroid out of orbit and on a vector for a near pass, as the green planet approached the closest point of orbit.

When Sawa Messa hove into view, the nest loaded into their shuttles, which were designed to make planetfall on one of the continent's smooth, arid plains. Most shuttle landings were successful; some were not. After the initial successful trip, the arrival of more nests to the new world occurred with every second rotation of Sawa and continued for eighteen rotations, until they stopped.

Communications from the Sawa Messa pioneers to Sawa's Regents of Queens went unanswered, and those on the new planet were left to wonder what had befallen their home world. Many young queens, who had braved the voyage to the new home world, suspected that it was a fight between the traditionalists, who decried the concept of leaving Sawa, and the modernists, who saw the exodus to Sawa Messa as the only way to save the soma.

Whatever the reason for the lack of communications and the end to the arrival of more nests, the expected support shipments of heavy technology and vital spare parts from Sawa were never forthcoming. So, in time, the nests were forced to adopt a much simpler level of existence, as parts for shuttles, communications, construction, energy, and medical equipment ran out.

The newly formed Fissla, the arbitrative council of queens on Sawa Messa, broke apart, and the nests resorted to competing against one another for resources. They were Dischnya, so they loved the arid plains, but soon after landing, some queens had sent numerous scouting parties into the huge belts of green forests that bracketed the plains on two sides. When not a single hunter returned, the young queens fell back on what the Dischnya knew best, and the nests of soma moved underground.

* * *

Nyslara was woken from her night's sleep by a polite rapping of sharp nails on the rock wall outside her inner abode.

"My queen, important news," Cysmana, the queen's personal attendant said, "A ship has been spotted crossing the dark sky."

"More of our people?" Nyslara asked hopefully, as she donned an embroidered royal robe that flowed to the ground, a slit up the back accommodating her magnificent whip-like tail, and joined her personal servant.

"No, my queen, the lookouts report a strange ship crossing the sky. They only caught a glimpse of it in the last rays of Nessila, before both of them passed below the horizon. The lookouts waited to see if the ship achieved orbit or passed on before they notified the sub-commanders. The ship was spotted again, as a dark object against the night's sky, moments ago, my queen, and the warriors believe that the aliens might intend a landing."

"Summon Pussiro," Nyslara ordered.

"Yes, my queen," Cysmana said and hurried away, the pads of her feet making a soft pat-pat across the compacted earthen floor.

Nyslara paced the front room, decorated and arranged for visitors. An alien ship, appearing in the sky, was not something she'd ever pondered. There was the ancient story of a ship visiting Sawa Messa before the Dischnya arrived, but the details were lost in the ages, and many queens believed it was unfounded and possibly invented as a tale to frighten the young.

Aliens who could travel between the planets and even travel between the stars, at will, would have power that Nyslara knew her soma couldn't match, much less overcome. A scratch of nails on the wall drew the queen's attention. "Enter, Pussiro."

"My queen," Pussiro said, curling his fingers into fists and placing them beside his hips, a sign of nonaggression among the soma, as he nodded his head in obeisance.

"Give me the benefit of your advice, Pussiro," Nyslara commanded.

Pussiro carried the scars of a multitude of skirmishes with other nests on his muzzle, shoulders, and arms. As a survivor of numerous conflicts, he'd risen steadily within the ranks of warriors until his appointment as commander of the queen's forces, several seasons ago.

"The ship in the sky would be vastly superior to our shuttle technology … when they were operable," Pussiro lamented. "It displays none of our rocket's extended tails of heavy exhaust gases, just bright circles of light at its rear."

"Do you anticipate the aliens will land, Commander?"

"With certainty, my queen," Pussiro said. His sad expression was accentuated by the slight graying of his muzzle, and it denoted one who had lived his life in successful devotion to his queen and having reached the pinnacle of his warrior career was now faced with the possibility of it ending in disaster.

"They will have superior weaponry, no doubt."

"No doubt, my queen. But we are not without our own craft. We have our tunnels, and we are many."

"I fear that will be little enough once the aliens decide they want Sawa Messa for themselves. Well, at least, we must warn the other queens. Dispatch runners to the other nests and ensure the queens are aware of the ship. The message from me is that they should take their soma underground and disguise anything left above ground … and do so quickly. The same must be passed to our soma."

"As you order, my queen."

"And, Pussiro, prepare the warriors."

"For what type of action, my queen?"

"The answer to that question we will discover together, Pussiro. Go, make haste."

The commander whirled, and the great claws of his hind feet scratched the hardened floor of the salon's entrance, as he hurried away.

Once alone, except for the ubiquitous presence of Cysmana, her personal servant, waiting quietly in the corner, Nyslara pondered the future of the nests. Her emotional reaction aimed waves of anger at the traditionalists, who, more than likely, would have been the ones to stop the exodus of the Dischnya from Sawa. By now, Sawa Messa could have been a bustling world with satellites, planet-wide communications, shuttle services to a space station, and perhaps even inner system transportation to the other worlds and moons of Nessila. *At least,* Nyslara thought, *we might have appeared as an advanced society to the aliens instead of a culture hiding underground, stranded on a new world, while we seek to rebuild a technological society.*

* * *

Pussiro emerged above ground, a cadre of sub-commanders, senior warriors, and more than fifty hunters close behind him. Word of the alien ship had disturbed the soma, and it showed in their furtive behavior. The warriors wanted to question their wasat, the queen's commander, but they took notice of the fur standing out on his face and crown. It was obvious that Pussiro was in no mood for questions.

Orders were hissed to hunters, who were to act as runners to the other nests. From packs on their backs, the hunters pulled their emissary masks, which were painted with jagged lines of blue and white to prevent them from being shot by the lookouts of the competing nests. After donning their masks, the emissaries darted away into the night, their powerful legs eating up the distances on the dry, flat ground.

More hunters were sent toward the western shore with orders for the skimmer crews to hide their boats and return underground. Finally, the warrior cadre was sent to search the surface. All soma were to seek refuge below and take anything small and portable with them. Anything large was to be disguised.

Soon, Pussiro was alone, and his thoughts mirrored those of his queen. As a veteran of hundreds of nest fights, Pussiro understood the strategies of conflict — creativity above all else, flexible command, surprise attack, and overwhelming force. But his question was this: What could all that knowledge and experience gain him if the aliens simply remained in the sky and slaughtered nest after nest, as if the soma were ceena?

-3-
Celus-5

It took sixteen years for Willem's interstellar investigation team to produce a list of possible habitable planets. The best candidates were narrowed to three planets most suitable for a new Haraken colony, and the data was presented to Alex and the Assembly. Since Celus-5 was Willem's preeminent choice, it was approved as the destination for the *Sojourn's* first voyage.

A small probe that was sent to the system had returned images of a world complete with multiple continents and hundreds of small islands, all of which were surrounded by extensive oceans. Two of the three continents contained great swaths of arid plains, located near the planet's equator. Bordered on the northern and southern sides of these grassy veldts were vast, solid stretches of red and green vegetation.

Originally, Willem approached Alex Racine, then Haraken president, for the funds to build an explorer ship. Knowing his days as president were numbered, Alex sought the Assembly's support for Willem's efforts, citing the opportunity for Haraken to add its first colony. It was the Central Exchange, owned by eight Haraken SADEs, which financed the building of the explorer ship.

The Assembly decided the expedition would require co-commanders: a human captain and a SADE. Informed by Rosette, a SADE who supported the Assembly's administration, Captain Asu Azasdau promptly applied for the position of the *Sojourn's* captain. Asu had split his time between his duties as an Assembly representative and managing his business, which was providing services for the passenger liner *Sternenvagabund* (*Star Voyager*). His liner, which had serviced the Confederation by transporting Independents to Libre for incarceration, was granted to the captain and crew when Haraken was founded.

However, Asu found the jobs of liner management and Assembly representative a far cry from the exciting days of the flotilla's escape from Libre, and he yearned for a return to the intensity of those times. As was common on Haraken with the community use of implants, when Asu submitted his request to the Assembly for the position of the *Sojourn*'s captain, all other interested parties demurred from participation — Asu was a well-liked and respected man on Haraken.

It was a foregone conclusion that Willem would be the mission's SADE, who would fill the post of co-commander, but Rosette submitted the idea to the Assembly that a second SADE was necessary. Her argument was that Willem would play an important role with the ground survey team, and that it would be in the expedition's interest to keep a SADE aboard the ship in the event of difficulties planetside. And, of course, Rosette submitted her name for the position.

Rosette had first supported Asu as the SADE aboard the *Sternenvagabund*. Later, when Asu was elected to the Assembly, Rosette threw her considerable talents into the fledgling Assembly's administration. From Captain Azasdau's first step aboard the liner, Rosette had been treated with nothing but courtesy and kindness. His treatment of her was exemplary, a wonderful change from the cursory and dismissive attitudes of Rosette's first two captains.

After becoming mobile, Rosette was inundated with the tasks of supporting the Assembly and her duties as a Central Exchange director. But despite the daily demands of her duties, Rosette always found time to support Asu in the little things. It was small repayment for the almost four decades during which her life, as the liner's SADE, was a true pleasure.

The Assembly accepted Rosette's suggestion of a second SADE on the mission, and she was added to the *Sojourn*'s roster.

* * *

"Captain Azasdau, here's my final roster," Willem said, sending the landing party list to Asu's implant and copying Rosette.

"I see you intend to take all four of the Swei Swee and our two journey crew members planetside," Asu replied.

"Ground surveillance has not produced any evidence of sophisticated or simplistic constructions of a society, and the creatures on the plains that can be observed are small in size. Furthermore, atmospheric conditions are nearly optimal. I see no danger to our two auspicious young people, and the Swei Swee can begin fulfilling their tasks to survey the waters."

"Then you're still intending to land near the single traveler location?"

"Could there be any better choice of site for our first landing?"

"I suppose not. That's all the crew has been talking about since Teague first spotted those dark travelers. Keen eye, that boy. But those ships raise a good many questions, and I'm hoping you'll find some answers ... preferably ones that aren't going to mean any of us harm."

"I must admit that this expedition's focus has grown far beyond my expectations. I was merely searching for a new, habitable colony."

"That's the problem, Willem. A planet that's habitable for one species might be preferable to others."

Asu and Willem regarded each other, but they kept their thoughts private. The discovery of the dark travelers, evidence of the Nua'll's passage, would generate turbulent waves that would ripple across the light-years to Haraken and the Confederation.

* * *

Willem planned to be planetside for approximately thirty days. Of the two travelers aboard the *Sojourn*, he would take the rear-loading shuttle. It was designed to carry heavy equipment, when necessary, and was constructed specifically to facilitate the ground survey scientists and techs.

The *Sojourn's* second shuttle served as a passenger carrier and could operate easily as a fighter, if need be.

Armed with the knowledge of the dangerous circumstances the New Terran colonists met when they finally made planetside, more than seven centuries ago, Willem was determined to conduct a thorough survey — atmospheric gas analysis, weather anomalies, soil testing for minerals and biota, water purity, microorganisms, and the potential of danger to humans from creatures large and small.

In determining who would be taken planetside, Willem attempted to approach the list as logically as possible, but he found a series of conflicting priorities. *Decisions were much simpler aboard the observation station when I was investigating distant stars*, Willem thought.

Willem knew he needed the Swei Swee to investigate the seas. They could shorten that aspect of the survey by tens of days, while he and the others concentrated on the land. However, for the Swei Swee, thirty days without a Singer was an unnecessary discomfort, and Willem was intent on treating the aliens as he would any of the crew, fairly and equally. If he had learned nothing else from Alex Racine, it was that, and it meant Ginny must be aboard the shuttle with the Swei Swee.

Dubbed Little Singer by the Swei Swee, Ginny was prized by everyone aboard for the light and laughter she brought to their lives. She had a way of enlivening any room she entered. Despite her humble beginnings as a deaf orphan aboard a space station in the outer rim of Sol, Ginny had bloomed into a beautiful young woman. Her hearing loss was repaired with the aid of Haraken medical nanites, restoring an innate perfect pitch, which enabled her to sing in the Swei Swee language.

Then there was the subject of Teague, whom Willem fervently wanted to protect. Every Haraken did, but Teague chafed at the attempts of those around him who tried to limit his activities in the name of preservation. And in these circumstances, any effort to dissuade Teague from traveling planetside was moot. Yes, Teague might engage in risky activities of his own, but if Ginny undertook an adventure that smacked of potential danger, he would not step 2 meters away from her side. In Willem's kernel, the answer was obvious: If Ginny was going, Teague was going.

From captain to SADEs to crew and even to the Swei Swee, it amused one and all to watch Teague deny what his heart felt. The president's son appeared aloof from Ginny's charms, treating her as a friend, a good companion, but it was all Teague could do not to follow her every movement with his eyes when she came within sight.

Teague and Ginny, Willem thought, *the pair acted with the synergy born of a quantum coupling.*

-4-
Pussiro

"Has all been made ready?' Nyslara asked Pussiro.

"Yes, my queen. The soma are below ground, and we've carefully disguised anything that was left above."

"And the ship?"

"It's poised far above us, my queen. Consensus among our lookouts is that the ship is too great in size to land. It must possess shuttles, which we expect will be used to land the aliens."

The thought of possessing shuttles to return to space at will — to travel the planets and possibly the stars — caused Nyslara to pause. She deeply lamented the slow retarding of her people's technical capabilities. Soon the knowledge of what once was possessed on Sawa would fade, and with the loss of knowledge and old stories, so would go the dreams of her soma. Then the possibility of retrieving their potential as a race would be lost.

"Have the runners returned with messages from the queens?"

"Most have returned, except for those journeying to the farthest nests. The replies aren't good, my queen," Pussiro said, casting his eyes down. "While they have taken your words of precaution to heart, disguising anything above ground and securing their soma below, none of them wish to join with us in repelling the aliens. Most believe their soma can best the intruders."

"Fools, old and young," Nyslara hissed. "They're gorged on their pride, intoxicated in the belief that they possess absolute power, but they've no idea what they'll face from these aliens.

"I believe they fear joining you, Nyslara. You rule a great and dominant nest. Joining you would diminish their standing and raise your own."

Nyslara hissed in reply and waved a hand in negation. She wanted to hear no more of their fears. "What's your plan, Pussiro, when the aliens land?"

"If we believe them to be the superior race and cower in fear, we'll have wasted our opportunity, and we'll be beaten before we even resist. So we will treat them as ceena and trap them," Pussiro replied, his eyes gleaming in anticipation of the coming encounter.

* * *

"A small shuttle is descending, Commander," a lookout reported to Pussiro.

"Where?" Pussiro asked. He was listening to the warrior on the underground communications network that was a simple string of wires and magnet-based receiver and mic handsets. Long gone was the soma's sophisticated comm network. When equipment failed, decades after their landing, repairs were impossible. The machinery necessary to create the replacement parts never arrived from Sawa.

"The ship appears to be headed for the water's edge near where the alien shuttle rests," the lookout added.

There was a pause and Pussiro could hear the hissing intakes of breath from the two lookouts, who would be peeking out from a concealed tunnel entrance. "Commander, the shuttle, which is floating in the air, is in the same shape as the ancient ship buried in the sands."

"Is it the same or merely similar?" Pussiro asked sharply, his mind racing and considering the possibilities.

"Exactly the same shape, Commander. Only, the ancient ship is dark, and this one has the colors of the great waters."

"Perhaps, the ancient ship possessed the colors of the waters, but it has weathered," the second lookout volunteered.

"Might the aliens have come looking for their comrades?" the first lookout asked. "Maybe it's not their intention to invade our lands."

"Keep a careful eye on them," Pussiro ordered. "I will want a great deal of detail about their every action. It will be crucial in determining how we react to them. Pass the order to every lookout who has a view of the landing site. No warrior is to break cover. They're to stay concealed." The queen's wasat returned the handset to the cradle and a furry hand stroked the whiskers on one side of his muzzle.

The nests never did find a trace of the aliens who had been aboard the three dark shuttles buried in the sands. Although the Dischnya estimated that the shuttles landed more than 100 years before they arrived, the general consensus was that there should have been some evidence of the occupants around the shore — equipment, flight suits, or bones. The shuttles were never searched, because, as far as the Dischnya were concerned, the ships weren't designed for access, which puzzled them.

Absent any evidence to the contrary, it became common conjecture that the shuttles were stranded, and others of their race had come to their rescue. But, if that had been the case, why were the aliens returning now, Pussiro wondered.

Since the Dischnya had been uncertain of the kind of technology the dark shuttles might possess, they were placed off-limits to the soma. None were to disturb the vessels for fear of releasing a contagion, or worse, an energy blast.

Pussiro ordered his support cadre to send warriors and trapping equipment to the tunnel exits nearest the ancient landing site, remaining underground, at all costs. Then he took off running, his powerful legs carrying him swiftly through wide tunnels shored with fire-hardened blocks of clay.

Knowing tunnel pathways intimately, Pussiro soon arrived at the lookout post that was nearest the landing site of the single dark ship. His swift pad strikes alerted the lookouts, who came to attention as Pussiro entered the hide. It was a small room that could accommodate about ten warriors, and, on the side farthest from the entrance, a ladder led to a simple periscope, the surface lens of which was camouflaged and could be detected by only the keenest eyes.

As the lookouts nodded their obeisance, Pussiro clambered up the ladder to take his turn at the scope. "It's landed on the plains, not on the shore," Pussiro remarked absentmindedly. "But where are the scorch marks from the engines?" he asked suddenly, turning the viewing glass left and right to search the area.

"There are none, Commander," one lookout remarked.

Pussiro turned to eye his warriors, his lips curling away from his teeth. A human might have confused it for a smile, but, for the Dischnya, it was a challenge.

"It's true, Commander," the second warrior declared. "It didn't fire engines. It didn't fly in at speed and land in a line to reduce its speed. It hovered in the air and settled gently to the ground without a sound."

Pussiro's lips covered his teeth, and he returned his eyes to the viewing glass. He knew they would be facing aliens with superior technology, but silent shuttles that floated to the ground without blasting engines made his blood run cold, and he quickly revised his attack strategy.

Descending the ladder, Pussiro yanked the handset off its cradle and whistled shrilly. It was a sound that issued from every handset and commanded the warriors to pick up. "The plan remains the same," Pussiro said after a brief moment to allow his warriors to come online. "But I don't want the aliens harmed. Their technology is many times superior to ours, and if we hurt them, that ship above us might be capable of taking revenge on this entire planet."

Pussiro replaced the handset and returned to the scope to watch the shuttle. The aliens had yet to exit their ship.

* * *

Orly Saadner leveled the traveler and halted in a fixed position 300 meters above the target area. He glanced at Willem, who was occupying the copilot position, and received a curt nod of approval. Orly patiently waited while Willem finished his final scan before choosing a landing site.

Tied into the traveler's controller, Willem was able to examine the local environment in great detail. "Pilot Saadner, the beach is much too narrow to accommodate our survey party and experiences too much tidal motion. The plains near the shore represent an optimal landing place. Here," Willem said, indicating a point on the controller's ground image, which was repeated in Orly's helmet display.

"It will be as you request, Co-commander Willem. I serve at your pleasure," Orly replied, tongue-in-cheek. Ever since Willem requested him for the *Sojourn*'s team, the SADE had addressed him as Pilot Saadner or Ser Saadner. But the New Terran emigrant thought of himself as Orly and asked Willem to refer to him in that manner, not that it had done him any good.

Orly was as jovial and affable a man as someone would ever meet. But, more important, he was a natural at a shuttle's controls, capable of putting the ship through acrobatic maneuvers that disoriented other pilots, which is why he was occupying the pilot seat of the survey traveler.

Easing the ship toward the ground, Orly continued to study the landing site, which was situated about 200 meters inland from the shore's embankment, which was marked by tidal surges. Below the shuttle was a small, flat hillock dotted with formations of boulders, some as high as 3 meters. Orly examined the prevailing wind data and chose to use the traveler as a windbreak, aiming the nose toward the beach but then cocking it at a shallow angle.

Captain Xavier Escobar, seated in the traveler's main cabin, was chafing. There were only three security escorts accompanying him. He'd requested eight personnel land with him, but was overruled by Willem. Not that the captain could disagree with Willem's reasoning, since the landing zone, in fact, most of the planet, appeared to be empty of dangerous creatures. But, Xavier and his people were tasked with the safety of the survey team. In his estimation, four escorts were five too few.

Xavier worked for the Haraken Security Directorate when he was approached by its co-directors, Alain and Étienne de Long, to provide security for the expedition. At first, Xavier thought the position somewhat beneath his capabilities, and he thought to offer other names in his place, but the fact that the twins had sought him out gave him pause.

"Who are the principals that will be aboard the *Sojourn*?" Xavier asked. His implant received a list from Étienne, and he quickly scanned it. "Oh," he said, drawing the word out as he exhaled. He had spotted the names of two SADEs, a university professor, four Swei Swee, the Little Singer, and Teague Racine. *Now I'm wondering if I'm qualified for the task,* he had thought.

The back half of the traveler was piled high with equipment — survey instruments, thousands of sampling containers, portable workbenches, temporary shelters for the scientists and techs, and much more. There wasn't much room for passengers, which is why Willem had limited the security force to a total of four.

"Captain Escobar, please understand that it's the primary mission of this first landing team to ensure that this planet is safe for a deeper and more thorough survey. We are but the first step. It's important to limit the number of individuals who will be exposed to danger," Willem had said. "This first group must be composed of as many technical people as we can accommodate."

"And the Swei Swee?" Xavier had asked.

"Who better to survey the shoreline sands and ocean waters?"

"And Teague?"

"You know as well as I do, Captain, that the Swei Swee need their Little Singer. So, you're welcome to tell Teague that he can't accompany us planetside. Please let me know how that goes." When Xavier hesitated, Willem commiserated with him. "That's the predicament we all face, Captain. Teague has his mother's face, but his father's build and temperament. He's polite but willful, and despite his protestations of a simple friendship with Ginny, he's devoted to ensuring her safety. That Alex Racine and Renée de Guirnon could convince me to take this menagerie of individuals ... Swei Swee, Singer, and son on our first expedition ... makes me think that I've adopted far too many human habits."

Orly landed the traveler, the interior lights brightened, and the scientists and techs went to work. Installed in the shuttle's rear shell was a single door, covering most of the traveler's rear, which swung down and formed the shuttle's exit ramp, as Willem deployed it. But a pair of plex-crystal doors, located behind the massive rear hatch, kept the passengers isolated from the planet's atmosphere. Inset in the doors were small sampling tubules that connected to instruments mounted on the doors' inner faces.

Everyone waited while the air samples were collected and tested. Every instrument aboard contained a tiny controller that could comm the results, on request, to an implant or SADE's comm. When the atmospheric quality tests revealed an acceptable range of gases for humans, despite the air's warm temperature and low humidity, the team breathed a sigh of relief. Step one of the survey was complete.

One piece of equipment was busy sucking great quantities of air through its intake and filtering out particles. The residue was delivered to one of the survey team's larger pieces of equipment, which was busy running DNA analysis on any living material, fauna or flora, and chemical analysis on everything else.

The crew took the opportunity to get a meal and drink from the food dispensers while they waited.

Security spent the time monitoring the shuttle's surroundings through the controller's hull sensors. Although the traveler shell's integrity was breached, due to the open rear hatch, and the ship no longer capable of charging its power crystals at anything approaching maximum, there was plenty of stored energy to keep the sensors and instruments running for several days. After that, the ship would need to be sealed again so that the shell could use the planet's gravitational waves to charge its power cells.

Xavier began to relax when after an hour of searching he and his team hadn't spotted anything remotely dangerous, although some of the large insects that were seen looked particularly menacing.

The completed DNA tests revealed more than one fundamental formation — some samples were composed of helix-style strands, but others revealed a hexagonal lattice. To the scientists, it was an indication that there were multiple life forms on the planet. More important, the different building blocks indicated that lifeforms had arrived on the planet from somewhere else, although it didn't mean that they were still around.

The upshot of the tests revealed that the present life forms presented no inherent danger to humans, and the medical nanites in the Harakens' bodies should be capable of handling contagions they might encounter. Dust samples indicated a host of tiny amounts of minerals and compounds in the air that indicated human's food plants would grow well in the environment.

The preliminary testing completed, the survey team made preparations to exit the traveler. Most would stay in close proximity to the shuttle, including Edward Sardi, a Haraken professor of physics and an import from Sol, and the majority of scientists and techs, who would set up the field tents, lab benches, and testing equipment.

A small group, which included Willem, Ginny, Teague, the four Swei Swee, Xavier, and a second escort, Corporal Keira Daubner, would undertake a short exploratory trip to the nearby shoreline and the site of the single dark traveler.

"I acknowledge that this survey trip is under your command, Willem, but I would ask that you heed any requests I issue that concern our people's safety," Xavier said.

"Rest assured, Captain, that I will take all your suggestions under advisement."

Xavier figured that was the best that he was going to get from the SADE, and he signaled Keira. <Stay close to Ginny, Corporal. I'll be next to Teague.>

<What about Willem?> Keira asked in reply.

<Two human teenagers need a great deal more protection than a SADE.>

When Willem signaled the team was ready, Orly opened the plex-crystal doors, which swung outward and tucked neatly against the inner hull. Security personnel exited first, silently stalking down the traveler's rear hatch, which had become the shuttle's gangway. Xavier blocked the path of the mission's personnel while his people scanned the area. When he received an all clear from his team, he motioned to the waiting survey team and joined his people on the ground.

The survey crew hurried to follow Xavier, not even bothering to grab a box or bag. Everyone was too anxious to see the new planet. While most of the team gazed about in wonder at the arid plains, covered with waves of dry grass and the odd boulder formation, Willem organized his group for the trip to the shore.

The SADE left Edward in charge of the scientists and techs, which would be based at the traveler's site and set off at a brisk pace toward the shoreline, but not brisk enough to keep up with the Swei Swee, who could smell the ocean breeze. Teague's harsh whistle halted the foursome's headlong charge ahead of the group, and they bobbed in excitement, while they waited for the Star Hunters to catch up.

Xavier nodded his appreciation to Teague for maintaining control over the anxious Swei Swee. It was bad enough the captain didn't have sufficient troops to maintain a secure cordon, but he didn't need his job getting more complicated by having his charges separate the moment they set foot on the planet.

At the bluff's edge, the Swei Swee paused to take in the sights — ocean swells breaking over a distant uplift, white-crested waves hurrying to the shore, dark sands covering the beach, and the rich, fecund smell of ocean life. Without waiting for their human companions, the foursome dove off the bluff, pulling in their legs and surfing down the embankment on their carapaces.

"I recommend the break in the ridge," Xavier said, pointing at a cut in the embankment that humans could navigate to access the beach. He wasn't above throwing Teague a stern glance, as if to say, "I thought you had control of your six-legged friends."

Near the water's edge, Bobs A Lot gingerly tasted the moist sand. <Good. But these are not the ancient waters,> he broadcast to the group.

When the Swei Swee viewed the images of the dark travelers buried in the sand, they hoped Celus-5 might have been their ancestral home, from which they had been kidnapped generations ago. Every hive member held a memory of the taste of the endless waters that had surrounded their cliff-based homes. Sadly, for the four Swei Swee, these were not the same waters.

Willem laid out the search parameters for the Swei Swee and the allotted time for their investigations, but he sent the information to Teague. It ensured that his directions were more accurately phrased. Teague whistled the orders to his alien friends, translating Willem's depth limit into water color, distance from shore into the far breakwater, which was possibly a reef or wall, and length of time into an angle change of the blue white star in the sky.

When Teague finished, the four Swei Swee whistled their understanding, warbled their goodbyes to Little Singer, and bolted into the breaking waters in search of prey and predators. Their entire foray, with all its accompanying sensory input, would be recorded in their new implants, and Teague and Ginny shared responsibility for collecting and uploading to the ship's controller the Swei Swee data after each exploration.

-5-
Attack

Pussiro's eyes were glued to the scope ever since the oddly shaped ship landed. Despite being a creature of the plains, part of him admired the cool blue, green, and cream colors that swirled softly through its exterior hull. But the warm tones of dry grass and ground with its browns and tans were home to him.

Envy mixed with fear flowed through Pussiro. He longed for the Dischnya to possess the advanced technology that the shuttle represented. At the same time, that level of science indicated an extremely advanced race, which warned of power that could easily decimate the nests.

Pussiro was about to relinquish the scope when he spotted the bulbous end of the ship breakaway from the hull and descend toward the ground. However, nothing more happened after that, and he allowed a lookout to replace him to maintain the vigilance.

Much later, after Pussiro had fallen asleep, a soft hiss woke him, and he jerked upright.

"Commander, the aliens are exiting their craft," the warrior whispered, and he stepped aside so that his commander could gain access to the scope.

Pussiro watched the entities descend a ramp and stand on his planet. His first emotion was one of relief. Nothing about the aliens appeared intimidating. In fact, they looked rather harmless — not large; no claws, teeth, or beaks to speak of; nearly hairless; not wrapped in armor; and not carrying identifiable armament. To Pussiro's mind, they resembled prey not predators, but still, they flew ships that moved without visible engines. *Do not be lulled into a false sense of security by your first impressions,* Pussiro thought, erring on the side of caution. *They can afford to appear without claws and let their tech speak for them.*

Flexing the scope's controls, Pussiro zoomed in for a closer look at the aliens as they examined the sky, ground, and far horizon. He was intrigued by the differences in skin colors, top knots, and statures. "Strange, these aliens," Pussiro whispered to his warriors. "They're not of the same soma."

"Two soma, commander?" one lookout asked.

"Three, maybe four, maybe more," Pussiro replied. The furrowing of his brow at the thought of the nests mixing echoed the frowns on his warriors' faces. The difference was that Pussiro's lips were not lifted in a grimace to reveal teeth, as were those of the lookouts.

Suddenly, Pussiro's body tensed, and the muscles of his hind legs bunched in a fight-or-flee reflex. His warriors, sympathetic to the wasat's reaction, crouched in defensive postures and sunk the claws of their feet into the hideout's hardened ground.

"By the life of our queen, it can't be," Pussiro hissed, as he watched a group of aliens form up and head toward the great waters. Pussiro spun and sprinted from the hideout, angling down passageways at breakneck speed and barking at soma to clear his path.

Behind him, one lookout and then the other took turns at the scope.

"What does this mean?" the young warrior said to his senior, the lips of his muzzle twisted to project his confusion.

"Great trouble for the nest," the elder warrior replied.

As Pussiro ran, he attempted to parse out the meaning of what he'd seen. The aliens were accompanied by ceena, but the relationship between them was unclear. His fervent hope was that the two-legged aliens had captured the six-legged creatures and trained them, similar in manner to that of the queen's feedwa.

But what if the ceena aren't slaves or pets? Pussiro asked himself. He noticed there were no leashes or restraints of any kind on the ceena. *What if they're allies of the aliens?* he thought, and that possibility spurred him to greater speed.

Pussiro ran with all his strength, and warriors, hunters, and workers alike wondered at the haste of the wasat whose strides were usually so measured and self-assured. Pussiro's destination was a small, seldom-used, hideout cut into the face of the small bluff that overlooked the waters.

The small room was empty when Pussiro entered it, and he brushed at insect webs and crushed some of the poisonous creatures beneath his padded claws. The scope was removed long ago. The location became useless when the Dischnya's hunt of the ceena chased the creatures out into the dark waters. Short, tough bushes, clinging to the bluff, hid the small hatch that Pussiro opened. He didn't have long to wait before the aliens arrived, the ceena sliding past his hatch, not more than a weapon's length away. Soon afterward, the two-legged aliens descended a path cut into the embankment by the feet of the Dischnya and came into view.

Pussiro was a keen observer of others. It was what had facilitated his mercurial rise through the ranks — that and his ferocious demeanor in battle. He employed that skill now, watching the aliens occasionally turn toward one another, but he couldn't hear anything they uttered until one of the bigger aliens, one not as tall as Pussiro but with more mass, whistled to the ceena. The four creatures whistled in reply, and then turned toward a small alien, whose topknot was the color of pale, dried grass, bobbing quickly before they raced for the waters. Their action in the presence of the small alien appeared to Pussiro to be the same obeisance the soma extended to Nyslara.

Pussiro felt fear creep through his body, driving deep into his bones. *We've dined on ceena since our arrival on Sawa Messa*, he thought. He closed the lookout hatch and sat heavily on the small bench, absentmindedly crushing a dangerous insect with a hard nail. In his mind, he replayed the whistles and warbles emitted by the ceena as they died at the hands of the nest's hunters — two generations of hunt, a multitude of creatures killed, and more whistles and warbles than could be counted — not the cries of simple prey, but the entreaties of intelligent entities.

Dropping his head into his hands, Pussiro attempted to collect his thoughts. It was not long before he pulled himself together. His duty was to his queen and his nest. If ever his soma needed him, it was now, even though what was needed had yet to form completely in his mind. His experience, as commander, told him that, at this moment, the aliens were vulnerable, and he knew his warriors must strike while the opportunity presented itself.

* * *

Bethany Latimer, the sergeant in Captain Escobar's command, left Corporal Smitty Lange, the junior security escort guarding the camp team, while she started a sweep of the area surrounding the traveler. She started close to the ship, moving out ever farther with each circle of the vessel.

Several times Bethany was forced to sidestep insects that scuttled toward her with claws extended or stingers hoisted high above their backs.

<Edward,> Bethany sent via her implant, <I don't know if you've noticed, but the insects here are extremely aggressive.>

<We've captured a few, Bethany, and are running analysis on the poisons we've extracted from the stingers, although there isn't much we can do about those attacking with claws. It doesn't seem to make much difference to these creatures that we outmass them by a few thousand times.>

<It goes to show you that even a ferocious attitude doesn't overcome all obstacles,> Bethany sent, her implant picking up her audible chuckles and transmitting them over the comm.

As Bethany's circle widened, she caught the barest hint of flash from a dried bush that looked in dire need of water, but she dismissed the speck of light as a piece of reflective mineral or some other anomaly. It was when she hadn't covered more than another 60 degrees of arc in her circle that she spotted another brief glint of light. This one was also at the base of another bunch of dried brush. After the second instance, Bethany kept watch for more of the telltale reflections, careful to glance across the bushes or watch from the corner of her eye. If the landing party was being observed, she didn't want to give her observations away.

<Captain,> Bethany sent. She was out of range via implant to implant, so the ship's controller automatically relayed her comm signal to Xavier.

<Go ahead, Sergeant.>

<I think we've got a problem, Captain. I've spotted little reflections that are located at ground level and coincidentally hidden at the base of dried brush.>

<Could it be reflective mineral deposits or trash?>

<Mineral deposits? Possibly, Captain. But trash, I doubt that, and trash left behind by whom? I haven't seen any indication of industrial material. Besides, the light bounces are bright. They have to come from polished metal or —>

<Or what, Sergeant?> Xavier asked when the comm went silent.

<Or glass, Captain, like the lens of a scope,> Bethany sent, her thoughts racing ahead, which flooded Xavier's implant with a continuous stream of images and partial impressions.

Xavier had taken Bethany planetside and left her in charge of the camp's survey team, because she was an experienced ex-Terran Security Forces (TSF) trooper and was as intuitive as they come when it came to trouble raising its ugly head.

<Sergeant, get our people back aboard the traveler,> Xavier ordered, breaking into Bethany's comm. <Make it casual. Don't signal the watchers, if they're out there. We'll collect the Swei Swee and head back ourselves.>

<Copy, Captain, > Bethany sent. She waited until her patrol circle passed the camp setup and she was on the far side of the traveler from where she'd spotted the reflections. Then she angled toward the camp tents. Two by two she commed individuals on the team and instructed them to slowly and casually board the traveler. <Don't take time to finish what you're doing or pack up your experiments. Board the ship and talk to each other about anything you like. Make it look casual, like you're having a relaxed conversation,> she instructed them.

Bethany warned Corporal Lange to take up a defensive position at the rear of the traveler. Both escorts had the same thought. It was a wonderful time to land on an alien planet, carrying only stun guns.

＊　＊　＊

<Willem, we must return to the traveler immediately. A security problem might be developing,> Xavier sent with urgency.

The SADE's head snapped toward Xavier, but the captain was intently scanning the low bluff that bordered the beach.

<Teague, retrieve the Swei Swee now,> Willem sent. <If you can't contact them, we must leave them behind and return to the traveler immediately. There are security concerns.>

Teague quickly stripped off his shirt, boots, and pants.

<Teague, we don't have any data on the safety of these waters,> Willem sent.

<Have to chance it, Willem. I must get closer to the Swei Swee. They're out of range, and I'm not leaving without them,> Teague replied, racing for the gently breaking waves, while Ginny scooped up his clothes. The instant Teague struck the water, executing a smooth headlong dive, he pinged his friends. His powerful strokes quickly carried him 80 meters from shore, where he made his first contact with Whistles Keenly.

Whistles Keenly surfaced, having received Teague's strident message. He dove back under and sounded the alarm to his companions, using both his shrieking whistle and implant to warn them to seek shelter. It was the Swei Swee's ancient call to make for the safety of the shore in the presence of dangerous sea predators.

Precious time was lost before the four Swei Swee finally broke surface. Three of them had been exploring the rocky bottom for sea creatures. They used their powerful tails to drive them at speed toward the beach. Swift Claws and Sand Flipper would come closest to Teague, and they angled to slip alongside him.

As his two friends passed Teague, he grabbed the front of their carapaces and was hauled toward the beach, bodysurfing over the waves. Teague released his hold when they reached the shallows, and the five of them waded ashore, only to freeze as a horde of aliens burst over the bluff and from a bolt-hole in its face.

Willem, who could process the extent of their danger faster than a human, sent <Everyone hold,> with all the intensity he could muster. It froze the hands of his security force, who were reaching for their stun guns. Slowly and carefully, Willem extended his hands up and away from his body, and the team imitated him.

More than thirty fur-faced aliens with long-barreled weapons surrounded the landing party at the shore. It was difficult to comprehend which was more intimidating, the ancient-looking weapons pointed at their faces from meters away or the up-curled lips, which exposed rows of sharp teeth in the aliens' snouts.

A gray-muzzled alien stepped forward, eyed Willem's hands in the air, and spoke to him. Willem didn't understand a word but he dutifully recorded the exchange, preparing to build a translation app. *Where are Julien, Cordelia, and Mutter, when you need them?* Willem lamented to himself. It was those three SADEs who had decoded the Swei Swee's whistling, warbling, and twittering language.

Six of the fur-covered aliens stood at the water's edge and pointed their weapons at Teague and the Swei Swee. The alien in front of Willem, whom the SADE took to be the leader, barked an order at those on the beach. In turn, the six warriors motioned with their weapons for Teague and the creatures with him to come ashore.

Teague started slowly forward, but the drool dripping from the jaws of several of the aliens as they eyed his friends scared him. He whistled shrilly, and the Swei Swee spun and dove back into the waves. That caused several of the aliens to bark harshly at Teague and gesture angrily with their weapons.

Holding his hands in the air and wading toward the beach, Teague tried to think calmly. His eyes glanced several times toward Ginny. Despite the dire circumstances, Teague couldn't help noting an odd thing. The aliens kept their sharp-clawed feet out of the water. In fact, if an errant wave crawled toward them, they would eye it with concern and step back quickly, while keeping their weapons trained on him.

When Teague reached the nearest warrior, a young-appearing one, the alien shoved the butt of his weapon at Teague's shoulder. With years of training by the de Long twins, his father's long-time security escorts, Teague reflexively crossed his body with his right hand to catch the weapon's wooden stock, which was aimed at his left shoulder. A more senior individual might have quit at that point, having defused the strike. Unfortunately, Teague was a teenager, and the young warrior, who wielded the weapon, was one of those who smacked his mouth noisily as he eyed the Swei Swee. So Teague rotated to his left, grasping the weapon with both hands and deliberately yanking it away from the alien. The result of his action was entirely unexpected.

With the weapon's strap wound around the alien's right arm, the creature was launched forward into the shallow waves. The weapon came loose, and it ended up in Teague's hands. Expecting to be shot in the next instant, Teague glanced at the other five aliens, while holding the weapon out to his side. However, instead of the warriors looking at him, they stared in horror at their companion. The alien warrior was in a meter's depth of water, but he was on his back, floundering and keening, as if he would drown or perhaps be eaten.

"Black space," Teague mumbled and tossed the weapon at the nearest warrior, who fumbled it and dropped it to the sand. Then Teague waded over to the panicked alien, grabbed him under the arms, and hoisted him bodily up and out of the water. Hard nails drove deep into the skin of Teague's shoulders, and he shouted in surprise and threw the warrior away from him. Unfortunately, that sent the alien into deeper water.

Howls of horror erupted from both the floundering youth and those watching from the safety of the shore. The din was ear-splitting and galvanized Teague to quickly wade over and snatch the struggling warrior by the back of what appeared to be some sort of makeshift armor. Then he walked ashore, dragging the creature behind him.

Stepping onto the shore, Teague, with one hand, stood the warrior up and pointed at his bleeding shoulder with the other. "Don't do that," he said forcefully, wagging a finger at the warrior before he let him go.

A burst of angry barks and growls issued from the alien's leaders, and the warriors backed away from Teague.

<Join us, Ser, if you're done drowning one of these weapon-toting, dangerous aliens,> Willem sent. He was happy to see Teague obey, although the boy strolled over, as if he intended to enjoy a nice day at the beach with an afternoon repast.

Ginny attempted to hand Teague's clothes back, but the leader issued more commands, pointing at the pile of clothes in her arms and wagging his finger at Ginny.

<Fortune is on our side,> Willem sent to his people. <The leader is quite an intelligent being. He understood Teague's admonishment to his nearly drowned warrior, and he just copied it.>

The alien leader spoke to Ginny, motioning her to drop the clothes, which she did. Then he waved his hand over the group, touched his body high and low, and pointed at Teague's clothes, lying in the sand.

<I believe we're being asked to disrobe,> Xavier sent. <The leader probably doesn't know which items on us might be used as a weapon or communicator. Get naked people, but do it slowly.>

The team stripped off packs, canteens, stun guns, boots, and clothes. When Ginny and Keira stood naked before the aliens, they elicited a great many yips and hisses, but a command from the leader silenced them. None of the Harakens missed the fact that the weapons previously trained on the women slowly moved away to aim exclusively at the men.

<Apparently, our alien dog men don't believe women represent a threat to them,> Keira sent with disdain.

<Another thought for you, Corporal, is that they might be a matriarchal society, and females are treated with great respect,> Willem sent. <Please do not make unfounded assumptions about these aliens. Our lives depend on learning their language and culture as quickly as we can, before they decide that we aren't worth keeping alive.>

* * *

Everyone at the traveler's survey site was privy to Willem's broadcast from the moment the aliens boiled over the plateau and descended on the small team on the shore. Most were transfixed by the action, but Bethany and Smitty cried out for them to abandon the masquerade and board the traveler with all haste. The scientists and techs were slow to respond, until they witnessed dried brush falling over, revealing open hatches, and aliens springing from the holes. Then the survey team scrambled for the traveler's ramp, while Bethany and Smitty provided rear guard.

"Sarge, tell me we can shoot," Smitty said, his voice strong and clear, as he backed toward the traveler.

"If they don't fire, we don't fire, Corporal. That's until they get too close," Bethany declared, as she swept the perimeter with her location app for any implants out of position. To her relief, every team member was either in the traveler or headed that way. "Inside the ship, Corporal. Hurry! Standby to signal Orly to trigger the plex-crystal doors first. They'll close the fastest."

Bethany could hear Smitty's boots pound up the gangway ramp. She wasn't going to make it in time. The aliens were covering ground at a tremendous speed, aided by the powerful musculature of their hind legs, and if she turned her back to run, they'd catch her.

Instead, Bethany backed up, extending her stun gun in front of her. She held her palm out, attempting to warn her attackers to stay away. But, either the enemy didn't understand her message or they were having none of it. Her boot heel struck the ramp, as she shot the first warrior, fervently hoping that the energy from her weapon wouldn't overload the alien's nerves and kill it.

Bethany continued to fell the aliens as she backed up the ramp into the traveler. She dropped eight of them until hands grabbed her from behind and yanked her backwards. The plex-crystal doors swung shut in front of her nose, and the aliens were left to pound on the transparent doors with fists or the butts of their weapons. The Harakens didn't need a translation to understand the harsh barking and growling thrown at them by the warriors, who were extremely irate at their quarry escaping capture.

<Close the ramp slowly, Orly,> Bethany sent. <There are aliens aboard between the plex and the ramp.>

Orly signaled the heavy rear shell of the shuttle to close at one-fourth its optimum rate. He wanted to give the creatures time to notice the ramp's activity.

The survey team watched first one and then another of the warriors stop their pounding, glance backward, and edge toward the ramp. A scarred muzzle marked an older individual, who issued a string of commands, and the aliens abruptly halted their attack against the plex-crystal doors, raced up the ramp, which had begun to point upward, and leapt for the ground. Unfortunately, one bright-eyed youth failed to heed his superior's command.

"Persistent individual, isn't he?" Smitty remarked, placing his face close to the plex-crystal to get a closer look at the alien, which only served to frustrate the warrior even more.

The scarred warrior, who now stood outside the ship, barked a final command, which brought the frothing youngster to his senses. The young warrior turned to find the top of the ramp only a few meters from closing and sealing to the ship's rear. In panic, he dropped his weapon and raced toward the opening. Leaping, he threw his body sideways through the gap, leaving a bit of fur on the sharp edge of the hatch and dropped over the other side.

Bethany signaled Orly to open the plex-crystal doors, and she snatched the alien's weapon. She intended to understand its capabilities, as soon as possible. Turning around, she bumped into a scientist, who carried a sample bag and a pair of tweezers. The man apologized and hurried to collect the piece of fur.

The scientist's efforts brought a smile to Bethany's face. *Good to see we have our heads screwed on tight,* she thought. But soon the smile was wiped off her face, and silence descended over the survey group, as they listened to the sound of something scraping over the entire hull.

<Orly, talk to me,> Bethany sent, handing off the weapon to Smitty and hurrying to the traveler's cockpit. She spared a quick glance to ensure that the specimen-collecting scientist had returned behind the plex-crystal doors and Orly had sealed the doors behind him.

<Getting an image now, Sergeant,> Orly replied.

When Bethany threw herself into the copilot's seat, she grabbed a helmet so that she could get a visual from the controller. "What's that?" she asked, unable to decipher the odd visual from the traveler's hull sensors.

"I believe you're looking at a net, Sergeant."

"A net? Do they think we're some sort of giant sea creature?"

"Whatever their thoughts, Sergeant, I recommend we liftoff."

"A net shouldn't stop us, Orly. We can tear it out of the ground when we lift," Bethany said confidently. "I think we should check in with the lieutenant and get new orders. This is a security problem now."

"Our choices might be limited, Sergeant." Orly said.

Bethany's helmet received a display of the traveler's power cells levels. "We're sealed up, Orly. We should be charging. Why are our levels dropping?"

"This is a new one on me, Sergeant, but my best guess is that the net they've thrown over us is made of some sort of conductive metal, and it's interrupting the shell's charging capability."

"And they would have anchored it to the ground," Edward said. He'd been standing in the cockpit doorway and listening to their conversation. When both individuals turned to stare at him, he added, "More than likely, the anchors are metal too. So the net isn't only interrupting the charging of the power cells, it's acting like an electrical ground, draining our cells through the shell."

"Orly, lift immediately," Bethany ordered.

"Sorry, I think it's too late, Sergeant. We've had the shell open all day. The scientists and techs have been running their equipment off the cells, and the crew's been using our refresher and meal dispensers. Once nightfall came, I intended to seal the ship and charge the power cells. We might have had enough to lift before the net was thrown over us, but it's been draining us incredibly quickly, and the controller now estimates that we're slightly underpowered to make orbit. And that's before we use up enough energy to break free of the net, if we even can."

"Orly, you're not making my day," Bethany replied, smacking the pilot's shoulder lightly to let him know her irritation wasn't aimed at him.

"We have another issue to deal with, Sergeant," Edward said.

"Oh, joy, I can't wait," Bethany remarked. It was her style that the worse a situation got, the more acerbic she would become. In a rare meeting with Tatia Tachenko, who witnessed a training exercise go south and Bethany's frustrated repartee with her commander, the admiral remarked that Bethany should get to know Julien, adding that the SADE and she had a lot in common.

"Orly can reduce extraneous power drains to buy us more time," Edward explained. "Then he can calculate how soon we'll need to crack the rear shell ... if it will be safe to crack the rear shell."

"Why would we need to ... black space ... we'll need air," Bethany replied, catching on to Edward's concern.

"Precisely, Sergeant. But the real question is this: Providing we can get the hatch wedged open, what will be the aliens' response?"

"He's got a point, Sergeant. They could fire their weapons through the opening," Orly said.

"I would expect the plex-crystal doors could withstand their fire, although I can tell you more, once we examine the weapon we captured," Bethany replied. "But my fear is that they could jam something heavy into both sides of the hatch, forcing us to surrender. But something about this attack seems off. Why didn't the aliens fire their weapons at us? They saw me drop eight of the comrades. They had to think I killed them with my ray gun." She laughed weakly at her reference to ancient science fiction stories.

"Perhaps, the weapons are for show, and they don't have the means of producing the items necessary to fire from the barrels?" Orly volunteered.

"Or perhaps, they had orders not to fire," Edward added. "Willem reported that no shots were fired at the beach."

While the two men pondered the gravity of their situation, Bethany hurried to the back of the traveler. She needed more information on the alien's weapon — whether it was armed and capable of firing, its armament type, and its potential destructive capability.

-6-
Captured

"Report, Commander," Nyslara ordered.

"The engagement was a partial success, my queen."

"Rather tepid tidings, Commander."

"We captured a small group of the aliens at the great water's edge, but one of their warriors, patrolling outside their shuttle, possessed keen eyes. We believe it spotted the reflection from our lookouts' scopes and warned the others, who've taken refuge in their ship."

"So the shuttle is gone," Nyslara lamented.

"That's the strange thing, my queen. We threw our greatest ceena net over the ship and staked it down. So far, the ship hasn't launched."

"Surely the aliens' technology could overcome a simple net of woven metal."

"You would think so, my queen. They could be waiting for the return of their companions."

"Perhaps," Nyslara agreed. She regarded the scene painted on the ceiling of her greeting room. It was a lifelike representation of the broad, arid plains, as the Dischnya first saw them. "How many soma were lost?"

"None, my queen."

"Better tidings, Commander. And what of the aliens?"

"The group we captured is being held in a storeroom on the nest's rim near the waters where we captured them.

"How many of them were killed?"

"None, my queen"

"Explain, Commander," Nyslara demanded. The encounters were not unfolding in any manner that she expected, and that was only adding to her frustration to find a safe path forward for her soma.

"In my experience, my queen, it's better to raid a nest and take the goods rather than kill the soma. The killing of another queen's people only breeds the desire for revenge. As I watched the aliens, it was evident to me that they carried no long weapons. At best, short weapons were strapped to their middles. I ordered my warriors to hold fire unless the aliens touched their pouches, where the weapons resided, if that's what they were."

"Were they weapons?"

"Not as we understand them, my queen. We've confiscated the ones possessed by the group at the water's edge and tested them, but no projectiles came out the end. Some of my subordinates believe they are only tools. But those who attacked the shuttle swear that they are the same instrument used on eight of our warriors, who were felled."

"You said none of our soma were killed, Commander," Nyslara hissed, and her lips curled away from her sharp teeth.

"And so they weren't, my queen," Pussiro said quickly. "After the shuttle closed, the warriors sought to carry their fallen comrades back underground and were surprised to discover they breathed and their hearts beat. A sub-commander reported that it was if the eight were in a deep sleep from which they wouldn't awaken. They were carried below, and, before I came here, I received a report that they were waking. It was said that they were groggy and disoriented, but otherwise quickly recovering.

"These strangers land on a foreign planet, and they don't bring weapons that kill. What type of entities are these aliens?" Nyslara asked herself before commanding Pussiro to continue his report.

"When we rushed the aliens at the waters and encircled them, they didn't fight. Instead, they displayed their arms as such." Pussiro held out his arms up and to the side, palms toward Nyslara. "Pardon my offense, my queen."

"None perceived, Pussiro." The gesture among the Dischnya was one of aggression, hands held high, and a position from which weapons or nails could strike.

"Why did you think this gesture meant the aliens didn't intend to defend themselves?"

"They're without claws, my queen. They wore coverings over their feet, and their forehands have soft, pink nails that don't extend beyond the digits. When they raised their limbs away from their technology, which resides around their middles and on their backs, I took this to mean that they didn't wish a confrontation."

"Oh, how clever of you, Commander. With no aliens or soma dead, you've left us room to maneuver. If we can communicate with the interlopers, they might be amenable to negotiations."

"That might be a challenge, my queen. Two warriors have been stationed inside the storeroom with the aliens, and four warriors are outside in the corridor. During the time that they have been under observation, they've not uttered a single word. They sit, all but one of them, who stands, and they say nothing."

"Are they without tongues? Are they mute?"

"We've seen tongues, although they are small and truncated. We heard speech, of a sort, at the water's edge when one of the male aliens tried to drown a warrior but then rescued him." When Nyslara's upper lip rose, demonstrating her agitation, Pussiro hurried on. "It might have been the warrior's fault, my queen. The alien appeared to have taken offense at a warrior, who prodded him. Before I could halt the action, the alien, who emerged from the great waters, tossed the warrior out past him. When the alien plucked him out, my warrior was panicked, and he sunk his nails into the male's shoulders. Then he was thrown into even deeper waters. The alien waded out and pulled him to shore."

Nyslara stared at Pussiro for so long that the commander ducked his eyes to the floor. "It happened as I said, my queen," Pussiro uttered softly.

"The alien came out of the great waters?" Nyslara asked with incredulity. "Did he have a ship, a skimmer, which was not capable of reaching the shore?"

"He had no ship, my queen," Pussiro said. He hissed softly, a sign of discomfort or exclamation, and eyed the exquisite painting on the ceiling.

"I'm waiting, Commander," Nyslara said firmly but quietly. She worked to control her temper, since it was obvious that the commander's encounter with the aliens had disturbed him.

"The alien rode two ceena to shore. In fact, four of them surfaced with him. But, while they were definitely ceena, they weren't exactly like ours."

"So the aliens have harnessed these creatures to work for them. Anything else, Commander?"

"Allow me to explain, my queen. I observed the ceena whistling to the aliens, and one of the aliens, the one who came out of the waters, whistled in return.

"A simple exchange … trained creatures begging for attention, and masters giving commands."

"Forgive me, my queen, but I must disagree. I witnessed the exchange on the shore. I would compare it to a discussion. It was clear to me that the aliens understood the whistles of the ceena … that they were communicating. After we surrounded the aliens and they threw up their arms as I demonstrated, the one at the water whistled, and the ceena dove back into the waters."

"Idiocy, Pussiro," Nyslara snarled. "What you're proposing is that the creatures we've hunted and fed on since we arrived on this planet have a language, which would make them an intelligent race. It'll take more than a few moments, observing an exchange, to convince me of what you're suggesting. Finish quickly, Commander. I'm becoming annoyed with this report."

"Yes, my queen," Pussiro replied, dipping his head. "I've already rotated the first two guards in the storeroom because they're disturbed by the aliens' quiet, especially one who is utterly still. I believe him to be the group's commander. According to reports, the alien hasn't moved a muscle … not shifted his stance, not changed his facial expression, not even blinked. I've ensured a senior warrior accompanies a junior one, when a pair is stationed inside the storeroom. The senior's years and experience should calm the younger warrior."

Nyslara regarded her wasat, a champion of innumerable battles, always fierce in the face of the enemy. Now, she saw concern, if not fear, and that caused a small element of doubt to befuddle her thoughts. She shook her muzzle, as if the action would clear her mind of the niggling feelings. "What of their appearance, Commander?"

"That's also disconcerting, my queen. They have four limbs, a head, and a torso, and they walk upright as we do. Except for small amounts on the crown of their heads, the aliens are hairless. But, most important, some aliens differ in skin color from one another."

"They're not of the same soma?"

"Not as we understand it, my queen. Even their bodies don't resemble one another. Some appear to be a match for any two of my warriors, and some are slender. And we believe there are two sexes among the aliens."

"They brought females? Are you certain?"

"I had them remove their coverings and instruments, until we had time to search those things for weapons and communications devices. Two of the aliens displayed most prominent breasts." Pussiro held his hands away for his chest to indicate the relative size. "While they do not possess the six nipples of our females, the capacity of the breasts would indicate that they could provide plenty of nourishment for a litter."

"Most disconcerting, Commander," Nyslara commented. Her head felt ready to burst with Pussiro's discoveries, and she felt ill-prepared to deal with the interlopers. Her assumption from the presence of two sexes hinted at the aliens' intention to colonize. *Why else bring females?* she thought.

"Come, Commander, I would see these entities for myself," Nyslara ordered, and she swept past Pussiro.

* * *

<It's a slug thrower, Lieutenant,> Bethany sent. The survey team was expending some of their precious energy reserves to comm the *Sojourn*. <We managed to eject the ballistic unit, and the techs took it apart. A mechanism strikes the back of a small casing, exploding a mix of chemicals, and projects a small metal ball down the barrel. It's a lethal weapon, Ma'am.>

Aboard the *Sojourn*'s bridge, Asu and Lieutenant Marie Soucis examined the weapon in the holo-vid. Rosette manipulated Bethany's implant view, rotating the weapon and adding the closeup view Smitty provided of the pieces of the explosive slug.

<Is this weapon meant to be a revered artifact, do you think, Sergeant?> Asu asked.

<You would think so, Captain, from the looks of it,> Bethany replied. <The wood holding the barrel and firing chamber appears to be worn down from decades of handling.>

<Captain, Lieutenant, the alien who dropped the weapon was a young one. I think it's a hand-me-down,> Smitty sent.

When Asu and Marie, who was also Méridien, looked at Rosette, she sent privately to them, <A New Terran expression for something used by an older sibling and when no longer suitable is passed to a younger sibling.>

<I would agree with Corporal Lange, Captain,> Bethany added. <But, while this weapon appears ancient, I've examined my recordings of the fight, in detail, and every weapon the aliens had is a copy of this model.>

<Sers, this evidence speaks to a race of intelligent creatures who has stagnated … that's unable to progress,> Rosette commented. <They demonstrate knowledge of a greater technology, which they have difficulty replicating. I would surmise that they didn't originate on this planet, but might have been marooned here.>

<Well, whoever these aliens are or however they got here, we have two problems to resolve,> Marie stated firmly. <Rosette tracked Willem's signal, which gave us his visuals and thoughts, as the aliens led him to a secreted cover in the ground. She lost the signal when the group descended below. The last thing we received was his view of a lengthy passageway, which means that the aliens could have taken our people anywhere underground.>

<So the tunnels are deep enough that even Willem's comm signal isn't getting through,> Bethany sent, expressing the thought on everyone's mind.

<Black space,> Smitty whispered.

<Just so, Corporal,> Marie commented.

<Our first concern has to be your ship, Sergeant,> Marie sent. <Pilot Saadner, have you attempted to open the rear clamshell at all?>

<No, Lieutenant, at the rate that net is sucking the energy from our cells I'm concerned we won't be able to open and close the hatch more than once or twice. While the sergeant and corporal believe our plex-crystal doors can withstand these weapons, we'll have to open the doors to circulate the air once we crack the hatch. But, none of us want these slugs banging around in the cabin, if the hatch is stuck open.>

<Understood, Pilot. Then that's what we must focus on, freeing your ship, and, if not that, at least protecting you so you can open the hatch to get air.>

<Lieutenant, if I may?> Edward sent. <The evidence points to a race of intelligent beings who are struggling to survive on this planet. I would have you note that no one is dead, neither the aliens nor us. We must not be hasty in whatever decisions we make.>

<Wise advice, Ser,> Rosette commented.

<Lieutenant, what are your intentions?> Orly asked.

<I'm ordering the second traveler down to assist you. You'll open the hatch when they're in position. The fighter pilot would have a firing position for any aliens who approached or aligned with the rear of the ship.>

<Might I suggest, Ma'am,> Bethany interjected, <that, following Edward's comments, you bring the fighter in over the ocean? Hover there, and let these aliens get a really good look at it. Then fire a beam into deep water. Let them know what type of armament our ships possess. So far, they haven't seen much from us except some stun gun shots, which by now have probably worn off.>

<Good idea, Sergeant,> Marie sent. <Standby, people, help is on the way.> Marie nodded at Rosette and the comm was closed.

* * *

The *Sojourn*'s captured crew hadn't traveled far underground before they were directed through an opening in the passageway and found themselves standing in a spacious storeroom. Shelves lined the walls and were stocked with all manner of goods, many of which were stone jars, their lids sealed tight with a waxy substance.

Two guards remained inside the storeroom with them, stationed near the doorway, which was closed off by a drape of fabric. At the present time, the curtain was closed, which Willem assumed was to prevent the curious from eyeing the aliens.

The captured team took woven grass mats from the shelves to sit on and protect their bare flanks from the cold floor, since the aliens had yet to return their clothes.

Willem continued to record everything — the surroundings, items on display, actions of the aliens, and the words spoken. Of particular note to the SADE were the furtive eyes of the guards, who chose to look everywhere else but at them, except for occasional glances at the Haraken women.

<We must look fairly odd to these people,> Willem sent. <They're furred, clawed, snouted, and of a similar coloring. Now regard us.>

The Harakens glanced around and saw multiple colors and shapes, flat faces, no claws, and no formidable teeth.

<I thought the events with Teague and the warrior, at the water's edge, to be quite telling,> Keira sent to her companions.

<You mean other than it being one of the more foolish things he's done,> Ginny replied, and her thought carried anger, which was meant for Teague.

<Besides that, which I agree with,> Keira sent, adding her emotional rebuke, <it was the warrior's reaction when he hit the water. It was shallow. He could have stood up, but his fright overruled his common sense.>

<These are a plains people, who live underground,> Xavier added. <Perhaps they have an enlarged fear of water.>

<When I picked him out of the shallows and he dug his claws into me,> Teague sent, <the alien's eyes were wild. At that time, he was completely disconnected from reality.>

<Captain, I could see that they might have a reasonable fear of the open ocean, but why be scared to death of knee-deep water? That doesn't make any sense,> Ginny added.

<The warrior's reaction was most unreasonable. It speaks to these people having an uneasy experience with the sea,> Willem sent.

Ginny glanced over at Teague, who looked stricken by Willem's words. <It might not be predators that these creatures are concerned about, Teague. It might be something else entirely,> she sent privately to him.

Unfortunately, Ginny's comments did little to quell Teague's dark thoughts about the possible fate of his four Swei Swee friends.

After little more than an hour, the two guards on duty inside the storeroom were changed. Once relieved, they fled as if racing for shelter. One of the replacements was the type of individual whom Willem was wishing to meet. The guard's muzzle was heavily scarred and tinged with gray, while his companion appeared quite young, as the first two warriors had been.

The SADE took a step forward, and the barrels of the guards' weapons swung toward him. Touching his hand to his chest, he said, "Willem."

The young warrior looked with surprise at his companion, but the older warrior hissed a dismissal.

Willem repeated his name and pointed at the older warrior, but was taken aback by the response. Both guards were snarling savagely and pointing their weapons directly at his face.

<Obviously, you don't extend your hands or fingers toward these people,> Willem sent to the others, quickly lowering his hand to his side.

<Look at their hands, feet, and teeth, Willem,> Xavier replied. <Those are dangerous weapons unto themselves.>

<So I guess pointing with your toes is a no-go,> Keira quipped.

The Harakens' audible chuckles put the guards on edge, but Willem noticed that, just like the first pair of guards, these two were occasionally glancing toward the women.

"Willem," the SADE repeated, touching his chest. Then he indicated the team's female security escort with his head, keeping his hands at his side. "Keira," he said. That brought the scarred one's muzzle around to focus on the female, and he nodded deferentially.

Ginny caught on and stood up. The guards' eyes flicked to her, but no weapons swung her way. Ginny placed a hand on her chest and spoke her name.

This time when the old guard nodded, he said, "Ginny," but it came out as Zhinni.

<What? The aliens prefer blondes,> Keira sent. <I'm jealous.> She possessed one of the prized Méridien genetic models — milk-white skin, dark eyes, and dark hair. She was a beauty in her own right, but, that aside, she was doing her best to keep the spirits of her companions up, including her own.

<Stands to reason,> Xavier commented dryly. <From what we've seen, there are only minor variations in these people's colorings. Basically, it's dark stripes in mostly the same general pattern, and the body colors range from dun brown to deep brown. A bright yellow color, like Ginny's hair, would attract a lot of attention.>

<Come to think of it, I'm happy I'm not blonde,> Keira shot back, adding a wink for Ginny.

Willem took the opportunity to indicate some mats on the shelf and spoke the Haraken word for it. The old warrior shook his head in negation and said, "bessach." When Willem repeated the word perfectly, the elder guard's eyes narrowed, but he didn't display any teeth. Willem took the opening and ran with it. He was able to learn nearly thirty words, before the warrior grew bored with the simple process.

Keira stood up and stepped forward. The guards' weapons, which had been lowered, were now pointed at her. She touched her chest and repeated her name. Both guards nodded their heads and did their best to affirm her name. They were more successful than they had been with Ginny's name, pronouncing it Hira.

<They're a matriarchal society,> Willem sent, recognizing the reason for the deference that the guards were paying the women, even alien ones.

<And so they should be,> Ginny sent. Her implant flooded with the mental chuckles that accompanied her companions' thoughts.

Keira stepped as close as she dared to the guards. Interestingly, they grew wary, but neither snarled or curled a lip at her. Then she stroked her hair, speaking the Haraken word. The elder guard quickly replied with his word. Keira went to her eyes next.

<Corporal, stay away from the nose, teeth, hands, or feet,> Xavier warned her via her implant.

Keira shifted to identifying arms, legs, and breasts.

Ginny edged forward and received a nod from both guards. By now, the barrels of the weapons were pointed overhead. She walked over to a shelf and searched for something to use to draw. An open pot of a dark substance, whose contents had dripped down the outside of the container and smelled of an animal by-product, suited her purpose.

Ginny held the pot up, and the scarred one named it. Then she knelt on the floor in front of the warriors, pulling Keira down beside her. Ginny dipped her finger into the bowl and made a single stroke on the floor. She held a finger close to her chest, careful not to point it at the guards, and spoke the word for one.

The guards exchanged expressions, which resembled rippling lips, and Ginny took that to mean they were confused. So she painted a second stroke next to the first one. Then she pointed at the first line and then herself, repeating the word for one. Next, she pointed at the two lines, then pointed at Keira and herself, and said the word for two.

The young alien twigged to it first, speaking excitedly to his partner, who nodded his agreement. The young warrior sat on his haunches, huge thigh muscles bulging the furred skin. He pointed a hardened, black nail at the first stroke and said, "diss" and then at the two strokes and said, "mess."

Ginny smiled in reply, and the young guard's head jerked back as if struck, and he sprung to his feet. Ginny and Keira quickly stood up too, and Ginny covered her mouth and lowered her head. "Zhinni," she heard the gray-muzzled guard say, and she looked up at him. He curled his upper lip slightly, tapped a sharp canine, and waggled his finger at her before he quickly pulled his hand to his side.

<Will you look at that, Teague? You're infamous,> Xavier sent. <The first interspecies hand sign on this planet, and it happens to be your remonstration signal of "don't do that.">

<Lessons learned,> Ginny sent to her friends. <No finger or toe pointing. Hands at your sides, at all times, and don't, under any circumstances, bare your teeth.>

To Ginny and Keira's surprise, the young guard squatted back down and dipped a dark nail into the pot, adding a third stroke.

When the women went to kneel on the floor, the scarred guard barked out, "Fellum, bessach, Zhinni, Hira."

Ginny and Keira could have clapped their hands and danced wildly, overjoyed at their success, but they kept still, with mouths closed and hands by their sides.

Willem nodded his understanding and brought two mats, tucking them under the women's buttocks for them to sit on.

The old warrior nodded his approval and then tossed his head to warn Willem away.

The young warrior chose to sit cross-legged on the floor, and Ginny and Keira adopted his pose.

<I'm not sure how comfortable I feel about this,> Ginny sent to Keira. <We're in our first alien meeting, sitting here naked, and exposing our private parts to the natives.>

Keira, on the other hand, who was raised as a Méridien Independent, when her parents were exiled to Libre, was much more comfortable with nudity than Ginny, a child of Sol. <I think we're fine, unless you see anything untoward raise its head.>

Ginny repressed the desire to giggle and resorted to covering her mouth with a hand. <Don't do that, Keira,> she warned, who had covered her mouth too. Both women looked at the old guard, who dipped his muzzle in assent at their efforts to observe his people's customs.

Before the young warrior could speak, Ginny motioned to Keira to stand up with her, and the young warrior joined them. She touched herself and repeated her name. Then she nodded respectfully at the old warrior and waited.

"Simlan, Tawas Soma, Sawa Messa," he said, assuming a proud and erect stance.

Ginny nodded her appreciation of the introduction and looked at the young warrior. He snapped to attention and announced, "Hessan, Tawas Soma, Sawa Messa."

<I would surmise that the aliens have introduced themselves by name, association, and something greater,> Willem sent.

Ginny repeated their names, nodding courteously to each. Then Keira and she sat back down, and Hessan joined them on the floor. The youthful warrior joined in the women's education with abandon. He worked through numbers and walked around the storeroom adding to the names that Willem had first learned. The women were fed questions by the other team members, and the vocabulary building went quickly.

At one point, Keira caught Hessan staring at her slender rear end. She looked pointedly at him, and the young warrior spoke to Simlan, who barked a laugh. Hessan explained something to Keira, but it didn't translate.

-7-
Prisoners

During Nyslara's trek to the storeroom, a lookout hurried forward. He bowed to her and looked expectantly at Pussiro.

"Make your report, warrior," Nyslara commanded.

Pussiro and the lookout stepped aside. The conversation went on and on, and Nyslara watched her wasat's mood shift radically during the exchange. *These events are so far beyond both our capabilities to predict*, Nyslara thought.

The warrior ran back the way he came, and Pussiro nodded to Nyslara, indicating they should resume their walk.

"The warrior has reported the arrival of a second shuttle, my queen. It attempted to rescue the first ship, which leads me to believe that our net has somehow pinned the first shuttle to the ground. Otherwise, why endanger their people when they know the capability of our weapons."

"Pussiro, you said no one was harmed in the initial encounter, and the soma did not discharge their weapons. How could the aliens know our capabilities?"

Pussiro ducked his head. In a battle against another nest, his warriors knew what was demanded of them, but the presence of aliens was eroding command control, and events were moving too fast to reestablish discipline in the ranks. "One of our warriors stayed too long in the ship. The hatch was closing, forcing him to drop his weapon so he could escape through the narrow opening."

Nyslara stared hard at Pussiro to the point that the commander's lips waffled in consternation. "Tell me about the second ship," she finally ordered.

"Yes, my queen. The new shuttle came in over the great waters and sat in the sky, unmoving for ten thiles."

"Unmoving and still no visible engine display?"

"None, my queen."

"What we could do with such technology, Pussiro. Our people could rise again. We could climb out of these tunnels and into the light where we belong."

"Agreed, my queen, providing the aliens do not eliminate every nest in retribution for our devastation of the ceena."

Nyslara's eyes lit in anger at Pussiro's comment. "You take the most inopportune times to remind me of the worst of our predicaments, Pussiro. It's good that you're a great wasat."

Pussiro nodded respectfully, saying nothing, deciding his great clawed foot would not fit beside the other one already in his mouth.

"Continue citing the details of the second ship's actions."

"The lookouts report that the ship tilted its nose down, and then the waters in front of it exploded in a giant spray. They said the spray reached over 50 shecks into the air. Then the ship did the same at the water's shore. The ground was said to have heaved and thrown material even higher into the air than that of the water's spray. The shore still glows where the aliens pointed their ship."

"What did it fire?"

"The lookouts say that some type of light, seen exiting the nose of the ship, struck the waters and later the shore. Afterwards, the ship circled over the one we netted and settled to the ground. Our warriors were commanded to shoot near the ships to frighten the aliens and keep them inside. But it pains me to report, my queen, that an errant shot wounded one of the aliens emerging from a hatch."

"Errant, commander?" Nyslara asked.

"The unit commander knows who fired the shot. The warrior is young, but he's known to be capable with his weapon."

"Was the alien killed?"

"That's unknown, but it's not believed so. Soon after our warriors' firing began and the one alien was struck, the second ship lifted off. It now hovers protectively above the first shuttle. With its great weapon, our soma must keep their distance. But they wait in their hideouts in case the hovering ship attempts to land again. It appears that no side has an advantage … for now."

"What of the young fool who shot the alien?"

"He's been disciplined. His formerly unmarked muzzle now displays the scars of his unit commander's rebuke."

"I would hear your opinion of the aliens' actions, Commander."

"I believe the aliens intended to demonstrate their power to us by firing into the water to ensure they had our attention. Then they fired onto the shore so that we would know the potency of their weapon against the land. They were warning us. It should be repeated, my queen, that the weapons they fired at my warriors did not kill."

"So, are these benevolent invaders, Pussiro, who intend to rule us gently, or are they cunning interlopers, luring us into a false sense of security about their intentions? I can't believe the Dischnya would be so fortunate as to receive aliens who were a passive species."

"I believe the answer to your musings, my queen, will be discovered quicker than we could wish."

"Well, Pussiro, we do have leverage. We have their ship pinned." Nyslara paused and regarded her wasat. "Hear me, Commander. You must be diligent and not let that shuttle loose."

Pussiro nodded his understanding.

"Also, Commander, we have their people. With these captives, it's hoped that we can discover what sort of aliens has landed. Come, hasten the pace, Pussiro. I'm anxious to learn."

* * *

The Harakens sat on bessach, the Dischnya mats, except for Keira and Ginny, who were squatting across from Hessan, a pot of the dark-pigmented material beside them and the newest drawings on the floor between them. Willem didn't need to see the figures with his own eyes.

Both women were continuously streaming their vision and thoughts to him via their implants.

Suddenly, the warrior leader, who led their capture, appeared in the doorway and barked a rough command. Hessan jumped to his feet and raced to his post. His head hung in shame when he was required to collect his weapon from Simlan before he could come to attention.

The leader stepped aside and a tall, regal-looking female stepped through the doorway. An intricately woven cloak surrounded her shoulders. It was held closed by a carved piece of animal bone. Unlike any other Dischnya, the Harakens had seen, her coat was a light tan, an almost milky color.

The Harakens came to their feet, and as one, they nodded their greeting.

Nyslara ignored their gestures and sniffed the air. It was rife with the smell of fossar, the rendering of fat from a small plains animal, which was used as a lubricant. She eyed the marks on the floor near the guards' feet and followed the trail of drawings across half the storeroom.

Pussiro's lips were rippling. He glanced once to Simlan, who stood erect and still. Not so for Hessan. The youth's digits were covered in fossar, and he trembled in anticipation of the severe disciplining to come.

"Commander," Simlan said, "as elder, I'm responsible for the actions of Hessan. Allow me to be disciplined for what has been done here while on duty." Simlan's muzzle was already marked with the scars of battle and discipline, whereas Hessan's muzzle was pristine.

Pussiro would have replied, but Nyslara extended a hand from her side with a single digit facing the floor, a signal for her wasat to wait. She continued to study the pictographs on the floor.

It was obvious to Willem that the entity in front of him, gazing at the drawings, was the leader of these people. That she was female fit with his estimation of a matriarchal society, and he hadn't missed the subtle hand signal she sent a warrior leader. "Willem," he said, nodding his head and placing a hand on his chest. He waited, but the female only stared at him with dark eyes.

Nodding to his left and right, indicating his fellow team members, he said, "Haraken." Then tipping his head toward her, the warrior leader, and the guards, he said, "Dischnya." This time, the female's long tongue came quickly in and out of her mouth, as if tasting the air.

Willem brought his arm up slowly, barely above his waist with his palm out, and indicated the older guard. "Simlan," he said. Doing the same toward the youthful guard, he said, "Hessan." Then the SADE touched his chest again, saying, "Willem."

Nyslara glanced around at the markings on the floor and at the fossar dripping from the hands of the female prisoners and her guard. She silently studied the alien, who spoke perfectly the Dischnya words. Then, making a critical decision, she extended her hind legs fully, rising to an impressive height, and said, "Chona Nyslara, Tawas Soma, Sawa Messa."

Willem touched hand to heart and gave Nyslara a leader's bow. The answering snort could have been an acceptance or dismissal, as far as Willem could tell. Nonetheless, he returned to an erect posture and glanced toward the warrior leader.

Nyslara barked a command, and Pussiro stepped up beside her. "Introduce yourself, Commander. This seems to be a day for firsts."

The Harakens watched the warrior leader rise to his full height and say, "Wasat Pussiro, Tawas Soma, Sawa Messa."

Willem greeted Pussiro in the same manner as Nyslara. This time he received a courteous dip of the head in reply.

<Now I know why Hessan was studying my bare ass,> Keira sent. <He was confused as to where I was hiding my tail. Look at hers.>

Keira's comment brought the Harakens attention to the impressive, scaled tail that extended below the back of Nyslara's cloak. While she stood still, it wrapped around her lower limbs, its tip resting on a foot, ostensibly a habit the female developed to keep it out of harm's way, especially since every Dischnya possessed great clawed feet.

Nyslara turned to Simlan. "What has taken place here?"

"My queen, it started with the one who calls himself Fellum. Simple words were taught. Then the females, Zhinni, the one with the bright crown, and Hira drew with the fossar. Hessan joined them, and I allowed it. Forgive me, my queen."

"Have the aliens learned anything of value that could hurt the soma?"

Simlan looked stricken. "Never, my queen. The aliens seem intent on learning our language. There was no exchange about our weapons, the number of soma, our tunnels, directions to their ship, or anything of a strategic nature."

Nyslara decided to test the intelligence of the aliens, especially the one called Willem. She could hear Simlan wasn't pronouncing the entity's name correctly, but she didn't think she could do much better. Nyslara pointed the claw at her primary in a drawing and eyed Willem, who gave her the correct Dischnya response. She continued to test him, touching drawing after drawing, including the hash marks, which indicated the number count. Willem didn't miss a one, and his pronunciation of the Dischnya tongue was perfect. The entire test was unsettling.

"Your guards have been busy, Commander," Nyslara said, continuing to examine the drawings. Indeed, they were benign, the type of things taught to mewlings soon after they demonstrated cognizance.

"They'll be severely disciplined, my queen."

"Not this time, Pussiro. I find your guards' efforts encouraging. Later, I would speak with them and learn more about what transpired here. Where is the one who whistled to the ceena and was injured by the soma's nails?"

"That's him, my queen," Pussiro said, indicating Teague with a palm upward movement of his hand.

Nyslara beckoned Teague forward, and she watched him stride toward her without hesitation.

"The arrogance of youth," Nyslara said to Pussiro when Teague stood before her.

"But if this is a youth, my queen, how large is his progenitor?"

Nyslara nodded her agreement and stepped around the young alien to observe her warrior's nail marks. She was careful to keep her clawed feet away from the soft, pink toes of the alien.

"Do you see this, Commander?"

Pussiro examined Teague's other shoulder. "I saw the alien's life fluids spill from these wounds myself, my queen. But these marks appear nearly healed and not scarred, as our flesh would be. In fact, the wounds seem to be fading away."

"I wonder, Commander. Is it their nature or their technology? We continue to discover more questions than answers about these creatures. I could wish for the advice of the Fissla — the thoughts of many queens might guide us better than my own."

"You have done well for the soma, my queen. We could wish for no other."

"Who knew, Pussiro, that a wasat possesses a tongue that could caress a queen?" Nyslara barked a laugh, but she eyed her commander for a brief moment. Soon she would need to give birth to a daughter to rule the nest, and Pussiro might be the perfect choice to sire the next queen.

Nyslara walked around Teague to stand in front of him again. "His eyes burn brightly, Pussiro."

"I believe the youth thinks of his four ceena, who were with him at the shore. They aren't his pets or his slaves. They're his companions, and they've been left in the great waters to fend for themselves."

"If your estimations are true, Pussiro, then this youth's shining eyes display a well of anger for us. Let's hope that he's an individual of no consequence, and that we haven't angered some powerful progenitor."

Nyslara shooed Teague back with an imperial toss of her muzzle. Then she indicated Keira with the palm of her hand and motioned her forward.

Keira stood absolutely still in front of Nyslara. She had a closeup view of the tall female, who possessed six teats, set in two rows, which were clearly visible through the opening in her exquisitely made cloak.

Nyslara closely examined the alien female, Keira, eyeing her breasts and her abdomen, as if searching for more of the former. At one point, she placed her snout next to a nipple and sniffed, then dismissed Keira too. "Definitely female, as you and your warriors have surmised, Commander. You can smell the difference between the males and the females, not that either scent is pleasant."

"I should point out, my queen, that one of the small tools we believe to be a weapon, which put the warriors to sleep, was worn by the female that you just examined."

"Interesting, both males and females are warriors or, at least, defenders of these aliens. Yet another discovery to challenge our comprehension of these creatures and their ways, Commander. Who is the alien that so frightened your young guards?"

When Pussiro nodded toward Willem, Nyslara beckoned him close. She eyed him and then leaned forward to sniff, her lips wrinkling along her snout. She traced a course across his shoulder and toward his hair, continuing to draw in air in short breaths.

"He has no scent, other than those found on Sawa Messa. How can this be, Pussiro?"

"I don't wish to state the obvious, my queen, but these are aliens. We can see that they aren't of one soma. Perhaps, they aren't a single species?"

"Is it possible that they have already mingled with the species of other worlds, possibly those of other stars?" Nyslara asked.

"It would explain why they possess ceena companions."

"Let's not venture into that discussion again, Commander, until we have more evidence of your conjecture." Nyslara's slight baring of teeth emphasized her point. She looked for a last time at the drawings on the floor and the collection of aliens waiting calmly before her. Curious to her was that their mannerisms weren't those of captives. There was no cowering. *They're confident in the eventual outcome of this encounter*, Nyslara thought. She had seen this attitude before. Committed warriors displayed it, knowing, if they were killed, revenge would be taken for their deaths. Taking all this in, Nyslara made one of the most momentous decisions of her rule, without knowing it.

"Return their coverings, Commander ... those you're sure are safe. Do so now."

Pussiro stepped into the passageway and ordered his guards to bring the aliens' coverings. The warriors had carefully divided the strangers' possessions into two categories — safe and suspect. Several warriors hurried into the storeroom, loaded with clothing, and at Pussiro's order, dumped everything at Willem's feet.

Willem gracefully bowed to Nyslara, thinking it time to demonstrate some of a Haraken SADE's abilities, not that the female leader would understand what she was seeing. Signaling each of his companions, at the appropriate time, Willem identified clothing by its embedded ID sensor and tossed it over his shoulder, targeting the individual by their implant.

The Harakens understood what Willem intended to do, and they calmly caught each item sent their way, dropping the pieces at their feet, until they had collected their allotment of clothes. Then they decided to do Willem one better, dressing simultaneously and in the same manner — left trouser leg, right trouser leg, left boot, right boot, and shirt.

Then Xavier called for a finishing touch, ordering a parade stance, and the Harakens snapped upright with hands behind their backs.

"An interesting display of capabilities, don't you think, Pussiro? Perhaps the aliens can give your warriors some lessons." The lips along Nyslara's jaw rippled in amusement. A quick glance at her wasat revealed his forehead was furrowed in concentration, as he sought to understand how the aliens had managed to coordinate their movements so perfectly.

"Prepare suitable accommodation for these captives, Commander. Think of them more as honored guests than as interlopers. See to their needs. You two," Nyslara said, turning to Simlan and Hessan, "are no longer on guard duty. You will be the alien's instructors. I will send you some of my advisors, who will assist you, but since you've earned the strangers' trust, you will be the face of the Tawas Soma."

Simlan and Hessan bowed, relief evident in their faces, and Hessan's knees finally stopped shaking.

"What about food, my queen? Do you think these aliens can tolerate our meals?" Pussiro asked.

"Another excellent question, Commander. I look forward to hearing how you solve the problem," Nyslara said and left the storeroom, her great cloak and tail streaming behind her.

* * *

Lieutenant Marie Soucis was laid out on a traveler's seat, which could double as a medic's exam table. A tiny device was attached to her temple, to induce unconsciousness, while the medical specialist, Yaki, probed for the slug embedded in the lieutenant's shoulder. Her officer's coat, a durable item in itself, managed to slow the metal projectile somewhat before it lodged deep in Marie's shoulder, cracking the bone.

Yaki extracted the slug and then ran his portable scanner over the area. He'd already sealed two bleeding arteries and reconnected several severed nerve endings. Painstakingly, he worked his way slowly out of the wound, fusing the tissue together behind him. The nanites in Marie's body would repair the rest, but it would take two days or more. In Yaki's opinion, the aliens fired an extremely primitive and ugly weapon.

The attempted rescue of the netted shuttle proved to be an unmitigated failure. The pilot, Verlan, had demonstrated the traveler's firepower, twice, ensuring the aliens were driven below ground, which gave Marie confidence in the mission's success.

It had been Marie's plan to have security exit the traveler first to provide cover fire for the techs, who were prepared to cut Orly's traveler free with portable torches. Verlan set the fighter down as close to the trapped shuttle as he dared, and Marie stood ready at the hatch with several troopers behind her. However, the hatch was barely open when the ship began to draw fire from the aliens' bolt-holes.

Marie continued to let the hatch drop open, since she couldn't detect any slugs careening off the hull. When the hatch was nearly halfway down, Marie leaned out to see where the shots were directed. That was a mistake. A slug ricocheted off the hatch's steps, and struck Marie in the shoulder. She fell forward onto the open hatch, grabbing her shoulder in pain and creatively swearing at the aliens and herself. Her compatriots reached out and hauled her back inside the ship

Bleeding and angry at being shot by primitive aliens, Marie's consideration of alternate rescue plans was cut short when Verlan called her attention to a group of natives, exiting a nearby tunnel and dragging a net behind them. Marie linked to the controller and saw the aliens hurrying toward their traveler's aft end. Choosing not to see their ship end up in the same predicament as the *Sojourn's* first traveler, Marie gave the order to liftoff and take up station over the downed shuttle.

Marie waved Yaki off when he tried to investigate her wound. Instead, she signaled Orly that he was clear to crack the rear hatch, if he could. Holding her comm open to Orly and Verlan, Marie sent, <Orly, don't worry about the natives shooting at your shuttle's aft end. I'm giving my pilot permission to render star services to any aliens who show their faces remotely near the rear of your ship.>

Verlan took up station over the downed traveler, as ordered, even as he thought to question Marie's directive. Haraken star services were the equivalent of funeral services, and, while he was prepared to execute the order, he didn't believe that vaporizing an intelligent, but primitive, species would be in keeping with the president or the Assembly's preferences for treatment of a native society, even if they had fired first and had taken their people captive. No one was dead yet, as far as he knew.

However, knowing the lieutenant was nursing a badly damaged shoulder from an alien weapon caused Verlan to decide to keep his opinion to himself. Besides, he'd just been informed that the lieutenant was under, having finally acquiesced to the medical specialist's entreaties to allow him to operate. So, Verlan mentally shrugged off the command, deciding that a beam shot 45 degrees off-target to frighten the aliens away was as good a tactic as any. *I can always apologize later for my poor fighter pilot skills,* Verlan thought.

* * *

Aboard the *Sojourn*, in the captain's cabin, Asu Azasdau studied the summary reports of Orly and Marie, his face dejectedly cradled in both hands — one ship stranded, five crew members captured, four Swei Swee unrecovered, and one lieutenant wounded. It was a sad state of affairs for what started as a scientific expedition.

The mission shuttle's predicament was locked in a stalemate. The *Sojourn* wasn't capable of landing on the planet, and its two travelers were now frozen in position. To allow the pinned traveler to keep its rear hatch cracked open, the second ship couldn't abdicate its station above the hapless ship.

In preparation for an extended siege, the scientists, techs, and security consumed much of their shuttle's remaining energy to prepare and store food dishes and pump water from the traveler's sealed tanks into containers.

On receiving the same reports, Rosette might have blanched, if she'd been capable of doing so. Sixteen years ago, she would have been installed in a liner's bridge, instead of, presently, replaced by a controller. Back then, if her ship's energy was drained, as it appeared was the shuttle's fate, her kernel, entwined in its crystal matrix, would have lost power, and she would have ceased to exist. While the shuttle's controller wasn't cognizant, the thought of its impending shutdown made her emotional algorithms cascade.

Asu studied the image of the hot, glowing sand where Verlan's ship fired to warn the natives. It dominated the cabin's holo-vid view in front him. The hole's fringe, the area closest to the water, had cooled, leaving an arc of blackened, glass-like silica.

When Asu accepted the captaincy of the *Sojourn*, he resolved to handle any issues that might confront the expedition. However, for the mission's personnel, it was fortunate that Asu didn't possess an excessive ego. He recognized when events progressed beyond his control and threatened to overwhelm the mission like waves repeatedly crashing over a drowning man's head. Asu had but one thought — they needed help, and they needed it soonest.

-8-
Sadesville

The Harakens called the small enclave Sadesville.

Alex Racine, Haraken's ex-president, called it a social disaster.

Truth was the SADEs didn't require the usual human living conditions — food dispensers, running water, refreshers, seating, and sleeping accommodations.

Two years after Alex won the SADEs' freedom, the first group of Confederation SADEs, who had completed their indenture period, elected to immigrate to Haraken, and the *Allora*, the Strategic Investment Fund's (SIF) overhauled passenger liner, landed 102 disgruntled SADEs on the planet. These SADEs wanted nothing more to do with the Confederation.

SIF was formed from the contributions of every Confederation SADE, who directed their stipends and profits from their share percentages to their SIF accounts. The fund was managed by eleven SADES, including Winston, and resembled the structure of the Haraken Central Exchange. And so it should. It was Julien who suggested the idea to Winston.

Haraken's Assembly had welcomed the first SADEs with open arms, but the populace had different reactions. Harakens came out to greet the newcomers, but their enthusiasm turned to surprise and then shock, witnessing the SADEs exiting two Exchange travelers, sporting bright skin colors and patterns, not to mention some of the oddest hair fashions seen anywhere in the human worlds. The SADEs meant their unusual appearances to celebrate their independence from the Confederation. But on Haraken, they were asking another group of humans to accept them.

It didn't take the new SADEs long to feel the chill of their reception, and they set about constructing their own small village. The problem was that the SADEs' concept of habitation wasn't a human one, and, in the beginning, they were uninterested in building accommodations for humans.

Improvements in Sadesville's social amenities were added slowly to host humans such as Alex Racine; his partner, Renée de Guirnon; Teague; Mickey Brandon, Haraken's premier engineer; Claude Dupuis, who constructed avatars for Z; Edmas, an engineering graduate; Jodlyne, who loved Edmas; and Emile Billings, a biochemist.

The new SADEs were fascinated by many of Emile's biochemical concepts and created a state-of-the art laboratory for his work. Much of their new fabrication and testing equipment had no equal anywhere on Haraken or most of the Confederation.

Still, trade was alive and well in Sadesville, and it served to integrate some humans with the newcomers. The SADEs needed components, power cells, power generators, and manufacturing equipment, although little else. They traded their skills as superb troubleshooters and analysts for credits, helping human entrepreneurs in their businesses. The new SADEs opened accounts in the planet's Central Exchange, which was owned and operated by Haraken's eight SADEs.

The *Allora* arrived in Haraken's orbit today, delivering a third group of SADEs to the planet, in as many years. It would bring the total of Confederation SADEs inhabiting Sadesville to 312.

Alex intended to meet with the SIF directors today and some of the more influential individuals among the Sadesville residents. He sought a means by which he could foster the integration of these new immigrants with the human population.

Walking down a passageway in one of Sadesville's warren-like buildings, Alex passed cubicle after cubicle. Most were empty, but some held SADEs, braced upright in their locked avatars. There were no doors on the cubicles, and there was barely room to turn around. From what Alex could see, none of the SADEs had bothered to personalize a space. It was still a first-come, first-served concept, even after years of habitation.

Alex entered the building's only conference room, a small area set aside for human visitors. He smiled at Winston and the few other SADEs. Then eerily, unless you were Alex Racine, every SADE, except Julien, froze. Alex looked to his friend, who held up a finger, to stall a response while he received the entire message.

At that same moment, Dane, an Assembly SADE and Exchange director, who was about to speak to Tomas Monti, Haraken's president, received the same message.

Fourteen days ago, aboard the *Sojourn*, Asu held a conference comm with Lieutenant Soucis and Rosette on his thought to place an emergency comm to Haraken.

Marie had concurred, sending, <Yes, we must inform the president.>

To which Asu had replied, <Agreed.>

<And Alex Racine,> Rosette had added.

<Most definitely,> Asu sent, readily concurring.

So, simultaneously, Alex Racine and Tomas Monti were informed of the emergency conditions of the *Sojourn*. Both of them learned that Alex's son, along with four other Harakens, was taken captive by an intelligent but aggressive species native to the planet, and the travelers were pinned in place, with time running short for the netted ship.

"No meeting today, Sers," Alex said quickly and spun around to leave, but he ran into an immovable wall that was his friend.

"If you please, Alex," Julien said. "The SADEs would have a few words with you."

Alex glanced over his shoulder, impatience written across his face. If Alex could have appeared aboard the *Rêveur* and fired its engines in the next tick of time, he would have done it already.

"Those SADEs, who can be freed from their obligations, stand ready to assist you, Alex Racine," Winston said formally.

"I don't have time to work out details with your people, Winston. Forgive my rudeness, but time is of the essence," Alex said. He turned around, expecting Julien to have anticipated his movement and stepped aside, but his friend continued to block his way.

Alex scowled, and Julien rendered an exact facsimile of Alex's expression on his own face. Alex's scowl deepened, as did Julien's.

"Teague is as important to Ser and you, as he is to me, Alex," Julien said quietly, taking the opportunity to reason with Alex since he had his friend's attention. "And I would exchange my existence to ensure his safe return, but I would not see you sacrifice your own without seeing the odds stacked in your favor."

Alex stared at Julien. He burned to shove past his friend and race for the *Rêveur*, but Julien and he had been through too much for Alex not to take time to listen to his crystal brother. Alex took a deep breath and exhaled it, placing a hand on Julien's chest where a heart would beat. Then he turned around and said, "Talk quickly, Winston."

"The *Allora* must return to Méridien, but only seven directors need be present to conduct SIF business. All other SADEs presently aboard our ship have volunteered to support the efforts to retrieve your people. In addition, those on Haraken who are unencumbered by business transactions are ready to join you," Winston said.

"That is, Ser, if you think 177 SADEs might be of assistance to your efforts," added Esther, who gave Alex an offhanded shrug, as if to say that there was the remotest possibility that there might not be one.

Alex extended Esther the briefest smile. SADEs could move faster, send signals farther, and calculate immensely more complex probabilities than any human could, not to mention their ability to survive without food or water. Alex turned his attention to Winston. "As soon as I'm aboard the *Rêveur* and have loaded the necessary supplies, we'll be breaking orbit. Anyone not aboard isn't going. Am I clear?"

"I'm sure that we'll be able to accommodate your schedule, Ser," Winston said politely, giving Alex a leader's salutation — hand to chest and a nod of the head.

Much of the fire drained from Alex's mind, and he looked around the room at the expectant faces, some appearing nearly human, and others resembling abstract art. "Thank you, all," he said. When he spun around, Julien no longer blocked his way.

Julien sent to Winston, <Two Exchange travelers will land shortly here to transport the locals to the *Rêveur*. Then the pilots will manage the transfer of the SADEs from the *Allora* to the *Rêveur*. Captain Lumley has been apprised of your arrival.> The last thing Julien did before turning to follow Alex was deliver a wink to Esther. <Well said, sister,> he sent her.

During Esther's visits to Haraken, she spent a great deal of time in the company of Cordelia and Miranda. She was determined to understand the nuances of human expression for her avatar, but, more important, she wanted to learn the subtleties of dealing with human emotions. Her positing of the question to Alex of the SADEs' value to support a rescue mission was just such an exercise in dealing with the anxieties of a distraught father, and she had acquitted herself admirably.

* * *

"It's critical that I inform you, President Monti, that every SADE has received this emergency comm, which means —"

"That Julien's already relayed the message to Alex Racine," Tomas finished for Dane. The frown furrowing Tomas' face quickly morphed into a look of horror. "Black space," he swore, having adopted the New Terran expression years ago. "Dane, transfer Asu's comm message to Admiral Tachenko, in case she hasn't received it. Tell her that Alex received the same message, and that I will be speaking to her immediately after I reach Alex."

<Talk quickly, Tomas,> Alex said in response to Tomas' comm request, which wasn't really necessary for Alex to send. It wasn't as if Alex was preoccupied with flying his personal transport home. Julien wouldn't let him pilot the little grav transport, having locked him out of the controller until Alex relented. So, Alex sat in the passenger seat, his arms folded across his chest and his mind reeling with dire thoughts of what might have happened to his son and the other Harakens.

<Alex, I can't imagine the emotional turmoil you must be experiencing, but I urge you to wait and speak with me before you make any decisions,> Tomas sent.

<I've already made the most critical decision, Tomas. I'll be launching the *Rêveur*, as soon as possible.>

<I know you don't want to hear this, Alex, but the *Sojourn*'s expedition is government sponsored. Those individuals at Celus-5 are our responsibility, and, in my authority as president, I'll be deciding which resources are sent to safely retrieve them.>

<I'm a private citizen, Tomas. There are no restrictions on where I can travel.>

<Know that if you travel to Celus-5, Alex, you'll be interfering with a government-sanctioned operation.>

<What are you saying, Tomas, that when I manage to free my son I should leave the rest of our people where they are so you can rescue them?>

<Alex, I need you to carefully think this through. You *are* a private citizen, who is without the resources to take on an indigenous population of aliens, who possess slug-throwing weapons and have proven they're willing to use them.>

Julien interrupted the discussion with a private message for Alex. <Ser, we might wish to return home once we've recovered Teague and the others. Perhaps, it would be wise to allow the president to express his concerns.>

Alex eyed his friend, who refused to glance in his direction. The fact that Julien was right, didn't improve Alex's mood, but, nonetheless, it was sage advice.

<Let me ask you a question, Tomas: Who, on your government staff, would you consider an alien expert?>

Tomas stared across his desk at Dane, who cocked an eyebrow at him. They both knew that the Harakens had only four alien experts — Teague and Ginny, who had been captured; Mutter, the Swei Swee's Hive Singer; and, of course, Alex, who held the allegiance of every whistling, six-legged, claw-snapping, four-eyed, Haraken Swei Swee.

<Thought as much, Tomas,> Alex sent, when the comm remained quiet.

<Dane, link Admiral Tachenko,> Tomas sent privately.

<Alex, I've just heard. I'm so sorry to hear this has happened to your family again,> Tatia sent when her implant signaled who was on the comm. <We'll get Teague, Ginny, and everyone back safely.>

<I was just explaining that to Alex, Admiral,> Tomas said.

<And how was that going, Mr. President?> Tatia asked.

Tatia and Tomas could hear Alex's throaty laugh, and Tatia sought to take advantage of it.

<I gather you're ready to launch the *Rêveur*, Citizen Racine,> Tatia sent.

<Citizen Racine, is it now?>

<Just establishing a starting point, Alex,> Tatia replied. <This situation will need firepower and a familiarity in dealing with aliens. Suppose you were approved to go along as an advisor?>

Everyone could hear Alex's low growl.

<Not the most diplomatic response, Alex,> Julien sent to his friend.

<And … what if my appointed officer was someone you could work with … someone who would heed your expert advice?> Tatia asked.

<Whom did you have in mind, Admiral?> Alex asked.

Both Tatia and Tomas felt as if they'd reached a delicate tipping point, and Tomas was hoping that whatever Tatia was about to suggest would start the rescue mission off on the right foot.

<As the alien advisor, Alex, wouldn't you agree that a carrier would be the wrong response?>

<Agreed.>

<And wouldn't you agree that a single sting ship with its four travelers would be about the right level of response, especially since the possibility of enemy ships in the area is remote?>

<If the *Sojourn*'s crew had spotted alien vessels, Asu would have mentioned them in his comm, and he wouldn't have risked a survey landing,> Alex sent back.

<Agreed. So one sting ship is all that's required, and you would be aboard as the advisor, yes?>

<One sting ship, yes, but I'll need to take the *Rêveur*.>

<Why, Alex?> Tomas asked.

<I have 177 volunteers who wish to accompany me.>

<Alex, I don't see how placing more civilians at risk is going to help the situation. This is a rescue mission, it requires trained and capable individuals,> Tomas pleaded.

<I understand your concerns, Tomas. I will limit the number of people aboard the *Rêveur* to a minimum crew.>

<Alex, if you have a minimum crew aboard, but still need the liner, who are the volunteers?> Tatia asked, suspicious of the large number.

<Well, I told the SADEs there was no need to join me, but you know how independent-minded they can be.>

This time, the comm was filled with Tatia's hearty laughter, as only the sound could erupt from a New Terran's heavy body.

<Your turn, Admiral,> Alex sent. <Which sting ship?>

Haraken had three of the lethal warships, which possessed a beam lance many times more powerful than a fighter's, could carry four travelers, and was equipped with both starship and grav engines. The design was a marvel of Haraken engineering.

<Well, I wouldn't want there to be any friction between my military commander and the advisor, so I was thinking Captain Reiko Shimada, with Commander Franz Cohen for fighter support.>

<Done,> Alex said quickly.

<Some ground rules, Alex,> Tatia sent back just as quickly. She'd worked too long with Alex not to know how his mind worked.

<Franz has command of all pilots, which includes those that will be aboard the *Rêveur*.>

<Acceptable. What else?>

<Most important, Reiko has mission command and will supersede Captain Azasdau and Willem's authority.>

There was a long pause, while Tatia and Tomas waited.

<It's worthy of consideration, Alex,> Julien sent privately.

<How long until your people are ready, Admiral?> Alex asked.

<Two days ... three at the most.>

<One day, then the *Rêveur* launches.>

<Agreed.>

When Alex dropped off the comm, Tomas sent, <Well done, Admiral, I thought we would never get Alex to agree to your proposal.>

<Oh, he agreed all right, Mr. President … to Reiko and a sting ship, but not to her ultimate authority.>

<But …> Tomas sent, but his thought stuttered to a halt.

<The Admiral's correct,> Dane sent. <Alex Racine adroitly implied his consent, but he never gave it.>

<Why that sneaky son of a New Terran … apologies, Admiral … but then why did you relent?>

<Because that's the best deal we're going to get, Mr. President. And I know Alex and Reiko. They can work together, and that's what we need.>

<Why did there have to be aliens hiding underground on Celus-5?> Tomas lamented, his thoughts betraying his mental anguish at the turn of events so many light-years away.

<I'll offer you the simple answer, Mr. President. We live in the same world as Alex Racine.> Tatia closed her comm, shaking her head in disbelief. For someone who had been a ground pounder in the Terran Security Forces, Tatia had a firm belief, at that time, that her people were alone in their corner of the universe. *It's getting mighty crowded out here,* she now thought, as she prepared to find a way to phrase Reiko's orders without contradicting the president's authority.

* * *

After receiving Asu's message, Alex decided to wait until he reached home before he broke the news to Renée, but, engrossed in completing a launch list necessary to ship onboard before getting underway, he'd failed to consider the fact that the emergency comm had spread across the entire Hellébore system. Every Haraken knew about the expedition's dire circumstances within a quarter-hour of the message hitting the farthest stations and mining posts. If any poor individuals were asleep, someone woke them to share the news.

Julien set the personal transport down beside Alex's house. In the fading evening's light, Alex could make out stacks of baggage on the broad porch and Renée perched on one of the larger bundles.

Without a preamble, Renée launched into a summary of her efforts. "I heard the news from Z. I've contacted your parents, and they'll watch Julien and Cordelia's young ones while we're away. Captain Lumley commed me that he will be aboard the *Rêveur* soon and make preparations for getting underway, including readying the owner's suite. His work is cut out for him since we haven't used the liner in over half a year. Our belongings are packed, and we're waiting for the arrival of one of the liner's travelers for transport to the *Rêveur*."

Alex listened to Renée reel off her accomplishments in a monotone fashion, and his heart lurched in sympathy for the pain she was enduring, knowing her son was in mortal danger. He strode up to her and swept his love into his arms, and Renée broke into tears, sobbing into Alex's shoulder.

"I want our son back," Renée said, her voice muffled by Alex's jacket.

"We'll do whatever is necessary to get him back safely, my love," Alex replied, holding her tightly.

"But what if he's already —"

"Don't say it, and don't think it, Renée," Alex said, cutting her off. "We have to be patient and hope for the best. We'll know more once we reach Celus-5." Alex heard his own words, and they failed to convince him. Then again, the words weren't meant for him.

As quickly as Renée started crying, she stopped. She snuffled a couple of times, and then announced, "Our ride is here."

Alex set Renée down and glanced over his shoulder at the traveler landing 60 meters from the house, its grav drive enabling a noiseless approach. Julien was marching toward the shuttle, even as the hatch opened. The first boots on the ground were three crew members, who hustled over to the porch, nodded a greeting to Alex and Renée, and grabbed some of the couple's belongings.

"Come, my love, time's a wasting," Renée announced, striding behind the first crew member, who was loaded down with several carryalls and making for the waiting shuttle.

Alex, still unsettled by his exchange with Renée, grabbed two large packs and followed in his partner's wake. At the hatch, he threw the packs up to waiting hands and then clambered aboard.

Alex expected to find the traveler nearly empty. Instead, it was packed with bodies and bags, and Alex was forced to weave his way through the crowded aisle to reach the front of the main cabin. Ahead of him, he could see hands touching Renée in sympathy as she made her way forward.

As the emergency message spread across Haraken, Alex received comm after comm from close friends, but he'd ignored them. If they weren't calls of sympathy, which he didn't have time or the desire to entertain, then they would be requests to accompany him, and he knew he would find it difficult to refuse their offers. In his own incommunicative way, Alex tried to be faithful to his statement to Tomas that he would limit the number of civilians who would accompany him. More important, he didn't want his friends exposed to dangerous circumstances.

As Alex stepped past crew members, who were trying to find places for their baggage, he ran his implant's locator app to see who was aboard. Crew were present, which he expected, but there were many others — human civilians.

<Renée,> Alex sent in consternation, <I told Tomas that I wouldn't invite civilians, except for a minimum crew.>

<Yes, Alex, our friends told me that you wouldn't accept their comms … a bit rude of you, my love. However, I *did* accept their comms and was pleased to accept their offers to join us. Your conscience can remain at ease. You haven't violated your promise to Tomas, and I never promised the president anything.>

Alex eased around some crates in the aisle. Mickey, Claude, Edmas, and Jodlyne sat in double pairs of facing seats. A small nanites-active pedestal was anchored to the deck between them, and a miniature holo-vid, a new Haraken invention, sat on the pedestal, displaying an intricate schematic.

The three men were engrossed in a discussion, with Jodlyne enjoying the fact that she was sitting next to Edmas. The two orphans had found each other in the ventilation tunnels of a Sol orbital station when they were young teenagers. It had taken Edmas longer than Jodlyne to realize that his feelings for her ran much deeper than that of a friend and fellow tunnel rat.

Claude, Z's primary avatar fabrication technician, looked up when Alex paused beside them. "We've been working on some exciting new avatar developments with Z," Claude said. "But you're taking our primary advisor and most of our intended clients with you. So we're following them out to Celus-5 and back in order not to lose R&D time."

"And what rescue mission can't use the best engineering team the planet has?" Mickey threw in.

Edmas, a graduate engineering student, nodded in agreement, and Jodlyne added an innocent and charming smile.

Alex's eyes narrowed slightly, and he stared at each man without saying a word before he moved on. Julien and Cordelia sat together, and she stood up and gave Alex a warm hug when he reached their seats.

Miranda and Z sat opposite the other two SADEs, and Miranda took a turn hugging Alex. However, she added just a hint of hip movement, which caused Alex to pull his head back and eye her.

"It's always best to distract a man from focusing too long and too hard on any one subject, dear," Miranda said, touching Alex's cheek and sitting down beside Z. The couple immediately returned to their conversation.

Alex found Emile Billings and Pia Sabine sitting together.

"The expedition might need an additional medical technician, especially with aliens firing slug-type weapons at our people," Pia stated firmly.

Alex's eyebrows rose in question. Pia knew that the *Sojourn* was well prepared for medical emergencies.

"Well, if truth be told," Pia added, "I'm not letting Mickey jaunt off to an alien world without me. I'm here to ensure that my partner does nothing foolish."

"As for me," Billings quickly added, "I'm in the middle of an exciting breakthrough. The SADEs and engineers, who are assisting me, will be aboard the *Rêveur*, and I'm anxious to continue my work. Most of these crates are from my lab. The rest is on another shuttle."

"And what does your wife say about you joining a rescue mission?" Alex asked.

Billings ducked his head and offered Alex a grin of embarrassment. "Janine said I'm to keep my butt safely aboard the *Rêveur*, and that if I get shot by an alien, she promises to finish the job if I'm not dead."

Alex had to smile at that one, surprised that he could do so after hearing the news of his son's capture. *Keep your thoughts positive, Alex,* he told himself mentally, *just like you told Renée.*

Renée was seated across from the twins, Étienne and Alain de Long, co-directors of the Haraken Security Directorate, initially responsible for the safety of the president and Assembly but, years later, expanding to become the planet's security force.

"And does the president know that you two have abandoned your duties to join this mission?" Alex asked.

"The Security Directorate is in good hands," Alain replied. "We've hired and trained superb subordinates. It's a lesson we learned from a good friend."

"And, as for the president, he's aware that we are, as you once put it so succinctly, Ser, on vacation," Étienne added with a grin.

"It occurred to us that a trip to an exotic new planet might make the perfect holiday trip," Alain deadpanned.

"Exactly," Étienne chimed in, "and since the *Rêveur* was headed in that direction, we asked Ser de Guirnon for a ride."

"She was charmingly accommodating," Alain said.

"We would have asked you, Alex," Étienne said, and the humor went out of his eyes, "but you appeared to be distracted."

"And you know how dangerous it is to be distracted on a critical mission," Alain added, and he too was staring at Alex with a stern look.

"Point taken, Sers" Alex acknowledged. He moved on to the pilot's cabin, missing Renée lean across the opening to place her hands on a knee of each twin. She smiled, and Étienne and Alain nodded their heads in acceptance.

Commanders Cohen and Valenko sat in the pilot and copilot seats. Alex knew about Franz, but Svetlana was unexpected.

"Commanders," Alex said, by way of greeting the pair.

"I believe it's allowed to hug a civilian," Svetlana said, rising to greet Alex. "My sympathies, Ser," she whispered in Alex's ear. "We will get them back safely or the aliens will regret it."

"They've made a mistake, Svetlana," Alex said, as she returned to her seat. "That doesn't necessarily mean the entire species has to pay the price."

"Understood, Ser, but if you wish revenge, I'd be happy to deliver the punishment."

"You'll be the first to know, Commander," Alex promised. That seemed to mollify Svetlana, who donned her helmet. Alex looked at Franz, who was wearing a slightly stricken face.

<Always good to know how your fellow officer feels about a situation, wouldn't you say, Commander?> Alex sent privately to Franz.

<I would have thought so ... until now,> Franz sent back. The furrow in his brow never disappeared, as he pulled his helmet on and prepared for liftoff.

"Thank you, Tatia," Alex whispered softly, as he returned to the main cabin. On this mission, his weapons master, Tatia, would be staying home. The discovery of more aliens had unsettled the population from the president down to the newest immigrant, and Admiral Tachenko would be ensuring the system was prepared to defend itself if there were more than just slug-throwing aliens in the Celus system. But Tatia was still taking care of him, having sent two of her best fighter commanders with him. Between Franz's cool, calculating style and Svetlana's out-of-the-box tactics, the rescue mission was well prepared, if force was required.

-9-
Alex and Reiko

Statements of condolences and well wishes for a safe return originated from Haraken and throughout the Hellébore system. Millions of messages poured into the *Rêveur's* controller from those planetside and from hundreds of thousands of captains, officers, pilots, station personnel, and crew across the system, as the liner sailed out of the system.

First Julien and then Cordelia, Z, and Miranda, sought to take the comm load from the ship's struggling controller. When even they were overwhelmed, Winston, Esther, Hector, and Didier picked up the slack.

<You were correct, Winston,> Hector sent during a lull in the onslaught of messages. <Alex Racine and Renée de Guirnon are indeed wealthy humans if we were to use the measure of those who care about them.>

Preparations to launch the *Rêveur* had proceeded at a phenomenal pace. The ship's minimal crew merely stood back and watched as Julien, Cordelia, Z, and Miranda directed the Confederation SADEs in the offloading of travelers and the transporting of baggage and crates to their destinations.

Mickey, Claude, Edmas, and Emile waited for their deliveries in the *Rêveur's* engineering suite, which, in its last iteration, had been Billings' biochemistry lab. It would become a lab once again, but of a different sort. The space would be shared between Emile's project and the engineering tests of Claude and Mickey. Six holo-vid projectors were unpacked and linked into the ship's controller.

The massive amount of data brought by the engineers and the biochemist was stored on portable crystals and was carefully handed over to SADEs to install under the suite's control panels along with a secondary controller, which was designed to aid their research and prevent pulling on the ship's controller. As the secondary controller came online and began a data integrity check, Mickey breathed a sigh of relief.

"Why were you so worried, Mickey?" Edmas asked. "If there were any problems with this controller, I'm sure Captain Lumley would have lent us access to the ship's controller."

"My young friend," Mickey said, clapping an enormous hand on Edmas' shoulder, "we're sailing with Alex Racine. The last thing you want to do is interfere with his ability to call on this ship for everything it's got when he needs it."

Edmas blinked in confusion and glanced toward Jodlyne, who was directing SADEs in unpacking, then storing the empty crates. "But we're just along for the ride, Mickey, aren't we? It's not like there's any expectation of trouble while we sit in orbit."

Mickey and Claude laughed so long and hard that Edmas blushed in embarrassment.

Claude was the first to recover and apologize to Edmas. "Ser, that man is the universe's greatest lightning rod for the unfortunate and lost. If I had to guess, I'd say the trouble on Celus-5 is greater than a pinned traveler and some captured Harakens."

"You can bet on that," Mickey added. He was a major participant in Alex's card games, of which the favorite one for New Terrans was poker.

Jodlyne paused in her efforts and stepped over to join the discussion. She left a female SADE, who had bright blue skin and long, orange hair gathered in a top knot, holding a 110-kilo crate in the air and waiting for further directions.

"Are you saying that this is more than a simple recovery of our people and a shuttle from a few backward natives?" Jodlyne asked, staring at Mickey. She watched the two senior men glance at each other.

"It might start that way, but there's a good chance it won't end that way," Claude said.

"And you're saying this simply because of the involvement of a single man, who's no longer a leader of the planet or the military?" Jodlyne continued.

The men exchanged another glance, which began to irritate Jodlyne. "That's ridiculous. The universe doesn't order itself around the actions of one human. That's ... that's mysticism."

Mickey smiled warmly in the face of Jodlyne's display and said, "There's always proof to the contrary." Claude and he returned to their work, leaving Edmas and Jodlyne to wonder what they had volunteered for, and, more important, who might be right.

<Well, Alex Racine went to the aid of a single Confederation SADE, Allora, and look what became of that,> Edmas sent to Jodlyne. <Speaking of SADEs, I believe you left Trixie holding a crate.>

"Oh, my, I'm so sorry, Trixie," Jodlyne said, hurrying back to the SADE. She was momentarily confused because the ID of the SADE pinged back as Lenora. "Please set that crate down over in that far corner. We'll stack these others on top of it."

"No need to apologize, Ser. I found the exchange most instructional," Trixie replied with an overly bright smile. Her pixie-like appearance was fostered by her unusual skin color and accented by pointed ears, and she was one of the SADEs who had yet to set foot on Haraken, having just arrived aboard the *Allora*.

"How so, Trixie?" Jodlyne asked.

"I served aboard a tiny station, orbiting a satellite-rich planet in the system of a far colony. Routine communications were the order of the day ... day after day, year after year."

"How old are you, if I might ask?"

"I'm young, as SADEs go. It's been fifty-seven years since I was created."

Jodlyne swallowed with difficulty. Trixie was the age of her mother, or, at least, she was the age of her mother if she had lived. Once sentenced to the corporate mines of Sol in the outer rim, life expectancy was measured in one to two years.

"You appear stricken, young Ser," Trixie said with concern. "Have I said something wrong?"

The words of Julien and Cordelia came back to Jodlyne. The newly freed SADEs, who immigrated to Haraken, were fragile beings. Robust in structure and computational analysis they might be, but their developing personalities and interactions with non-Confederation humans needed careful coaching.

"No, Trixie, what you said reminded me of my mother, whom I lost at a young age."

"I am sad for you, young Ser. I felt a similar loss a few years ago when the Confederation Council ruled against a newly created SADE —"

"By the name of Allora," Jodlyne finished. "I thought what happened to her was tragic."

"Then we are in agreement, young Ser. The universe is not an equitable place."

"But if we help one another, it can be a better place," Jodlyne said, reaching out to take Trixie's brightly colored hand.

"Then we are in agreement again," Trixie replied, adding her electric smile. "Let us return to work before the lash falls on us for our slothfulness." When Jodlyne looked at her in confusion, Trixie added, "I've found the most wonderful collection of ancient vids and stories onboard this ship. Ser Racine and Julien have collected them."

Jodlyne received a link to the library in her implant. "Come, young Ser, let us apply ourselves. Two most anxious humans wait on us to launch."

* * *

Hours ago, Captain Reiko Shimada stood on the bridge of the sting ship, *Tanaka*, and observed the *Rêveur* break orbit. Earlier, Commander Franz Cohen reported to her that the travelers and pilots were aboard both ships. Despite his people and ship's readiness, the *Tanaka*'s crew was still transporting equipment and sundry material via supply shuttles. Knowing this was a critical rescue mission, Reiko aimed to be ready for almost anything. She had been caught short once before and had vowed never to be found wanting again.

Now, Reiko, with Franz by her side, watched the *Rêveur* on the holo-vid, an ever-widening gap forming between the liner and the sting ship, which was still in orbit around Haraken. "Do you think I should comm Alex and ask him to wait?" Reiko asked Franz.

"If I might offer a piece of advice, my heart," Franz replied. "Think of Alex as the president and then imagine how he would take that suggestion."

"But he isn't the president, anymore," Reiko objected.

Franz's face broke into a wry grin, and he shook his head in negation. "Imagining Alex with a title was for the benefit of your imagination ... to help you picture him that way. In Alex's mind, he never really was the admiral or the president. Those were titles that circumstances forced him to carry."

"So whom do you believe him to be?"

"Alex was, and always will be, the uncomplicated, explorer-tug captain, who was required to play extraordinary roles. Thinking that he's no longer president will only confuse matters for you. Instead, think of the man who discovered that the aliens destroying the Confederation were slaves to a higher power and who used economics to force your government to reconsider its policies. Our alien advisor is the same man who rescued the derelict, foreign starship that flew into New Terran space."

Reiko glanced at Franz. His words hadn't cleared the questions she had about the roles Alex, as advisor, and she, as mission commander, would share. *I'm pleased one of us is happy,* Reiko thought, watching her lover gaze into the holo-vid, the *Rêveur* stretching out its lead, and a smile on his face.

Mentally glancing at the latest reports in her implant from the ship's crew chiefs, Reiko calculated she could launch the *Tanaka* in five more hours. The sting ship, with its grav drive, could accelerate much faster than the liner, and she had the controller run computations. The answer pleased her. The *Tanaka* could catch the *Rêveur* before it reached the outermost planet's orbit. That the two ships would make the jump to Celus-5 together gave Reiko an opportunity to enjoy her own smile.

∗ ∗ ∗

Alex slowly paced the width of the *Rêveur*'s bridge.

With the help of the SADEs, Captain Lumley had seen the ship squared away in record time. Francis assumed they would wait to hear from Captain Shimada, who would send a signal when they were to break orbit, but one look at Alex's face had told Lumley that launching at the earliest possible opportunity would be the wiser decision.

<I've always felt it a shame that we couldn't harness that energy to drive the ship so much faster,> Julien sent to Renée, as the two of them watched Alex stalk the bridge. <I'm sure if we'd been successful, we might have achieved, at least, a 10 percent increase in acceleration.> Unfortunately, Julien could see that his attempt at humor did nothing to soften the pained expression on Renée's face.

<I'm as worried as Alex, Julien,> Renée sent in return. <I can't help thinking that it's taken too long for Asu's emergency message to reach us and we'll arrive too late … something awful will have already happened to Teague and the others.>

<Ser, in the face of overwhelming odds, our people wisely chose to surrender, and it must be noted that the natives allowed their capture instead of firing their weapons. This begs remembering. And let's not forget, there's a SADE among the captives. This stacks fortune in our favor. Willem will be doing everything possible to find a safe solution to their dilemma.>

On another loop of the bridge, Alex glanced up, noticing that Winston, Esther, Hector, and Didier were standing at the four corners of the bridge, with locked avatars. <Julien,> Alex sent. <What are the SIF directors doing?>

<They're observing, Alex,> Julien sent in reply.

<Observing what?>

<Not *what* but *whom*. They're observing you.>

Alex eyed Julien, his stare demanding more details. Julien was tempted to wait for Alex to ask the next question, knowing precisely how long he could draw out the suspense before Alex lost his patience. But this wasn't the right time for their games.

<The SIF directors have positioned themselves in the four quadrants, so they can monitor your facial movements and body language from all angles, Alex, and they're beaming this information plus your communications to the other Confederation SADEs,> Julien explained. <They've singled you out as the human model they wish to emulate. I attempted to convince them to choose a worthier candidate, but you know how stubborn SADES can be.> Julien ended his explanation by adorning his head with a tall, pointed, black hat, labeled dunce, and he added a brilliant smile to contradict the idiotic display.

Alex barked a laugh at his friend and returned to his thoughts, while he continued to circle the bridge.

<Julien, what was the purpose of your strange headgear. It appeared farcical in nature,> Hector sent.

<It was meant to distract Ser Racine,> Julien replied.

<But shouldn't you be aiding him in solving the problems he will face at Celus-5?> Didier asked.

<I am helping him,> Julien replied. <Harakens, who are comprised of ex-Independents and New Terrans, are governed as much by their emotions as by their reason. In this regard, they vary greatly from the humans that you dealt with in the Confederation. If unchecked, emotions in situations like this, where a couple's only child is at risk, can override the mind's ability to examine the problem dispassionately. Humor, in its many forms, can ease the tension, quiet the raw emotions, and allow the mind, which is now in a more relaxed state, to be more creative in solving the issue.>

<Who taught you this, Julien?> Esther asked.

<Experience and a desire to protect my friend,> Julien replied.

<So you observe your friend, and if you perceive an imbalance, you attempt to correct it in any manner you can,> Winston sent.

<Precisely,> Julien replied.

<You've done these things for Alex, but has he been able to assist you in return?> Esther asked.

<Oh, yes,> Julien replied, sending to the SADEs the signature algorithm Cordelia and he had created. It exploded in the kernels of the four SADEs in a beautiful, ever-evolving, kaleidoscope of color before fading away. <He taught me to love life.>

"We can always try talking to the alien leader," Alex said, offhand, as if he was speaking to himself.

"In whose language?" Julien asked, recognizing Alex's frustration was getting the better of him.

"That's what Cordelia and you are for," Alex replied.

"And how long do you think these aliens will stand still while we learn their speech and mannerisms, Alex?" Cordelia asked.

"So we wave a white flag," Alex replied, his temper growing.

"What if the aliens' symbol for attack is a white banner?" Julien asked.

"Okay, Julien, you suggest an idea," Alex said heatedly, throwing up his hands.

"Apologies, Alex, but I haven't a viable plan and neither do the other 180 SADEs aboard this ship, who've been following this conversation."

"Where's our devious one when we need her?" Alex asked, returning to pacing.

"Admiral Tachenko is protecting Haraken, which is her rightful duty," Renée said. She was just as unhappy about Tatia's absence as Alex, but Renée didn't want the admiral thought ill of because she wasn't present.

"With so little information, Alex, I'm sorry to say, we must wait until we arrive on-site and see how events unfold before we can make intelligent plans. To paraphrase you, this game must be played one hand at a time," Julien said.

Unfortunately, Alex wasn't satisfied with that answer, and he continued to pace. He worked at clearing his mind, putting all thoughts of Teague aside, and considering the problem from a detached perspective. In his implant, he deconstructed the emergency message, which contained detailed information about the events that had unfolded planetside, and constructed a matrix of action-reaction responses of both entities — humans and aliens. Questions as to why a side made a particular choice was pinned to many of the matrix's points. One question caused Alex to stop pacing and focus on Julien. "Why holes?" he asked.

<Is this an example of stress, the inability to formulate an entire sentence?> Didier sent to the other three SIF directors.

<Observe,> Winston replied, and he linked them into the comm stream between Julien, Cordelia, Z, and Miranda.

<They're examining the original probe's data and the *Sojourn*'s preliminary survey reports,> Hector noted.

<What you're witnessing is a shortened form of communication developed between Alex and Julien, which has been adopted by the other Haraken SADEs, especially these four. It's an example of the intimate connection that any one of us could achieve with a human, and it's a lesson that those of us recently from the Confederation must embrace,> Winston sent.

<Weather?> Alex asked over his comm.

<No unusual weather patterns have been detected by any of our reconnaissance,> Cordelia sent in reply.

<Temperature?>

<Again, negative,> Z added. <The air circulating around the equatorial area, where the plains are located, is warm but certainly not intolerable.>

<Huge, carnivorous animals?>

<No, Alex,> Miranda replied. <Only small fauna have been detected, and most of those were registered by thermal imaging during the darkened hours.>

Alex resumed pacing, but stopped after a few steps. <That leaves only adversaries.>

<There is another possibility, Alex,> Julien replied. <Perhaps it's an inherited trait. This species might have been stranded on the planet, and they continued to practice their cultural habits.>

<Then answer me this ... if the aliens have such a limited level of tech now, how did they reach Celus-5?>

<I would propose a single ship with drive problems, requiring its captain, crew, and passengers to abandon ship. They've only their shuttles,

and the potential to manufacture repairs to their tech is unavailable to them,> Z theorized.

<A probable explanation,> Alex allowed. <But if I follow your supposition, Z, then this species would have been on Celus-5 for generations. It would have taken that long to descend from a space-traveling species to one toting primitive weapons around, as our people have discovered. And later generations would have eroded the original cultural leanings. By now, the aliens should have come above ground and constructed shelters, if not buildings. There's no obvious reason for the species not to come out into the open. Speaking of which, why not move into the enormous green swaths that border the plains?>

<Unknown,> Julien replied.

<I'm betting on adversaries, Julien,> Alex sent in reply.

<Most instructive,> Hector commented privately to the Confederation SADEs.

*   *   *

"Sir, you have a ship to ship comm," Captain Lumley announced. Despite his recent years on Haraken, Lumley's deeply ingrained habits, such as referring to superiors as sir, originated from decades of service aboard Sol's United Earth ships. "It's Captain Shimada and originates from the *Tanaka*'s bridge. The sting ship broke orbit, and the captain is accelerating the warship at maximum."

"On bridge speakers, Captain," Alex replied.

"Hello, Alex," Reiko said, when her view screen displayed the personnel arrayed on the *Rêveur*'s bridge.

"Greetings, Captain Shimada and Commander Cohen," Alex replied formally.

"I'm assuming that you launched much earlier than us, Alex, knowing that with our grav drive we could catch you before you jumped," Reiko said.

"Actually, the thought never occurred to me, Captain."

Reiko took a breath and exhaled slowly and quietly. Another recent Sol immigrant and an ex-commodore of the United Earth forces, there was much about Harakens and Alex Racine, in particular, that she was still trying to understand.

For Alex, these would be the occasions when Renée would urge him to be patient or cautious, depending on the situation. Instead, she stood beside him, her hand in his, wearing the same determined expression he wore.

"Alex, I've been ordered by President Monti to assert my authority as mission commander, and I'm reminding you of that because the responsibility for any mission failures will ultimately fall on my shoulders."

"And Tomas expressed the same request of me, Captain," Alex replied.

<How is it that I'm speaking about the president's order and Alex refers to them as the president's request?> Reiko sent to Franz.

<Alex is trying to tell you, in polite terms, where he stands, regardless of your orders,> Franz sent back. <You're correct that mission responsibility is yours. My advice is to take charge, and run this mission as you think best, and not as you believe you've been ordered. Remember that it was Admiral Tachenko who chose you for this job and who knows both Alex and you extremely well.>

"In contrast to the president's orders, Alex, my admiral said that she expected me to get the job done no matter what I had to do," Reiko said.

"So what are your intentions, Captain?" Alex asked.

"I was in this situation more than once when I commanded a United Earth destroyer, and every time I tried to follow orders, my ass ended up in a bind. So, I'm going to follow my intuition, and it tells me to depend on an alien expert when dealing with aliens. So, I'll follow your lead, Sir, until such time as I feel it compromises mission integrity. Fair enough?"

"That's something I can live with, Captain. Thank you."

"It's the least I can do for the man who saved my solar system and brought me my partner, but please don't make me regret this decision, Sir."

"Can't promise that, Captain," Alex said, smiling for the first time in the conversation, "But I'll try."

-10-
Incarceration

The captive Harakens were sharing their usual gruel of stewed tubers. It was hard to tell who was more disgusted by the concoction, the jailers or the prisoners.

Initially, the Dischnya guards were confused by their prisoners' refusal to eat, but Simlan and Hessan listened intently to Willem's entreaties, finally bringing a display of the soma's raw foods. They watched Willem nibble each item, except for the skinned animals, which he left untouched. Much to the guards' surprise, Willem could crunch and split wild grains in his teeth, spitting the pieces into his discard bowl after rummaging them around in his mouth.

Finally, Willem pushed a multitude of items forward and indicated the prisoners would eat these foods.

Unsure of how to prepare the limited food selection, Pussiro ordered a small cookstove brought into the Harakens' front room, along with cooking pots and utensils. He had no choice but to give the prisoners blades with which to prepare the hard tubers, but Simlan and Hessan were careful to hand out and retrieve the knives before and after each period of food preparation.

Then there was the odd eating ritual of the prisoners, at least from the Dischnya's point of view. The prisoners faced one another in a circle, taking a few bites from a bowl and passing them to the individual next to them. Round the circle the bowls would go until they were empty.

What the Dischnya didn't know was that Willem was attempting to disguise his unique nature. He sat with his back to the guards and went through the motions of eating, but the nearly flat spoon never touched his mouth. It was the other Harakens, who cleaned out Willem's bowl for him.

Xavier worked to choke down his portion to keep his heavy New Terran body fueled. He tried pretending the odd-tasting mixture was a favorite Haraken dish, but he was never able to convince himself. More than once, he thought he was going to heave his partially consumed meal into the circle's middle.

On the other hand, Teague exhibited the appetite of a growing young man, often eyeing the others' bowls for remains when they were set down. Ginny's bowl always contained a leftover bite or two, and she felt a warming in her belly when Teague snatched it up and smiled at her.

After the meal, female Dischnya whisked away the cooking pot, utensils, and bowls to be cleaned and later returned. Then school was back in session.

The Harakens had been moved twice from their original storeroom. The first time was to please Nyslara, who wanted to show her alien captives better treatment in the hope that some sort of relationship could be established before the situation deteriorated. The second time was to find the largest classroom Pussiro could supply.

By Nyslara's order, Simlan and Hessan were in charge of the captives' comfort and education. Several of Nyslara's advisors, nest elders, were added to the mix to support the two warriors. But Nyslara defined everyone's roles succinctly when she said, pointing first at Simlan and Hessan and then at her advisors, "These two lead, and the rest of you follow. Am I understood?"

Simlan and Hessan's elevated statuses didn't go to their heads. Instead, they were extremely nervous, directing the advisors the first day to take seats on bessach along one wall and observe. But the warriors' confidence returned when they resumed their discussion with the aliens. The advisors hissed in amazement at Willem's perfect pronunciation of the Dischnya language, and the aliens' ability to learn quicker than mewlings, even faster than cubs.

Soon the advisor count grew, as the first group began participating in what became a bidirectional educational process, with the Harakens and Dischnya alternating the roles of teachers and students. During this time, on Pussiro's orders, was when the school was relocated to a large, bare room. At the end of lessons, the captives were returned to their comfortable, well-decorated rooms to rest and sleep, while soma cleaned the marked floors and walls of the classroom and prepared the space for the morrow's lessons.

One day, while Simlan and Hessan led the group back to their rooms after the day's lessons, Willem's calendar app pinged. He'd marked the date when he thought Captain Azasdau would have sent an emergency comm, once it was obvious the natives didn't intend to release their captives. Allowing for the comm's transmission time, rescue preparations, and the return trip, Willem calculated that Haraken ships might make orbit as early as tomorrow.

If anyone were to examine Willem's calculations, they would see that he only allowed a single day from receipt of the message to the launch of a rescue vessel. *Regardless of the president's response, the* Rêveur *will break orbit with all speed,* Willem thought, a wry smile forming on his face.

Willem considered the rescue's timing couldn't have been more opportune. His grasp of the Dischnya language and culture was sufficient for him to act as translator and negotiator. *Now, if I could only anticipate what Alex Racine might do once he arrives. But, I would have more success contemplating the origin of the universe,* Willem thought.

Hessan glanced at Willem, when the SADE chuckled. It was an odd noise to the Dischnya's warriors, who made no equivalent sound.

* * *

For many days after the mission shuttle was pinned, the scientists and techs were kept busy with the analyses of their samples, while Orly, Bethany, and Smitty were bored to tears. Guard duty fell to them, and they kept a continual watch on the rear hatch, which was cracked open a few degrees. But, when nothing happened after the first few days, their intense wariness turned to mind-numbing tedium.

Once the second traveler took up station above them, there were no more assaults on their ship or even visible movements from the natives.

Occasionally, Lieutenant Soucis ordered Verlan to lower her traveler until implant contact could be made with the netted ship, since there was no more energy left in the mission shuttle's power cells to accommodate comm calls.

Marie kept those aboard the pinned traveler up to date on the various plans to free them, none of which came to fruition. Time was slowly running out for the crew trapped in the mission shuttle. The food from the dispensers, packaged in haste into specimen collection containers when the net was first thrown over them, was consumed. The dried, emergency rations in the expedition packs were gone too, and now the people were sharing the last of the water.

Orly's greatest lament was that there was no energy available to open the plex-crystal doors and lower the hatch so that the survey team could surrender. *Not the best time to discover a design flaw,* Orly lamented, *that we don't have a means of manually operating our doors and ramp.* He compared their predicament to unfortunate miners, who were trapped underground, and despite everyone's best efforts, help wouldn't arrive in time to save them.

Several times, the Harakens aboard the grounded vessel received comm signals that Lieutenant Soucis was testing the aliens' resolve, and they were preparing to land. Although the crew aboard the pinned traveler couldn't hear the descent of their sister ship, they could hear the barks of the slug-throwing weapons and the whines of projectiles bouncing off the traveler's shell. The natives remained at their posts.

After the third attempt to land, Verlan reported to Marie that he couldn't recommend a fourth. "Lieutenant, those strikes from the alien slugs are chipping away at our shell," Verlan said. "They're creating so many small cracks that they're compromising the hull's integrity, which is reducing our charging rate. If we keep taking hits, Lieutenant, our charge rate will fall below threshold, which will mean we'll reach a point where we'll have to decide between staying on station and making for orbit. If we choose to stay on station, then eventually we'll be forced to land to charge our power cells sufficiently to make orbit.

"And, if we land," Marie supplied, "the natives will ping their slugs off our shell until we can't ever lift, or they'll net us like our friends down there."

* * *

There was a third group of stranded Harakens — Bobs A Lot, Sand Flipper, Swift Claws, and Whistles Keenly. While the Swei Swee weren't prisoners or in danger of starving to death, they did feel abandoned. Their society was one of community. To be separated from the intimacy of the hive, or, in this case, the crew, which substituted for the hive, was tantamount to incarceration in an emotional prison.

Watching from the shallows, their eyestalks peeking above the breaking waves, the four Swei Swee saw their life-long friend and Little Singer, along with the others, forcibly led away by strangers.

<Hunters,> Swift Claws had signaled the others. Eyestalks had retracted into carapaces, and the Swei Swee sought deeper waters, lest the hunters come for them.

Hours later, after dusk descended, the foursome crawled stealthily ashore ready to flee back into the waters at the first sign of danger. A dark night, one without a moon to add its light, enabled the Swei Swee to fade into the background. They crept slowly across the sand, intending to make for the mission's shuttle.

It took them hours to work their way up the embankment and across the grassy plain. Their six walking legs enabled them to move noiselessly, while eyestalks searched the ground in the dim starlight for proper placement before the next legs were moved.

Bobs A Lot was the first to spot one of the natives' lookouts. He froze and signaled the others. <The hunters are in the ground,> he sent.

Swift Claws' four eyestalks swiveled around him, searching for what Bobs A Lot saw. With a lurch of his double hearts, the Swei Swee realized he was straddling a lookout post. The optics of a viewer extended outward between his second and third legs. Had he been a half-meter to the left, he would have been discovered.

The safety of the ship was still hundreds of meters away. The Swei Swee studied the ground with their keen eyesight, wondering whether they could cover the distance safely. Unfortunately, while they waited motionless, they caught the subtle movements of many natives' viewers, as the lookouts scanned the night.

<Many hunters,> Sand Flipper sent.

<Too many,> Whistles Keenly agreed.

<Can't reach the traveler with comm,> Swift Claws sent, and each of the others tried without success.

<We must seek shelter somewhere else,> Bobs A Lot said. When the others agreed, eyestalks extended to their farthest length to peer behind each individual to observe the path taken. Walking in reverse, the Swei Swee slowly retraced their steps off the plains.

When the foursome gained the embankment's edge, they spun around and raced down a cut in the hill to the beach. Then they scurried along the shore, seeking a place to shelter. They spotted a small cave, which had been carved out by the sea. It was a snug fit for the foursome and wasn't the most comfortable place to spend the night, but it offered them a place of refuge for now.

In the morning, the Swei Swee fished the shallows for small catches to maintain their strength. They found the taste of the ocean's prey to be tolerable but not exciting. More and more, the flavors of their faux fish that they consumed aboard ship appealed to them, which was due in large part to the efforts of Alex, who constantly suggested recipe changes to the scientists who managed food stock production. He attempted to guide the scientists toward a means of capturing the flavors of the Haraken sea creatures. With twenty years of experience at greeting ceremonies, Alex was well acquainted with the tastes of fresh-caught, raw fish.

After the Swei Swee's morning meal, they floated just offshore and discussed their options. Two hours later, they were absolutely nowhere with regard to creating a plan that might conceivably save them. It was obvious they couldn't reach the traveler without the ground-dwelling hunters intercepting them.

The idea was proposed that they did possess weapons, their claws, and, if they closed on the natives, they might fight their way to the shuttle. But Swift Claws' proposal was shot down. First, killing a few native creatures might endanger the captives, if they were still alive. Second, having observed the net over the shuttle, it was thought that the ship wasn't the best destination. But Bobs A Lot had perhaps the most fundamental objection. He warbled that based on the number of hideouts they had spotted the tactic would most likely lead to their deaths.

"We must wait to be rescued," Sand Flipper warbled in lament.

"Yes, the Star Hunter First will come for us," Bobs A Lot replied. The fact that Alex was no longer admiral or president mattered not one whit to the Swei Swee. He was and would always be the Star Hunter First, who led the People to freedom.

"Then we must return to our mission's purpose," Swift Claws whistled.

"Agreed," Whistles Keenly replied. "We have questions about these dark travelers that require answers."

These four Swei Swee had never seen dark travelers. However, since their time as younglings, riding the matrons' backs, the adults sang tales of them, and Mutter, their Singer, sang of the People's time in captivity, of the slavers, the Nua'll, and of the great battle fought to free the People.

As night fell on the Swei Swee's third day since their separation from the crew, they slipped out of the cave, deciding to explore the ship that Willem's team chose to investigate. They swam in the shallows until they could crawl quickly from the waters into the lee of the half-buried fighter.

No visible entry into the traveler was found, but that was expected. The matrons would have opened the hull at ground level when the ship landed, or so the songs said, but the ship was now buried in sand to its midline.

Sand Flipper wasted no time digging a trench along one side of the fighter, the one nearest the waters. Great mounds of sand flew behind him, and the other Swei Swee spread out to keep watch, while their companion searched for the entry. Unfortunately, fortune was not with Sand Flipper.

By dawn, he'd failed to find the opening. Celus' light brightened the sky, and the Swei Swee retreated to the safety of their cave.

That first night at the dark traveler established the Swei Swee's routine — dig at night, retreat at dawn to the cave, sleep half the day, fish in the afternoon until dusk, and then make their way back to the ship. They split the night into two shifts, alternating a single digger, while the others kept sentry duty.

It took the Swei Swee nine days to find the entrance. First, it was deep below the surface near the front of the ship, an unexpected location, and second, it was on the side away from the shore, which confused the Swei Swee even more. If the craft had been abandoned in all haste, then the side nearer the waters would have been the logical choice for the exit.

In Swift Claws' excitement at finding the entrance, he nearly blew a shrill whistle but stopped at the last moment. Reverting to his implant, he sent, <I have the matrons' opening.>

<It must wait,> Bobs A Lot sent in reply. He had the sentry position on the top on the embankment and was the first to see Celus' rays warming the horizon's edge.

As the Swei Swee hurried back to the cave, Sand Flipper warbled, "How will we see inside the ship at night?"

"We could use a shiny or bright material to reflect light into the interior during the day," Whistles Keenly suggested.

"Because of the ship's position and the entry site so far down in our trench, Celus would need to be directly overhead," Bobs A Lot reasoned.

"Too dangerous," Swift Claws whistled. "The hunters would spot our efforts."

Suddenly Sand Flipper skidded to a halt. "Maybe we don't need to bounce light into the interior. If the ship landed soon after exiting the master ship, the power crystals might contain some charge. The People would have shut down power before exiting, and there would be nothing to drain the cells."

Swift Claws whistled a note of derision. "Even if the traveler contained power, we've never operated one of the ancient versions. How would we even know the difference between powering the lights and firing the beam?"

During the remaining trip to the cave, the Swei Swee argued Sand Flipper's idea among them. Over Swift Claw's objections, the other three chose to change the next day's cycle. Before Celus climbed high in the sky, they fished briefly and then swam to the traveler.

Bobs A Lot was the first to crawl through the dark traveler's entrance. His carapace brushed the opening's upper edge, and a portion of the ship's hull crumbled. His eyestalks swung to the rear, as fine pieces of shell rained over his back.

When the Swei Swee hives were first captured, they decided to build the dark traveler shells in an artificial manner and designed them to breakdown if, for some reason, they were no longer the ones flying the ships. It was the ultimate act of revenge against their masters, the Nua'll.

The foursome crawled into the ship's interior, feeling their way to the bridge panel. They waited for their eyes to adjust to the faint light entering by way of the matrons' hole. Eventually, the Swei Swee could make out the controls on the bridge panels.

<We're here,> Swift Claws sent to the others. <Which of you original thinkers imagines they know which control to touch?>

The others ignored Swift Claws' sarcasm while they examined the various items on the board. Bobs A Lot noticed a small icon, covered in dust, next to a panel button. He blew on it, scattering dust, and sets of eyestalks craned his way to observe what he'd found.

<Images,> Sand Flipper sent.

That brought Swift Claws crowding forward and soon all the Swei Swee were blowing their breaths across the panel and trying to decipher the glyphs next to each control.

<Here,> Whistles Keenly sent, and eyes stared at a small icon that looked like a semicircle with rays projecting downward from the round side.

They continued to observe the glyph until Swift Claws became impatient and sent, <Well, you found what you were looking for, but it's not going to activate itself. Push it.>

Whistles Keenly's eyestalks separated. One pair turned toward Sand Flipper, and the other pair twisted in the opposite direction to regard Bobs A Lot. <Yes,> both Swei Swee sent to Whistles Keenly, who reached out a true hand and hesitantly tapped the button.

Immediately, a bank of lights embedded on the upper median ridges of both sides of the ship and running down its entire length lit up. Having acclimated to a dim interior, the lights were blinding. Eyestalks were yanked into carapaces and nictitating membranes were slammed shut. Slowly, stalks emerged, and eyes adjusted.

The identifying icons on the panel were now lit, including a power level display near Swift Claws. <I think I'm looking at the energy levels left in the power crystals,> Swift Claws sent. <If I'm reading this correctly, only a few percent of the energy remains in the crystals.>

<With these power levels, the lights could be used for many days, if we wish,> Sand Flipper sent.

<Are you thinking we could stay here?> Bobs A Lot asked.

<No,> Swift Claws sent with urgency. <If the hunters see our trenches they will come to investigate, and we would be trapped.>

The others warbled their agreement. Thoughts of having a dry and comfortable place to hide in the day had overridden their focus on the priority issue — hunters roamed the shore, and they were dangerous.

A small squeak issued from Whistles Keenly. Observing his eyestalks were pointed to the rear, the others swung theirs in the same direction. Several small noises escaped the breath ways of the other three.

In a crumpled heap, toward the rear of the traveler, lay the remains of a hive member. The Swei Swee edged their way to gain a closer look at one of their distant cousins. Small animals and insects had eaten the flesh and much of the leg joint material. It gave the body a disassembled appearance.

<Look at the carapace,> Swift Claws sent. A huge crack ran from the front diagonally across the back and separated the two halves by several centimeters.

<He couldn't flee,> Bobs A Lot lamented.

Sand Flipper poked one of the male's claws and whistled softly. The claw was nearly half again as large as his, and instead of the blues and greens that ran through his claws, this one was dark blue and even more sharply pointed than his.

<Are these of the People?> Whistles Keenly sent. It was the thought on every Swei Swee's mind. Yes, the body was that of a six-legged, clawed, carapace-ensconced individual, but the coloring, size, and fine details of the body were not those of the Haraken hives.

<If they are, then this is how we appeared before generations passed while our People were held captive,> Sand Flipper sent.

<Imagine what could be done with a set of claws like these,> Swift Claws sent, which elicited a round of amused warbles from the others.

<So what do we do now?> Bobs A Lot asked.

<We can't stay here,> Swift Claws sent. He wanted to be sure his comrades heard him this time. While he had been wrong about coming back to the traveler in the day, he was sure the ship would become their deathtrap if they stayed. To his relief, the others agreed with him.

<We should seek them out,> Sand Flipper sent, and Bobs a Lot and Whistles Keenly sent their agreement.

Swift Claws regarded the broad, dark carapace and the enormous claws of the body in front of him and wondered if it wouldn't be safer to wait in the ship and take their chances against the hunters.

-11-
Rendezvous

Asu waited impatiently in the bay's airlock of the *Sojourn*. When Rosette notified him that two Haraken ships had transited outside the system, Asu nearly wept with relief. The next three days passed achingly slow, as he waited for the *Rêveur* and *Tanaka* to rendezvous with his ship.

Now, two travelers, one from each ship, were on approach to the *Sojourn*. Asu and Rosette had updated Alex and Reiko on the status planetside, sharing their ship's view of the netted traveler and the fighter maintaining vigilance overhead.

The ship's twin bay doors slid open, and Celus, in the far distance, shone brightly through the opening. First, one shuttle and then the other eased into the bay, and the crew chief closed the doors and pressurized the bay. No sooner had the green telltale flashed in the airlock than Asu was through the airlock hatch.

Reiko was first down the hatch steps of her traveler, and Asu greeted her and warmly shook her hand. Then he spotted Alex jumping to the deck with a resounding thud and turning around to help Renée down, and Asu hurried over.

"Alex and Ser, I'm so sorry for the worries my expedition has caused the two of you," Asu said humbly.

"These events aren't your fault, Captain," Alex replied.

"Thank you for saying so, Alex, but I must accept some responsibility for not being more careful in the survey of the planet before initiating the first landing."

"And whose idea was it to land and start the ground survey before a more thorough aerial reconnaissance was completed ... your mission co-commander, perhaps?" Alex asked. When Asu ducked his head, Alex had his answer. "Thought as much," he added. "Captain, are you aware of the new, shall we say, power arrangement?" Alex asked.

"Yes, Alex, I was informed privately by Captain Shimada."

Alex glanced at Reiko, and she responded by straightening her shoulders and lifting her chin.

"Yes, Captain Shimada is thorough like that," Alex commented drily. "Well, Mission Commander, what do we do next?"

Just that quickly, Reiko found herself unseated by Alex. She had commed Captain Azasdau to ensure he had understood her assignment, as dictated by the president — the power arrangement, as Alex had called it. And for her forwardness, Alex had dumped the responsibility for the first decision squarely in her lap.

"I suggest we convene on the bridge and study the situation," Reiko said with conviction.

The *Sojourn*'s bridge became quite crowded. While Reiko left her pilot and crew aboard the *Tanaka*'s traveler, Alex's people trooped behind him. In addition to Renée, Alex was followed by Mickey, Claude, Edmas, Jodlyne, and eight SADEs.

After a lengthy discussion, which only served to rehash the information everyone already knew, Alex grew impatient. "Captain Shimada, what's your first priority, and how do you expect to accomplish it?"

"I think we should recover that pinned traveler. They're out of food and probably out of water by now."

"Agreed," Alex replied. "And your tactics?"

<Easy, my love,> Renée sent privately. <Reiko is over her head in this situation, and you're putting her on trial.>

<Patience, Renée,> Alex replied. <I'm reminding Reiko of her promise to allow me to lead with the strategy and tactics until such time as my actions place the mission in jeopardy.>

Asu looked hopefully at Reiko, waiting for her to suggest the one thing that he hadn't thought of that would save his people.

Reiko studied the holo-vid intently. That the natives hid in tunnels presented a major obstacle. That they were obviously many in number was the second, and they possessed slug-throwing weapons and weren't shy about firing them was the third. Short of turning the area surrounding the netted traveler into slag with the beam from one of the *Tanaka*'s fighters, she had no idea how to rescue the grounded shuttle.

Finally, Reiko relaxed her shoulders, placed her hands behind her back, and raised her eyebrows at Alex. "You win, alien advisor," she said. "I defer to your wisdom and experience."

"It's not about who wins or loses, Captain," Alex said gracefully. "The best idea wins."

It was Alex's turn to study the holo-vid, and, after some thoughtful moments, he looked at Julien and said, "Their weakness is line of sight. They want to stay in their tunnels and shoot from concealment. If they can't see, they probably wouldn't shoot."

"We were hoping for some sort of major weather event, Alex," Asu said. "But, in the entire time we've been in orbit, the weather has been quite orderly."

"Then we need to make our own," Alex said. "Something akin to a whirlwind that will obscure their vision."

The holo-vid's display shifted to a view from above the netted traveler.

"Z," Alex said quietly, in response to Asu and Reiko's puzzled expressions.

Four travelers, noses pointing at one another and positioned like fan blades, descended toward a point between the netted shuttle and the lookout locations, which surrounded the ship for about 190 degrees. When the travelers were about 100 meters above the ground, they rotated onto their sides. Then turning like the blades of a fan around a central point, the travelers spun faster and faster. Numbers appeared in the holo-vid display — velocity, downward air pressure, and lateral wind speeds at ground level.

At one point, with the travelers spinning in a blur and the wind speed approaching 132.8 kph, Reiko said, "That's all well and good, but my pilots can't execute those maneuvers."

"We can," came the chorus from Julien, Cordelia, Z, and Miranda.

"And all of you have piloting experience?" Reiko demanded, before she thought her question through. "Sorry, that was an ill-considered question."

"Actually, I don't, dear," Miranda said, "but I'm a fast learner." She gave Reiko a brilliant smile, which made the captain feel even more foolish.

"And a rescue ship, Z?" Alex asked.

A fifth ship appeared in the center of the swirling travelers and descended through the fan's center to touch down.

"We would need a pilot and sixteen crew to cut the tie-downs simultaneously, Alex," Z said.

Reiko shook her head at what was being planned, and said, "Walking in those wind forces and unable to see … that would take —"

"More SADEs," Alex said. "Glad so many of them decided to accompany me," he added, turning to regard Winston, Esther, Hector, and Didier, who touched hands to chests and nodded heads in acceptance of Alex's appreciation.

"One more problem," Asu said.

"Of course there is," groused Reiko.

"That alien net must be made of some metal, possibly iron. It's somehow grounded the hull, conducting the power cells' energy back through the shell."

"Well, there's a design flaw, Mickey," Alex said, glancing over at the engineer.

"Who knew that it would take primitive aliens to demonstrate the errors of my team's effort?" Mickey remarked. "Well, if that net is conducting, it's more than likely a comparatively soft metal. With a SADE's strength, a pair of cutters would be the better implement rather than a burning tool. I can have my people build a set of these in a couple of hours."

"Do you carry spare traveler power cells aboard, Captain Azasdau?" Julien asked.

When Asu agreed that he did, Z said, "A pilot and seventeen crew … all SADEs."

The Haraken SADEs boarded Reiko's traveler. They would employ the *Tanaka's* travelers as the blades. The SIF directors rode back to the *Rêveur* with Mickey, Claude, Edmas, and Jodlyne. Since Alex, Renée, and Reiko were staying aboard the *Sojourn*, a replacement shuttle transferred from the *Rêveur* to the *Sojourn*.

Aboard the *Rêveur*, the engineers and techs set to work building heavy cutting tools, and Mickey had an eye-opening discussion with Claude, who was the original builder of the avatars. Claude and Edmas still constructed Z's many fantastical requests.

"Claude, since these will be hand tools … no pneumatics or motors … I need to know what pressure a SADE can apply to determine the handle length. We can make them as long as they need."

Claude pinged Z with the request, and the SADE pulled up a *Sojourn* vid and estimated the thickness of the cable, the probable metal density, and the force necessary to quickly slice through the cable.

"Mickey, 45 centimeters should do it." Claude said, relaying Z's answer.

Mickey frowned and plugged the length into one of his implant's engineering apps. "That would mean a SADE would be able to generate a force of —"

"Hush, Mickey," Claude said quietly. Then reverting to his implant, Claude sent Z's calculations of the tensile strength of the cable and the force required to cut it.

Mickey reviewed the data and stared at Claude. Then he glanced toward Edmas, whose eyes were regarding his boots.

"I would ask that you don't share this data with anyone else, Mickey," Claude whispered. "Direct the techs as to the design of the cutters and leave the engineering specs out of it. The SADEs would prefer that humans weren't aware of their avatar's strength."

"Besides Edmas and you, who else knows about this?" Mickey asked.

"Jodlyne, since she knows more about Edmas than he knows about himself," Claude replied, which caused Edmas to blush a deep scarlet and Jodlyne to offer a warm smile to her young lover. "And, of course —"

"Alex," Mickey whispered, cutting Claude off.

"Yes," Claude agreed.

"Hmm ..." Mickey said with a sigh, as he considered the revelation. Finally, he said, "I can see why they want this kept quiet. But hearing this now, after all this time, makes me wonder what else they've been hiding."

Claude, Edmas, and Jodlyne waited patiently for Mickey's response. Finally, the engineer said, "Forty-five centimeters it is, and that's all that needs to be said."

Mickey headed to the engineering suite, and the three were left behind to regard one another.

"Secrets are difficult things to keep," Jodlyne said.

"And the longer they're kept, the worse it is when they come out," Edmas added.

"Remember, young Sers, the population of our planet no longer consists of Independents, as it was on the day we founded Haraken. There are many New Terrans now, who were not raised with SADEs, and they aren't so willing to accept the SADEs as the gentle citizens that they are."

Aboard the *Rêveur*, Winston met with the Confederation SADEs in the landing bay. He shared the plan and asked for volunteers to add to the count of the four SIF directors, who would lead the effort on the ground.

<Would you not deem this mission as having a high probability of lethality for us?> Oliver sent privately to Winston.

"Yes, I would describe this plan as extremely dangerous to any exposed individuals, who would be those cutting the cables and delivering the power cells," Winston replied vocally. It was a hint to Oliver, who had yet to make it planetside on Haraken that he was to communicate openly with the other SADEs. "The possibility of a mortal wound is small, but the natives' weapons could disable your avatars, which would lead to your capture."

"The study of the slug-throwing weapon is inconclusive," Linn said. "It's not known whether the projectile could penetrate our chest and smash the kernel, ending our life."

"You're correct. The data is minimal," Esther replied. "All these things are possible, but we won't be exiting our shuttle until visibility is nearly zero. We'll navigate by coordinating between our ship's controller and its map of the exact positions of the net anchors."

"We need a pilot, who will remain aboard, and thirteen more volunteers. Please signal me with your willingness to join the four of us," Winston said.

<Now what do we do?> Winston sent privately to Esther, Hector, and Didier. <Everyone volunteered.>

In less than three hours from the time the decision was made on the *Sojourn*'s bridge, the pieces for the rescue were in place, and four travelers exited the *Tanaka* and one from the *Rêveur*. Julien, Cordelia, and Miranda, slaved their ships' controllers to Z's and linked with him. The SADEs' proposed maneuvers could only be accomplished with the aid of extremely sturdy avatars and ultra-fast controller coordination. Humans were too fragile and not quick enough.

* * *

The one telescope the Tawas Soma possessed, which was rescued from the nest's shuttle, was trained on the first alien ship to arrive from the time it took up station above them. It also tracked the descent of each shuttle.

As the system's star, Nessila, crested the horizon, an advisor hurried to inform Nyslara that two more alien ships now resided beside the first. The queen sent a runner to wake Pussiro, and, reluctantly, he eased from the warm embraces of his two mates and climbed off the comfortable pad.

Despite the anxiousness of those early hours after wakening, the morning turned to boredom. Pussiro took the opportunity to meet with his sub-commanders to discuss tactics. Afterwards he sat down to a meal, but the shrill of the receiver in his quarters interrupted the first bite. The lookout warned that the aliens were on the move.

Pussiro replaced the receiver in the cradle and raced to the forward lookout post, which had called him. This was the event the commander was anticipating and fearing, at the same time. The aliens were landing in force to rescue their comrades.

A snarl escaped Pussiro's muzzle as he ran. Simlan and Hessan were achieving great progress in understanding their captives and teaching the aliens the Dischnya language. Nyslara had hoped to begin the bargaining with those in the netted ship, but that idea might now have been thrown into jeopardy.

The two lookouts jumped aside as Pussiro burst into the tiny room. "Status," he barked, as he climbed up to the scope.

"The advisors on the telescope report that five shuttles have left the ships above and are descending," the senior warrior on lookout reported. "Their destination appears to be the grounded shuttle, Commander."

Pussiro rotated the external eyepiece of the scope upward. He waited, the sharp claws of his right foot tapping nervously on the scope's ladder, and he didn't have long to wait. Five shuttles descended into view, but rather than land, they formed a pattern, pointing their noses at one another. The shuttle, which had guarded the netted ship, slid up and out of sight.

A hiss issued from Pussiro's lips as he watched four of the ships rotate onto their edges and swing around an invisible center. Faster and faster they went.

At first, Pussiro felt a soft breeze on his face. This was midday when the heat was its greatest, and air shouldn't be stirring. Then the breeze stiffened, and, soon after that, dust blew around the scope and stung his eyes. It was not much longer before Pussiro lost sight of the spinning ships. This lookout was one of the closest posts to the netted shuttle, and, if his vision of the ship was fouled, then the others were too.

When the dust and debris blowing into the lookout's opening became too great to tolerate, Pussiro retracted the scope and closed the hatch, locking it behind him. He jumped for the receiver and issued a general alarm to the posts facing the shuttles to close down rather than risk damaging the scopes' lenses.

Pussiro's hand rested on the cradle after he hung it up. *Clever,* he thought. *Whoever you are up there, you're a devious commander. You'll rescue your soma without firing a shot.*

* * *

The Haraken SADEs monitored the g-forces on their travelers and themselves, as they increased the spin rate. While the fighters possessed fantastically strong shells, they'd never been tested in this way. There was no data to monitor to tell the SADEs when to cease the spin rate's increase. As for their own bodies, the inertia compensator limit for humans was already surpassed, and they could feel the mounting pressure on their more sensitive areas, such as the orbs of their synthetic eyes.

Linked to the travelers' controllers, Z could accurately determine the ground's rising wind speed and the shrinking visibility distance created by their spinning ships. He, for one, was wishing that he was wearing his Cedric Broussard suit. The monstrous, New Terran-style avatar was built to more exacting standards than the Exchange director's avatar he presently inhabited.

<Now,> Z sent to Oliver when conditions were optimum.

Winston had selected Oliver to pilot the fifth shuttle since his experience, among the Confederation SADEs, was the most extensive, having more than a century and a half of controlling starship passenger liners. Oliver was pleased to be of service in the rescue operation, and his attitude was a common theme among those SADEs immigrating to Haraken. Their primary intention wasn't to leave the Confederation; it was to relocate to Haraken where they would have the opportunity to experience life to the fullest. In this manner, they were more akin to the Independents, who were being incarcerated on some unknown colony for their desire to live outside the Confederation's societal norms.

Oliver was exacting, as he followed Z's data, dropping his traveler down the wheel's center. The air disturbance in the windstorm's eye was minimal, but, when he approached ground level, visibility dropped to near zero. Oliver depended on the controller's contact with the ships above to maintain his position in the center of the wheel and to know when he was due to touchdown.

<Exit,> Oliver sent to the seventeen SADEs, waiting in the main salon, when his traveler settled on the ground.

Winston cued the hatch open, and sixteen SADEs poured out of the ship with cutters in hand. Last out of the hatch was Trixie, her arms wrapped around a traveler's power cell, housed in a transport container. She signaled the hatch closed when she jumped free of the ship.

Every SADE was running multiple algorithms. There was no signal to guide them to the netted traveler. Neither the ship's controller nor the humans' implant comms were responding to hails. Instead, the SADEs employed a mapping algorithm, which held the positions of the netted shuttle, their originating ship, and their individual destinations. The difficult part was navigating by taking equally measured steps despite the wind's attempt to blow them off course.

Despite the difficulties, every SADE reached the netted traveler — some on target and some contacting the net's edge and feeling their way along it to their assigned tie-down. Half the SADEs were required to circle the ship, via the bow, to reach the tie-downs on the ship's starboard side.

The cutting tools worked with ease. Within ticks of the last SADEs slicing through their cables, those positioned on the leeward side of the ship hauled the net off and chopped it into small sections.

Winston signaled Z that the trapped traveler was free, and the Haraken SADE reduced the spin rate of the four travelers to the point where the SADEs on the ground gained some visibility and could sprint back to their shuttle.

-12-
Trixie's Rescue

Trixie signaled Winston that she reached the traveler's aft end, and he wished her fortune, as he and the other SADEs raced for safety aboard their ship.

Hanging onto the power cell's elongated container strap, Trixie tossed the precious cargo up and over the top of the ramp. She eyed the 3.5 meters to the top and jumped for it. Grabbing the sharp edge with her hands, she hauled herself up to lay lengthwise along the ramp's 15-centimeter-thick edge.

With a heavy pack on her back, Trixie couldn't fit through the narrow opening. She performed an intricate set of maneuvers, gripping the ramp between her thighs while she wriggled out of her pack and dropped it to the shuttle's deck. Then she pulled the container back up by its strap, holding it with one hand, while she squeezed through the opening and twisted in the air to strike the deck feet first.

<I'm inside,> Trixie sent to Winston and Z, her signal picked up by the travelers' powerful comm systems. <Still no response to my pings on the occupants' implants or the ship's controller.>

Having received Winston's signal of all clear, Oliver lifted the ship up through the wheel's center.

Z waited until Oliver's ship gained altitude above them, then he quickly slowed the four spinning travelers, bringing them to stationary positions. Then the five SADE pilots spread out into overwatch positions, relieving Lieutenant Soucis' ship to return to the *Sojourn*.

Inside the freed traveler, Trixie regarded the closed plex-crystal doors. This was why she was selected for this aspect of the mission and why she carried a pack of tools. Mickey and Claude would have been the perfect pair to accomplish this task, but unfortunately, humans couldn't cross the open territory in the sandstorm, much less vault to the top of the upturned ramp.

On Trixie's Confederation outpost, when she was known as Lenora, she managed the mining operations on several metal-rich moons. The massive ore-dredging machinery was automated, but often required servicing due to the harsh operating environments. Trixie would send bots to manage the repairs and oversee their operations. As a SADE, she was superb at her job, but her contact with humans was limited to the occasional comm she received from her administrators. In a word, her existence was isolated and torturously lonely.

When news arrived that Trixie would soon be liberated, she was ecstatic, but, soon after, time crawled slower and slower with the passing of every day. She busied herself reviewing the ancient vids Julien had shared with Winston. The image of a fabled, blue-faced fairy caught her attention, and she submitted a request for her avatar to be patterned on that creature.

Had the rescue operation reached the downed shuttle, two days earlier, Trixie would have found the plex-crystal doors ajar. It was necessary to open them to allow air to flow into the main cabin once the ramp was cracked. But, as the water ran short and the crew became listless, Bethany, waiting until the last moment, triggered the doors closed. The techs had jury-rigged the power cells of security's stun guns into the doors' actuators, warning Bethany that she had enough power for only one operation. Bethany believed she had no choice — closing the doors was necessary to prevent the natives from having access to the shuttle, its technology, and its passengers.

Staring through the traveler's transparent doors, Trixie was concerned for the humans, who lay slumped in seats or in the aisle. She could detect the humans' implants, but there was still no comm reply. She updated those above her, sending, <Every human is alive, but they're unconscious. Vital signs are extremely weak, especially those of Ser Sardi, the physicist, and Ser Tallen, a senior scientist.>

The controller was offline, which meant Trixie couldn't signal the doors open, and she couldn't reach the ship's power cells, which, in this transport model, were located behind the pilot cabin's bulkhead.

Kneeling on the deck, Trixie pulled a laser cutting tool from her pack. Using the traveler's schematics stored in her memory, courtesy of Mickey, Trixie located a section of bulkhead panel and sliced into it, exposing power cabling. There was no concern for live wiring, since the ship was drained of energy.

Trixie attached the power cell to the bulkhead below the cutout, container and all, with a tube of strapping nanites. When the thick liquid stream of nanites touched the metal wall, it took on its properties. Three loops of nanites later, the container was firmly held in place. Attaching the power cell's leads to the traveler's interior cabling was the job of another tube of nanites that fused the leads into the ship's power system.

Trixie waited a few moments for the ship's power sensors to restore the safety relays in the circuitry. Then she signaled the pilot's board to reboot the controller and waited until the unit completed its startup diagnostics and confirmed ready. <I have power, and the shuttle is ready for liftoff,> Trixie broadcast. Then in the next moment, she sent, <I spoke too soon. The ramp is jammed. It's not closing.>

Scrabbling across the deck on her knees, she examined the base of the ramp and discovered dirt and debris filled the creases formed by the ramp and the lower portion of the shell. Trixie had nothing in her pack that could be used to blow out the material. Worse, time was wasting. One of her algorithms kept track of the humans' vital signs and several were extremely weak and heralded imminent failure.

Knowing the plex-crystal doors could seal in atmospheric conditions but not against the vacuum of space, which would risk the humans' lives, Trixie made a snap decision.

<Standby,> Trixie broadcast. She ordered the controller to liftoff. When she had several hundred meters of altitude, she lowered the ramp completely and launched the traveler into a horizontal spin but not so fast as to injure the comatose humans.

With the shell's integrity breached, the ship's actions were quickly draining the new power cell. Nonetheless, Trixie used a small fraction of the power to open the plex-crystal doors and flood the main salon with fresh air. Her sensors registered the huge buildup of carbon dioxide that flooded past her from the main cabin. As soon as the debris cleared the ramp's creases, Trixie sealed the ship.

<Z, I have 28 percent of charge left on the power cell,> Trixie sent. <Do I need to wait to gain more charge before I can make orbit and dock with the *Sojourn*?>

<Your margin of safety will be minimal,> Z replied. <But the humans' lives depend on urgency. In a worst-case scenario, you'll make orbit before you lose power, and we can use the tethering beams of the *Rêveur* to pull you into the bay.>

<Lifting now,> Trixie replied. It was good that the traveler's controller was as sophisticated as the SADEs could design, since Trixie had never personally piloted one. But she did know how to assign responsibilities to intelligent machines. She located the *Sojourn* in the controller's telemetry and directed it to rendezvous with the ship, utilizing the most efficient power management flight possible.

Knowing there was nothing she could do to aid the humans, Trixie locked her avatar in place and waited out the tense moments as the traveler made for space.

* * *

Aboard the *Sojourn*, medical specialists and techs assembled in the corridor outside the starboard bay. Trixie landed the traveler, with 1.5 percent charge remaining in the power cell, while the med crew danced from foot to foot, anxious for the bay to pressurize.

The first medical team rushed through the airlock just as the traveler's rear ramp touched the deck. Trixie stood aside, as humans rushed past her armed with syringes to pump oxygenated fluids and nutrients directly into bloodstreams. The next medical unit to board the ship held med-readers and sensors, which were attached to the survey team's temples to monitor brain activity and deliver more detailed bio information.

Trixie was dismayed to watch the medical teams work to resuscitate two of the scientists. They were the oldest members of the expedition —

Edward Sardi, a physicist from Sol, and Ullie Tallen, a Méridien who had investigated his fair share of planets for the Confederation. Both men yearned for one more adventure before they settled down to quieter lives.

Efforts to revive the two men went on for the better part of half an hour, while around them the other survey members were carted off on grav-gurneys. Finally, the medical teams called a halt. The two elders, Edward and Ullie, had participated in their last adventure. Both men expressed hopes that they would find alien life on Celus-5. Their wishes were granted in a manner they could never have imagined.

While the specialists waited for the return of two more grav-gurneys, Trixie threaded her way through the crowded aisle to Ullie's body. The elderly scientist lay in the aisle, and she bent down to touch the cheek of the centenarian. <I'm sorry I was late,> she sent to him. Then she visited Edward, who occupied a seat, which was in the reclined position to treat him. <You came from a faraway star, leaving your home, to live in a better world among the Harakens. I hope they brought you pleasure, as I hope they will bring me. Goodbye, Earther.>

* * *

Alex waited for Trixie in the corridor outside the landing bay. Her hair and clothes were covered in dust and small bits of vegetation. She looked a mess, and the sadness on her face added to her distraught appearance. Trixie halted in front of him and studied his face, and Alex could only guess at the myriad thoughts flooding through her kernel in those few moments.

"I regret, Ser, we were not in time to save them all," Trixie said, her eyes locked on Alex's.

Another SADE in a fragile moment, Alex thought. The Confederation SADEs lived lives of boring repetition and yearned for the freedom that could be enjoyed on Haraken. But with that freedom came emotional challenges many of them were not prepared to face. "Walk with me, Trixie," Alex said, taking her arm.

Trixie thought it odd that a human would attempt to guide her, the mass of her avatar negating any such effort. But Alex Racine's hand felt oddly comforting, and so she was careful to walk so as to ensure she did not pull free.

When Trixie realized that she was being led toward the medical suite, she suffered a moment of fright. Her first thought was that more humans had died, and she would be forced to face more of the SADEs' failures.

Alex signaled the medical suite's twin doors open and motioned her inside. The emergency room was crowded with medical specialists, techs, and the rescued. Trixie conducted a quick head count by visuals and implants. The numbers matched — everyone taken from the traveler was alive in the suite. She smiled in relief at Alex, and he smiled back at her.

When the rescued survey team saw Alex step into the suite, they struggled to sit up, straighten their clothes, and brush hair from their faces. It was the least they thought they could do to show respect for the man who created their world.

"Rest easy, people," Alex said. "I wanted you to meet someone. While many people took part in planning your rescue, twenty-two SADEs were responsible for its execution. And this individual, Trixie, deserves a great deal of credit. Through her ingenuity, she gained access to the shuttle, resurrected your dead traveler, unclogged a jammed ramp, and flew you to safety. And I might point out one unusual fact … this was Trixie's first experience as a traveler pilot."

Alex's last statement caused laughter, weak as it was, to ripple through the room.

In the bed nearest to them, a young New Terran-built tech reached out a hand to Trixie, and she took it gently. "Who knew that blue skin and orange hair could look so lovely," he mumbled.

Trixie was unsure of what was expected of her and would have remained rooted where she stood, except for Alex's gentle nudge forward, as he sent, <Talk to them.>

The next nearest bed held Sergeant Bethany Latimer, who held out her hand to Trixie. "Well done, Trixie. You have my thanks too."

On around the suite Trixie went, listening to the comments of the rescued, who shook her hand or touched her arm in passing. Many days ago, aboard the *Allora* and on her way to Haraken, Trixie wondered what sort of welcome she would receive in the new society. Saying goodbye to Edward and Ullie made her want to flee back to the Confederation, but listening to the voices of these brave individuals, who had signed up for the expedition to investigate a new world, told her that the people she was joining were wonderful, if not a bit crazy.

At one point, Trixie, almost giddy due to the enthusiastic reception, turned to speak to Alex, but the man had disappeared. <Thank you, Ser,> she sent. In reply, she received the image of a winking eye.

* * *

"One problem down, two to go," Marie Soucis commented. Her shoulder was fully healed, thanks to Haraken medical techniques, and she was standing on the *Sojourn*'s bridge with others, dissecting the events that took place planetside.

"What is it, Alex?" Asu asked. He had watched Alex replay Willem and Sergeant Latimer's recordings of their encounters with the natives over and over on the holo-vid. Everyone else was intensely involved in the discussion, except for Alex.

<My love, it's polite to respond when you're spoken to,> Renée sent when Alex continued to stare at the beach scene.

"We've more than the two problems you're mentioning, Lieutenant," Alex said, never taking his eyes off the holo-vid. "Recovering the captives and our Swei Swee will be our first operation."

<The madman is preparing to take us into the unknown again,> Alain sent to his crèche-mate, Étienne.

<And it's about time! The tasks of the Security Directorate are becoming unbearably tedious. The work's reminding me of our time in the Confederation,> Étienne replied.

<The stars forbid,> Alain sent with mock horror.

"Does anybody else think that there's something odd about this planet and these people?" Alex asked.

"You mean that the natives have primitive weapons, suggesting that they would be an aggressive race, but they held their fire during both encounters … except, of course, when they shot the lieutenant," Bethany quickly added. She was seated at a bridge operations position, still too unsteady to stand for long. But as Captain Escobar knew well, Bethany wasn't one to shirk her duty because of something as mundane as a near-death experience.

"I was thinking about that," Marie chimed in. "When we opened the hatch, I heard a large number of weapon reports. I should have heard most of them pinging off the hull, but my recording shows that there was only the one … the one that happened to ricochet off the steps and hit me."

"You think that was an accident, Lieutenant?" Reiko asked.

"If it was, some individual is in trouble for violating orders," Marie replied.

"So how does an undeveloped race get to the slug-throwing weapon's stage, but act with a sophisticated war mentality by taking hostages when they surrender?" Alex asked.

"Is that pertinent now, Alex?" Reiko asked.

"It might be the key to how we get the hostages back unharmed," Alex replied.

Most on the bridge thought the captives might already be dead, because no one had seen or heard from them since the day they were marched off the beach, but no one was foolish enough to utter that thought in the presence of Alex and Renée.

"Julien," Alex said, proposing a scenario, "a society demonstrates dissociation between their weapons level and battle tactics. Then strangers land on their planet, aliens in their minds, and these people realize the newcomers are superior beings, who possess vastly advanced technology."

<I perceive Alex's intent,> Esther sent to the other SIF directors, who were stationed in the four corners of the bridge, as had become their habit to observe Alex. <He describes a problem in the broadest of terms, which allows Julien to analyze a great many factors to present solutions. In return, Alex receives a host of possibilities, many more than a human might think of in so short a time, allowing him to select those concepts he intuits to be most likely.>

"The appearance of space-traveling aliens should generate awe and probably fear, first and foremost," Julien replied. "If my society was composed of nothing more than cunning predators, I would seek to destroy the visitors, never doubting that I could win the fight. But, if I was an intelligent leader of people, who only sought to survive, I would seek a solution that kept my people safe and free."

"So, by choosing not to kill our people, their leader keeps all options open," Alex mused.

"Precisely," Julien replied.

"That requires we find a means of bringing the leader out into the open so that we can communicate with him, her, or it," Alex said.

"It will be a he or she," Bethany replied. "When the youngster, who was banging on the plex-crystal doors, climbed back over the traveler's ramp, he flashed a healthy bit of equipment at me," she said, grinning.

"Well, Julien and Cordelia, you might have the opportunity to learn a second alien language, but it would have to be accomplished in record time if we're to save the hostages. That's providing, of course, that Willem hasn't done so already. My bet is he's more than proficient by now," Alex said.

The holo-vid blanked and was replaced by a vid, displaying a top-down view of the netted traveler before it was freed and a broad section of plains and boulders in a 190-degree arc out from the shuttle. Alex linked into the *Sojourn's* controller to discover that Z and Miranda were driving the display. Suddenly, Alex's comm became a party line, as everyone on the bridge linked into the controller.

Small translucent circles dotted the plains. They varied from deep red to light yellow.

<The colors represent variables for the potential targets,> Julien sent. <The deeper the shade, the more likely the lookout was active and monitored.>

Z and Miranda used the crews' implant recordings and the shuttles' controller records to piece together where the natives had emerged when they attacked or where their scopes had been spotted.

"We have sixty-eight potential hidden tunnel posts, with thirty to forty locations possibly manned, at any one time, although we can't tell how many natives in total might be in those holes," Z announced.

"And how will this help us?" Asu asked.

"We're thinking, Captain, that we should simply relieve the poor dears of their weapons," Miranda said.

The entire human contingent on the bridge stared at Miranda, who displayed the most charming smile, quite pleased with her suggestion.

"I'm sorry, I must have missed something," Reiko said. "We know that these native weapons can kill. We don't know exactly where they will be, at any one time, and we don't know how many will be there when you open their lookout hatches. Just how do you intend to relieve them of their weapons? Walk up and ask them?" Reiko was sure everyone else would agree with her feelings that the plan was absurd, except she didn't expect Alex to laugh. "What?" Reiko challenged.

"Sorry, Captain," Alex replied, using a hand to wave an apology, while he tried to control his laughter. "I just had an image of us standing in front of a pile of native weapons and waiting for their leader to come out of one of their holes and ask for them back."

Hector walked between several of the Harakens. He circled the bridge in a haphazard manner, nearly bumping into several people. By the time he was making a second more erratic orbit of the bridge, people were signaling him, asking if he was all right. Those unused to living with SADEs were wondering if they were witnessing their first breakdown of a cognitive digital intelligence.

As Hector walked, more like stumbled, past Alex, he received a quick wink. <You know us too well,> Hector sent to Alex. Despite being discovered, Hector made a third and final wander around the bridge before he stopped, surveyed his human audience, and said, "And you know who and what we are. Yet, you were still absorbed by the strangeness of the show. Only one human commented on my farce."

Everyone turned to regard Alex. He gave them his usual gesture when he had nothing else to add, a shrug.

The holo-vid display suddenly added three travelers, descending and landing among the dots on the plains. Julien was driving this scenario. From out of the shuttles poured 181 white dots. They wandered around the fields seemingly aimlessly, but anyone with an eye for detail could see that their travels took them closer and closer to the colored dots, which marked the lookout posts.

"We have a three-to-one advantage for potential targets, and a six-to-one for occupied tunnels, Ser," Z noted. Despite the general Méridien appellation, everyone knew who he was addressing.

"Security and medical specialists think that there's the possibility those slugs can penetrate an avatar's casing," Bethany said. Her comment cast a sudden pall over the conversation.

"What we need is a means of distracting the natives. It must appear so random that they're more interested in observing us rather than shooting at us," Miranda said into the quiet. "I've always found beguilement amazingly effective in disarming a target."

"I believe we can provide just such a scenario," Julien said. "And, by we, I mean Cordelia and me."

"Us?" Cordelia asked.

"Who better?" Julien replied. "Or synth-skins are holo projectors. Imagine the effect on the natives if they were to observe our appearances continually changing."

Realizing the unique characteristics of Julien and Cordelia's avatars elicited a round of excited murmurs from the Confederation SADEs.

"My next avatar will have that capability," Trixie called out, her eyes lighting up at the thought. She had been standing quietly near the rear of the bridge, fascinated by the discussion. In particular, she was surprised that the reason for Hector's erratic movements did not occur to her. *How quickly will my thinking change when I live among the Harakens?* Trixie asked herself.

-13-
Swei Swee Contact

Following their discovery of the remains aboard the dark traveler, the Swei Swee journeyed farther and farther every day away from the safety of shore into deep waters in search of those who had escaped the Nua'll's travelers. Each day of search left them exhausted, and, when they finally crawled ashore in Celus' fading light, they settled on the sand to rest before hauling their exhausted bodies off to the cave.

The foursome was forced to space out the search days, spending one day searching the shallow waters for food and resting before they would take up the quest for their lost People.

Many days into their quest and returning from their longest trip outward, the Swei Swee swam over dark waters when Bobs A Lot found himself the focus of an enormous predator rushing at him from below. He uttered a shrill warning to his comrades and raced for the surface, hoping to leap from the water and elude his attacker. Two of his eyes were focused on the fast-approaching surface, and two were faced backward measuring the narrowing distance from the onrushing fish's multiple rows of sharp teeth to his trailing tail.

From seemingly nowhere, a blur of dark bodies intercepted the predator from multiple directions, striking savagely and quickly at the huge fish. It gushed blood from deep, multiple cuts in its flesh, staining the water an orange yellow color. Severely injured, the fish broke off its attack and headed back into the deep, trailing enough body fluid behind it that Bobs A Lot anticipated the creature had met its end.

Bobs A Lot broke the surface, and his eyes searched for what he hoped were rescuers and not more predators. Then, directly in front of him, two pairs of eyestalks emerged from the waters followed by an enormous dark blue carapace. The Swei Swee was enormous compared to Bobs A Lot. Nictitating eyelids blinked away salt water, and four eyes stared at him.

"Friends, allies, hive mates," Bobs A Lot whistled, trying to think of how else to communicate to his lost cousin before he was rendered into small pieces by the individual's incredibly huge and sharply pointed claws floating just below the surface.

Bobs A Lot's comrades surfaced slowly behind him, and a swarm of the planet's giant Swei Swee emerged behind their comrade.

Everything about the Celus-5 People said aggression. Their pelagic coloring of dark tops and silver gray underbellies spoke of deep water entities, who rarely ventured into the warm shallow waters, which were the haunts of the Haraken People. Bobs A Lot wondered if they ever climbed ashore. Their carapaces were more streamlined, and their tails were longer, broader, and less flexible, capable of driving these People much faster through open water.

The lead individual whistled a response, and, to Bobs A Lot's dismay, he wasn't able to understand the message.

<I think he's requesting our hive name,> Sand Flipper sent to the others.

<Whistles Keenly, you respond,> Swift Claws sent. <Perhaps, he will understand you better.>

Whistles Keenly sang the hive's name and its lineage, which named the leaders before they were called First. He was back eight generations when the massive, dark individual in front of Bobs A Lot let loose a shrill whistle. It was followed by a string of whistles and warbles that the Haraken Swei Swee struggled to comprehend.

<I think he knows our ancestry,> Sand Flipper commented on the comm. <That would mean these individuals escaped the same Nua'll ship that held our People.>

The leader of the Celus-5 Swei Swee whistled and his hive members turned around. The leader gestured with a huge claw, indicating the Haraken Swei Swee should follow them, but the foursome hesitated, undecided whether to return to shore, where they might be recovered by the survey team, or follow the Celus People, continuing their investigation.

After a confusing exchange, the two groups separated. The Celus-5 People returned to the deep, and the Haraken Swee Swei returned to shore. The foursome was disappointed and tired. Having found their lost cousins, they were faced with the intervention of centuries of time, which had eroded the ability to understand one another.

"Is this how the Star Hunter First felt trying to communicate with our hives for the first time?" Sand Flipper lamented, as he and his companions hauled themselves onto the sand and collapsed in relief.

"In two days, we can try again," Swift Claws urged.

"If we can find them again," Bobs A Lot whistled.

Whistles Keenly warbled his humor, and Bobs A Lot let loose a shrill whistle in reply. He was in no mood for his comrade's humor.

"I meant no slight, Bobs A Lot, but do you believe that in the vast expanse of endless waters these Swei Swee just happened to be nearby when you're desperate for aid?" Whistles Keenly sang back. Twelve eye stalks swiveled his way, and he warbled again.

"They've been watching us," Swift Claws said, understanding what Whistles Keenly was saying.

"We've been swimming into deep and obviously deadly waters, exhausting ourselves for days on end, and you're telling me that they've been watching us for much of that time?" Sand Flipper whistled in anger. He stood up and spun around twice, sand flying everywhere, to demonstrate his annoyance. It was a poorly thought-out action, as it necessitated that his comrades crawl back into the water to rinse off the sand that covered them.

* * *

Several cycles before the hive saved Bobs A Lot, Dives Deep had burst from the waters onto the hive's floating youngling dome, whistling and chattering so quickly that few could understand him.

The hive's First, Wave Skimmer, had commanded calm with a shrill whistle and the nervous chattering was stilled until Dives Deep could deliver a full report. He told the hive that he had spotted four, small, blue green colored Swei Swee.

That evening, the hive discussed what was to be done. Many males urged the four small Swei Swee be sent to travel the endless waters. It was their opinion that their stunted size and blue green carapaces indicated they were merely decoys of the land hunters, who continued to bring their mobile surface craft deeper and deeper into the endless waters in search of the People.

The fear pervading the hive caused the youngest females and some matrons to opt for cutting the dome's anchor, disguised though the floating structure was, and move it to a new location, lest the land hunters find them.

But Wave Skimmer had overruled those who sought the small ones' deaths and those who were panicked into whistling for the nest's relocation. His decision was to observe the strangers and learn more about them. For days, hive members shadowed the foursome, noting their habit of searching every other day and adopting the same routine.

During one of their observation days, Long Eyes had objected again that these strangers were only tools of their enemy and should be destroyed. To which Wave Skimmer had whistled, "Where are the land hunters' mobile rafts, which should be following them? And if we were to contact them, what harm could be done to the People if we never lead them back to the hive?"

Wave Skimmer was distracted by his conversation with Long Eyes when Dives Deep had whistled for their attention. A maga was headed for the surface, aiming to attack one of the small ones.

It was when one of the strange Swei Swee spotted the predator and whistled the People's ancient alarm to seek shelter that Wave Skimmer doubted the four were land hunter decoys, and he had ordered his companions to attack. A single maga, even a large one, was no challenge for five full-grown males. Wave Skimmer did think it a shame that none of the strikes crippled or killed the fish. The sweet-fleshed creature could have fed the entire hive for the day.

In the evening, Wave Skimmer spoke to the hive of the encounter with the small Swei Swee, who they had been observing. His story of the endangered little one's ancient call changed the minds of most of the hive, the matrons and young females, most of all.

But Wave Skimmer's next announcement generated great concern. He said, "I will approach the foursome in the shallows where they feed. We dare not lead them to our nest until we know more, and I can't have an extended conversation floating in the middle of the dark waters, where we can be ambushed from predators. The only opportunity lies in my approaching them, and, if necessary, going ashore."

None of the hive had ever set foot on the shore. Stories abounded about males who lived generations ago and were thought to circumvent the land hunters by going ashore where thick growths of trees pushed to the edge of the beach. But once they entered the forests, they weren't seen again.

As the First, Wave Skimmer's dilemma was whether to tell, and, if so, what to tell the Firsts of other hives. Time was when a hive would number eighty or more members before a new hive would splinter off, but those days were long gone. Hiding from the land hunters was paramount and that required a smaller hive, which could shelter in inventive ways — floating nests far out in the dark waters, or caves accessible only by diving through water-filled tunnels. With this strategy, it meant the loss of fewer People, since, once discovered by the land hunters, the eggs and younglings would be defended to the last hive member.

* * *

The Haraken Swei Swee hadn't ventured into the deep for several days after their encounter with the Celus-5 People. The size and ferociousness of the fish that attacked Bobs A Lot had stunned them. It was plain that they were ill-equipped to compete with the vicious predators of this planet's dark waters.

The foursome chose to fish in the early morning, as soon as Celus lit the horizon, quickly filling their gullets before scurrying back to the cave to hide. It was a boring existence, but none of them could come up with a better plan.

One afternoon, Sand Flipper left the cave to immerse himself in shallow water and relieve his full bladder when something caught an eye. Another eyestalk swiveled to focus on the objects, and it was soon joined by the remaining two.

<Travelers,> Sand Flipper sent to his comrades, and the other three hurried from the cave to join him. The group watched the ship in overwatch position make for orbit. Then four travelers formed a wheel, spinning faster and faster, and a fifth vessel descended between them.

<Willem sent that his ship was netted,> Bobs A Lot shared. <They must be trying to free it.>

"Five travelers," Swift Claws whistled excitedly. "Help has arrived."

Sand Flipper floated in a meter-depth of water, as the foursome watched and waited for the outcome. It wasn't long before the windstorm, which had blown dust over the embankment and onto the shore, abated and then stopped. Soon after that, five travelers rose into the air, and the mission's survey shuttle sailed out over the waters. The foursome, forgetting their own danger, whistled their approval, as the transport traveler extended its ramp, spun in a circle, sealed up, and lifted skyward.

Suddenly, Sand Flipper was knocked in a somersault clear out of the water. The impact left him lying on his back and struggling to right himself. He could hear the screaming whistles of his companions, but with his eyes closed and stalks pulled into his carapace against irritating sand, he couldn't see. There was a tumble of feet around him, and he heard Swift Claws whistle, "Why? What have we done to hurt you?"

A sudden stillness descended following Swift Claws' cry, and Sand Flipper took the opportunity to flip himself upright and blink the sand from his eyes. The giant Swei Swee, who faced Bobs A Lot days ago, was poised over him. The male's sharp, dagger-like claws were poised high in the air to deliver killing blows. Sand Flipper's companions ringed him, extended to the full height of their walking legs, with their claws raised in defense. It was a brave but ludicrous demonstration. The undersized Haraken Swei Swee had little to no chance of defeating the enormous male staring down at them.

Sand Flipper warbled a plea to be spared.

That the small Swei Swee were prepared to sacrifice their lives to protect their hive mate caused Wave Skimmer to pause, and in that small moment of time, reason reasserted itself. He dropped his claws, as did the small ones, and all settled lower on their walking legs.

Wave Skimmer couldn't understand why the small Swei Swee would cheer the return of dark travelers, even though the ones he just saw were no longer dark. The hive's stories, passed down through the generations, told of the world traveler that had captured them, imprisoned them in the giant sphere, and from which the People escaped when the opportunity presented itself. It was made clear that the dark travelers were constructed by the Nua'll, except for the hulls, which were Swei Swee built.

It had been Wave Skimmer's thought that these blue green Swei Swee, who mirrored the colors of the travelers he'd just seen, must still belong to the Nua'll, and they meant to betray the hives and recapture them.

Wave Skimmer whistled, warbled, and tweeted his confusion and frustration, voicing his desire to understand the circumstances of these four Swei Swee and the appearance of the strangely colored travelers.

What ensued was one of the stranger conversations in the annals of the universe — the same species, generations apart, and from different worlds, with both sides struggling to understand each other.

Most of the conversation took place under a rocky overhang, which pleased both sides for the small amount of protection it offered from the land hunters.

Sand Flipper drew a circle, uttering, "Nua'll," which caused Wave Skimmer to rear up.

Bobs A Lot quickly drew an "x" across the sphere and whistled, "Nua'll travel the endless waters."

"Entirely?" Wave Skimmer asked, settling back down.

"The sphere and all aboard," Whistles Keenly replied.

"Swei Swee?" Wave Skimmer asked, retracing the "x" across the sphere with the point of a claw.

<I think he's asking who destroyed the sphere,> Bobs A Lot sent.

"Swei Swee and Star Hunters," Sand Flipper whistled.

"Star Hunter travelers ... blue and green," Swift Claws whistled, pointing a claw into the air to indicate the ships that Wave Skimmer had seen. "Friends of the People."

"Star Hunter First and Swei Swee First share greeting ceremony," Bobs A Lot said excitedly, displaying the characteristic action that gave him his name.

"Star Hunters appear like these land hunters?" Wave Skimmer asked.

"No, Star Hunters are humans ... not like these," Whistles Keenly replied. "Star Hunter First and youngling, Teague, swim with the People in the waters of our home planet, Haraken."

"Humans swim?" Wave Skimmer asked, incredulous at the news.

"Not good like the People, but they enjoy the waters," Whistles Keenly tweeted.

Wave Skimmer settled to the sand, tucking his great walking legs under him. The words of the small ones were difficult to absorb. For generations, the People were the only intelligent life in this planet's waters, save for a small, cunning, furry animal that fished the seas, but the two species left each other alone. Then the land hunters had arrived, and the lives of the People descended into chaos. They were forced to flee the shores and make their way to deep waters and hidden coves. Many People were taken captive before the hives developed a new way of existing.

"Humans are friends of the Swei Swee. Humans are powerful hunters, who have taught us many things," Sand Flipper said. "Come," he added, running down the beach.

Wave Skimmer reluctantly followed the small Swei Swee, who waited for him on the other side of a rocky outcropping.

"Warble something quietly to me," Sand Flipper entreated. When Wave Skimmer complied, the little one scurried back to his companions, and Wave Skimmer followed.

The Celus Swei Swee was standing in front of the foursome when the three, who had been left behind, warbled copies of his words — not just the words, but exact copies of his voice. "How?" Wave Skimmer whistled, stunned by the repetition of his warble.

"We speak our thoughts to one another," Bobs A Lot explained.

The power of the Star Hunters, who seemed capable of incredible things, even defeating the Nua'll, according to the little ones, seemed unbelievable to Wave Skimmer. Suddenly a thought occurred to the First, and he excitedly whistled his query. Unfortunately, it was too complex for the foursome to follow. So Wave Skimmer drew a traveler in the sand. "Humans," he whistled, please to see the foursome bobbing and warbling in agreement.

Wave Skimmer drew another shape. It resembled the head of the creatures that the Haraken Swei Swee saw capture their friends. "Land hunters," the First emphasized. Next, he drew the outline of a Swei Swee and tapped a claw to his carapace's underbelly. "Land hunters search the endless waters for the People."

The statement confused the Haraken Swei Swee. "Why search for the People?" asked Bobs A Lot, who was mixing his human education with the Swei Swee's words.

"Search, kill, eat," Wave Skimmer whistled angrily, forgetting that they were all in danger by standing on the shore. That his words caused the foursome to shrink in horror gave Wave Skimmer a bit of comfort, despite his fury. It was another signal that these Swei Swee did not come to the planet to harm his People. Wave Skimmer pointed at the traveler and drew a line in the sand to the image of the land hunter, whistling, "Humans send land hunters to search the endless waters."

<He wants the Harakens to destroy the species that captured our friends,> Swift Claws sent to his companions.

<We can't promise that. We're not the ones to decide that,> Sand Flipper replied.

<Five travelers landed to rescue our mission shuttle,> Bobs A Lot sent. <There must be a sting ship or the *Rêveur* overhead.>

<Maybe both,> Swift Claws replied.

<Someone whistle something to this enormous male. He's getting agitated while waiting,> Sand Flipper sent.

"Star Hunters are powerful. They will ensure the land hunters search for the People no more," Bobs A Lot whistled to Wave Skimmer. Suddenly, he was bombarded with messages from his companions, wondering how he could promise that.

Wave Skimmer spun about and dove into the waters, spraying sand over the Haraken Swei Swee.

The foursome rinsed off, while they wondered where the giant male had gone. No sooner had they shared the thought, than the Celus Swei Swee emerged from the waters with a small fish pinched in his claw. They watched as he expertly stripped off a filet.

"With a greeting ceremony, we'll bind your words of promise to protect the People of this world given to me, Wave Skimmer, this day," Wave Skimmer whistled, asking for their names.

<Now, you've done it,> Swift Claws sent to Bobs A Lot.

<I don't want to be on this planet if the Star Hunter First isn't above us,> Sand Flipper sent.

Bobs A Lot stood up on his walking legs, sending, "You warble as foolish younglings. Teague has been taken. The Star Hunter First will have come, and he will not let the land hunters hurt these People." Lifting his claws into the air, Bobs A Lot introduced himself and heard Wave Skimmer warble in good-natured humor at his name.

The three others quickly introduced themselves, and the fillet was shared among the five.

"A male of my hive will maintain vigilance every day at the break between the deep waters and the shallows. When the humans are ready to fulfill your promise, send word, and the hives will come," Wave Skimmer whistled. Then he whirled to dive into the waves. His powerful tail was stroked with considerable effort. The First was anxious to reach the safety of the dark waters. The time he'd spent on shore had caused him a great deal of anxiety.

"There are a few problems with your promise," Sand Flipper warbled sadly, facing Bobs A Lot. "We must be rescued first."

"Even then, the Star Hunter First must decide whether to fulfill your promise," Swift Claws added.

"Do you doubt our leader will wish to protect these People?" Bobs A Lot challenged.

"No," Swift Claws replied. "But it might not be within his capability to come to their aid. What if these land hunters are many in number, formidable, and occupy the entire planet?"

"A telling point," Whistles Keenly said, joining in the discussion. "If the problem is too great for our ships, what will become of the rescue mission? Our crew members might be rescued, but this planet could quickly be left behind."

Bobs A Lot settled onto the sand, dejected and warbling a lament.

"Come," Swift Claws whistled. "We're too exposed out here. Let's return to the safety of the cave." His claw thunked Bobs A Lot's carapace in passing, hoping to encourage his companion.

-14-
Masquerade

Pussiro reported to Nyslara that the aliens freed their netted ship without firing a shot or allowing an encounter with his warriors.

"How is that possible, Commander?" Nyslara demanded.

"Better you should ask me, my queen, how the aliens can create a windstorm with their ships that threatened to scratch our precious scopes and blind the eyes of our lookouts."

Nyslara found Pussiro's words impertinent, but she allowed them to pass. Too much about the aliens was disquieting.

"Come, Commander, we need to speak with our alien captives," Nyslara ordered.

Willem and the other Harakens were housed not far from the queen's chamber. Their schoolroom, which is where they were at this time of day, was even closer. When Nyslara swept into the room, the advisors, guards, and Harakens leapt to their feet.

"Fellum, I would speak with you," Nyslara announced.

"Yes, my queen," Willem replied in the Dischnya language.

"Your nest mates have arrived," Nyslara said, pointing a long digit at the room's ceiling.

"How many more ships have arrived, my queen?" Willem asked.

"Mess," Pussiro replied.

Two, Willem thought. He didn't know how to ask about the shapes of the ships, so he picked up the drawing pot, which had replaced the pungent bowl of fossar they first used, and handed it to Pussiro.

Fortunately, Pussiro knew exactly what Willem was asking, and he squatted on his haunches to draw the ships he had studied in the nest's telescope.

Willem pointed at the elongated, gourd shape of a sting ship and said, "Fighting ship. Nest killer." His words drew hisses from Nyslara and Pussiro, and the jaws of Simlan and Hessan fell open. Pointing at the other shape, Willem said, "Leader." Then he pointed at Teague and added, "Progenitor of youth."

That a male who had produced an offspring the size of Teague was a leader made sense to Nyslara and Pussiro. Strong, large, and cunning were always traits of warrior commanders.

Word of the aliens' effortless reclamation of their shuttle had spread quickly throughout the nest, and Nyslara was sure the prisoners would have been privy to the whispered words. That she lost a valuable negotiating prize was one thing. That Willem and the other captives knew it was another thing. Nyslara stared at Willem, who held her gaze. *You know who has come for you, Fellum,* she thought, taking in his confident stance and expression.

A question formed in Nyslara's mind but was interrupted by the buzz of a receiver, and Simlan leapt for it. He listened for a moment and then gestured with the receiver to Pussiro. Soon after Pussiro communicated with the caller, he hung the comm device up, snarled, and said, "The aliens are landing in force, my queen." He turned to leave, but a command from Nyslara stopped him.

"I wish to view these aliens for myself, Commander. Have Fellum brought with us. You might have need of him if there are to be words exchanged with them."

* * *

Five travelers descended on the plains of Celus-5 and settled to the ground in a rough arc, curved toward the greatest density of native hideouts. A group of humans and four SADEs disembarked from the centrally placed traveler and marched forward about 20 meters, then halted. From the other four shuttles, 177 SADEs poured out and formed a broad half-circle behind the central figures.

"This has to be the stupidest thing I've ever done," Reiko remarked, standing near Alex. She couldn't help fingering her stun gun's handle, even though Alex made her agree not to pull the weapon unless absolutely necessary.

"You mean more stupid than ramming a battleship with your destroyer," Franz quipped.

"Remind me to discipline you later, Commander," Reiko shot back.

Franz would have replied, but thought better of it. The grin on his face, which he was sure Reiko noticed, would have to do.

Étienne and Alain, standing near their principals appeared relaxed, however that was anything but the case. They were practicing breath control techniques to remain calm and keep from touching the butts of their weapons, as their minds screamed at them to do.

The SADEs locked their avatars, not knowing how long it would take to get a reaction out of the ground-dwelling natives. To an entity, you couldn't say they were disappointed that their clever ruse of snatching the aliens' weapons wasn't accepted by Alex. Their analysis revealed that the plan had a high probability of success. But Alex replied that there remained the possibility of injuries or deaths on each side, which was unacceptable, adding, "Yes, the locals have employed force and intimidation, but we're not going to respond in kind. That only creates a state of escalation, which never leads to peace."

So instead of the masquerade, employing shifting synth-skin decoys, and the coordinated response to intercept the lookouts, the entire group of SADEs stood patiently waiting to see how Alex Racine's idea would play out.

* * *

Pussiro led Nyslara and an entourage to the lookout post that would give them the best view of the plains where the alien shuttles had landed.

When the commander entered the small room, the warriors jumped aside and saluted him, but then braced to rigid attention when, most unexpectedly, Nyslara, with her long robe, stalked in behind him.

"My queen," Pussiro said, gesturing to the scope and offering her the first look.

Nyslara's lips rippled along her muzzle in amusement and anticipation. She hadn't used a lookout scope since she was young, when her mother was still queen. She took two steps up the ladder, took the viewer in her hands, and brought it to her eyes. The warriors had the scope focused on the central aliens, and Nyslara got a good look at Willem's would-be rescuers.

"Commander, I believe you understated your point that these aliens were not of the same nest," Nyslara said. She stepped down and nodded toward the scope.

Pussiro jumped up, adjusted the lens position, and hissed soundly. Not only were there the expected size differences, but arrayed around the central figures was the most bizarre collection of skin and hair colors Pussiro had ever seen.

"Could there be more than one species?" Pussiro asked Nyslara, taking a moment to look her way.

"Does it matter, Commander? Whomever or whatever they are, those who surround the leaders, which I take to be the ones in the center, are supporting them."

Pussiro accepted that with a quick curl of his lip. He wasn't satisfied with the answer, but this wasn't the time to debate it, especially not with the queen. Instead, he returned to studying the aliens through the scope.

Nyslara motioned the two guards outside the post to wait with her retinue. "Commander, I note that you've yet to call out more warriors to the lookout positions. Why is that?"

"These aliens are capable of expending tremendous power, according to Fellum, and yet they've been careful not to use it against the soma. Even our warriors, who were shot in battle, recovered later. Perhaps, they only needed something from this planet ... something that they would have gotten and then left, but we interfered."

"Perhaps, the one thing they wanted was our planet, Commander," Nyslara replied.

Pussiro turned to regard Nyslara, nodding his acceptance of the different point of view, but his thoughts were headed in an alternate direction. "My queen, if the aliens wanted this planet, couldn't they just have taken it? The shuttle that guarded the netted one demonstrated its power over both waters and land. It alone could have wreaked havoc on our nest. Now, Fellum says that one of the ships in orbit is mightier than these shuttles."

This time, Nyslara had to agree with Pussiro's line of reasoning. The aliens' actions resembled none of the Dischnya's internal struggles, which were highlighted by fierce conflicts between nests for greater territory and resources. In Nyslara's opinion, that confounding unpredictability made them dangerous.

"What is your plan when they attack the nest, Commander?" Nyslara asked.

"You mean if they attack now, my queen?"

"Of course, now, Pussiro. Are you losing your wits?"

"When they attack with what, my queen? Only several aliens wear the tools on their middles, which we take to be their weapons and which don't kill. The rest appear unarmed." Pussiro barked a command and the senior warrior, who had been on duty in the lookout, hurried into the room. Pussiro nodded at the scope and stepped aside. The warrior stepped onto the ladder, but he kept his eyes on Pussiro.

"How far have the aliens advanced since you last viewed them?" Pussiro asked.

The warrior, a veteran of the lookouts, marked movement on the plains by comparing enemy positions to the rocks, which dotted the landscape. Before he turned over his sentry's duty to his partner, a much younger warrior, he'd carefully marked a small rocky outcropping near the massive figure in the center of the group when they had assembled. He was fully prepared to report on the alien's deployment and their advancement. Now, locating the same pile of rocks near the feet of the broad alien, he said, "Commander, the leader hasn't moved since assembling his soma." The warrior scanned left and right. He'd taken the time to memorize the placements of several figures, who were remarkable in their coloring. "Commander, not only has the leader not advanced, but it would appear that most of his soma have not moved."

"If they haven't advanced, they haven't moved," Nyslara snarled with impatience, which immediately had the warrior dropping his muzzle and ducking his eyes. To her surprise, Pussiro shot her an irritated look, the edges of his lips rippling in consternation. Nyslara was reminded that she was interfering with the commander's underlings.

"Explain," Pussiro commanded.

The warrior's head snapped up, responding to his wasat's order. "Commander, I noted the exact positions of several aliens. With this large a number, I thought they might try a fade tactic." The lookout was referring to a favorite Dischnya maneuver to present a large force to the lookouts of another nest and then slip some warriors out of the force to flank the enemy. Because the warriors in a soma were so similar in appearance, the technique was quite successful when performed well.

"And," Pussiro prompted.

"Unless my eyesight is failing me, Commander, the aliens I marked haven't moved a muscle … same position on the ground and same body position. It's … it's —"

"Uncanny," Pussiro finished for the warrior.

"It's unnatural," Nyslara said softly. Then she drew her body up to her full height, her tail cutting back and forth. "So now what, Commander?" Nyslara demanded, fervently hoping Pussiro didn't ask for her opinion.

"Now, my queen, I take Fellum, and we talk to the aliens," Pussiro replied. He bowed briefly to Nyslara, walked into the corridor, and ordered Simlan, Hessan, and Willem to follow him.

＊ ＊ ＊

Alex was thankful for his Haraken-fabricated clothes. The fabric wicked away his sweat, keeping him cool in the hot sun.

Reiko was about to ask Alex how much longer they would wait when the entire assembly received a SADE's broadcast, reporting movement in the ground and its exact position.

A cleverly concealed hatch opened and one of the native creatures climbed out, stood still, and slowly held his hands out to his side, palms toward the group.

<That's not a coincidence,> Alain sent on open broadcast.

<Smart,> Étienne replied. <He's copying Willem's gesture, the one used by our people when they surrendered at the beach.>

Alex waved the native over to him, but, instead, the alien gestured toward the bolt-hole, which brought Willem climbing out. A slender cable encircled his neck, the other end of which was held by a gray, muzzle-scarred individual. A third creature climbed out of the hole and stood waiting beside the older one.

Those closest to Alex could hear the knuckles popping on his tightly curled fists, as he took in Willem's treatment.

<Ser,> Willem sent to Alex. <I will guide you in your negotiations and translate the Dischnya language, as best I can, but first you need to calm yourself. These people are terrified of you and are merely taking precautions so as not to lose another precious bargaining tool.>

Alex slowly blew out a deep breath and unclenched his fists, and the twins relaxed ever so slightly. <Willem, are the others okay?> Alex sent privately.

<We've been treated well, Ser, and have been participating in a language and cultural exchange of sorts.>

Knowing that the news was good, Alex sent it on to the Harakens. Renée's relief and warm thoughts flooded into his implant. Alex sent to Willem, <I'll speak in our language and use pantomimes to demonstrate

my requests, and you can translate between us. That way, we won't give away our implants.>

Willem sent the Harakens a map of the discovered Dischnya's tunnels, marking a series of points — the tunnel they entered after capture, the storeroom where they were held, their newest accommodations, and the extended classroom. The map was annotated with accurate distances between the marked points, but the relative angles were estimates. <Apologies, Ser, but the tunnels often curve, and I had no comm reference point by which to determine navigational parameters.>

<Well done, Willem,> Alex sent.

Alex gestured again for the natives to approach him, but his gesture was imitated by the first individual, who had climbed out of the bolt-hole.

After a short discussion between Willem and Pussiro, Willem called out, "The wasat, the warrior commander, wants to meet halfway, Ser, and he insists on only meeting with three of you."

After a short debate, Alex, Reiko, and Étienne stepped forward to meet the natives, much to the consternation of many in the Haraken's ranks.

< Alex, Reiko, and Étienne,> Willem sent in the open, <there are several etiquettes that must be observed when in the presence of the Dischnya. Don't smile or otherwise bare your teeth. Don't point your finger at an individual, and any hand gestures should be kept close to the body with the palms facing them. Actions to the contrary are signals of aggression.>

Pussiro was introduced to Alex Racine and Captain Reiko Shimada, but not the third individual. Then again, he didn't need an introduction. As slight as the alien appeared, his watchful eyes said warrior, and, if he accompanied the leaders, his capabilities would be formidable.

During the initial greetings, Pussiro was surprised by the aliens' display of Dischnya amenities. His suspicious mind connected small disparate items. Willem had learned the Dischnya's mannerisms, and now his people exhibited the characteristics, but Pussiro couldn't conceive of a means by which Willem had the opportunity to communicate to his people.

The alien known as Alex Racine stood directly in front of Pussiro. He appeared to be unique among his people. Pussiro was taller than the male, who had no prominent teeth or dangerous claws. But his girth and bulging muscles warned Pussiro that if the alien closed on him, his back would be broken in a heartbeat. The alien's eyes were narrowed and glanced occasionally from him to Willem, and Pussiro could imagine the heat inside him from the treatment of his comrade. *Be angry, Alex Racine, that redness in your mind will keep you off balance,* Pussiro thought.

"Willem, tell Pussiro that I want the return of our people now," Alex said.

After a quick exchange with Pussiro, Willem said, "The commander wants to know if you're the leader and speak for your people."

Alex was tempted to say yes, but that would complicate matters between Reiko and him. Instead, Alex gestured to his right and said, "Captain Shimada has mission command."

Willem recognized the confusion that Alex's response would generate for the commander and tried his best to interpret the statement in a manner Pussiro would understand. To Pussiro, he said, gesturing toward Reiko, "Captain Shimada represents the people of the vessels above. She commands the sting ship, the nest killer. The leader of our people is on a planet far away and rules a soma many times greater than all the Dischnya on Sawa Messa."

Pussiro eyed the tiny alien, the commander of the strangers, and his lips rippled in amusement. In his mind, she was neither a queen nor a warrior commander. He spoke to Willem, who relayed his words. "Pussiro finds Captain Shimada unsuitable as a representative with whom to negotiate. Apologies, Captain."

"Alien misanthrope," Reiko mumbled. "Willem, tell the commander that he has a choice. Deal with us fairly, whether he feels it appropriate to talk to aliens or not or deal with our ships' beams. We don't take kindly to the kidnapping of our people."

Willem took pleasure in baring some teeth as he translated Reiko's words.

Pussiro was caught off guard by the threatening message from the tiny alien and the rude display of teeth by Willem. In his world, only the more ferocious of foes displayed aggressive behavior, and her size negated a fair comparison. Pussiro's attention was diverted away from the tiny captain to the enormous alien, whose hand was raised over his head. He imitated a ship diving for the ground. Then he made a sound like the sizzling of meat on a cooker, and a second, massively explosive sound escaped his lips as he indicated the ground being thrown into the air. Then he pointed an intimidating finger directly at Pussiro, retracting his hand to make a slicing motion across his throat. His final motion was the baring of a huge grimace.

The alien's message was clear to Pussiro, as was its insulting method of delivery, and Pussiro couldn't resist the affront, snarling his own challenge.

Alex started to speak to Willem, but Pussiro was issuing his own reply, which required Alex wait.

"Sers, Pussiro said only the queen may free what the soma possess, which includes us. Furthermore, he says that none of you are worthy to meet with the queen."

Pussiro snarled a command and Simlan pulled on Willem's cable. The Dischnya backed up, taking Willem with them, and climbed down into their tunnel.

<Apologies, Sers,> Willem sent, before the tunnel hatch closed. <There is much that is foreign about these people, which will complicate our negotiations.>

Reiko glanced up at Alex. "Sorry," she said. "I didn't think standing on protocol as the mission commander would screw up the negotiations."

Alex didn't reply to Reiko's comment. Instead, he was staring into the distance. <Renée, Julien,> he sent, <you're the ones who've watched and read the ancient stories. Who would make the better queen, Cordelia or Miranda?>

-15-
Confrontation

Nyslara had never seen Pussiro so agitated in her presence.

"Bad enough we are invaded by aliens, but the soma are so honored as to receive truly strange ones," Pussiro raged.

The comment had Nyslara's muzzle twitching. "I believe, Commander, that the terms alien and strange go hand in hand."

Pussiro stared at her, as if she had raked his muzzle, but he soon turned to pacing her chambers again.

That will require replacement, Nyslara thought with lament, watching Pussiro's great clawed feet cut into the room's finely woven rug.

"If you're done fuming, Commander, your queen waits to hear more details about your encounter other than the aliens are strange."

"Your pardon, my queen, but how can I deal with these creatures when I can't understand their ways? I addressed the large male, who I believed to be the leader, but was told that their commander is the smallest female you've ever seen."

"Interesting. What did she have to say?"

"She threatened me, saying that the prisoners must be returned or we would face the consequences. Then the enormous one made motions with his hands of a ship attacking and destroying us, and he had the effrontery to bare his teeth at me."

"Did he demonstrate these poor behaviors beforehand?"

"That's the odd thing, my queen. From the moment of greeting, etiquette was carefully observed, as if they knew our ways."

"So think, Pussiro, what would have caused the male to react that way?"

Pussiro thought for a moment and then ducked his head before he looked up at Nyslara. "It might have been me, my queen. When the tiny female was introduced as the commander, I might not have paid her the courtesy due her."

"Might not or did not?"

"Did not, my queen."

"Males," Nyslara snorted. Nests were governed by queens for just that reason to balance the aggressive tendencies of the wasats and their warriors.

"So how did you leave the talks, Commander? What comes next?"

"I don't know, Nyslara," Pussiro said with a pained expression. "I told them that only a queen could choose to free what the soma held and none of them were worthy of meeting with you."

"That's the sum of your talk, Commander? You've left these powerful invaders with a slap of your claws across their muzzles?" Nyslara's eyes flashed. She was tempted to do the same to Pussiro, but she swallowed her anger with great difficulty. "Well, Commander, either this will be over quickly when the aliens burn out our nest, or they will demonstrate more intelligence than you have and return to speak with us one more time. If we're given another opportunity to negotiate, I'll be the one speaking with them."

"My queen, we can't risk you in the open. You have no daughter!" Pussiro exclaimed, aghast at the thought of risking their only female in the nest's great unbroken line of queens.

"The soma will have no use for a queen, or I for them, if the nest is turned to cinders by the aliens' ships, Commander," Nyslara shot back. She stood with hind legs fully extended and tail thrashing.

Pussiro realized he had overstepped his bounds and extended obeisance to Nyslara.

"I have one more piece of information for you, Pussiro, which might awaken your senses to what we face. While you were above ground, a lookout reported a most unusual observation. The warrior, who delivered the message, was the senior over the junior who shot the alien exiting the ship. He used his scope to focus on that same alien in the group you faced. To verify his observation, he called two other warriors, who had been with him during the fight. All three confirmed that the female was the one who was shot. Not only does she live, but she bears no semblance of injury ...

this despite earlier reports that she was struck in the shoulder and fell forward onto the shuttle's hatch."

"How is that possible?" Pussiro said quietly, his forehead furrowed in puzzlement.

"It demonstrates what I've been trying to tell you, Pussiro, and why it has to be me who speaks for the soma. Our traditions, even our courtesies, must be set aside so that we truly hear the words of these aliens. Our asset is Fellum, and we must heed his advice."

* * *

Days passed without action from either side of the conflict. Classroom lessons for the captives continued as if their comrades had never arrived. It was entirely unnerving to Pussiro, who had expected an immediate retaliation by the aliens. In the intervening time, he had done his best to prepare the nest for the attack.

The receiver next to a sub-commander whistled. He snatched it off the wall, listened, and hung it up. "Commander, the aliens are landing again," the sub-commander announced.

Pussiro confirmed the landing location, which was the same as before, and hurried to tell the queen.

Nyslara called to Cysmana, her attendant, and wasted no time donning her best robe and adorning her person with the trappings of her supreme position, a necklace of gemstones, arm bracelets, and a headdress of rare flight feathers from birds captured at the green's edge.

Pussiro was pleased to see that Nyslara stopped at a nearby gated room to snarl a command to her feedwa. The queen's twin dogs were raised to respond only to her and were often used as protection when two queens met in truce.

The soma deserted the corridor at the approach of Pussiro and a group of his sub-commanders. Not because of the warriors' presence, but because they announced the coming of the queen and her feedwa. The aggressive beasts were highly protective of their mistress and allowed none of the soma near her.

At the same lookout site, Pussiro examined the display of shuttles and aliens, seemingly identical to the previous positions of ship and individuals. The commander shook his head, trying to clear his mind of his unreasoning fear over the nature of the aliens. He managed to display a more confident expression when he signaled Nyslara that all was ready, breaking open the hatch, and stepping above ground first.

Nyslara signaled her male dog up the ladder, and the lizard-like creature scurried up it with ease. The second one eyed her, anxious to follow, and Nyslara waited a moment before she signaled the female, who was the feistier of the two dogs, to test its obedience. She hadn't used the feedwa in more than an annual and wanted to ensure she had firm control over her. Finally, she nodded, and the female tore up the ladder.

"Fellum, queen's dogs, feedwa, dangerous. Don't approach Nyslara or her feedwa," Simlan warned. Hessan and he climbed the ladder next, bringing Willem with them. Simlan had apologized to Willem when he extended the cable noose to him, but the alien nodded his acceptance and placed the restraining leash over his head and tightened it. Hessan ducked his head, disturbed by their treatment of someone who long ago had lost the appellation of alien and become much more than an acquaintance.

* * *

The Harakens arrayed themselves in the exact same positions as before, hoping to unnerve the natives. This time, they substituted the mission shuttle for the standard traveler at the center of the five ships. After it landed, the aft ramp was deployed.

Alex, Renée, Reiko, Julien, and Miranda waited in front of the assembly. They watched Pussiro, the commander, climb out of the tunnel's entrance. Then first one and then two odd-looking creatures scampered out of the ground. The animals had a similar coloring to the natives the

Harakens had seen, but these creatures walked on four legs, possessed powerful tails and elongated snouts, filled with long, sharp teeth, which they seemed intent on baring.

Following behind the creatures walked a tall, robed female, decked out in her finery. She towered many centimeters over Pussiro and carried herself in a regal manner. She snarled a command, and the creatures scampered to her sides.

<Now, that's a queen,> Reiko shared with her companions via comm, noting the long, tapered tail that curled around the female's feet, when she came to a halt.

<Let's hope our display is at least as impressive,> Renée replied.

<Keep a careful eye on the queen's beasts,> Étienne sent to Alain. <They have a hungry look about them.>

The Harakens watched the native queen step forward about 5 meters, giving her warriors plenty of room to climb out of the tunnel. They brought Willem with them. Then the threesome circled wide to take up a position a couple of meters off Pussiro's side, placing the commander between them, the queen and, most important, her dogs.

Alex signaled Z, and the Haraken's presentation began. Cordelia descended the mission shuttle's ramp, seated on a makeshift throne created by Mickey and some techs. The throne floated on four grav pallets hooked together to form a platform.

Z had transferred to his Cedric Broussard suit, his massive New Terran-built avatar, and walked beside the platform, as a queen's administrator would.

The entire scenario was designed by Julien and Renée, who were the aficionados of the ancient fantasy stories. In consideration of who would play the part of the queen, it was decided that Cordelia, with her holo-vid capable synth skin, could add some of the beguiling touches the role required.

Interestingly, some of the more fantastical touches came from Trixie, who had spent the trip immersed in the *Rêveur's* library of ancient stories. Those dealing with fantasy intrigued her the most. She designed a series of displays Cordelia could employ around her head, depending on her emotional reactions during the negotiations. In addition, Trixie urged Mickey to install hidden lights in the throne that would be linked to a controller.

"What's the purpose?" Mickey had asked Trixie.

"For whatever Cordelia wants," Trixie had replied. "Or do you dare disobey a request from our queen, mortal?" she added, giving Mickey an infectious grin.

"I hear and obey the word of my queen," Mickey had replied, bowing courteously to Trixie, who had giggled at the response and danced away.

Nyslara watched the approach of the aliens' queen, for that was whom she thought the female must be. What captivated Nyslara's attention was the swirl of light atop the queen's head. The colors echoed the light of Nessila as it broke the morning's horizon. Tendrils of brighter streaks coursed through the glow.

Leaning toward Pussiro, Nyslara whispered, "And you thought the male you dealt with was big." She nodded toward the alien who walked beside the throne-seated queen.

"Let's hope they get no larger, my queen," Pussiro whispered back.

Comparing herself to the awe-inspiring display of the alien queen, Nyslara felt drab and insignificant. Nonetheless, she rose to her full height, determined to serve her soma with the best of her ability. *If we're to be ruled by these aliens,* she thought, *I hope they're benevolent.*

The throne, bearing the alien queen, and her escorts stopped behind the same figures who had stood before Pussiro last time, and Nyslara made to step forward, but Willem hissed a warning.

"Apologies, Queen Nyslara, but we wait for an invitation," Willem said. He stepped forward to the length of his restraint. Simlan took a tentative step along with Willem, ensuring the cable wasn't taut on his alien friend's neck.

Willem delivered a courtly bow to Cordelia in imitation of the vid he'd received from Julien and stood patiently waiting.

"The amenities, Queen Nyslara and Commander Pussiro," Willem urged. When the two Dischnya delivered a tentative nod of their heads, Willem whispered, "Not the best of beginnings."

Nyslara and Pussiro's eyes dilated at the sight of the golden crown of light over the alien queen's head shifting to blood red with orange highlights and growing larger.

"The Haraken queen says that she understands your ways are not hers," Willem said, as the crown of lights changed again to return to its original display.

"How did you speak with her, Fellum?" Pussiro demanded.

Willem tapped his temple. "All my people can communicate this way," he said.

Many pieces fell into place for Pussiro. He glanced at Nyslara, the lips of his muzzle trembling with concern for the fate of the nest.

"Steady, Commander," Nyslara whispered. "These aliens have power beyond our comprehension. It's my intent to borrow some of it, and lift our Dischnya out of the ground and into the light once more."

"The Haraken queen comes," Willem said. "It's a great honor." He bowed again as Cordelia's grav-powered throne slid forward, Z in step beside it, and Alex and the forward company keeping pace in front of it.

What the Dischnya couldn't know was that their every whispered word was translated and communicated by Willem to the entire Haraken assembly with one purpose in mind — to facilitate the retrieval of the hostages. Eventually the ruse would have to be explained, but that would be after the crew was rescued.

When the grav-throne came to a halt, Z stepped to the front of the pallets and assumed the most intimidating stance he could imagine. Then Cordelia stood up. She had borrowed a small app that was used in her holo-vid shows for Haraken citizens to echo her comms to Z. The throne lights pulsed in time and color with her words and her emotions.

Nyslara, Pussiro, and poor befuddled Simlan and Hessan stared at the intimidating display of lights from the alien queen, and then her giant attendant spoke to them. "Her majesty, the queen of Haraken, says that her people are never to be held in bondage ... by any species."

If the Dischnya's jaws had been capable of reaching the ground, they would have struck with resounding thwacks. The queen's attendant spoke in the tongue of the Dischnya with the same fluency as Willem. Pussiro glanced at Willem, and their alien captive tapped his temple again.

In the silence that followed, Simlan eased out another half meter of cable, which allowed him to drop his hand by his side, as if that hid the fact that he was the one restraining one of the Haraken queen's people.

Simlan and Hessan glanced at each other. Both fear and relief somehow showed in the furrow of the youth's brow and the rippling of his lips. Simlan could understand that. Hessan was grateful not to be holding the cable, but he felt that the two of them would pay the ultimate penalty for Willem's treatment.

"How do we know that once your people are returned, Queen of the Harakens, that you will not destroy my entire nest?" Nyslara asked. Moments later, the attendant relayed the queen's reply, which fascinated Nyslara.

"Our queen asks if any of Nyslara's people have been hurt," Z said.

When Nyslara replied in the negative, Z said, "That is your answer."

A long sigh escaped Nyslara's muzzle, fluttering her lips in passing. "Release Fellum," she ordered. She was looking past Pussiro at Willem when the alien reached up and snapped the cable around his neck like it was thin piece of animal hide. Pussiro, who also witnessed the display, whipped his head to Nyslara and back to Willem, and both Dischnya principals heard the chortling of Simlan and Hessan, which ceased when Pussiro eyed them. Much to the Dischnya's surprise, Willem stayed beside them.

Nyslara waited for a response from the Haraken queen, but the female remained in that motionless manner, which Willem could adopt. After a few more moments, when nothing more happened, when no more words were said, Nyslara ordered the warriors to release the other captives. In her mind, it made no sense to free one and keep the others. She hoped she'd saved her soma and not delivered them into slavery, but she envisaged a cable restraint around each Dischnya neck, and a shiver ran up her spine.

Willem had told the Harakens that Nyslara had sent for the hostages, and an eternity passed for Alex and Renée while they waited for the return of their son.

Ginny and Keira were the first to emerge from the tunnel opening, shading their eyes and blinking from the bright light of Celus. Close behind them came Teague and Xavier.

Alex's message hit the four of them while they were still waiting for their eyesight to adjust and before they could take in the assembled sides. Once received and with eyes watering, the group walked with decorum to stand beside Willem.

The heads of the feedwa came up at the new scents offered them, but a word from Nyslara brought them to heel. *Strange*, the queen thought, *my dogs never took an interest in Fellum*. She tucked that inconsistency in the back of her mind to be considered later.

Willem kept his eyes on Nyslara, and when the queen indicated with a quick wave of her muzzle toward the Harakens, the SADE sent a short message to his fellow hostages. The five Harakens stepped forward, stopped, and nodded their appreciation to Nyslara, who accepted their thanks as her due. Then the group walked quickly forward to be welcomed by their comrades.

The Dischnya watched as the released aliens were touched or enfolded in arms, accompanied by prodigious displays of teeth. *Aliens and alien mannerisms*, Pussiro thought, admiring the restraint his captives exhibited while communicating to his people and observing the Dischnya's amenities. Their efforts gave him hope for the future of the Tawas Soma.

What happened next confused the Dischnya as little else about the aliens had done. The alien queen's crown of light disappeared. She threw off her cape and descended her throne to stand beside those in front of the assembly. Her throne was disassembled, and four conveyors underneath it were transported back to the ship. Then the central figures advanced toward them.

When the aliens stopped in front of them, the large male known to them as Alex Racine standing foremost, Nyslara's eyes narrowed. "You have no queen," she said.

"No," Alex replied in Dischnya.

"And you speak our tongue," Nyslara said.

"You taught Willem," Alex replied.

Nyslara glanced to Willem and back to Alex. There were many questions that she wanted to ask, but there were more important issues to discuss. "You're the leader of your people?" Nyslara asked.

"Our words to Commander Pussiro were true. Captain Shimada commands," Alex said, indicating Reiko. "I'm an advisor."

"I have advisors," Nyslara acknowledged. "None of them are treated by the soma as you are by your people."

"I was the leader of my people," Alex replied.

"For the Dischnya, a queen leads until her death or her daughter takes it from her."

"It's not so with my people."

"Many things are not the same between our people."

"True words, Queen Nyslara," Alex replied

"Are we your subjects now, Alex Racine? Will my soma wear restraints and do your bidding?"

"As you said, Queen Nyslara, our ways aren't your ways. We don't subjugate populations … soma," Alex corrected. "We didn't —" <Willem, I'm running out of Dischnya vocabulary,> Alex sent. <Please explain that we didn't know this planet was inhabited, and we'll be leaving them in peace as soon as we've conducted a couple of important investigations.>

"Our leaders have questions, and answers must be found," Willem translated for Alex. "When they're discovered, we'll be departing Sawa Messa."

"What questions?" Nyslara asked. Part of her was still waiting for the aliens' powerful weapons to end the lives of her soma. That they might actually leave and take their knowledge with them scared her more than the thought of immediate death.

"Willem, explain that there are two," Alex replied. "There are three ships like ours, but dark, buried on their shores. We need to examine them and would like to know of their beginnings."

While the groups were talking, they'd edged closer. The female feedwa, who was tempted by the scent of the new creatures, took the opportunity to taste them. Her extraordinarily long tongue lashed out at Renée.

Faster than a human or Dischnya eye could follow, Miranda snatched the offending tongue and held it firmly in her grasp. The female dog whimpered, and Nyslara's lips trembled with mirth. "Met your match, have you?" she growled at her feedwa.

Alex signaled Miranda, and the SADE released the animal's tongue.

Nyslara barked a harsh command and the feedwa slunk behind her. The male nipped the female's flank, a rebuke for placing them in disfavor.

"The ships you speak of were here long before the Dischnya arrived," Nyslara said.

"Arrived?" Reiko asked, when she heard the translation from Willem.

"Yes, Captain," Willem replied. "In the Dischnya language, this planet is Sawa Messa or second home. Sawa is the next planet starward and their home world. It would seem that they began a migration due to adverse environmental conditions on Sawa. I've yet to discover what actually happened, but, suffice it to say, after several landings, the flights were halted. The Dischnya here on Sawa Messa have been stranded for two or three generations."

Suddenly, the odd pieces of information about the natives completed a puzzle for Alex. "You have my —" Alex started to say, but when the Dischnya vocabulary failed him, he requested Willem's help again, sending, <Willem, please convey my sympathies to Queen Nyslara for the predicament of her people.>

"Alex Racine feels great pain for the Tawas Soma, whose lives have been harsh on Sawa Messa, isolated from the soma of Sawa."

Nyslara stared at Willem, surprised by the words he expressed. When Willem nodded gravely at her to underline the sentiment, she glanced at the huge alien male and then back to Willem. There followed a rapid exchange between Willem and Nyslara, with the SADE struggling to keep up with the queen.

"Apologies, Ser," Willem said to Alex. "The queen's questions are pushing the limits of my education. I believe she is confused by your name. Anyone of rank in the nest, as the Dischnya refer to their society's organization, has a title. She thought that perhaps Alex was your title and wanted an equivalent name in Dischnya."

"And your response, Willem?" Alex asked.

"I explained that, at one time, you were commander of all Haraken warriors. Later, you were the leader of the Haraken soma. Now you're just Alex Racine."

The Harakens, who knew Alex well, broke out in laughter at the thought of the man, who created their world, being thought of as just Alex.

Nyslara and her Dischnya drew back at the audacious display of teeth, and Alex sent a quick warning. Humans and SADEs apologetically either snapped their mouths shut or covered them with hands.

"No offense was meant to you or your soma, Queen Nyslara," Alex said, holding his hands slightly away from his body, palms toward her. "Their display was meant for me."

"Their rudeness was meant for you, Alex Racine?" Nyslara asked, evidently quite confused.

"Among our soma, this display is not rude," Alex replied. Human laughter wasn't always meant as a kindness, but Alex didn't think this was an appropriate time to communicate species subtleties.

Behind Nyslara's back, Hessan bared his teeth briefly at Simlan in imitation of the aliens, and his senior cuffed him lightly across the muzzle. But the lips of both trembled in mirth — partly for the jest, but most of all for the thought that they might not die today at the hands of the aliens.

Nyslara continued to speak quickly to Willem, who queried Simlan. Nyslara gestured the senior warrior forward and Willem and he dove into a conversation. Eventually, they squatted on the ground, with Hessan and the other ex-captives joining the exchange.

<Willem, is this critical, at this time?> Reiko sent in the open.

<Apparently, Captain, it is to Nyslara. She refuses to address Ser as simply Alex Racine,> Willem sent in reply.

<I'm able to supply myriad alternative names for our exalted one,> Julien quipped.

<That might be quite true, my learned friend,> Willem replied, <but I think none of them would be acceptable to Nyslara or Ser himself.>

<Good one, Willem,> Reiko sent, and the comm was filled with laughter over the exchange.

<You have a challenge to your position as the driest wit, Julien,> Alex sent privately.

<And it's a welcome thing to learn,> Julien admitted.

<Yes, my friend, I think both of us can rest a little bit easier, knowing that, given time, humans and SADEs can learn to be comfortable in each other's company.>

The group, drawing in the dirt with pieces of stick, the ground now covered in a host of crude drawings, nodded in agreement and stood up. Simlan approached Nyslara, ducked his head, and whispered to her. She considered his words and nodded her approval.

"Dassata Alex Racine," Nyslara announced. Her Dischnya echoed her pronouncement.

"The queen has titled you Dassata, Ser. As close as I can approximate the Dischnya term, you're now known to them as a peacemaker."

<I told you, my love, that the universe was waiting for you,> Renée sent privately.

Alex's comm was flooded by humans and SADEs, who sent their congratulations. It was a tiny moment in human history, but it punctuated one man's desire to build bridges between intelligent species. Not a single Dischnya had been killed, and the two humans who lost their lives chose to forego actions that might have harmed the natives, despite the danger it presented to them.

<Most appropriate, my friend,> Julien sent, when the wave of compliments ended.

"Dassata Alex Racine," Nyslara said. "You asked only one question."

"Four of our soma are missing," Alex replied. He signaled Julien, who stepped forward, holding a portable holo-vid in his hand. When he activated it, the hisses of the Dischnya were audible. Pussiro stared at the instrument intently, envisioning its uses.

The holo-vid displayed Julien's vids of the four Swei Swee, at various times aboard ship. It was a good thing that fur hid the Dischnya's skin color. Otherwise, the Harakens would have witnessed them turning the purest white. Nyslara, Pussiro, and Simlan were doing their best to remain absolutely still and give nothing away. But behind Nyslara, Hessan's soft cough of regurgitation, which he managed to swallow, was heard.

"These are your soma?" Pussiro asked.

"Harakens are many soma united together," Alex explained, and he waved his hand at those assembled around him, careful to keep his arm low and his palm facing out. "Willem, please augment our request," Alex added.

"The four soma, who Dassata speaks of, live in the great waters, Commander. Those ships, buried on the shores, were once flown by their progenitors many generations ago. Dassata is asking if you've seen these four."

"They were seen at the shore," Pussiro said. "Teague whistled at them, and they fled into the waters. That's the one and only time when my warriors saw them."

"We will be at the shore for some time before we leave," Alex said. "We will trouble your nest no longer, Queen Nyslara."

"Dassata Alex Racine, I would speak with you again when Nessila is high," Nyslara said. She wanted to talk to the alien peacemaker now but needed time to order her thoughts.

"Yes, I will come here," Alex replied, pointing at the ground. "Your lookouts can warn you when I land."

Nyslara nodded her acceptance, and she and her soma watched the aliens climb into their ships, which, without a sound, lifted into the sky and were gone.

Pussiro regarded Nyslara, his forehead heavily furrowed in a frown.

"You're wondering, Commander, what Dassata will do to our soma when he discovers the Dischnya have made war upon the ceena, who he considers part of his nest."

"That was my thought, my queen."

"It was my thought too," Nyslara replied softly. She turned to reenter the tunnel, her tail whipcracking across the muzzle of the female feedwa, who yelped in pain.

-16-
Alex and Teague

After the meeting with Nyslara, the discussions aboard Alex's traveler were heated, and Teague was at the center of them.

"What do you mean you haven't found them, Captain?" Teague cried out. He was standing in the aisle, hands on his hips, and towering over a seated Reiko.

"I believe my comment was self-explanatory, Teague, and, while I know these are close friends of yours, let me remind you that you are a journey member, and I'm the mission commander." She punctuated her comment with a captain's stare, designed to put overreaching crew in their places.

Teague was about to issue a hot retort when he received Julien's comm. <An intelligent human knows when an argument is lost and retreats until a better opportunity presents itself.> Teague threw his hands in the air and stomped back to take a seat beside Ginny. Alex and Renée sat facing the teenagers. Teague glanced at his parents. His mother looked concerned, but his father was frowning.

"Dad, can't you say something to the captain?" Teague complained.

"I believe more than enough has been said to Captain Shimada, Teague. Our Swei Swee haven't been found, but we've been unable to mount a serious search for them. The Dischnya possess dangerous, slug-throwing weapons. They seriously injured Lieutenant Soucis when she tried to lead an operation to free our downed traveler."

"The Dischnya trapped a traveler?" Ginny asked.

"There's much that's happened while the five of you were held hostage. I always found it to be of great value to be brought up to date on the latest reports, to make more informed decisions," Alex said, eyeing his son.

Immediately, Teague reached out to Julien and Ginny contacted Cordelia for a synopsis of the events that took place above ground, during their time in captivity.

Alex and Renée sat quietly, while the two young ones were deep in their review.

When Teague finished, he sent an apology to Reiko.

<Apology accepted, Teague,> Reiko sent in reply. <You can see we were quite busy taking care of the issues in order of priority. Had we waited any longer to free the netted traveler, we might have lost more than two good people.>

"Teague, tell your father about the warrior's reaction at the shore," Ginny urged.

Teague wasn't sure what value the story held for his father, but Ginny's expression insisted.

"Well, it was odd, Dad. I was coming out of the water when I ran into these warriors, who were waiting for me and the Swei Swee. The odd part was the way they were looking funny at my friends."

"Funny? How, son?" Renée asked, and both Alex and Renée received a short vid of the warriors.

<They're drooling in hunger,> Renée sent to Alex, shocked at what she saw.

<Let's not voice that opinion just now, my love,> Alex sent in reply. He too was unsettled about what he saw, but mentioning it to Teague would only upset him further. The last thing Teague needed was to envision the land-based aliens considering his friends as food.

"So, I whistled to the Swei Swee to seek shelter," Teague said continuing his story, "which upset one warrior, who swung his weapon's butt at my shoulder."

"Which you took issue with, despite being surrounded by weapon-toting natives," Ginny remonstrated.

The expressions on his parents' faces made Teague duck his head. He would rather Ginny hadn't underlined that part of the story. She was always doing that to him. He'd be having a little fun, enjoying the excitement of a dangerous stunt, and she would be warning him to be careful.

"Yes, well, anyway," Teague continued, throwing Ginny a reprimanding look, which she ignored, "I blocked his swing and snatched the weapon away from him. When I did, it yanked him off his feet and launched him out into the shallows. Dad, you should have seen this warrior lose his mind when he hit the water. He panicked beyond all reason. He wasn't even in waist-deep water, but he was shrieking and whining like he was about to die. I had to fish him out. When I did, he dug his nails into my shoulder, and … and …"

"He threw him into deeper water," Ginny finished for Teague.

Alex had to cover his mouth to keep from laughing, but that didn't stop him from receiving a glare from his partner.

"But I fished him out again," Teague objected.

"Teague told the warrior off once the two of them reached the shore with a gesture like this," Ginny said, wagging a finger at Teague, "and then pointing at his bleeding shoulder. When we made a mistake of showing our teeth to the Dischnya, it was pointed out to us, using the exact same gesture, that we had displayed bad manners."

"Captain Escobar remarked I had become infamous, having become the first human to teach the aliens a new gesture, which happened to be a remonstrative one," Teague added.

The lights in the main cabin brightened, and Commander Cohen announced their arrival aboard the *Sojourn*. Moments later, the telltale at the hatch signaled the bay was pressurized, and the Harakens filed off the ship and groups moved through the bay's airlock. Teague headed for the bridge, but a signal from Alex stopped him.

"We will begin a full-scale search for our Swei Swee tomorrow, first thing in the morning, Teague. But for right now, and except for Willem, of course, you and the other ex-captives have appointments with medical."

Teague looked at the medical specialists, who were standing by, Pia in front. He took a breath to object, but Ginny truncated that protest with a swift punch in his arm. "Ow," he uttered, glaring at Ginny, who glared right back at him. "Guess we're going to medical," Teague said, rubbing his arm and following Pia, who hid her smirk at Ginny's antics.

Ginny flashed a bright smile at Alex and Renée and then ran to catch up, linking an arm with Teague and rubbing the spot she hit.

<What seems so familiar about that scene?> Julien sent to Alex.

<You should be quiet,> Alex sent back, adding an image of Julien with his face fully encased in a mask.

Julien returned the image as a vid. He was seen turning blue, his head slumping and passing out since Alex failed to provide an opening for the mouth.

<As if you need to breathe,> Alex shot back and received an altered vid. In this version, Julien's head righted, and his face resumed its natural coloration. But his eyes blinked in confusion, as if he was unsure what to do next — the mask remaining in place.

<Oddball,> Alex remarked, slipping an arm around Renée's waist and laying a hand on the back of Julien's neck, as the threesome walked to the bridge. Their buoyed spirits were reflected in the sense of relief, circulating throughout the fleet, at recovering the hostages, especially after suffering the losses of Edward and Ullie.

In quick order, the medical specialist checked out the returned captives and, much to their surprise, pronounced them healthy, although suffering from slight weight loss, most evident in the New Terrans.

Cleared from medical, Captain Escobar and Corporal Daubner hurried to join the conference about to take place on the *Sojourn*'s bridge. Reiko thought that the next steps were obvious, but since Alex seemed lost in thought, she kept her opinion to herself and waited.

"Alex, there are several things that Corporal Daubner and I wish to discuss," Xavier said, choosing to start the conversation. "Willem has done a wonderful job of learning the native's language, but I believe there's a bigger picture that must be considered when dealing with the Dischnya."

"Yes, Ser," Keira added. "There's something odd about the concept of an underground nest on this planet. I get it that this is the way they might have lived on Sawa, but they're not on Sawa, and they haven't lived there for generations."

"You mean why are the Dischnya living underground when there seems to be no reason for it?" Alex asked.

"Exactly," Xavier exclaimed.

"Well, I, for one, am interested in finding our four missing crew members and leaving this planet to the Dischnya as soon as possible. They can keep their confusing society," Reiko said. She expected a swell of support, but no one showed an interest in seconding her comment. *Or not,* Reiko thought.

"In contrast to the Captain's opinion, I'd like to request permission of Nyslara to spend time investigating her planet. This is Haraken's first exploration mission, and there is much for us to learn," Willem said.

"Willem, I believe that Nyslara's conversation with Dassata tomorrow will be enlightening and will provide you with answers without voicing a request," Julien commented.

Alex frowned at Julien's use of his Dischnya title, but his friend wore the most innocent expression on his face, which Alex knew was about as far from the nature of Julien's thoughts as the enormous distances between stars.

"Captain Escobar, what were your other concerns?'" Alex asked.

"I'll let Corporal Daubner describe it. She found it," Xavier replied.

"For many days, we were held in a storeroom, where we initiated an ongoing conversation with our two primary guards, Simlan and Hessan, who you saw at the meeting, standing behind Nyslara and Pussiro," Keira began. "Ginny and I were drawing images on the floor with some stinky, dark pigment that I think was boiled down from animal parts. Once we earned the trust of our two guards, which took a while, I went looking among the shelves for something else to use for drawing. In the back and high on a shelf were a set of large, shallow bowls that were stacked together. I thought there might be something inside them, so I took them down."

Keira paused and looked at Xavier, who nodded his encouragement to continue.

"I didn't pick up on it at first, Ser," Keira said. "But the platters were light. It's when I held them over my head to see if they were wood or some other exotic material that I noticed the pattern in the base. They were Swei Swee carapaces, Ser. From the size of them, they were younglings." Tears of anguish formed in Keira's eyes. "I'm so sorry, Ser."

Alex shared Teague's images of the warriors staring at the Swei Swee when the five captives were taken. "As you can see by the interest of the warriors, combined with Keira's news, the Dischnya have been harvesting the Swei Swee, as a food source, since they arrived on planet. I don't need to tell you that this information must not be shared with my son, right now, or Ginny, for that matter. But this does mean that there is the distinct possibility that the Swei Swee, who inhabited those dark travelers, might no longer exist."

Alex let those thoughts sink in, and then he brought everyone back to their next priority. "However, first things first. Captain Shimada, I believe we have four crew members to rescue."

"I was thinking the same thing myself," Reiko replied. "We'll put a pilot and copilot aboard each traveler and launch eight of them, keeping the mission shuttle and one other shuttle aboard this ship. The pilots will slow cruise the coastline, alternating duty with the copilots, until they locate them."

* * *

Franz Cohen was chatting with his copilot as he boarded his traveler. He would be in command of the squadron's search for the four missing Swei Swee. He spotted Teague by his height and distinct body shape, sitting head high over his seat back, and Franz had no doubt he would find Ginny seated beside him. ·

Nodding briefly at the two teenagers as he passed, Franz noted that they both held pilot helmets. Not that they would be flying, but they could aid in the search. The remaining crew aboard would take feeds from the controller via their implants, which didn't possess the sophisticated controls and viewers in the helmets.

Franz knew better than to ask Teague or Ginny whether they had Captain Azasdau or Captain Shimada's permission, much less Alex's, to join the search — he knew they would be extremely cooperative, lest it endanger their permission to be aboard. If Reiko had been lost planetside, no one could keep Franz from taking a front-row seat in the effort to find her. And Teague grew up with these four Swei Swee. To him, they were brothers.

After exiting the mother ships in orbit, the travelers descended planetside, targeting the point where the Swei Swee were last seen. Franz split the eight travelers into two groups, one to head north along the coast and the other to head south. Two ships in each group would hover over the shoreline, while the other two would spread out over the waters, one surveying the shallows and one following the edge of the dark waters.

The travelers moved ever so slowly, per Alex's advice that the Swei Swee could stay underwater for up to 0.35 hours and travel hundreds of meters during that time. The crew in the main salon rotated shifts as time passed, as did the pilots, although the controllers did all the flying once they were programmed.

Everyone's eyes in the helmets or implants were focused on various wavelength feeds from the controller. Most were in the visual spectrum, but some thought that a Swei Swee on the surface might have absorbed more of Celus' light. Warmed by the star, the carapace would appear at a different temperature than the waters surrounding them and might stand out under thermal imaging. Still others monitored for disturbances or wakes that might indicate a Swei Swee swimming below the surface.

In each traveler, the crew was emotionally feeding on their recent successes. Despite the loss of two mission members, they successfully recovered an entire shuttle of their people and every captive. Finding the four Swei Swee would complete their efforts.

Unfortunately, the cave where the Swei Swee hid was far up the coast from the original point of attack. The foursome chose it because of the bluff above and the thick growths of tall trees that supplanted the grass and shrubs of the plains. It was their thought that the land hunters wouldn't have ventured into the forests where their underground tunnels would be challenged by the deep tree roots.

To further complicate the searchers' efforts, the Swei Swee's visible exposure time was minimal. They fished briefly at Celus' emergence over the horizon and quickly returned to the cave and, hidden beneath the rocky overhang, a traveler would need to pass within 50 meters for the ship's controller to pick up their implants.

* * *

It was Wave Skimmer's turn to monitor the little ones. He'd alternated the surveillance days of the strange Swei Swee with Long Eyes and Dives Deep. On the prior evenings before his turn, Wave Skimmer would receive the reports of the activities of the foreign Swei Swee before leaving the following morning to watch them from where the dark waters broke to form the shallows.

What Wave Skimmer noticed, as the days passed, was that while the little ones' routine didn't vary, their exposure time in the water lessened each day, and Wave Skimmer recognized the signs. They were separated from whatever they considered their hive, and, detached as they were, there was no community support for them.

It was the calling of Swei Swee males to search the waters every day to support themselves and the hive's females, who tended the younglings and eggs, and the search could only be conducted during the light of day. Duty drove every member of the hive. But these four Swei Swee had no duties to perform for their hive. They could only wait, and they were sleeping more with the passage of every day. It was Wave Skimmer's thought that if the foursome were not discovered soon, they would grow too weak to fish. Lethargy would follow, and, soon after, they would travel the endless waters.

Long Eyes reported one evening that when he left his watch, as light faded, he'd seen eight travelers on the horizon. He kept watch for a little while longer, as he returned to the hive, with a pair of eyes turned backward and staying on the surface — a dangerous maneuver for a Swei Swee in the open waters. Long Eyes noted that the ships halted their movement along the shore as dark fell.

Today, when Wave Skimmer assumed his post, he was barely in time to catch the foursome returning to their cave. They couldn't have had time to each catch more than one or two small fish. As the day stretched on, Wave Skimmer dove, caught fish, and fed.

When the star was at midday, the ships cruised into Wave Skimmer's view. The travelers, which mirrored the colors of the shallow waters, approached the cave. To Wave Skimmer, it was obvious the travelers would be far past the cave when the light faded from the day. The little ones would crawl out the next day and never know they had been missed.

Wave Skimmer warbled a small apology to his mates and younglings, if what he was about to do would send him to travel the endless waters. With a powerful thrash of his tail, he launched toward the shore. His six-walking legs stroked the water like sets of triple oars, adding to the speed created by his tail. The Swei Swee First appeared to skim across the surface of the water — underlining the name given to him by his matron.

* * *

<Black space, would you look at that?> a crew member sent on open comm. She tagged the point of interest in the controller, which tracked the highlighted object, as the subject moved.

Franz ordered the ships in his group to halt, and pilots synced their controllers, focusing their telemetry on the broad back of the dark carapace of a Swei Swee, who appeared to be walking on the water, as he raced toward shore, his massive claws raised high in the air.

<I'd say we're looking at a survivor of those dark travelers,> Franz sent to his shuttle group.

<Is he signaling us?> another pilot asked.

Orly looked at the wickedly pointed claws and remarked, <Who says he's signaling? Remember that these Swei Swee are generations removed from ours. He might be trying to catch the giant flying fish in the sky.>

<Commander Cohen, land immediately,> Teague sent with intensity, forgetting he had no authority in the matter.

Franz offered a quick plea to the stars for their support and ordered the other ships to maintain position, while he dropped his traveler to the deck. The only place to land was a short stretch of sand, bordered on both ends by prominent rock formations. The shoreline was steep, and rather than set down parallel to the waters, which would have lent a 30-degree tilt from side to side to the shuttle, Franz chose to drop the bow into the shallows. Exiting the traveler through the port's rear hatch would mean that the crew could keep their feet dry.

The traveler had no sooner settled onto the sand than the hatch was triggered. Checking his personnel app, Franz saw that it was Teague exiting the ramp with Ginny right behind him. <All other crew remain aboard,> Franz ordered.

<I've got them,> Sergeant Bethany Latimer sent to Franz, as she jumped out behind Ginny, which gave Franz a modicum of relief.

Teague was forced to circle the traveler via the bow, since his view of the dark Swei Swee was blocked. Both Ginny and Bethany called out for him to wait, but unfortunately, they were speaking to a male teenage brain, operating on an entirely different wavelength.

Wave Skimmer slowed his rush to the shore when the ship settled to the sands. Suddenly, a creature, which walked on two legs, as the land hunters did, raced around the front of the ship. He stripped off coverings revealing soft, white flesh, so unlike the dark coloring of the land hunters. Nonetheless, Wave Skimmer came to a halt, his claws raised protectively in front of him.

"Wow," Teague murmured when he got a real-world view of the giant Swei Swee, with its killing claws raised high in the air. The two stared at each other, six eyeballs taking in the differences between what they knew and what they were seeing — for Teague it was a comparison against the Haraken Swei Swee, and for Wave Skimmer it was the land hunters.

Wave Skimmer was debating whether to dive for deep waters or lead the pale one toward the cave. Besides a concern for his own safety, Wave Skimmer didn't know if the entity in front of him had come to rescue the little ones or not. Hive loyalty won out. Strange as the coloring, size, and build of the foursome appeared, they were still of the People, and Wave Skimmer was a First, dedicated to protecting his hive and the People.

Teague saw the Swei Swee hesitate and then drop its claws. It came wading toward him, growing larger with every meter covered. Unlike the Haraken Swei Swee, who, in a normal stance on even ground, came to Teague's waist, this male had to bend its eyestalks slightly down to stare Teague in the eyes.

Regarding the huge Swei Swee, Teague belatedly considered his dash from the traveler. He was reminded of his father's words, repeated so often to him — the less time you give yourself to consider your options, the quicker you will hasten toward an ill-considered decision or action.

Wave Skimmer and Teague were poised only several meters apart, each waiting for some sign from the other, when a sweet clear note of greeting rent the air. Wave Skimmer split his stalks, half on the pale alien and half searching for the source of the whistle. Two more aliens stood beside the ship, neither of them colored as were the land hunters.

Another note of greeting issued from the smaller of the two creatures. It was pure and comforting, and Wave Skimmer couldn't help but warble in reply. The little alien waded into the water, headed toward the white one in front of him and requesting his name.

"Wave Skimmer," the First whistled, and then warbled, "Have you a name?"

"The People of my world call me Little Singer," Ginny whistled in reply.

Wave Skimmer ignored the white one, who was, at the moment, standing still. *Little Singer,* he thought. *The People wouldn't have named the creature lightly.* The little one whistled her delight in meeting him, asking if he was a First, and he acknowledged that he was, rising on his walking legs to his full height.

Ginny momentarily faltered when the giant Swei Swee rose, taking pride in his position as the hive's leader, but she quickly resumed wading, intent on getting to Teague. She would burn his ears later for his foolish rush from the ship, but, for now, she wanted to be near him, and, if possible, protect him.

"We search for four of the People lost to us," Ginny whistled.

"Friends, comrades of mine," Teague added.

The white one's barely understood comment made sense to Wave Skimmer and explained the creature's rush into the waters. It ran to search for and protect members of his hive, despite the fact that he carried no means with which to aid them. As a hive member, the alien made no sense to Wave Skimmer. It had neither tail nor multiple legs with which to speed through the water or claws with which to fight.

"Have you seen them?" Teague whistled, but the eyes on the dark, male Swei Swee blinked rapidly, a sign of confusion.

"He can't understand you, Teague," Ginny said, reaching Teague's side and holding on to his arm. She repeated the question.

"Follow me," Wave Skimmer whistled.

Both Teague and Ginny sent comms — Teague to Franz and Ginny to Bethany — each relayed the conversation and that they were following a hive First, Wave Skimmer, to the Haraken Swei Swee.

Bethany stood on the shore, seriously conflicted. She would give her life to protect the two youngsters, but, if the Swei Swee were to become aggressive, she would need to be close to him for her stun gun to be effective, and, in her estimation, that wasn't going to happen. The enormous male kept nervous eyes on Teague, yet, in contrast, allowed Ginny to walk beside him. *Little Singer*, Bethany thought. She slowly waded to the shuttle's bow to keep the three of them in sight.

As soon as the threesome neared the cave, Teague picked up on his friends' implants and he raced forward, surprising Wave Skimmer, who had yet to indicate where the little ones hid.

Both Teague and Ginny disappeared into the cave, and Teague rushed back out moments later, able to reach Bethany, who relayed the request to Franz.

Wave Skimmer whirled and dove into the waters, stroking quickly for deeper waters. It didn't take him long to spot the prey he sought. A flash of his tail drove him forward and a quick thrust of his claw speared the 1-meter long, succulent fish. He hurried back to shore as a group of the aliens came around their ship towing a platform that floated in the air. Wave Skimmer warbled his amazement and hurried forward. He was too large to fit in the small cave, so he whistled to Little Singer for her attention.

Teague sprinted out of the cave, nearly running into Wave Skimmer's enormous claw, which the Swei Swee extended to block Teague's rush.

The First held up the wriggling fish, and, this time, he understood the pale alien's whistle of appreciation. Wave Skimmer expertly stripped the fish of its skin and then pulled off two fillets. He chopped each fillet into several pieces, dropping them into the white one's outstretched hands, who then ran back into the cave.

Teague fell to his knees in the cave floor's soft sand. His four friends were weak and feeble. He laid his pile of fish on a rock, and he and Ginny held small pieces against each Swei Swee's mouth parts. Only Swift Claws and Sand Flipper began to chew immediately.

Taking a piece of flesh, Teague squeezed the fish with all his might. The succulent flesh gave up its juice, which dribbled onto Teague's other hand, and he tipped the liquid into Whistles Keenly's twitching mouth parts. He was rewarded, moments later, by a gentle lapping on his palm.

Ginny tried the same maneuver, but she couldn't exert enough force to squeeze any liquid out. She smacked Teague on the shoulder and swapped pieces of fish. Crabbing around to Whistles Keenly, Ginny tore Teague's pulverized piece into tiny chunks to feed him, while Teague dripped juice into Bobs A Lot's mouth. It took much longer before Teague got a response, and he nearly wept with joy when he did.

The two humans slowly fed the entire fish provided by Wave Skimmer to their friends.

Crew waited outside the cave, at a respectable distance from Wave Skimmer, who split his stalks between eyeing the cave front and watching the groups of aliens and their floating platform.

Finally, Wave Skimmer watched the two individuals exit the cave. Little Singer told him the four would survive, and he raised his claws in celebration. At the same time, the aliens behind him let out strange screeches, and Wave Skimmer spun to take the charge. Little Singer's whistle for calm stalled him. She explained that her hive mates were celebrating the news that the foursome lived.

The pale one approached Wave Skimmer, and, in a strange gesture, held out his true hands to him, with the tips pinched together and waited.

Ginny whistled to the Celus Swei Swee, "Teague, the youngling of the Star Hunter First, who helped to free the People, held by the world traveler, waits to greet Wave Skimmer in the manner of our world called Haraken."

Wave Skimmer's eyestalks extended to their full length to take in the pale one in front of him. Singers, little or otherwise, do not tell untruths. He realized the four young Swei Swee whistled the truth. The world traveler, the giant sphere that the hives had fled, was gone, destroyed by the small, pale hands of those who stood around him. Wave Skimmer warbled in humor at his earlier thought that these creatures had no means by which to stand and fight.

Teague waited patiently for Wave Skimmer to process Ginny's words. Then the huge Swei Swee held his claws out even with Teague's pinched fingers. Teague balled up his fists and smacked the top of Wave Skimmer's claws, but unlike the Haraken Swei Swee's ceremony, Wave Skimmer returned the greeting and his heavy claws smacked down on Teague's fists.

It was all Teague could do to keep from crying out, and Ginny didn't know whether to be alarmed or laugh at Teague's actions. It was one thing to be Alex Racine in his prime smacking the claws of the Haraken Swei Swee; it was another thing for a youth to attempt the same thing with an alien First, who was an order larger than those he knew on Haraken.

<I heard bones crack,> Bethany sent to Franz. She had relayed the entire scene to him. <Better have Pia standing by. She has her work cut out for her.>

Franz sent the message to Captain Azasdau, adding the fact that the Swei Swee had been found, alive but barely so.

Wave Skimmer turned to Little Singer and pleaded for her help.

"We know the land hunters are the enemy of the People," Ginny whistled, using Wave Skimmer's words for the Dischnya. Despite Alex's request that the information not be relayed to Teague and Ginny, they were aboard a ship, and gossip had a way of spreading around a ship like air seeking vacuum. "The Star Hunter First resides in a ship above us." Ginny added. "He won't let the land hunters hurt the People anymore."

"Will your leader destroy the land hunters?" Wave Skimmer asked. A pair of eyestalks watched the floating platform carry out one of the little Swei Swee, who warbled softly to him. The aliens' methods were mystifying, and Wave Skimmer was in awe of what they could do for those who were injured.

"You're a First," Ginny said, seeking to prevent Wave Skimmer from putting her into a corner. "You know that no hive mate speaks for a First."

Wave Skimmer warbled his agreement. The Little Singer spoke true words. "I will greet the Star Hunter First," he whistled.

"Two days, at day's first light, here on the sands," Ginny replied.

Wave Skimmer whistled his agreement and, in one motion, whirled and launched 7 meters out into the waters.

The Harakens watched Wave Skimmer, with his unique characteristic of walking the water, skim across the shallows, and then dive into the deep.

Ginny turned to examine Teague, who held his broken hands at his side. Tears in his eyes began to fall, whether from relief that his friends were safe or pain from his injured hands, she couldn't tell. Ginny calmly wiped away his tears, as a medical specialist injected a pain killer into the side of Teague's neck. Then she walked back to the traveler beside Teague, as another Swei Swee was carried from the cave on a second grav pallet.

-17-
Many Nests

It was early morning when Alex checked in with the mission's Swei Swee medical specialist on the statuses of the recovered foursome.

"Credit must be given to Terese Lechaux, Dassata," Davi said. "Her instructions for medical emergencies that might befall the Swei Swee were exhaustive. I must admit that I thought many of them unnecessary, but throughout yesterday evening and morning I have been exchanging plasma bags for the four of them. Swei Swee body fluid ... who would have thought of that?"

"Terese," the two men said quietly, laughing together.

"Then they're stable?" Alex asked.

"They'll be fine, Dassata. Medically, it was a lack of fluids and food, although Teague has been explaining to me that much of their condition was due to an encroaching malaise. Something about being separated from their community. However, I expect them to make a full recovery within a few days."

Alex was trying to ignore the use of the Dischnya title by the crew, but he was fighting a losing battle. Harakens had twenty years of history, during which they addressed Alex by an appellation. Offered an opportunity to adopt a new title for him, even an alien one, the crew members had seized on it.

Stepping outside the medical suite, Alex found his son waiting for him. Teague's hands had undergone hours of work by Pia and her team to restore order to the bones. He was young and carried nanites in his blood since the day he was born. He would be completely healed within another day.

"I'm going with you to meet the queen," Teague said, his tone demanding.

"That's not a good idea, son," Alex replied.

"Yes, it is. I have a few things to say to her."

"That's why it's not a good idea, Teague. You need to stay here."

"You're not mission commander. I can ask Captain Shimada," Teague said, defiantly.

"Shall we go wake the captain, son?" Alex asked mildly. He understood Teague's anger after learning that the Dischnya were mortal enemies of his beloved Swei Swee, but the last thing Alex needed was to have his temperamental son in a delicate conversation with the queen. He wasn't even sure what he was going to say.

Teague knew his father had called his bluff. He wouldn't dare go above him and ask the captain. First and foremost, the captain would defer the decision to his father, and, second, he wouldn't want it known that he had tried to circumvent his father.

As the son of the famous Alex Racine, Teague felt he lived in a conundrum. *No one knows how to treat me,* Teague fumed internally. But that wasn't true either, he admitted. Humans and SADEs close to Alex treated him as a normal teenager. His problem was that their consideration didn't often match his desires. Sometimes they angered him by not paying him more deference, and then, at other times, they were generous when he felt little need for their attention.

"Son," Alex said, reaching up to cup his boy's neck with a warm hand. "Your friends are sleeping and recovering. When they wake, you should be there. It will mean a great deal to them."

Teague let go of his anger with a sigh. "Who will accompany you planetside?" Teague asked.

"The smallest number I can get away with," Alex replied.

"That should be the entire mission's roll call," Teague replied with a twist of his lips, attempting to repair the moment with his father.

"Probably what they want," Alex replied, a small smile on his face. He was inwardly more than pleased that a crisis with Teague was averted. *Sometimes I think you're growing up too fast, my son,* Alex thought, *and other times I can't wait until you grow out of this phase.*

* * *

Pussiro stood in Nyslara's front chambers. He was breathing hard, having run at top speed to the queen to deliver the report he'd received from some far hunters, who used mirrors to signal the news back to the nest.

"There can be no mistake," Pussiro said, working to catch his breath. "The hunters are sure of what they observed, my queen. One shuttle from a flight of four landed on the shore. The hunters were at the green's edge but could see clearly with hand scopes. Teague, Zhinni, and another exited the ship, as an enormous male ceena came out of the water. The hunters thought the ceena was poised to strike Teague until Zhinni whistled to him."

"Whistled to him?"

"Yes, my queen, as Teague did on the shore to chase his ceena back into the waters."

"Go on, commander."

"According to the hunters, Zhinni and the ceena spoke, and he led Teague and her to a cave. The aliens recovered their four hive members from a small cave. They carried them out one by one on their floating platforms."

"Remember, Pussiro, the aliens refer to themselves as Harakens. We should too."

"Yes, my queen. A final note, if you please. The ceena spoke with Teague and Zhinni for considerably longer and Teague conducted some sort of ceremony with the ceena … like this." Pussiro balled his hands and smacked down on the empty air. "He struck the claws of the ceena, and the creature struck Teague's hands in return."

Nyslara considered Pussiro's report. Despite her desire to refute the concept of ceena as intelligent creatures, the evidence was overwhelming in the contrary. She gazed up at Pussiro, her eyes sad, and asked, "Do you think Dassata knows?"

"I can't see how he wouldn't, my queen, now that we know the ceena whistling is a language. The Haraken's four missing crew must have come in contact with our ceena, since the large male appeared to be waiting to signal the Haraken shuttle. And who knows what information was exchanged between them before the rescue. Also, I spoke in detail to Simlan and Hessan, asking them to recall if our captives ever asked about the ceena. Simlan recalls Hira taking down shell plates in the storeroom. He said that when Hira lifted them in the air to look at the bottom, she seemed disturbed."

"So Hira recognized the origins of the plates," Nyslara confirmed.

"Undoubtedly, although it could be said that we came by them naturally … after their deaths."

"Plausible, unless the Harakens know something different. Have the soma ever found dead ceena on the shore?"

"Not that I know, my queen. Our soma had to capture and kill them."

"Then you have your answer, Commander. Dassata knows. He'll probably not even bother to keep the meeting tomorrow." Nyslara sat down heavily on a small stool, enabling her to wrap her tail around its base.

Pussiro felt awkward, standing above his queen, so he squatted on his haunches. "If Dassata does come, what will you say?"

"For that, my trusted Commander, I have no answer."

* * *

Just before Celus reached its zenith over the plains, Alex boarded a *Sojourn* shuttle. He didn't quite have his way, concerning the size of the landing party. Franz sat pilot and Orly copilot. The twins sat behind Alex. Pia and another medical specialist sat near the back of the main salon with a host of equipment. Captain Escobar, Sergeant Latimer, and Corporal Daubner sat near the hatch, as if they were ready to repel boarders. Completing the entourage were Julien and Willem, who sat across from Alex.

Alex was grumbling to himself. His entourage looked more like an invasion force than a negotiations party. Despite the extended size of his escort, Alex set some hard ground rules for them. The majority of the people were to remain either aboard the shuttle or close to it. "This will be a tough conversation for the queen," he told them. "We will be discussing a sensitive subject, one she won't wish to have in front of underlings."

"I've reviewed much of the information about the local hives, captured by our Swei Swee, Teague, and Ginny," Willem said. "It does not bode well for negotiations. To quote Wave Skimmer, he expects the Star Hunter First to eliminate the land hunters."

"Nyslara carries the burden of generations of her people, which have hunted the Swei Swee. It's an unfair predicament for her," Julien said.

"The plains are running out of food, as far as I can tell," Willem added. "And judging by Wave Skimmer, the Celus Swei Swee have migrated out into deep waters, as far away from the Dischnya shoreline as they can get."

"Which begs that nagging question: Why are the Dischnya ignoring the forests?" Alex asked.

"They aren't indigenous to this planet, Alex," Julien said. "There is a high probability of microbes in the humid environment of the forests that might be dangerous, if not deadly, to the Dischnya."

"Possible," Alex agreed. "Willem, whether we stay for an extended time or not, I want some mission information collected immediately. Map the continents closely with an eye to discovering the Dischnya's habitat range."

"Your intent, Dassata?" Willem asked. When Alex groaned at the use of his title, Willem replied, "As we are about to meet the queen, I'm merely adopting my role as translator, including the title by which she will refer to you."

"Acceptable reasoning, Willem, if you were human," Alex replied. "But you're a SADE and can switch your role in the wink of an eye, if not faster."

"Then I'm uncovered," Willem said, adopting a sad face and hanging his head.

Alex looked at Julien, who wore a huge smile and was sprouting sprinkles from the crown of his head to fall in a fountain's pattern to his shoulders.

"A wonderful performance, was it not?" Julien asked.

"We thought so," said Alain. Étienne and he were leaning over Alex's seatback. They had been warned by Julien to watch Willem.

"I'm practicing my acting," Willem said, perking up and smiling at the twins for their compliment.

Alex grinned and shook his head in astonishment. Which human aspects the SADEs chose to adopt constantly amazed him, and, of all humans, he knew them best. Sometimes, Alex truly understood why other humans failed to comprehend the SADEs' mannerisms. There was no telling what they might copy next. They were still experimenting with their freedom and would be doing so for the rest of their long lives.

* * *

The traveler's cabin lights brightened, but Alex didn't move.

Everyone aboard remained seated. Bethany glanced at Xavier, he signaled with his hand to stand down and stay in place.

One of the intimates of Alex's world, Pia, was busy chatting with her lover, Mickey Brandon, who was aboard the *Rêveur*.

<I've told Alex, more times than I count, that I'm happy not to be occupying his boots,> Mickey sent.

<You won't hear an argument from me, lover. What peace agreement is going to be equitable if one species has spent generations killing another and, worse, consuming them?>

<But, let's think back, Pia. Would you and I have recognized the Swei Swee as an intelligent species, many years ago, when we first saw them?>

<Probably not, but then again, I didn't envision us killing them and eating them.>

<You forget, love, we thought the Swei Swee were the true perpetrators behind the deaths of billions of Confederation citizens. If Alex had never

thought to capture a dark traveler and speak with those aboard, we might never have discovered the truth.>

<Which is why I'm a medical specialist and you're an engineer, love, and neither of us wants to be Dassata.>

When Pia saw Alex stand, she quickly signed off. Security gathered at the hatch, and Étienne and Alain bracketed Alex.

Alex still wasn't sure how to approach the upcoming and difficult discussion with Nyslara, but he figured he still had time since they had arrived early. However, an open comm from Franz announced that the queen and commander were waiting at the agreed-on spot, and Alex wondered what that meant if the two of them were more anxious than him.

<Anyone else in sight or any weapons visible?> Xavier sent to Franz.

<No other Dischnya or weapons, Captain,> Franz sent in the open.

Bethany and Keira exchanged quick glances. Keira's expression said surprise; Bethany's said doubt.

Alex exited the traveler and strode, with his ground-eating stride, across the 50 meters to where Nyslara waited. Julien, Willem, and the twins kept pace with Alex, while security fanned out to provide three points of coverage.

"Dassata's people are on the defensive. They're anticipating trouble," Pussiro hissed to Nyslara.

"And why shouldn't they?" Nyslara replied. "They've discovered that we've hunted their nest mates since we've been on this planet."

"I urge you to reconsider, my queen," Pussiro said. His words whined like that of a pup.

"You have been a most faithful commander, Pussiro. I need you to stand by me one more time. Without you by my side, I believe I might fail at this crucial moment."

"But we don't know what Dassata will say, my queen. Your actions might not be necessary."

"I know what he will say, Pussiro, and I have this one, and only this one opportunity, to end this for the good of our soma."

Pussiro would have pleaded further, but a hand signal from Nyslara silenced him, as Dassata approached.

The SADEs stopped 3 meters away from Nyslara, and the twins flanked the group, but Alex marched right up to Nyslara.

The queen had never expected anyone to approach her so closely, especially not an alien. Dassata was a muzzle's length from her nose, and his eyes drilled into hers. They smoldered with pain and indignation.

Pussiro was shocked by the confrontation, but it was obvious that Nyslara was right. Dassata not only knew of the Dischnya's past, but his queen had only this one opening to save the nest.

Nyslara slowly reached up and removed her feathered headdress, handing it to the commander. Next, she unfastened her beautiful cloak and laid it over Pussiro's extended arm. Then something Nyslara never thought she would ever do in her life — she fell to her knees and spread her arms out to the side, palms toward Dassata, imitating the Haraken gesture of surrender.

Alex heard Nyslara's words, but they were enveloped in such husky tones that he couldn't understand them. <Willem,> he sent.

<Julien, help,> Willem sent. <I'm not sure what the queen is saying. The sentence structure is too complex.>

<Willem, integrate what you see with what you can understand. Alex can clarify with questions, if necessary.>

<Dassata, Nyslara is admitting to a great injury by the Dischnya against the ceena,> Willem sent. <I would surmise that there isn't a Dischnya word for crime, and ceena is, in all probability, their name for the Swei Swee. It's my consideration that the queen fears Dassata will punish the entire nest for their transgressions, and she is offering her life for those of the Tawas Soma.>

<An unexpected turn of events,> Julien sent to Alex.

<Well, first things first,> Alex sent in reply. <I can't have a critical discussion with a female, especially a queen, while she's on her knees at my feet.> "Stand," Alex said to Nyslara in Dischnya.

Nyslara rose. She was tempted to step back from the alien face, but her courage never faltered, and she kept the muzzle-close distance. Dassata continued to stare at her, probably deciding the means by which he would take her life and whether he would destroy her nest before or after her death.

Nyslara's hopes that her sacrifice would be accepted began to fade as the silence dragged on. *I will be the last queen of the Tawas Soma,* Nyslara thought, *but I want my soma to live.* She'd prepared Pussiro to proffer the nest to Sissya, the queen of a large nearby nest, when she passed. Sissya was a young queen, and the possibility of more than doubling her nest size could overwhelm her. In that instance, her Pussiro would be a welcome addition, especially since Sissya was without a mate.

<Julien, I'm coming up short for ideas,> Alex sent. He'd been prepared for a heated discussion, even an outright argument, but not this.

<I have none, Dassata, except to suggest that we go home.> Julien sent an image of caricature starships, shrieking, as they sped out of the Celus system.

Julien's droll sense of humor made Alex's lips twist up at one corner. It would have become his lopsided smile, but he was trying to prevent a display of teeth. "Oh, black space, why me?" Alex moaned, and there wasn't a Haraken within hearing distance who wasn't commiserating with him, but, nonetheless, chose not to relieve him of the responsibility.

"Nyslara dies. New queen kills ceena," Alex said, accusing Nyslara of an empty gesture.

"Nyslara dies. Tawas Soma is no longer," Nyslara replied calmly.

Alex looked at Willem in confusion, and the SADE stared back, his expression blank.

Pussiro barked a command, and Simlan and Hessan exited a hideout tunnel entrance and came running, each carrying a few short, sharp sticks. They hesitated slightly at the sight of Pussiro holding the queen's garments, but hustled to her side, when she uttered a command.

Soon, Simlan, Hessan, and Willem were on the ground drawing and talking.

<A millennium of technological development, and we're reduced to deciding the fate of species by scratching in the dirt,> Alex lamented privately to Julien.

<The desire to communicate in any form is the mark of sophisticated cultures, my friend. Who cares whether it's conducted over a holo-vid or pictographs in the soil?>

At one point, the discussion on the ground became animated, then heated.

<Uh-oh,> Alex sent to Julien. <I think communication might have broken down.>

When Nyslara's warriors jumped up, she was prepared to interject, but Pussiro touched her elbow lightly, and she closed her jaw with a snap.

Simlan and Hessan walked over to a broad section of bare ground and drew a group of small figures. Then they moved to a new area and repeated the action. Simlan motioned Willem over to them, and all semblance of a two-party arrangement degenerated as everyone stood around the threesome, who was engaged in an earnest discussion.

Simlan drew an "x" through one group of figures, and Hessan drew a line from that bunch to the other. All the while, Simlan chattered away, and Willem heated crystal in an attempt to understand the Dischnya concept.

Both Alex and Nyslara sought to interrupt at the same time. Following his mother's teachings, Alex gestured to the queen to speak first. But before Nyslara could utter a word, Willem exclaimed, "I understand." He uttered a few phrases to Simlan and Hessan, who thumped their chest with open palms, signs of approval.

"Well, Dassata, the situation has gotten much more complicated," Willem said.

"Of course it has," Alex grumped.

"If Nyslara dies without a daughter, and, at present, she has none, the matriarchal succession of the nest ends. That was the reason for the queen's statement that, upon her death, the Tawas Soma will exist no longer. Her nest will be offered to another queen."

Alex stared at Willem, and the SADE could only say, "I'm afraid so, Ser. In fact, Simlan and Hessan don't even know the total count of nests. Apparently, the Dischnya have continued to spread across the plains for generations."

"How many nests, Nyslara? How many queens?" Alex asked.

"Thirty-six by name," Nyslara replied.

"By name?"

"Thirty-six queens and nests known by name to Nyslara," Pussiro explained.

"How many names not known?" Alex asked.

"More, not many," Pussiro replied.

"Why don't you know?" Alex asked the commander.

"Each queen … each nest fights to defend its territory."

<And who picked this planet to land on?> Julien sent out to the small group, but he was eyeing Willem, whose eyebrows tweaked in recognition of the singular honor.

<To quote Dassata, who was our admiral, at the time,> Willem sent in reply, <in the moment, all indications pointed to it being a logical decision.>

Alex sighed as if the weight of Celus-5 had fallen on his shoulders. Nyslara's offer of sacrifice was useless, even if he had been prepared to accept it, which he wasn't. Now, Alex had no idea how many of the nests hunted the Swei Swee or if the queen, who inherited the Tawas Soma, would take up the killing even if her nest never participated in the first place.

Nyslara saw Dassata whirl his finger in a circle at her. "Nyslara, come," she understood Dassata to say, as he turned and marched off toward his ship, his soma following in his wake.

"Do nothing until you hear of my death, Pussiro. I believe Dassata will not fail to inform you," Nyslara said. Pussiro sought to hand her robe back, but she shook her head at him, and then, with a ground-eating lope, caught up to the alien peacemaker.

Pussiro watched his queen disappear with the aliens, and he held her headdress in front of his face. Many rises of Nessila ago, he had detected a mating scent from Nyslara when he was in her presence. It was faint, but it was there. Pussiro knew he would have had to give up his mates and pups to accept Nyslara's offer, but he was aware of a sub-commander, who admired them. He was an excellent warrior, without mates of his own, and his battle-scarred body proved his worthiness.

-18-
Queen's Sacrifice

Closely following Dassata, Nyslara climbed aboard the shuttle. The interior was oddly comforting, reminding her of the nest's tunnels. However, near the front of the ship, Dassata halted, eyeing the vessel's chairs and glancing down at her tail, which was wound around one leg. He moved his shoulders in some sort of gesture, which she didn't understand, and simply remained standing with her.

Nyslara braced herself against the ship's movement by grasping the top of two chairs, but since Dassata stood with his arms folded, she released her grip and imitated him.

"Tell me about queens, about daughters, and about nests," Alex asked.

Willem, who stood behind the queen, broke the complex request down into its parts and amplified each point for Nyslara.

For a half hour, the conversation continued as Nyslara explained the succession of queens, the fate of the soma if the succession was lost, and the constant struggles between the queens to protect their nests and precious resources.

The more Nyslara explained, the more questions occurred to Alex. But their discussion was interrupted by the brightening of the main cabin's lights.

Nyslara heard Dassata say that they were to leave, and he gestured behind her. The soma, the Harakens she reminded herself, were leaving the ship by the same exit. *So the aliens aren't perfect and invincible,* Nyslara thought, a huff escaping her muzzle. *Even their technology breaks down.* Nyslara was feeling a little more confident, until her great claws touched the hatch steps, and she looked around.

Everyone behind Nyslara and on the *Sojourn's* deck waited while the queen assimilated what had just happened.

Pia eyed Nyslara's neck, the fur bristling. *Culture shock, in the worst way,* she thought with sympathy.

It was several moments before Nyslara could collect herself and descend the hatch steps to the deck. Her claws made a clacking sound against the ship's metal alloy. The smells in her muzzle were foreign: the ship, the Harakens, and things she couldn't even identify.

Alex's implant chronometer told him it was three hours before evening meal, and he intended to continue his education with Nyslara on the Dischnya before the meeting with Wave Skimmer tomorrow.

<Mickey, I need a stool for dinner aboard the *Sojourn* at our table. Get someone here or aboard the *Rêveur* to make one and install it,> Alex sent. He included two images, one of Nyslara and another of her scaled tail, as it wound around her leg.

<Oh,> Mickey replied. <We'll get on it. You haven't got a shot of the … of the point of attachment?> When Alex cut the comm instead of replying, he muttered, "Guess not," and immediately accessed the ship's extensive library for images that might help him with his design.

Alex led Nyslara through the ship at a slow pace, since the queen was taking time to examine everything in detail. He did clear the passages of crew so that Nyslara wouldn't be forced to pass people in the corridors. The lift to the upper deck seemed to be a treat to the queen, and Alex could envisage how Nyslara was imagining the technology helping her people.

On the bridge, Alex introduced Captains Azasdau and Shimada, and then he activated the holo-vid, requesting Willem display the plains area, which crossed the entire continent, from ocean to ocean.

Nyslara hissed at the sight erupting before her eyes, but as the image zoomed in to show an area of great waters, shore, and nearby arid land, she recognized many of the rock formations. Her eyes gleamed, as she realized she was looking down from the sky at her nest's territory. "Tawas Soma," she said, poking a hard, black nail into the image, which zoomed into to a single rock formation. She snatched her hand back and eyed Dassata, waiting for his outburst of anger.

Several of the soma surrounding Nyslara uttered that strange alien sound she heard directed once at Dassata, but they held their hands over their mouths to prevent the display of teeth. "This time it's me, who's served your soma's gesture," Nyslara huffed.

"Yes, but no harm is intended," Alex said, and he placed his hands in the holo-vid, separating and closing them slowly so that the holo-vid responded to his actions, zooming out and zooming in. Then he gently rolled a finger, first one way and then another, across the face of the image, and the holo-vid shifted view.

When Dassata indicated she should try it, Nyslara tentatively tried manipulating the alien device. In short order, she was moving the display around, looking at her world, as she had never seen it. Suddenly control was taken from her, and the original image was projected.

"Tawas Soma," Alex said, and when he touched the point where they had met, a yellow dot appeared.

Again, Nyslara was offered to use the alien display. She set her nail on the coastline, and yellow bloomed under her dark nail. Carefully she drew an outline around her nest. Each queen knew her territory intimately.

"Another queen," Alex said.

When Willem explained Dassata's request, Nyslara drew Sissya's territory, which bordered her own. Her finger drew in blue, this time. Nyslara didn't need any more prompting. She concentrated on the display, zooming in and out to spot key formations, which helped her plot the territories that she knew. Near her nest's rooms, Pussiro had built a miniature replica of the territories and identifying formations bordering each nest, as reported by the messengers. It was how every queen spied on her neighbors, under the guise of the blue white messengers' flags.

In the earliest of her drawings, the borders were precise and often heavily convoluted, revealing her intimate knowledge of those territories nearby. Each nest was outlined in a different color. When Nyslara spoke the name of the queen and soma, small lines appeared in the territory, and she took those to be the aliens' language.

As Nyslara continued to define territories farther and farther from the Tawas Soma, her shapes became blobs or boxes, indicating the nests' boundaries were not well understood. When she finished, the territories ended halfway across the continent, far from the other shore. She looked at Dassata, and said, "All that is known."

Alex nodded his understanding. Then he picked up the discussion where he had left off when they landed aboard the *Sojourn*. When Alex's app chimed for meal time, he motioned Nyslara to follow him, and more than a couple of crew members were treated to the sounds of stomachs rumbling from Alex and Nyslara as the two passed.

* * *

Nyslara thought of the amazing sights she saw aboard the alien ship. Her heart ached for all that her soma might have possessed, if she could have only brought these things to them. But, having told Dassata everything she knew of the territories, it was her thought that her usefulness to him was ended. Part of her was resigned to her fate; part of her wanted to fight, to tear at the aliens, and win her freedom.

Doors slid apart in front of Dassata and the scent of food assaulted Nyslara's nose. She inhaled deeply, her muzzle tingling from myriad new and welcome smells. The Haraken soma sat on chairs around tables, much as her warriors ate. She followed Dassata to a table, fitted with more chairs, and she envisioned herself standing while the aliens ate. *Unless I'm to be the one who is served for the meal,* thought Nyslara.

Dassata stopped at the head of a table, as was his right, and he indicated a bare area next to him, opposite where she stood. Rounding the table, Nyslara spotted a stool with a single leg, anchored in place. Its seat was round but with a cut out at the rear. She glanced at the alien leader, who nodded at the stool, as he took his own seat. Nyslara, who was accustomed to lying on cushions to dine, unwound her tail and gingerly lowered herself onto the simple seat. Her tail exited nicely though the cut out, and she relaxed as she wound it back around her legs, nodding her appreciation to Dassata for his efforts.

Willem, who had an exacting knowledge of the Dischnya diet, had compared the queen's needs to their own fare. She would have a strong preference for lightly acidic food, as the Dischnya preferred preserving much of their food in salt or an acidic liquid, made from a local plant.

Food was served to Nyslara, and she sniffed the plate. The smells made her mouth water, and she smacked her jaw in anticipation.

<This will take some getting used to,> Reiko sent privately to Xavier, as the table watched and listened to the queen's unorthodox table manners.

Nyslara snatched up a piece of food, tossed it to the back of her mouth, and swallowed it whole. She did that several times, picking through the plate for tidbits of interest. Belatedly, she noticed the Harakens using tools to eat with that sat beside their plates. Dassata's mate offered her a cloth and imitated wiping her fingers. After Nyslara did so, she picked up a tool and speared a chunk of food from her dish. But, the bite dropped to the table when the tool struck a long canine.

The dink of Dassata's eating tool on the table caught Nyslara's attention. She watched him pick a piece of food from his plate with his fingers and stuff it into his mouth, grunting in satisfaction. The lips of Nyslara's muzzle rippled in humor. She dropped her tool, plucked the offending piece of food off the table, and gulped it down. Then she returned Dassata's grunt of pleasure with one of her own.

The table watched Alex and the queen consume dish after dish, but even she quit before Alex finished his meal.

Nyslara looked across the table at Dassata's mate. Ené, she called herself. The queen knew that she was not speaking the alien's tongue correctly, but many of the Harakens' sounds were difficult for the Dischnya's muzzles, filled, as they were, with sharp teeth and long, thin tongues. Nyslara thought Dassata chose one of the slightest mates she had ever seen. Then again, the way Dassata admired the female made her seem many times more important than her size.

A hearty belch escaped Nyslara's lips and the Harakens resorted to their odd noise, accompanied by the covering of their mouths with their hands. But she didn't mind. If this was to be her last meal, it had been a fine one, as befitting a queen. For that small mercy, she was grateful.

* * *

Afterwards, Nyslara was led to a small room. No curtain concealed the doorway. Instead, metal, such as she saw throughout the ship, slid aside at her escorts' approach. When the door closed behind her, Nyslara surveyed the simple accommodations. It contained none of the fine trappings of her rooms. No woven carpets decorated the floor or the walls, and the ceiling was unpainted.

Attached to the room was a personal space. Careful testing revealed a source of drinking water and the ability to carry her waste away. When she tried the controls of the large stall, she was inundated with a liquid and jumped from the stall with a shriek. Fabrics hung nearby, which allowed her to dry off. Nyslara eyed the mist pouring from the little metal head. She was loath to step into the stall to switch it off, not wanting to get wet again. To her relief, it turned itself off. *Some alien technology I don't want for my people,* she thought, shuddering as she dried her fur.

The long day had taken its toll on Nyslara, and she eyed the bed with longing. When she placed a knee on the bed, it moved under her leg, and she leapt back with a snarl. Placing a hand on the bed produced the same result, but she kept it there, adding a second hand beside the first. She tested the bed in many ways, trying to understand the reason for its movement. It occurred to her that this was to be the manner of her death. The bed would enfold her, and she would suffocate.

In the end, Nyslara chose to accept her fate with dignity, and she lay on the bed, turning on her side and curling her tail over her. The bed moved, as it had always responded to her pressure, and she gathered her courage, awaiting the end. Soon, the caress of the bed eased Nyslara's fears and lulled her to sleep. Her last thought was that this was a most comfortable way to die.

* * *

Alex and Renée were in the refresher together. It was Renée's idea. Alex was seated, and Renée stood behind him, slowly scrubbing his neck, shoulders, and back, allowing the warm moisture and soothing massage to lessen the tenseness in his muscles and help him think.

Renée halted her ministrations, as a thought occurred to her. "I forgot to tell Nyslara's escorts to demonstrate the cabin's facilities to her."

"She'll figure out the sink and the toilet, and she won't need the refresher. The Dischnya must have their own means of cleaning their fur, but it isn't with water. The warrior that Teague threw in the ocean freaked in less than a meter of water. I don't know if these people fear the sea or if they just don't like getting wet."

"Are you taking Nyslara to your meeting with Wave Skimmer?" Renée asked, as she resumed her efforts.

"I thought about letting the two of them fight it out on the beach, winner take all."

Renée paused, glancing down to see Alex's face, not sure if he was making a jest or not. From the frown on his face, it was clear that he wasn't. Realizing that the refresher and her touch were failing to help Alex think, Renée signaled the refresher's shutdown, and the two of them dried off and climbed into bed. They chatted for a while, but Renée was soon asleep. She woke hours later to find Alex staring at the overhead.

"Can't sleep?" she asked. Alex's response was a small shake of his head. She propped herself up on an elbow and studied her partner's face. "Well, my love, if you can't sleep, then you should make yourself useful to me."

Renée eased on top of Alex, and they quickly fell into their intimate routine. Their implants engaged, relaying to each other what they felt and fostering a mental intertwining of lovemaking that few could imagine.

Much later, it was Alex who was fast asleep, and Renée who was wide awake. She listened to the sound of his deep breathing, pleased that she had brought him a small measure of peace. *The rest is up to you, Alex,* she murmured, tracing the outline of a deep pectoral muscle with a finger's soft touch and laying her head on his chest.

-19-
Wave Skimmer

Nyslara's keen hearing woke her to the hiss of her domicile's metal door sliding open. She jerked upright, surprised to be still alive. Her escorts gestured toward the facilities room, and she took the opportunity to eliminate waste and sip deeply of the water flowing from the post. Nyslara hoped for another meal, but such was not to be the case. Her escorts led her through metal tunnels, and they entered the odd room that transported the Harakens up and down within the ship.

As a queen, Nyslara was affronted by the lack of information shared with her about the ship, but, as a prisoner, she accepted the indignity. She and her escorts traversed more metal corridors to wait in the small room with its view of the cavernous space where she had exited the Haraken's shuttle, which had whisked her from the world below. The question of the tiny room's purpose burned in her mind, but she refused to ask the alien warriors, who stood next to her, not wanting to appear weak and ignorant. *It's just as well,* Nyslara thought, *I would speak, but they wouldn't understand me or, if we could exchange words, their answer would be too strange for me to comprehend.*

The escorts stayed within the room, but they motioned Nyslara toward Dassata, who stood alone beside his shuttle. She strode with dignity across the intervening space and, without urging, climbed aboard the shuttle, her claws screeching against metal, as she clambered up the steps.

The ship's interior was filled with Harakens, and, despite their presence, Nyslara walked to the front of the room where she considered a queen had the right to stand, regardless of what fate she would meet today. Dassata walked through the shuttle to stand beside her, and the lights dimmed, as they had before.

Nyslara expected to be transported to another Haraken ship or somewhere on the plains below. But when the room brightened and she exited the shuttle, the last thing she expected to find was sand beneath her feet, with the great waters lapping the nearby shore. Fear clenched her guts, and bile rose in her throat. Somehow Dassata had discovered the Dischnya's great terror — that of drowning.

Nessila was brightening the horizon, but hadn't yet revealed its orb. To Nyslara's relief, Dassata did not approach the waters, but Ginny did. Her whistle split the morning's still air.

In response to Ginny's call and much to Nyslara's horror, the seas boiled with ceena. Hundreds of huge, dark carapaces churned the shallows as the creatures raced for the shore. Most stopped where their walking legs could lift their bodies clear of the waters, but three giants scurried forward to gain dry sand.

During Nyslara's lifetime, she'd only dined on the lower legs of the ceena, the prized portions. She'd never imagined the size of the huge beasts, which possessed them and loomed over her now, the claws clacking furiously. Her legs trembled in fear at the sight of the three monsters.

In a moment of clarity, Nyslara, as queen, recognized a greater concern than that of her own life. The number of male ceena in sight was more than twice her warriors. The soma had thought the Dischnya's hunt decimated the population, thinking only a few individuals remained — apparently, not so. It underlined Dassata's point that the ceena were of his soma. The ceena must be intelligent creatures if they could hide so cunningly from the nest's hunters, who rode skimmers to collect them.

"You stand with a land hunter, Little Singer," Wave Skimmer whistled in accusation.

Before Ginny could reply, Alex's quiet whistles and warbles caught the First's attention. "This is the Swei Swee you described, Little Singer?" he asked Ginny. "A leader who doesn't bother with introductions?"

Wave Skimmer, Long Eyes, and Dives Deep eased down from their extended walking legs, and eyestalks twitched toward one another at the rebuke.

"I'm known by the People of my world as Star Hunter First. My familiar name among Harakens is Alex Racine. I would know with whom I speak."

Immediately reminded of Swei Swee courtesies, Wave Skimmer and his hive mates introduced themselves.

"I'm pleased to find the People surviving on this planet," Alex whistled. "Your skill and cunning, exhibited by escaping the world traveler, are a compliment to the People."

"The Star Hunter First's words are of comfort to our hives. Little Singer said that you freed the People and destroyed the world traveler," Long Eyes whistled.

"We helped the People achieve the destruction of the world traveler and send its inhabitants to travel the endless waters," Alex replied.

Dives Deep spun around and relayed Alex's message to the host that waited, which consisted of Firsts and two key males from each hive. The Swei Swee responded with shrill whistles and snapping claws, held high in the air. The din was horrendous, and it set Nyslara to trembling afresh. She glanced at Dassata, who bared his teeth fully at the ceena. Only his lips were crooked, as if his short muzzle suffered from an injury. *Before my death, I must know what this expression means,* Nyslara promised herself.

"Why have you brought a land hunter to our meeting?" Wave Skimmer asked.

"Among the land hunters, a female is a First," Alex whistled. "This is Nyslara, the First of her people. She has offered herself as a sacrifice to the Swei Swee to appease your anger and call an end to the hunt."

"One female," Dives Deep whistled in derision. "The People have lost hive members for more than a hundred annuals. How is her offer equal to that suffering?"

"Even if we were to accept this female's offer of sacrifice, Swei Swee don't kill for the sake of killing," Long Eyes whistled.

"Didn't you kill the land hunters when they found your hive younglings?" Willem asked.

"We destroyed their platforms," Wave Skimmer replied. "The endless waters took them."

<How convenient for the Swei Swee that they can say they didn't kill the Dischnya. They simply allowed them to drown,> Julien sent to Alex.

<What would you do if someone tried to kill Cordelia?> Alex sent in reply.

<Destroy them with my own hands and own the deed,> Julien replied fiercely.

<Remind me to be extra polite to your partner, my friend. Now, can we focus on solving the convoluted politics of this planet's peace?>

I'll extend my apologies later, Alex, Julien thought.

"If that's your usual means of defending your hive, then I suggest you take this First out beyond the shallows and let the endless waters claim her," Alex whistled.

Willem was translating for Nyslara, whispering into her ear. When the conversation turned disastrous, her ears twitched and then laid back.

"Would this stop the land hunters from taking the People?" Long Eyes asked.

"No, there are many nests of the Dischnya, as they are called," Alex replied.

"Are all their Firsts offering themselves to us?" Dives Deep asked.

"No, the People are offered only this one." Alex gave Nyslara a push forward.

The queen stumbled, her legs failing to support her, and Wave Skimmer reared up on his walking legs, distressed at his enemy's proximity. He snapped his claws in warning and was pleased to see the female land hunter fall to her knees. The fear evident in her eyes was the same look of horror the land hunters displayed when the Swei Swee swamped their mobile platforms and knocked them into the dark waters.

"Little Singer promised the Star Hunter First would destroy the land hunters," Wave Skimmer whistled in frustration.

Ginny's piercing whistle brought every entity up short. "Wave Skimmer must be past the age of sentience," Ginny chastised, which produced angry whistles and warbles of humor from the Swei Swee. "Wave Skimmer was told that the Star Hunter First would not let the land hunters hurt the People any more. I didn't say he would destroy them."

Wave Skimmer lowered his walking legs farther, which brought him closer to the land hunter, causing the female to scuttle back until she was near the feet of the Star Hunter First. He snapped a single claw at her. The gesture was beneath the dignity of a First, but decades of fighting the land hunters and protecting his hive had driven him past the point of observing the People's first contact courtesies.

"Little Singer whistles the truth. That's what she said, but it wasn't what I hoped to hear," Wave Skimmer apologized. "Will the Star Hunter First protect the People of this world, as Little Singer says he protects the hives on his world?"

<And there you have it, my love,> Renée sent to Alex. <Once more, the universe calls on you to build another bridge.> Her thoughts were laced with mirth and an outpouring of warmth.

"What will Wave Skimmer do with the life of this land hunter?" Alex asked, focusing on the negotiations.

"Before the land hunters came," Wave Skimmer whistled, "we lived lives of contentment, lives of peace. It has always been the People's hope that we could return to those times, someday. If the Star Hunter First can bring peace to this world and protect the People, then Wave Skimmer pledges to follow as he directs us."

Dives Deep spun around and addressed the Firsts, relaying a summary of the communications and Wave Skimmer's pledge to obey the human leader.

Wave Skimmer faced the host of Firsts and whistled, "Will the hive leaders follow the Star Hunter First?"

Unfortunately, a resounding chorus of assents was not forthcoming. Many whistled questions and Wave Skimmer fielded one after another.

Monitoring the tone of the questions and answers, Alex could see that he was losing the Swei Swee's approval. Given time, it might come, but it would be much later.

Another of Ginny's whistles caught everyone's attention, and Wave Skimmer, Long Eyes, and Dives Deep spun around, heeding a Singer's pure sounds.

Ginny marched out into knee-deep water, and Alex sent a command for everyone to hold.

"If your hive has a Singer, raise a claw," Ginny whistled. She waited, but not a single limb was lifted into the air. She glanced back at Wave Skimmer and his claws were lowered. "Was my request misunderstood?" she whistled with a touch of derision. Warbles of apology filtered back to her. The Firsts had heard her, but the Little Singer was pointing out a great lament of the hives.

"When the People were chased permanently into the dark waters, our Singers, over time, traveled the endless waters, and the hives produced no more of them from our younglings," Wave Skimmer whistled.

Ginny waded over to stand beside Wave Skimmer. She was forced to stare up at the giant First, but her hands were on her hips, and the eyestalks of the leader were drooped in sorrow. She turned to face the assembled Firsts, who floated in the shallows, and whistled shrilly to them. "You have no Singers, because the People have no harmony. Your lives are spent in hiding. The Star Hunter First offers you a way out of your misery, but you warble like younglings. What will it take for you to agree to our help?"

The Firsts threw questions at Ginny, but she stood resolutely in the shallows refusing to respond. When she had enough, she raised her hands for silence and received it. "I will grant a favor to the People of this world, if you will embrace our help. I will stand on this shore, every evening, and sing for the hives."

"No," Teague shouted. He would have leapt to stop Ginny from continuing to utter her promise, but two heavy hands held his shoulders pinned in place. When Ginny first waded into the shallows, Z was told by Alex to prevent Teague from interfering.

<This is Ginny's choice,> Z sent to Teague. <She has a right to live her life as she chooses.>

"The shores of these plains will be a place of guaranteed refuge for the People," Ginny added.

There was a stunned silence from the Swei Swee. The only sound was the gentle lapping of waves on the beach.

When Nyslara heard the translation of Ginny's offer, she marveled at the courage of the young alien, and the heat of that emotion forced her to her feet, as she sought to regain her dignity. "Fierce pup," Nyslara commented to Dassata.

"Ginny reminds us all of what it takes to win peace," Alex replied.

"Now, what say you, Firsts?" Wave Skimmer whistled loudly. He spun and dove cleanly under Little Singer's legs, and Ginny's rear end plopped down on his carapace. She grabbed the leading edge, laughing loudly. The First raised her up, as high as his walking legs would go, and his eyestalks were bent straight forward, daring the other Firsts not to accept Star Hunter First and Little Singer's offers.

Whistles of approval cut the air. The promise of the Star Hunter First was intriguing, but the People had endured a century of pain and devastation, and it made them leery that their safety could be ensured. But the opportunity to hear a Singer again was too tempting to resist, and, if the Little Singer stood on the shore, the Star Hunter leader would ensure her protection, making the shore safe again for the People.

As Ginny was bounced on the back of Wave Skimmer in celebration, Alex leaned over and whispered to Nyslara, "What can I say, Queen of Tawas Soma? The Swei Swee have refused your offer. Your life wasn't payment enough for the losses they've suffered." Alex received a small amount of satisfaction from the confusion written on the queen's wrinkling forehead and rippling muzzle after Willem translated his words.

Wave Skimmer returned to the shore, and Alex helped Ginny down. Her face was flushed, and she was grinning ear to ear with her success.

Celebrate now, Ginny. The reality of what you've promised will sink in later, Alex thought, smiling at Ginny's moment of joy.

"Return to your hives, Wave Skimmer," Alex whistled. "When I've secured the promise of peace with every land hunter First, you will be informed."

"A member of my hive will stand guard just beyond the shallows each day," Wave Skimmer whistled. When Alex nodded, the First whistled and his males dove into the waters behind him. Faster than Nyslara could have expected, the entire assembly disappeared, diving to the safety of the shallow's bottom, while they made for the dark waters.

"Everyone aboard," Alex shouted.

Z released Teague's shoulders, and Ginny fairly skipped up to him, but Teague's angry glare wiped the joyful smile off her face. Ginny would have said something to Teague, but he whirled and stomped off to the traveler.

"Well, that moment of celebration was short-lived," Renée commented to Alex. "My son is not demonstrating his best side."

"And it will probably get worse," Alex lamented, as he indicated to Nyslara to return to the ship. "But my concern is with Ginny. The Swei Swee agreed to follow my lead because they would have access to a Singer, and you can bet that they believe they'll be safe because we'll ensure her safety. This surely can't get any more complicated."

"Let's hope not, Dassata," Julien commented drolly. "But for the life of me, which promises to get shorter every year I spend in your company, I must admit that my mind is boggled by the intricacy of this puzzle, and I await Dassata's most enlightening solution to the dilemma."

"You're boggled?" Alex growled.

"Interesting word … conjures up all sorts of impressions, don't you think?" Julien replied and gave Alex a brilliant smile but received a scowl in return.

* * *

Inside the traveler, which was returning to the *Sojourn*, emotions roiled again.

Teague sat opposite Ginny, in a four-seat section, rather than sitting next to her. Renée took Teague's usual place and was in an earnest discussion with Ginny about her promise to the Celus Swei Swee.

Julien glanced at Teague. The youth was fuming, and he refused to look at Ginny.

Nyslara stood beside Dassata in the narrow corridor between the ship's chairs. She no longer braced herself, having already become accustomed to the lack of motion during the alien shuttle's flights. She couldn't understand what the individuals were saying, the ones who held Dassata's attention, but it was obvious that they were focused intently on Zhinni.

To Nyslara, Teague looked like a pup, whose food was taken from him. The youth was seated directly beneath Nyslara, and she could smell the mix of scents rising from Dassata's progeny: anger, fear, and the desire to mate.

Nyslara glanced at Dassata, who was eyeing his progeny with frustration. With a leap of intuition, Nyslara suddenly saw her world through his eyes: the nests fighting one another for dominance, the Dischnya hunting the ceena, and both sides composed of a multitude of leaders, most of whom would be reticent to accept a truce. She looked behind her and caught Willem's eye, and he immediately came to her side.

"Fellum, I would speak a sentiment to Dassata," Nyslara said.

Willem missed understanding the keyword in Nyslara's statement, and it took a few exchanges before Willem comprehended the entirety of Nyslara's wish. He ducked his head and covered his mouth, as the nature of her comment struck home.

"I will be pleased to share your words with Dassata," Willem said. "Alex, the queen wishes me to convey an observation to you."

Alex, who had been listening intently to the exchange between Renée and Ginny, turned his attention to Willem.

"Nyslara believed her role as queen to be a most challenging one, perhaps the most difficult one on this world. Now, she understands that honor belongs to you, and she happily grants you that honor."

To Nyslara's surprise, those within hearing of Willem's words, barked harshly, bared their teeth, or made gurgling sounds in their throats. That Dassata displayed his teeth, with the odd twist of his short lips, as he gazed up at the ship's ceiling and that Willem had covered his teeth when he heard her request, gave Nyslara a sudden insight into the aliens' behavior.

Among the Dischnya, aggression was always beneath the surface, which is why the soma within a single nest practiced self-control and observed the amenities. Nyslara realized these aliens had little or no fear of one another. Fingers could point and teeth could be bared without concern. She glanced around her and saw Dassata's soma were focused on him, observing his reaction. He tried with difficulty to hide the expression spread across his face and failed to do so.

Then Nyslara mentally leapt to make one more interspecies realization. A leader, such as Dassata, would not be that way simply because he landed on her world; he must have always been that way. And, if Nyslara expressed a wish to never wear his cape of power, then it was most likely that his soma would have said the same thing, perhaps many times. Inadvertently, she'd spoken an old truth of the Harakens.

Understanding what her comment meant to those around her and basking in relief of a reprieve from a watery death, Nyslara loosed a loud bark and bared her teeth wide at Dassata. Suddenly, those around her repeated their raucous sounds with even greater enthusiasm, much like warriors celebrating a victory when the amenities could be ignored, and Nyslara joined them, barking and hissing.

That's when Nyslara saw Dassata's control burst. His attempts to observe the amenities for her sake were over, excused by her own display, and he echoed the sounds of those about him. The timbre of Dassata's sounds were those of the Dischnya's drums, beat to summon the soma to defend the nest.

Soon after, quiet returned to the shuttle, and Nyslara was left with much to contemplate.

* * *

After exiting the ship once more into the Haraken's cavernous room, Nyslara found herself seated at a table with many of Dassata's key people. The special stool she used during her meal now had a place at this table, or, at least, she thought it was the same one. The odd thing to Nyslara was that while all maintained their places at the table, including her, Dassata felt no such desire. He stalked the room as if he was looking for something. It reminded her of Pussiro when he worried over a battle plan. Recall of her wasat gave Nyslara's heart a momentary twinge. *I should have made you my mate when there was still time for us,* Nyslara thought.

Alex stopped his pacing and eyed the table. His people — Renée, Julien, Asu, Reiko, Willem, and Xavier — waited patiently for him. Unfortunately, his efforts to wear down the cabin's decking hadn't produced any insightful ideas that would resolve the planet's thorny issues.

"Nyslara, do the queens meet in conference?" Alex asked. He waited while Willem worked out the subtleties of the question.

"The queen says that if it was permitted to display herself, as the Harakens do, she would be barking with laughter," Willem replied.

"I take that as a no," Alex said, staring at Nyslara, whose lips rippled with humor.

"According to the information we've gathered," Julien said, "the Dischnya are latecomers to Celus-5 or Sawa Messa, as they refer to it."

"Which begs the question: What were their societal traditions on their home planet?" Asu asked.

Nyslara listened to the ship's leader speak. She was captivated by his color, so deep and dark. He sat beside Dassata's mate, and the two of them were in contrast in more ways than she could have imagined. *Alien soma,* she thought with a small shake of her head.

"Nyslara," Alex said, "did the queens meet on your home world?"

"It's called the Fissla," Willem said, glancing back at Nyslara to ensure that he was reproducing the term correctly. Nyslara had pronounced it by sliding her long tongue in her mouth. "It would appear to be similar to a council or assembly."

"Why not here?" Xavier asked.

"According to the stories of the first queens to land on Sawa Messa," Willem translated, "a Fissla was formed but fell apart when the flights of new soma and supplies ended. Soon after, the queens focused their efforts on defending their territories from the incursions of other nests."

"Did the Dischnya live above ground on Sawa Messa, in the beginning?" Reiko asked, pantomiming walking her fingers above her hand.

"Nyslara says yes," Willem explained. "As fights between nests broke out, the soma dug tunnels to protect their resources. Later, they dug rooms to keep the females and pups safe. Soon, the entire nests were living below ground."

"What stops us from calling a new Fissla?" Asu asked.

"Nyslara wishes to know what reason could be given the queens to tempt them from their nests," Willem replied.

"Do you communicate with the queens in any way?" Renée asked.

When Willem translated the question, Nyslara became animated and launched into an extended explanation. At one point, Willem signaled Asu for his reader. He showed Nyslara that she could draw on the instrument with a stylus, but that only confused her.

Something the queen was saying about a warrior's face gave Willem an idea, and he sent an image of Hessan from his crystal memory to the reader. Nyslara lit up when she saw her warrior's face. She picked up the stylus, bent over the reader and began drawing. Her lips rippled at the pleasure she felt, playing with the alien toy.

When Nyslara finished, she commented to Willem, who filled in white where Nyslara pointed. She looked up sharply at him, since he hadn't touched the stick or the instrument. Tentatively, she touched her temple and Willem nodded his agreement. Nyslara blew out a huff and continued pointing at portions of her drawing, and Willem filled in the blocks as required.

"Emissaries," Willem said, handing the reader to Alex and sending the image to everyone at the table. "What the queen has drawn is a ceremonial mask worn by each individual to announce to a nest's lookouts that they come in peace to speak with the queen."

Alex examined the image of Hessan wearing an elongated mask of blue and white stripes. "It stands out," he said.

<And it isn't white,> Julien sent privately to Alex, reminding him of the discussion they had soon after they launched from Haraken.

"How many nests does an emissary visit?" Reiko asked.

Nyslara held up a single finger on each hand, as she answered Willem's question.

"One emissary to each nest," Reiko said, recognizing the pantomime, and Willem affirmed her guess.

"So the queens have a means of communicating, using emissaries, but that doesn't supply us with a means of enticing the queens to the Fissla," Alex said. He didn't realize that he was staring at Nyslara, as his mind pondered the problem.

For her part, Nyslara was entranced by Dassata's eyes, which peered into her. A thing she occasionally bestowed on her soma and her commander was forgiveness. She never thought she would be seeking it for herself, especially not from an alien leader.

Images of Sissya and Chafwa came to Nyslara's mind. Two more different queens, she couldn't imagine — Sissya, young and impressionable; Chafwa, aging and intractable. The question Nyslara asked herself was how she might entice the likes of both of them to a Fissla. Suddenly, an idea occurred to Nyslara.

Alex saw the queen's eyes light up, and he grinned at her.

Nyslara watched Dassata bare his teeth wide at her, and she huffed in reply, and then opened her jaw and curled her lips away. If Dassata wanted to compare teeth, she would show him a Dischnya's formidable set. She added her own chortle to let him know she was adopting his Haraken habit. Dassata clapped his hands and the boom from both his hands and voice were ear-splitting, and Nyslara couldn't help joining him in celebration. They were two leaders solving problems together, a lost practice on Sawa Messa.

When Alex and the queen finished enjoying themselves, Xavier looked between the two of them and held up his hands, indicating that a little more information should be forthcoming.

Nyslara began a long conversation with Willem, outlining her idea.

"The queen says that she was impressed by your shuttles, as any Dischnya would be," Willem said. "If Dassata would carry her emissaries to other nests, land, and let them deliver invitations to the queens to attend a Fissla, she is sure that the majority, if not all, would accept."

"Yes," Alex shouted enthusiastically, clapping his hands together again, the sound careening around the room, and held his arms wide.

The similarity of the extended arms to the Haraken's gesture of surrender completely defeated Nyslara's attempt to understand. "Is Dassata annoyed?" Nyslara asked anxiously of Willem.

"Your pardon, my queen, Dassata is overjoyed at the idea."

Picking up on the queen's confusion, Renée addressed Willem. "Please tell Nyslara that Dassata displays that mannerism when he's most pleased by a person's efforts. In his excitement, he typically would hug the individual," and Renée pantomimed closing her arms tightly.

The translation produced a growl from Nyslara, and not a friendly one.

<There you have it, my love,> Renée sent to Alex. <Some females are just beyond your charms.>

-20-
Queens' Invitations

The Tawas Soma lookouts reported to the wasat that a Haraken ship was landing near the meeting site. While they waited for Pussiro's arrival, they were astounded to see their queen exit the shuttle, which immediately departed.

As Pussiro jogged toward the lookout post, he was joined by a sub-commander, who relayed the warrior's update. In response to Pussiro's order, the sub-commander commed the queen's attendant, Cysmana, requesting she fetch the queen's cape and headdress, and tell her a warrior would guide her to the lookout.

Nyslara felt exposed, walking in the open without escorts or feedwa, but she strode resolutely toward the nearest lookout post. In the distance, she saw the hatch pop open. Two warriors jumped out and ducked their heads in greeting. Before Nyslara could wonder why they didn't race to her side, Pussiro leapt out from behind them, and he raced across the ground, closing the distance to her in no time. He skidded to a stop in front of her, dipping his head in obeisance.

"You've returned, my queen," Pussiro said in amazement.

"You're not normally prone to stating the obvious, Pussiro," Nyslara said, but she cuffed his muzzle softly, which brought his head up sharply. "Come. I have much to tell you, and then you and I have much to do." The two of them walked side by side back to the lookout post and through the tunnels, headed toward her rooms. Along the way, the soma, surprised by Nyslara's return, chuffed at her, sounding their pleasure at her safe return.

"You faced a ceena," Pussiro said, when Nyslara spoke of the meeting on the shore, amazed that the queen survived.

"Three of them, Commander," Nyslara replied. "And I can't tell you which left a greater impression on me ... their enormous size or their intelligence. I was provided with a translation of the conversation. What the leader, Wave Skimmer, wanted most of all for his people, which he called a hive, was their safety. The assembled leaders have accepted a proposal of sorts that protection will be provided for them. It's complicated and involves Zhinni, but that explanation can wait."

"Protection for the ceena?" Pussiro asked.

"Their name is Swei Swee," Nyslara said, but it came out more like a pair of short whistles than words.

"Appropriate," Pussiro commented, comparing the sound to the manner in which the ceena communicated.

"You wouldn't believe who the Swei Swee revere."

"Dassata?"

"Certainly, he's respected. It's known by his soma and was communicated to the local Swei Swee that he freed many of the hives through the destruction of a giant sphere and lent them sanctuary on his home planet."

Pussiro stopped dead in his tracks, his great claws seeking purchase on the tunnel's hardened floor. "You spoke of the sphere to the Harakens?" he asked.

"I didn't. The time was not appropriate. It might become so later."

"You were speaking of the Swei Swee's admiration," Pussiro reminded Nyslara.

"Yes. It's Zhinni."

"Our Zhinni ... the little female with the topknot the color of Nessila?"

"Do we know of another, Commander?" Nyslara replied, the skin surrounding her muzzle rippling. Her world had been turned upside down by the aliens' arrival. One moment she was prepared to defend her nest to the bitter end, and the next she was offering herself in exchange for her soma's lives. Then, much to her great surprise and relief, neither Dassata nor the Swei Swee accepted her offer of sacrifice. Now, once again, she was walking beside Pussiro. That in itself was pure pleasure — she had missed him terribly.

Nyslara knew she had an opportunity to unite the queens in peace, and, better than that, it might provide the means by which the Dischnya of Sawa Messa might rise again into a developed society, conditional, of course, on receiving the Haraken's help. *Have no fear, Dassata, I want your goodwill, as much as you want mine,* she thought.

"Why is Zhinni favored?" Pussiro asked, after he'd digested Nyslara's comment.

"Fellum says she's known by the Swei Swee on her home world as Little Singer."

"But would the ceena on Sawa Messa know this?"

"According to Fellum, the Swei Swee of our waters knew of her capabilities by the sounds of Zhinni's whistles. She's a perfect imitator of their hives' singers."

"Why would they honor an alien over their own singers, my queen?"

This time, it was Nyslara, who halted to regard Pussiro. Three days in the company of the Haraken aliens had drastically altered her perspectives. But Nyslara realized that if her commander's point of view hadn't shifted, then certainly her soma's perceptions wouldn't have either. It gave her an idea of the impediments facing her to successfully form a Fissla.

Pussiro saw the frown form on his queen's brow. During the long walk to her rooms, he'd detected subtle changes in her, some good and some odd. She was calmer, mellower than he'd ever seen her. The cuff on his muzzle was one indication. But, more important, she was less dictatorial and much more thoughtful. Now she waited for him to act in the same manner.

The first image that came to Pussiro's mind was the pile of steaming ceena legs served to Nyslara as a delicacy. Others were the ceena hunters' reports of lives lost, and their strange stories of the whistles and warbles from dying ceena — young, females, and males. He shuddered and fur rose along his entire body.

"Yes, Commander," Nyslara huffed softly, taking in Pussiro's reaction. "We've been hunting, killing, and feeding on an intelligent race, which had done no harm to us before we attacked them and drove their entire race into the great waters."

"If I stood in Dassata's place and knew what he knew, I might burn every Dischnya nest into an empty, black hole," Pussiro said, and he shook his head, trying to clear it of the Swei Swee images he'd called forth.

"Then we're fortunate that this alien is a wiser leader than you or me, Commander."

Nyslara's attendant, Cysmana, met her in the tunnel, holding out her royal robe to her, but Nyslara waved her off. The female's confusion was displayed in her face and body. Nonetheless, she fell in behind her queen and wasat, carrying the robe in front of her as if it was a stately object, belonging to the nest, whether Nyslara wore it or not.

Pussiro halted again, as a disturbing question occurred him. "If Dassata is as informed as you say, then why did he release you, my queen? Not that I'm not pleased to see your return ... for the soma's sake, of course."

Nyslara glanced down. When Pussiro was embarrassed or otherwise attempting to disguise his feelings, the primary great claw on his right foot rose, as if the effort could hide his emotions. It stood upright. *So you're personally pleased by my return,* Nyslara thought, *and more than just a little.* "We're going to summon a Fissla, Commander."

"My queen —"

"Pussiro, we're never going to reach my rooms if you keep halting our progress," Nyslara teased. "Never fear, there is a plan in the works. We'll be working with Dassata."

Nyslara strode on, and Cysmana glanced up at the wasat, who was rooted in place, bewildered and uncertain. Then she hurried after her queen.

* * *

It took a significant effort on the part of the Harakens to coordinate the emissaries' dispersal operation. The ships in orbit carried a total of ten travelers, but the captains and security voted heavily for risking only part of them on the ground at once. No one knew what the reception would be for each ship as it touched down at six, seven, or more nests.

Willem added a piece of logic to the planning stage, stating that each emissary would need to be accompanied by a SADE to manage translation. "While many of you carry my dictionary in your implant, I carry a significant amount of data pertaining to conversational circumstances, interpretational conjectures, and other ancillary information," Willem said. "Only a SADE can carry that much data and make use of it when translations with the Dischnya get stretched thin. I recommend six travelers and six SADEs."

"Who would be the sixth after Julien, Cordelia, Z, Miranda, and you?" Alex asked.

"Rosette," Willem replied, looking at Asu.

"Why not any of the others who've accompanied us?" Alex asked. He knew the answer, but Asu needed to hear it from a SADE. The captain was quite protective of Rosette, as she was of him.

"Our appearance, to a great degree, Ser. The six of us are not easily distinguishable from humans in our usual avatars," Willem replied, but he glanced at Z, who still wore his Cedric suit.

"I'm sure the Dischnya will simply mistake me for Dassata's older and heavier brother," Z riposted.

"Much older," remarked Julien.

"And much heavier," added Cordelia.

Alex, the only one who maintained a constant link and secondary conversation level with the SADEs during the planning meeting, enjoyed sitting on the sideline as a visual war broke out with Z and Miranda pitching images against Julien and Cordelia, who responded in kind. It was over in a few ticks, but hundreds of static images and short vids flew between them in that tiny breadth of time.

"Asu, if either Rosette or you are against this, I will understand," Alex said gently.

"It's her decision, Alex," Asu replied, but everyone could see he was uncomfortable with that statement.

"Security will be aboard every traveler," Xavier said, "and I will be aboard whichever ship Rosette rides in, Asu."

The *Sojourn*'s captain nodded his head in appreciation of the gesture.

"Rosette agrees," Julien commented.

"Then it's six each of travelers, emissaries, and SADEs," Reiko announced.

"The emissaries' reception at the first nests will be a strong indicator of the challenges that this operation might face," Xavier said.

"And they'll be in great danger," Lieutenant Marie Soucis added, rubbing the shoulder that was wounded, despite the injury's complete healing. Captain Escobar ordered her to remain aboard the *Sojourn* for this operation while he traveled planetside. As he phrased it, circumstances were too precarious to have both officers down below, at the same time. Marie was able to keep abreast of events, during her recuperation, by staying in communication with Rosette and receiving a full stream of Willem's vid.

"But Nyslara's Dischnya have acted as the queen's messengers before," Reiko objected.

"Who will be stepping out of alien ships, this time," Xavier riposted.

"True," Cordelia added. "Who's to say that the lookouts won't think that what they're seeing before them isn't an emissary but an apparition … an alien disguising itself as a queen's messenger.

"It was tricky enough trying to guess the maneuvers of our enemy when they were human," Reiko complained. "I don't know how you people twist your minds to accommodate the machinations of aliens." To which, the table responded by turning to regard Alex, many with grins on their faces, and he shrugged his shoulders in response.

"Great, we're saying we have only the one alien expert. But what about the SADEs?" Reiko asked, glancing around the table.

"Don't look at us," Cordelia replied. "We were too busy celebrating having escaped certain destruction at the hands of the last group of aliens to think about the inconsistencies that Alex saw."

"But, Julien, I heard that you agreed with Alex," Reiko said.

"Yes, I did support his theory, even though I worried for his sanity, but the man saved my life. I owed him a certain amount of leeway."

"Traitor," Renée shouted good-naturedly, and Julien grinned at her.

"Okay, so one alien expert and a lot of believers. Sometimes, I think it would have been smarter, if not safer, to have stayed home." When Franz threw Reiko a hurt look, she quickly added. "Except for you, my heart. You're worth a trip across the galaxy."

"Good save," Renée commented, chuckling.

"Back to work, people," Alex announced. "Nyslara said that she sends an emissary to each nest, and she estimates we'll land at thirty-six or more nests. Each ship takes its load of emissaries, drops them, one at a time, at the assigned nests, and then returns to recover them in order."

"What if the emissaries run into trouble?" Willem asked.

"And what could we do for them if they do?" Xavier replied.

It occurred to everyone that they would be safely ensconced inside their ships that could lift skyward at the slightest hint of danger. But once the queen's messengers left the shuttles, they would be at the mercy of foreign nests, whose soma might be in a state of paranoia after sighting an alien ship landing in their territory.

"Is there nothing we can do to support them?" Marie asked. Silence greeted her question, and she shook her head in regret.

"Remember, Marie," Alex said softly, "both we and our ships are alien. It's Nyslara's estimate that this is the only means by which we can gain the queens' attention and impress on them the importance of attending the Fissla, and she knows these individuals best. We can only hope the emissaries will be a familiar enough sight, despite exiting our travelers, that the lookouts will hold fire and escort them to their queens."

* * *

Franz, Svetlana, Orly, Verlan, and two other pilots set their travelers down in arcs on either side of a seventh shuttle at the usual meeting place outside the Tawas Soma nest.

Alex, Willem, and Z strode out to meet Nyslara and Pussiro, who hurried from a lookout post to join them.

"Dassata," Nyslara greeted Alex, "we're ready. I've prepared forty-two emissaries and believe the number will be sufficient."

After Willem's translation, which took some effort on his part, he relayed Alex's instructions to divide the messengers among the six ships that he pointed out.

Pussiro barked a command and blue-and-white-masked warriors hurriedly climbed out of the tunnel entrance. As the emissaries reached Pussiro, he divided them into groups, as directed by Willem, ordering each to climb into the indicated shuttle. In no time at all, the last emissary disappeared into the sixth ship.

<I thought Nyslara's drawing was crudely exaggerated,> Alex sent privately to Willem.

<As did I,> Willem sent in reply.

Instead of a façade designed to fit tightly over the face, the emissary masks reached a good 30 centimeters above the crown of the head and dipped down into the chest, the blue and white alternating and jagged stripes creating a bizarre display.

<It seems obvious now,> Alex sent. <You want that mask to stand out so the lookouts don't shoot first and realize their mistake later.>

"The Fissla will be joined in three cycles, Dassata, when Nessila is high overhead," Nyslara said, dipping her head and striding back to her nest.

Pussiro nodded as well and seemed about to say something but changed his mind. Then he hurried after Nyslara's retreating back.

"That was interesting," Alex remarked.

"Yes, our commander seemed intent on expressing a thought," Willem replied. "His body language was less hostile than usual, most relaxed."

"Maybe he's just happy to get his queen back. I know I would be," Alex replied, smiling.

"I would be too," Z added, thinking of Miranda.

* * *

Each pilot carried Nyslara's layout of the nests, as she had laid it out on the *Sojourn*'s holo-vid and as originally reported to Pussiro and her by the emissaries. Alex divided up the thirty-six known locations among five of the pilots.

But it would be Svetlana's job, piloting the sixth traveler, to scout the territories beyond the known nests and attempt to insert the emissaries. Willem rode with Svetlana to manage the translations with these messengers.

The pilots flew lofty arcs. They were ordered not to appear shooting low across the ground, frightening lookouts prematurely. So the pilots vaulted their travelers skyward and set down on a nest's fringe, allowing the emissary to exit the craft, proceed 10 meters away from the ship, and halt. He would wait for a hatch to pop open and a warrior to gesture him forward. In the case that slugs were thrown the emissary's way, his orders from the queen were to leap for the ship's hatch.

High overhead, Svetlana overflew the last nest marked by Nyslara and continued on. The aim was to plot the unknown nests as she worked her way eastward, as the Harakens had defined the north-south poles of the planet. The travelers' controllers were programmed to detect the telltale circles that indicated the round hatch covers. Once Svetlana discovered the most eastern nest, she would work her way back west, dropping off emissaries.

The pilots kept in contact with the *Sojourn*, where Alex and the captains intended to monitor the emissaries' progress and reroute the pilots as necessary.

It was a few hours before Svetlana and Willem finished their survey. Of course, they had no way of knowing exactly where one nest ended and the other began, but Nyslara's information indicated that the nests were similar in size to one another. The queen had given Willem a long rambling explanation as to why this was, but Willem had professed to Alex that

Nyslara's recital was way beyond his translation capabilities, stating that he thought the queen was educating him on the social dynamics of a nest.

At the farthest edge of the Dischnya's expansion, Svetlana, who was monitoring closeup images of the ground in her helmet, said to Willem, who sat in the copilot seat, "Let me know where you want me to set the ship down."

"I see potential lookout hatches but they appear to be overgrown not just camouflaged," Willem replied. Nonetheless, he directed Svetlana to a bare patch of ground.

The first emissary exited the hatch slightly confused. Along with his fellow warriors, Haffas had sat quietly in his chair, awaiting the motions of the alien craft and more than a little apprehensive. Now, much later, he was stepping out of the ship onto strange ground without having felt any movement. Haffas squared himself and his mask and marched the ten paces forward, as explicitly directed by his commander and repeated by the queen. Over and over, it had been stressed to the emissaries that they were to follow their instructions exactly, and, in case of trouble, take orders from those Harakens who spoke the Dischnya language.

Haffas glanced back at the ship and received a nod of approval from the Haraken called Willem. He stood in the rays of Nessila until he could feel the heat cooking his skin through his thick fur. Occasionally, he sipped on his flask, trying to prevent a buildup in his bladder. Relieving himself on the grounds of a foreign nest without permission was tantamount to marking his territory and was known to have started wars between nests.

"No response?" Willem asked. He stood directly behind the emissary, and Haffas jumped in the air with a yip. The emissary hadn't heard or smelled Willem's approach.

"Fellum, no," Haffas scolded. "Walk to greet soma at the muzzle, never at the tail."

Willem apologized and zoomed his eyes in on what appeared to be the nearest disguised tunnel entrance. Many small things did not seem right to him. He instructed Haffas to return to the ship, and he walked up to the nearby brush, which covered a hatch. Willem expected to find it locked tight, but it gave with a screech as he pulled on it.

A rotting stench swept past him. It might have doubled a human over, retching to clear passageways, but, as a SADE, Willem pulled a couple of tests through his nose and mouth to analyze the scent. It was the smell of decayed meat, a great deal of it. Willem let the hatch drop and returned to the ship.

The moment Willem stepped aboard the traveler, six muzzles pointed overhead, sniffing the air. The emissaries growled softly at the scent of decaying Dischnya.

"The nest is dead," Willem announced.

"Not a war," Haffas said. "A queen takes a nest … adds soma to hers … her territory expands."

"Perhaps illness among the soma," Willem said, hazarding a guess.

"It has happened before," Haffas allowed.

Closed up in a tunnel system without an infrastructure to deliver running water or remove waste was inviting calamity, Willem reasoned.

Svetlana lifted the traveler, flying low, this time, toward the west, and Willem and she scanned the ground for signs of disguised outposts that weren't heavily overgrown with brush.

A second time, Svetlana set down, and Haffas exited the ship to wait for recognition. Before Nessila had even begun to warm the crown of Haffas' head, a lookout hatch popped open. Four warriors climbed out. None of them carried slug-throwing weapons. Instead, Haffas saw long blades, worn at the waist, and the warriors carried odd weapons made from the trees of the green.

No gesture to step forward was given Haffas, so he stayed where he stood. Eventually, an elderly queen, supported by what Haffas presumed to be her heir, climbed out of the tunnel and eyed him. The queen beckoned him forward, and Haffas walked slowly and with measure toward her. He delivered an emissary's greeting, dropping to both knees several lengths from her, an indication of nonaggression.

Inside the traveler, Willem watched anxiously, analyzing the reception Haffas was receiving. The queen kept him kneeling for a long period, while she eyed both the emissary and the ship. Willem could see the jaws of the elderly queen and the young female heir moving and earnestly wished he could hear what they were saying. Several times, Haffas gestured at the traveler.

Finally, Haffas received permission to stand and was invited inside. He beckoned to the shuttle to lift, wanting the queen to see that he wasn't a lowly warrior, but a true emissary. Much to his relief, the ship lifted immediately, turning slowly toward them and even dipping its nose, first down and then up. It was a nice gesture to the queen, and Haffas mentally thanked the female who guided the alien vessel.

"One down," Svetlana said, as they swung south to an area that might hold a second nest.

"I would prefer that you use an alternate phrase, Commander," Willem remarked.

Svetlana laughed heartily but nodded her head in understanding.

It took much of the day before the rest of Svetlana's emissaries were deployed, and she circled back to the site of the first drop-off.

"Oh, black space," Bethany uttered. She was the first to spot the figure on the ground.

Haffas had been staked out. His throat was cut, and his emissary mask lay at his feet.

Svetlana turned to Willem. Her former statement, uttered as a simple count, now haunted her, and guilt was written in her face.

"Your words did not elicit this, Commander. Do not fall on superstition. This has occurred due to the baseness of the people we face."

<We will recover him,> Willem sent to Bethany and Svetlana.

The traveler landed close to Haffas' body, and Bethany triggered the hatch open. She eyed the scene and when she spotted no movement, she signaled Smitty Lange to follow her. Willem exited the hatch on their heels.

When the three Harakens reached the body, Willem yanked up the first two stakes with ease, despite the fact that they had been driven deep into the ground with Haffas' limbs heavily lashed to them.

A hatch flipped open when the third stake came free from Willem's effort, and three warriors jumped out with their weapons pointed at the

Harakens. It was obvious the old queen's warriors thought the sturdy stakes would buy them time while the aliens sought to recover the body.

A veteran of a Dischnya fight, Bethany knew the warriors wouldn't recognize the small shiny item in her hand as a weapon. They would believe they'd surprised unarmed aliens.

<They're using crossbows, Sergeant,> Smitty sent. He was itching to stun the warriors, but Bethany gave him explicit orders to wait until they were fired on.

<Explain,> Bethany shot back.

<Spring-tensioned weapons that fire a wood shaft tipped with metal or stone. They can be extremely deadly.>

Bethany and Smitty remained frozen, but Willem grabbed the last stake, which caused one warrior to growl a warning, and the SADE froze with a hand on the piece of wood. He slowly straightened and faced the warrior who uttered the words.

"Your queen has broken the emissary's truce," Willem growled. "This puts the lives of her soma in jeopardy from all queens."

The warrior looked as if he had been struck across the muzzle. Hearing the Dischnya language spoken by the alien stunned him, and his lower jaw hung slack.

"Lower your weapons while we recover our emissary or the metal tools in my soma's hands will put you to sleep," Willem threatened.

A stalemate existed, with both groups eyeing each other and no one making a move. Movement at the hatch caught Bethany's eyes, and several more warriors bounded out. They tried to encircle the group, but Willem uttered a warning growl, one he'd recorded from Pussiro, and the warriors halted and carefully retreated to join their comrades.

The old queen and the heir climbed out of the tunnel. She sniffed the air to catch the alien scents and growled her own warning. "Go," she ordered. "Leave your messenger where he lies. The Fossem Soma declines the Fissla. We don't heed the words of aliens."

<Get ready, Sergeant,> Willem sent to Bethany. <You have my permission, as mission co-commander, to fire first.>

Bethany relayed the message to Smitty, and the two pretended to relax, straightening out of their crouches, and lowering their stun guns. It worked, the warriors relaxed a little too.

"And we, who brought this emissary under the mask of truce, do not recognize an old, embittered queen, who does not obey the laws of the Dischnya. We will take this one with us," Willem ground out in his best Dischnya.

The aged queen's eyes burned with hate, and she snarled a reply.

<Now,> Bethany sent. The three Harakens dropped to the ground, catching the warriors off guard, and Bethany and Smitty opened fire. Several arrows were loosed in panic, the warriors trying to regain the enemy in their sights, but the six of them stood little chance against fire from two sophisticated alien weapons.

A portion of Bethany's stun gun beam overlapped a warrior and struck the old queen in the side. She fell to the ground, unable to rise, and spit vitriolic at the three Harakens.

The two security personnel kept their weapons trained on the tunnel entrance and watched the scope follow their movements. In the meantime, Willem asked the young female Dischnya, "Who are you?"

"I'm Posnossa, heir to the Fossem Soma," the female replied, standing fully erect with her tail thrashing proudly behind her. But, soon she lowered herself to stare at the queen, withering on the ground and clutching her numb side. Then she gazed at the bodies of the nest's warriors. "Not every soma was guilty of your emissary's death."

"And those who are guilty have yet to be judged and punished," Willem said, closing Haffas' eyelids gently. "Listen to their breathing."

Posnossa knelt at the side of the nearest warrior. She placed a hand on his chest and felt it rise and fall. Looking carefully at the others, she could see the same was true. "You speak the truth," she said to Willem.

"I always speak the truth. We're called Harakens, and we don't kill unless we must."

Posnossa hung her head. Pointing at the queen, she said, "This one ordered it. She said the emissary couldn't be Dischnya if he stepped from an alien ship."

"He was Haffas of the Tawas Soma, a brave warrior, who brought you an offer to meet in Fissla."

"So he said. But our queen said he lied … said it was a trick to take the nest." Posnossa studied the scene of the murdered emissary, the sleeping warriors, the three strangers, the alien ship, and her mad matriarch. "The invitation to the Fissla is real?" she asked.

"It's as Haffas told your queen," Willem replied. "The Harakens wish to unite the Dischnya and help raise them out of the ground." It was a slight exaggeration on his part, and he silently asked Alex for his forgiveness, but deep in his crystal core, Willem wanted to be a part of the peace Alex wished to bring to the planet.

"Chona Posnossa, Fossem Soma, will attend the Fissla," the young female declared. When the old queen hissed at the presumption of her heir, Posnossa swung around and raked a clawed foot across her mother's throat, slashing it open. Blood poured from the wound, and, in moments, the old queen uttered a death rattle. Posnossa dropped to both knees and hung her head, saying, "The queen of the Fossem Soma begs forgiveness for your emissary's death."

"Attend the Fissla. Speak for peace, and you'll receive our forgiveness," Willem said. He yanked the last stake free with one hand, picked up Haffas, and started back to the ship.

Bethany and Smitty backed up slowly. The sergeant spared a glance for the torn throat of the old queen, while the corporal snatched the emissary mask off the ground.

Posnossa watched the ship silently lift and fly away. The hatch near her opened and warriors flooded out. One by one, they knelt at her feet, long tongues licking her fingertips and tasting the scent of the new queen. Word spread quickly among the soma that the old queen was dead, and Posnossa ruled the nest. It was a relief to most. The killing of an emissary had shocked them. A drastic change was needed, and the young queen was a welcome sign of that.

Svetlana and Willem's work to recover the other emissaries continued without further incident.

Overhead, aboard the *Sojourn*, forty-three nests were identified, with two wiped out from some sort of disease. Of the forty-one queens who met with emissaries, thirty-four agreed to attend the Fissla, including the young queen, Posnossa.

-21-
Fissla

Nessila was low on the horizon when the Tawas Soma lookouts passed the word that the Haraken ships were returning. Pussiro ran ahead of Nyslara, who loped behind without her headdress and robe. Pussiro noticed that the queen wore neither since returning from her time with the aliens. Seven ships perched again on the plains, as the queen and wasat emerged from the lookout post.

"This was too soon for them to return," Pussiro said. "The plan must not have worked."

"Do not judge the Harakens by Dischnya standards," Nyslara replied. "It might not be too soon for the return of these aliens."

Alex and Willem strode from their separate ships to meet with Nyslara and Pussiro. After a short greeting, Alex laid out the count of the nests for Nyslara, and the queen's eyes grew with interest. "The queens of thirty-four out of forty-one active nests have agreed to attend," she said with enthusiasm. "We've done well, Dassata, much better than I had hoped."

Willem completed the translation for Alex and then delivered the bad news about Haffas. About that time, the emissaries emerged from Svetlana's ship. Haffas was laid on a grav pallet, his mask over his face, covering the jagged slash across his throat. Bethany and her trooper walked alongside the pallet.

"A good warrior," Alex said simply.

"I thought many more of my soma would die," Nyslara commented. "Your ships were more impressive than even I supposed."

Alex only nodded slowly to Nyslara when he heard her words through Willem, as Haffas' body was carried past.

"Mates?" Alex asked.

"Diss," Nyslara replied, raising a single digit. "I will find her a new warrior."

At Alex's urging, Bethany related the story of Haffas' death, the exchange with the aging queen, the brief fight, and the death of the queen from her heir's claw.

The remaining emissaries gathered behind Nyslara, their masks in their hands, while warriors carried Haffas below to prepare for his burial. She turned and reviewed them. As she spoke, the Harakens watched their muzzles lift, their stances straighten, and chuffs escape their lips. Then she asked a question and seven warriors stepped forward. She interrogated them thoroughly.

Alex glanced at Willem, but the SADE shook his head. Either he couldn't hear them, which Alex doubted, or the discussion was beyond his capabilities.

The seven warriors stepped back into the ranks and, at a command from Pussiro, they hurried into the tunnels.

"The trend is clear," Nyslara said to Willem and launched into a longer explanation.

"It would appear, Ser," Willem said, "that Nyslara questioned the seven emissaries who visited the queens who refused to attend the Fissla. She sees a trend. It was the eldest of the queens who refused the offer. Four of those queens are without female progeny, meaning they have no heirs."

"How did the emissaries discover that four of them had no daughters?" Alex asked.

When Willem relayed the question, Nyslara tapped a dark-nailed finger alongside her muzzle, and Alex nodded his understanding.

"Nyslara believes that the older the queen, the less she trusts the concept of the Fissla, possibly thinking it to be a trap, but not going so far as to kill her messenger," Willem continued. "She emphasizes that the four aging queens, who are without an heir, present problems. I'm not sure of this next part, Ser, but she's speaking of something that goes wrong with the soma if left without a queen for too long. That's the point at which she tapped her skull."

<Willem, pursue this subject with the queen when you have time. I'm not sure that it impacts the Fissla, but it might be of importance later,> Alex sent.

* * *

Aboard the *Sojourn*, later that evening, the arguments in the captain's salon grew heated about the arrangements for the Fissla, and this was only among friends. Alex voiced his ideas, but security objected. The captains volunteered their plans, but most everyone objected to those. On top of it all, the SADEs, as Winston explained it, wanted to be present at this historic event to observe the proceedings firsthand.

"Willem, let's discuss security concerns," Xavier said, attempting to take control of the discussion. "Who attends a Fissla?"

"From each nest, Captain, the queen, the wasat, and one warrior," Willem replied. "An emissary precedes his two principals, wearing the mask of truce."

"Won't they have to cross the territories of other nests, Willem?" Reiko asked.

"Undoubtedly, but that is the risk every queen will take except for Nyslara and those whose territories are adjacent to her. Let's hope that none of them meet the fate of poor Haffas," Willem replied.

"Willem, describe how the Fissla proceeds," Alex requested.

"The queens' council is ringed by their wasats, who act as bodyguards. The emissaries form a broad ring around the group and act as another layer of protection. The queen, who called the Fissla, in this case, Nyslara, leads the meeting."

"Do the queens discuss any other subjects beside the one Nyslara will present?" Renée asked.

"I don't know this, Ser," Willem replied, "but I will seek an answer. I have several subjects to pursue with Nyslara."

The group went back to the general discussion about who would be present for the Fissla. In the end, Alex lost every argument — to the SADEs, to Xavier, to Renée, and to the captains. For a brief moment, Alex regretted not having the president's power but only for a brief moment. Looking around the table, he realized that it was no longer necessary for him to be in charge and have his way. His people were capable of making their own decisions, wise ones at that, and directing their own paths, and he couldn't have been prouder of them.

* * *

Two days later, the Harakens landed a couple of hours before the appointed meeting time. The Tawas Soma had set the field with tents. The tops were covered with woven cloth. The edges fluttered in the breeze. Underneath the tents, the ground was layered with bessach. The greater tents displayed soft pallets for the queens, and already twenty-nine queens, including Nyslara, reclined on these comfortable mats, lapping at drinking bowls. Their commanders lined the tents' peripheries, and the emissary warriors waited in small shades set up for them in a wide ring 10 meters farther out.

When the Haraken's ships came into view, the queens rose and congregated to watch the alien ships land, anxious to observe the occupants, as Nyslara had spent much of the morning describing them. Two of the strange entities stepped down from one of the ships, both remarkable in their differences from the Dischnya. One queen murmured to the others, "Dassata," and others nodded in agreement. There was no mistaking the figure that Nyslara's tales told of the alien peacemaker. The queens watched Nyslara and her wasat hurry to meet the odd-looking pair.

"A good turnout, Nyslara," Alex said to the queen, when she stopped before him, bowing her head gravely in greeting.

"Dassata is pleased to see this number of queens assembled," Willem translated for Alex.

Alex watched Nyslara glance back at the assembled group, but when she faced him again, she was frowning. "What's the matter?" Alex asked.

"Dassata wishes to know the reason for the furrows in your brow, Nyslara," Willem said.

The queen glanced at Pussiro, who replied, "Lookouts report sighting four queens near or entering the Tawas Soma territory. They've traveled far."

"The count is at thirty-three, Ser, with the queens that the lookouts have observed entering this nest's territory."

"And the thirty-fourth?" Alex asked.

"Which queen is not seen?" Willem rephrased for the queen.

"Chafwa," Nyslara replied. "Her nest borders the Tawas Soma. It's important that Chafwa attends the Fissla."

"Why?" Alex asked when he heard Willem.

"Chafwa's soma are large in number," Willem said to Alex after he received the queen's reply. "She's an older queen, and her voice will carry great power. Her nest also hunts the Swei Swee."

Nyslara's words struck Alex hard and reminded him of the Fissla's purpose.

The queen saw Dassata's short muzzle tighten. The muscles along its edge flexed and distended the flesh. The Haraken leader wanted an agreement from the queens that the ceena would be hunted no more, but a consensus among chona would not be easily reached simply because he desired it.

* * *

The Harakens returned to their travelers to enjoy the cool comfort while they waited for the arrival of the last queens. In the two remaining hours before the Fissla was due to start, four more queens, including Posnossa arrived. Finally, Chafwa and her wasat, Foomas, led by an emissary warrior, strode across the grounds to join the assembly. The warrior doffed his mask and took up his duty, as a member of the Fissla's peripheral guards.

As had been orchestrated with Alex, Nyslara opened the Fissla. "Each of the queens who accepted my offer is present. The Harakens, who you think of as aliens, have identified forty-three nests. Two are dead from the taking, and seven queens refused to attend. These people …" Nyslara said, indicating the travelers with a wave of her hand.

The queen's gesture was a cue for the Harakens. Franz's ship controller relayed the image to his helmet, and he passed the signal to everyone on open comm. The entire assembly of Harakens flooded out of their ships, but stayed close to them.

At the aliens' coordinated display, hisses issued from many of the queens and several recoiled, backing up several steps. The wasats and warriors tensed, their clawed feet gripping the bessach or soil for purchase to launch themselves in defense of their queens.

"These aliens have capabilities far beyond our imagination," Nyslara continued, "and we've discovered that the ceena are part of their soma."

"Impossible, the ceena are not thinkers!" Chafwa snarled.

"It has been proven to us beyond doubt, Chafwa," Nyslara said calmly. "The Harakens travel with ceena in their company. They're called Swei Swee."

"This is a trick to prevent the Mawas Soma from harvesting the ceena so that the Tawas Soma will be the only hunters," Chafwa challenged.

"Your words might have force, Chafwa, if I called this Fissla of my own volition. I didn't. The one we call Dassata requested this council of queens. He wants peace for his soma … an end to the hunt, and his ships have the power to burn nests to blackened holes if we continue to attack the ceena of this world."

"You speak of power beyond our vision, Chona Nyslara," Foomas said, from the edge of the tent.

Pussiro's neck hairs bristled. Wasats did not speak at a Fissla, but Chafwa was a powerful queen, and she allowed her commander much freedom.

"Queens of the Fissla, we've witnessed the power of the alien ships," Nyslara replied, deliberately not addressing Foomas. "If you require proof, we can lead you to the shore where a wide stretch of sand is now a smooth, glassy black hole. The destroyed surface, which you will see that no soma could have created, will convince you of their power."

"How many of your soma died encountering the aliens?" Chafwa asked.

Nyslara knew the old queen was wondering if the Tawas Soma had been seriously weakened and was ripe for a takeover. "Many of my warriors fell to the aliens' weapons," Nyslara replied, and then she bared her lips to reveal her teeth just the slightest, as she added, "But later, they rose."

Growls and hisses of incredulity escaped the queens' muzzles at Nyslara's words.

"Nyslara speaks the truth," Posnossa said into the noise. The young queen surprised herself. She hadn't wished to voice her opinions during the Fissla, not wanting to attract the attention of older queens who bordered her territory. "My matriarch killed the emissary sent to us and staked him out. The aliens sought to recover his body, as was their right, since they brought him to our nest. My mother would not have it, and our warriors attacked them. Six warriors went down; six of them recovered."

"And why is your matriarch not here, Posnossa?" Sissya, a young queen, asked.

"It was time for the heir to lay a mad queen to rest and assume the robe of power," Posnossa replied, and every queen knew what she meant. In most cases, the handover of a nest's control was orderly, and sometimes it wasn't."

"Shouldn't we hear from the aliens if we're to believe these stories?" Chafwa asked. She leaned back on her pillows and stared quietly at Nyslara. The other queens discussed what Chafwa said, and soon they were requesting exactly that from Nyslara.

"One among the aliens speaks passable Dischnya," Nyslara said. "He'll translate the words of Dassata, who will speak directly to you." She stepped off the bessach and raised her arms to Alex, waiting by his traveler.

"Time to get the show started," Alex murmured, as he stepped forward to join the Fissla with a small retinue in his wake.

The queens rose from their pillows at the approach of the aliens. Sissya eyed the leader of the group, impressed by his breadth, and then her eyes traveled to another, walking slightly behind him, who was even more formidable. "Do they get any larger than those two?" Sissya hissed to Nyslara, indicating Alex and Z.

"Let's hope not, Sissya," Nyslara replied.

Alex waited while Nyslara introduced him to the waiting queens. A detail he'd observed about the female Dischnya gave him evidence as to the emotions they were experiencing. It was their long, scaled tails — some lay relaxed behind the queens, some curled tightly about their legs, and others swung slowly to and fro.

As Alex spoke to the queens, Willem delivered translations on the fly. "You might not wish to hear what I have to say to you. Nonetheless, the requests of my people are simple and twofold," Alex said. "First, the Swei Swee of this planet are not to be harmed. They are of our soma, and we'll take any measures we deem necessary to ensure their safety."

Alex heard the hiss of the old queen, who was the last to arrive at the Fissla. Chafwa, Nyslara called her.

"To accommodate our first request, the Dischnya must change their ways," Alex continued. "Your food source is too scarce to support your growing nests. There are better ways to feed your soma, and we'll teach you these ways. But, if you want this, then we require that the queens agree to live in peace … your fighting must end."

The first point was easily accepted since most of the queens had no access to the great waters. So, the hunt for ceena was not an issue. It only required the agreements of Nyslara and Chafwa. But Dassata's second request astounded them. His words were simple, but what he asked was monumental in scope. To end nearly a hundred annuals of fighting just because aliens wished it seemed absurd.

"You ask for our pledge that we won't hunt these creatures you call your soma, Dassata, requiring the Dischnya put aside their way of life," Chafwa said, as she stepped forward. "What do you offer in return?"

"What do the queens want in return?" Alex asked.

"The gift of your alien capabilities for the soma of Sawa Messa," a voice said from the back of the tent.

When Willem asked who spoke, Foomas walked around the tent's edge to stand beside Chafwa. "I speak in my queen's name."

Hisses and snarls of dissent issued from the queens at the impertinence of Chafwa's wasat. Besides Chafwa, only one other queen hadn't reacted. Nyslara watched Chafwa quietly and with interest, wondering what the old queen gained by fomenting dissension among her peers. Whatever her reason, it was an impediment to what Dassata sought.

Without uttering another word, Chafwa and Foomas pulled short-barreled slug throwers, which were hidden from sight in their clothing. Haraken security forces were still drawing their stun guns when the twins fired at the queen and her wasat. Beams hit their targets even while slugs exploded within the Dischnya weapons, despite the fact that the queen and her wasat moved first.

The queen's heavy metal pellet struck Alex in the upper chest, and the wasat's slug threw Alex's head back sharply, dropping him like a stone to the ground. It was Étienne's beam shot that struck Foomas as he fired and threw off his aim by centimeters. Foomas was known among his soma as a deadly shot.

Even though Chafwa and Foomas instituted the fight, growls echoed from the Dischnya ranks at the thought that the aliens had killed some of their own during a Fissla. Desperately Nyslara cried, "Halt! These two aren't dead. The alien weapons don't kill."

Sissya and her wasat knelt by the fallen pair and checked for signs of life. "Nyslara speaks the truth," Sissya called out. "They breathe and show no wounds."

"It's as I spoke earlier," Posnossa declared. "Six of my warriors were struck by these alien weapons, and they rose later with no ill effect."

While the Harakens held the Dischnya at bay with drawn stun guns, Z, faster than the eye could follow, scooped up Alex, as if he was a baby, and raced for the mission shuttle. With its large ramp, it would accommodate a fast ingress. SADEs parted like waves in front of him, and the combined mass of Alex and Z thudded the ground with Z's every swift step.

Pia raced after the pair but quickly fell behind. Suddenly, she was hoisted in the air. "Times a wasting, dear," the medical specialist heard Miranda say, and soon they were covering ground in a blur.

Svetlana, who had been standing by next to her traveler, heard the shots and received Z's determined comm to the assembly to clear way. Her ship was next to Orly's, where her location app indicated Z was headed, and she took off at a dead run.

"Medical emergency, Orly," Svetlana sent, recognizing he was sitting in his pilot's seat. "Move over, I'm flying." She made it up the ramp only moments before Z, even though she had a 30-meter headstart on the SADE.

<Awaiting your clearance, Z,> Svetlana sent, while she snatched a helmet and readied the controller for liftoff.

Z judged Miranda's speed and signaled Svetlana to lift, copying Miranda, who was still 12 meters away.

Miranda linked into the traveler's controller to track Svetlana's flight orders. The traveler was lifting and spinning, while the ramp was rising. At a flat-out run, Miranda corrected her course and leapt for the ramp, throwing Pia and her combined weight into a twist to ensure that they were firmly planted against the ship's spin, while the ramp closed behind them.

Pia doubted they could have made the leap. So, as her feet hit the deck, she said her thanks to Miranda and hurried to Alex's side. Z reclined a seat to lay Alex on it.

* * *

Part of Renée's mind howled for her to race after Alex, but she stood rooted in place, sending an urgent open comm to the Harakens to stand still. She wouldn't allow Alex's efforts to be undone this way and went so far as to block comm transmissions, good or bad, from Svetlana's flight. She could ill afford to be distracted. Renée glanced toward Julien. They could read the pain in each other's faces.

The twins and security continued to cover the queens and wasats with drawn weapons, daring anyone to move. The Dischnya were quiet, after it was proven that the two perpetrators of the fight still lived. It crossed the minds of most of those called to attend the Fissla that the treachery of Chafwa and Foomas would spell their demise.

<Willem, translate for me,> Renée sent, as she fought to gain control of her emotions.

"If my partner is … dies," Renée said, addressing the queens in a choked voice. "I would see your nests turned into great black holes in the ground. Isn't that the Dischnya way? Repay an attack with one of your own? It's fortunate for you and your soma that this isn't Dassata's way, and I will act in his stead, as he would wish me to do. All of you stand still, while my soma search for more weapons."

At the translation of Renée's words, Chafwa's emissary warrior broke from his shade and bolted for his nest's territory. He barely covered 50 meters when he had the misfortune to pass close to a Tawas Soma lookout post. Three of Nyslara's lookouts leapt out of the tunnel and tackled Chafwa's warrior. Soon, Nyslara's warriors had the emissary warrior's hands trussed behind his back. One of the lookouts displayed the emissary warrior's long blade. It was another breach of Fissla's ancient rules.

Snarls and growls greeted the discovery, and several emissaries left their posts to collect the traitor. The Tawas Soma lookouts stood where they had caught the runaway, since they were forbidden to approach the gathering. Once the emissaries affirmed that the traitor carried a sheath under his vest that fit the knife, they left the weapon with the lookouts and hauled the prisoner back to their shades. Tying their captive's hocks together, they lowered him to the ground.

During the silence that followed the attack, Esther sent a comm to the Confederation's SADEs. <What should be our response?>

<I'm unsure,> Winston replied.

<Our purpose here was to intimidate the Dischnya by show of numbers,> Trixie sent in the open to her fellow SADEs. <I believe Dassata would desire that we don't get involved.>

To this, Winston could add no more. So, he seconded it.

<Start your search, Captain,> Renée sent.

Xavier and his people investigated every individual carefully and thoroughly — queens, wasats, and emissaries. More than one Dischnya felt an intrusion into sensitive areas, but none objected. No other weapons, slug-throwers, or blades were found.

"Ené, mate of Dassata," Nyslara entreated, when the search ended. "The Fissla has been dishonored. Allow the Dischnya to discipline those who've forgotten its sacred rules, so that we might demonstrate our intentions to you to abide by Dassata's requests."

"Why should I believe that justice will be dispensed?" Renée asked, after hearing Willem's translation. "The Dischnya shot and critically injured an alien. What's one of us mean to you?"

"There are no words of mine to give you, Ené, which you would take as truth," Nyslara replied. "But you can believe this. The queens standing before you attend their first Fissla. If the Dischnya's traditions aren't upheld, there can never be another. Punishment will be given … must be given … according to our laws."

Renée tried desperately to think of what Alex would do if their roles were reversed.

<Alex always looked past the moment, the obvious, to see what followed or lurked underneath, in both the good and the bad, Ser,> Julien sent to her. <Has every queen trespassed or just one of them and her people?>

<You think I should leave justice in the hands of the Dischnya?> Renée replied.

<I think you should do what your conscience dictates, Ser, not what's driven by your pain and anger.>

<So don't order Reiko to bring the *Tanaka* down and turn the plains black,> Renée sent. Despite the anger that warped her thoughts, there were elements of sadness and capitulation.

Nyslara watched Ené's eyes burn into her, but no words were exchanged. Nyslara could hear the shuffling of clawed feet on bessach behind her. The queens and wasats were growing restless, waiting for the

Harakens' reply to Nyslara's request. Many were probably thinking that if they were to die, they would prefer to die fighting.

"I will leave judgment of these three to the Dischnya," Renée finally said.

When Willem translated Ser's words, there was visible relief among the queens and wasats. Young Posnossa was especially relieved, having hoped for a longer reign than it appeared she would have had several moments ago. She wouldn't have ruled for three full days if Dassata's mate wanted revenge, which, in the Dischnya's eyes, she would have every right to demand.

"Tomorrow, Ené," Nyslara said, bowing gravely to Renée. "Judgment will be rendered when Nessila lights the day."

Renée nodded curtly, turned, and headed for her transport. Willem commed everyone to board the ships.

As the Harakens walked away, Nyslara blew out a long breath and heard the queens and wasats do something similar. She spun around and stalked over to the body of Chafwa. She could understand Ené's anger, as she wanted nothing more than to rake her claws across the unconscious queen's throat.

Nyslara requested the queens bind Chafwa, and Pussiro asked the wasats to do the same to Foomas. Then Nyslara sent Pussiro to order soma to fetch water and food. The discussions surrounding the judgments would be long and heated, and Nessila's emergence over the horizon would come sooner than anyone expected.

-22-
Aftermath

Svetlana's destination was the *Rêveur*. There were no better medical facilities for humans on any of the three Haraken ships.

Orly might have objected to being demoted to the copilot's seat, except Svetlana's formidable reputation preceded her. Using his helmet's connection to the ship's controller, Orly took the opportunity to learn, carefully following Svetlana's maneuvers. Her takeoff was unorthodox, but she was shaving fractions of time off her flight, even as she notified the *Rêveur* that Alex Racine was injured and unconscious.

Historically, New Terran pilots, such as Orly, were trained to lift and take the shortest route to space. Instead, Svetlana exhibited her Haraken fighter pilot training. She queried the controller for the shortest flight time to the *Rêveur*, and they sped across the landscape, barely edging over a mountaintop, to intercept the liner, which was close to the planet's horizon.

Pia bent over Alex, examining the wounds. She requested Z turn Alex over to see if the slug in his chest had exited.

"There's no need, Pia. I felt for that wound as I carried Ser here. The projectile is still inside his body."

Of course, you did … and a million other things as you ran, Pia thought, chastising herself. At this time, both humans and SADEs would be experiencing heightened emotions. Only humans would have to fight to concentrate on what to do next — not so for the SADEs.

Pia dug in her med kit and produced a tube of specialized medical nanites, which were designed to seal a wound with a temporary patch and stop the bleeding. These nanites wouldn't attempt repairs. They'd stay in place until a medical specialist signaled their disassociation. Then they'd enter the body and join those nanites already present in the body. These dual-purpose, medical emergency nanites were designed by Terese, specifically for the *Sojourn*'s mission, and brought to fruition by the SADEs. Terese could never have guessed that the first patient to receive her invention would be Alex.

Pia examined the ugly head wound. Pieces of bone stuck up at odd angles. The meninges, the protective tissue layers surrounding the brain, were pierced. Pia paled and her hands trembled. Inside, she wailed at the horrendous circumstances that had placed the life of Alex Racine in her hands.

Suddenly, Miranda's head intercepted Pia's sightline. The SADE rotated a single eye over the wound and then, lifting her head, said, "Under magnification, I detect three bone fragments near the surface. However, assembling them virtually, they are insufficient to encompass the damaged area. My conclusion is that there is a fourth, much smaller piece that lies on the plains of Celus-5 or —"

"It's lodged inside the skull or possibly deep in the brain," Pia completed for Miranda.

"What's to be done first, dear?" Miranda asked quietly.

Pia reached up and touched Miranda's cheek, grateful for her calming influence. <Svetlana, how long until we dock?> Pia sent on open comm.

<The *Rêveur* is 3 kilometers out, people,> Svetlana replied, her voice flat and neutral, while she concentrated on reaching the *Rêveur* in the shortest amount of time.

"Z, no pressure on this head wound during transport," Pia said.

"Understood," Z replied.

After receiving Svetlana's emergency comm, Captain Lumley oriented the *Rêveur* to place an empty bay broadside to her flight path. He thought to move his ship closer to her, but knowing Svetlana well, he knew that he stood a zero chance of guessing the thoughts going through her mind.

The *Rêveur*'s docking protocols required traveler pilots to enter the bay aft first and settle to the deck before any action was taken by the flight chief. Svetlana, Z, and Miranda scrapped those regulations. Svetlana brought the fighter in nose first, and Z signaled the bay doors closed before the ship touched down on the deck. Once inside the bay, Svetlana performed the dangerous maneuver of spinning the mission shuttle in a half-circle to point the aft end directly at the bay's airlock.

The bay doors closed, and Miranda triggered the bay's pressurization. Meanwhile the *Rêveur*'s medical specialists waited in the airlock. Svetlana eyed the air pressure and signaled the ramp to drop even before her telltale flashed ready.

Z held Alex in his arms, cradling the head to prevent jostling and waiting for the ramp's descent. Pia stood anxiously nearby. The ramp was in a horizontal position with another 15 degrees to drop to the deck when Z took off. Algorithms churned as the SADE calculated trajectories, mass, and his avatar's response, allowing him to cushion his impact on the deck as he jumped clear of the ramp and minimally disturbed his precious cargo.

As Z raced across the deck, he signaled the medical team to clear way and overrode the airlock protocols to open both hatches. The crew members barely had time to jump aside as Z barreled past them, headed for the medical suite, and the specialists took off after him.

Pia saw Z jump, and her eyes beseeched Miranda.

"I love a woman who learns quickly," Miranda said, scooping Pia up and tearing after Z. Miranda signaled the specialists to stand aside as she passed them in the corridor. Neither Z nor Miranda bothered with the lift. Instead, they took the stairwell up the three decks to the medical suite, their legs churning and taking the steps three at a time.

Pia commed Z and indicated on which medical table he should lay Alex. Miranda and Pia entered the suite just as Z was gently lowering Alex on a table outfitted with equipment prepared for the more grievously injured.

The full-body medical scanner Pia positioned over Alex delivered its images to a controller, which prioritized his injuries. The slug in the chest nicked an artery and required immediate attention. Pia sent a command to the medical controller, which signaled her patch over the chest wound. The nanites released their bond on one another and assumed their secondary purpose, quickly disappearing into the body.

Pia called for the controller to select a tiny arterial sleeve from within its medical supplies. "Miranda," Pia said, "you're going to play surgeon."

"Not my favorite role, dear," Miranda replied, linking to the controller. She studied the first item on the surgical priority list and the scanner's imagery of the arterial bleeding. Immediately, she shunted the controller into a passive state and directed the tips of the delicate surgical arms into Alex's chest cavity.

Miranda's eyes were open, but she kept her vision app in a low priority state while she focused on the scanner's imagery, which displayed Alex's body and the controller arms. Gently, she slipped the open sleeve around the artery at the site of the nick and, as its two edges touched, the sleeve sealed and shrank to tighten against the artery. Days from now, the sleeve would be dissolved by the medical nanites in Alex's body — long after the artery was repaired from the inside.

"The controller can do the rest, Miranda," Pia said gratefully, when the device confirmed zero blood loss from the artery.

"Nonsense, dear, what a controller can do, a SADE can do better and faster." Miranda glanced down the controller's code, examining the next steps for the chest. She undertook the process of sealing muscle layers, small bleeders, and skin from the inside out with the surgical laser tool.

At one point, Z looked at his hands, whose fingers hid sleep darts or whatever loads he required. He spread the massive digits apart, and designs formed in his crystal kernel about other tools, such as surgeon's instruments, that he might incorporate in the next avatar's iteration. As the list of possibilities grew, he yanked himself back to the here and now, realizing he was trying to occupy his mind to defeat the feeling of an impotent bystander at this critical time for Alex.

Miranda completed her work on the chest, and Pia linked to the SADE, who was peering into Alex's skull injury. "I need the three bone fragments you mentioned, Miranda," Pia said, placing a small dish of liquid near the SADE. "Place them in this dish in their original orientation to one another but separate them by a centimeter or so."

As Miranda fished out the bone fragments, Pia realized the tremendous advantages a SADE surgeon offered over a medical controller. Miranda's eye magnification and precise hand control, coupled to the controller's knowledge base and imager, could create an unsurpassable amalgamation of tools. It gave Pia ideas for surgery's future. *If I'm going to have one,* Pia thought. She wondered where she might live if she was the medical specialist who lost Alex Racine.

After Miranda retrieved the third fragment, Pia requested an extreme closeup of the wound from the SADE. At the same time, Pia rechecked the scan. The metal slug wasn't present. It hadn't penetrated the skull.

When Miranda heard Pia's trembling sigh of relief, she surmised the reason for it. "But, Pia," Miranda said, "you should have known the slug wasn't in Alex's brain. Everyone is aware of the great hardness of this dear man's skull."

Pia released a strangled giggle at Miranda's jest. Realizing the extent of her tension, Pia took a deep breath in and exhaled. Then she focused on the work.

The fourth piece of bone was driven backward between the skull and the outer layer of the meninges, the dura mater. Miranda's close magnification revealed that the next two layers of the meninges were bruised but not penetrated. The SADE glanced at Pia, who said. "We need that piece of bone removed as carefully as possible."

"But of course we do, dear," Miranda replied, not any happier than Pia to be the one responsible for the operation. In a cascade of events, Miranda linked to Z, who was embedded in the medical controller. He merged the scan image, real time, with the controller's medical directives and laid them in Miranda's kernel, essentially generating the exact intertwining Pia envisioned.

Miranda located the tool attachment the controller would have chosen to retrieve the bone fragment but passed over it in favor of another one. She closed her eyes, since her sight would be useless in locating the bone fragment unless they opened Alex's skull — a barbaric concept for Haraken or Méridien medical specialists.

During the entire procedure, Z rotated the scanner to provide Miranda the best possible view, as she closed on the tiny piece of bone. Every movement of arm and hand was calculated by Miranda to minimize the impact on surrounding tissues. Rarely had she run so many algorithms in concert for such a simple procedure. But she certainly wasn't going to be responsible for injuring the man any more than the queen and her wasat had already managed to do.

The tip of the tool merged with the scanner's view of the fragment, and Miranda eased the injector rearward, which sucked the fragment to the tool. Then she slowly withdrew the bone and laid the piece in Pia's dish in its proper orientation to the other three. Pia ordered the controller to repair the dura mater layer, but Miranda cancelled it and managed the job herself.

When Miranda finished her work, Pia checked the scanner's output for any signs of bleeding and was pleased to see none. The bruising of the meninges would be repaired by the nanites in Alex's body.

"Do we replace the bone fragments now, dear?" Miranda asked. She'd reviewed the controller's procedural steps, but there were a host of variable conditions to consider before proceeding, and the SADE didn't have the experiential memories to understand their application.

"Not yet," Pia replied, closing a lid over the dish and placing it carefully in a medical containment unit. She signaled the controller to lock it and added a safeguard so that it couldn't be tampered with by a human, even accidentally. From a tube of nanites, similar to those used on Alex's chest wound, Pia placed a semi-permeable seal over the open area in Alex's skull. "This seal will allow seepage if there's any swelling of Alex's brain from the concussion. *When* Alex recovers," Pia said with determination, "we'll dissolve the seal, implant the bone fragments, and apply some synth-skin, genetic copy, of course, for his scalp so that his hair will regrow."

In her haste to treat Alex, Pia hadn't applied a temporal device to Alex while he was out. The slug's impact rendered him unconscious, and he remained so. She attached one now in case Alex woke in an agitated state. At this point, there was nothing more to be done but monitor Alex's condition and wait to see if irreversible damage had been done to his brain.

The medical team went about their jobs, cleaning up from the operation, removing Alex's clothes, and closing the medical table's case over him to allow the controller complete imaging access to the patient.

Pia found a place in the suite to rest, and a specialist hurried to fetch some hot thé for her.

Miranda stood beside Z, choosing to hold his hand, which the two of them found comforting.

Z sent an update to Julien, trusting his friend would know when to deliver the news to Renée.

* * *

Renée, always the calm one when it came time to exit a traveler, stood at the hatch, impatient for the bay to pressurize. Franz, Julien, Cordelia, and Willem were all monitoring the exterior pressure and the hatch so that Ser did not trigger it prematurely.

Julien had communicated to Renée the news that Alex was stable but still unconscious. "We must wait, Ser," he said, adding, "I believe fortune is in our favor. I calculate his skull is probably of sufficient thickness to withstand almost any alien, slug-throwing weapon."

Renée had burst into tears, hugging Julien and burying her face in his chest.

<My next avatar will be capable of producing those,> Cordelia sent to Julien, as she watched Renée cling to her partner. <It's such a poignant gesture of an individual's raw emotions that all of us should be capable of demonstrating it.>

Julien couldn't agree more. Inside, he was fighting to maintain control of his emotional algorithms. He felt as if he was suffering some sort of cascade failure in his code. *We've come so far along the path with Alex,* he thought, *that we're becoming as vulnerable as humans to the loss of one another.*

When the bay's controller signaled pressure equalization, five signals triggered the hatch open. Rather than climb down the steps, Renée leapt to the deck. Julien barely had time to drop the energy in a section of grav plate to relieve Renée's impact.

Just as Z and Miranda had done, Julien cleared the way for Renée. Both sides of the airlock were triggered open, despite safety protocols. Cordelia spared a moment to warn those in the medical suite that Ser was on her way, and Franz requested Captain Azasdau collect Teague and Ginny for transport from the *Sojourn* to the *Rêveur*.

Renée burst into the suite and ran to the medical table. She placed her hands on the case, frustrated that she couldn't touch her beloved partner and feel the warmth of his skin. Tears streamed down her face, and she turned to stare at Pia, who started to break down.

"We've done the best we could, Ser," Pia sobbed.

Renée enfolded her good friend in her arms. "I know that, Pia," she soothed. "Alex knows that." Realizing the pain others were suffering, Renée set aside her own grief and took up Alex's role. She walked up to Z, who she couldn't hug while he was ensconced in his considerable Cedric suit. Instead, Renée gripped his shoulders and stood on her tiptoes to kiss his cheek. "Thank you," she said.

Z merely nodded, unable to choose fitting words from his extensive library.

"And you, dear," Renée said, standing in front of Miranda and copying her inimitable speaking style, "are invaluable too." Then, she hugged the SADE.

"The dear man deserves our best efforts," Miranda replied.

"That he does," Renée replied.

Julien entered the suite and signaled to everyone that they should give Renée some time alone with Alex. Pia picked up her reader, which rendered a feed from the controller, which, in turn, monitored Alex via the temporal attachment and the 3-D scanner. Then she slipped out of the suite with Z, Miranda, and the medical team.

Julien started to leave too, but he was halted by Renée's signal. Turning around, he saw her sitting on a couch and holding out a hand to him. He sat beside her, taking up her hand. The two of them kept their vigilance in silence — two old friends in need of each other during the worst of times.

<Don't you dare torture me this way, Alex,> Julien sent to his friend. <We're supposed to have, at least, another century and a half before we part, if then.> He waited, but there was no return comm from Alex's implant. While they kept watch, Julien monitored Alex's vitals incessantly, scanning for changes and trends in hopes of alerting Pia to something of

value to assist her in reviving the human, who had come to mean so much to him.

* * *

By the early morning, there was no change in Alex's condition, and Renée was asleep on the couch, a coverlet spread over her by Pia.

<Ser,> Julien sent gently, sorry to see Renée anxiously sit up, worry lining her face. "No change, yet, Ser. I wondered if you thought it would be appropriate to observe the Dischnya's disciplining of the three perpetrators."

"Is anyone going down?" Renée asked.

"One shuttle, piloted by Franz, will be headed planetside with several SADEs, security, and the twins."

"Shouldn't I be there?"

"Every Haraken would understand if you weren't there, Ser."

"Yes, but would he?" Renée asked, pointing at Alex.

"To that, Ser, I would say: What would Dassata request you do?"

"Exactly," Renée replied. "Give me a few moments to refresh and change. I'll meet you in the bay."

"We'll be ready, Ser," Julien said, never quite as proud of Renée as he was then. *Courage, Ser,* he thought as Renée hurried from the suite.

-23-
Judgment

Pussiro gently woke Nyslara. She and every queen had less than a quarter of the dark period to rest. The deliberations took them into the early morning hours before a consensus was reached. What Nyslara observed was that the younger the queen, the more likely she was to work toward agreement. It was the older queens, who had lived most of their lives at war with other nests, who distrusted others' suggestions.

"Yes, Pussiro?" Nyslara asked, her eyes having difficulty making out his image, backlit by the pale torchlights, but his scent announced him.

"The lookouts have spotted the descent of a Haraken ship, my queen."

"They've come to observe the punishments," Nyslara whispered. "That, in itself, is good, but they're early. Wake me again at dawn." Then Nyslara tucked back into her warm pillow bed and pulled her robe over her.

Since they landed before dawn, the occupants of Franz's traveler tilted their seats back and napped, except for Franz, who along with the SADEs monitored the Fissla tents.

<What do you believe the judgments will be?> Willem asked his compatriots.

<What do I want them to be,> Miranda sent back, <or what do I think the Dischnya will do?>

<Either one,> Willem replied.

<My bet is that they'll be the same,> Z replied.

<Imagine that your culture has slid backward for a century,> Julien replied. <You live underground in primitive conditions, fighting with other tribes over scarce resources, because you've lost the technology to elevate your people. Along come aliens, who can cure that, and the only thing these aliens ask for is peace ... peace between the nests and peace for intelligent sea creatures. But before that discussion can take place and a

consensus reached, three members of your society threaten to rob you of those hopes by breaching your sacred rules and committing an act of violence. What would you do?>

Julien's rhetorical question left the SADEs dwelling on their own thoughts and patiently waiting for Celus to rise.

When the rays of the system's star pierced the dark sky, Franz sent over an open comm, <We have movement.> Humans and SADEs tapped into the controller for a view of the Dischnya tents.

<I'm going out,> Renée sent. She signaled the hatch open and climbed down the steps.

Renée expected to lead her people to the tents, as Alex always did, but she was so tightly encased in bodies it was difficult to see where she was going. "Everyone, stop," she said, halting her steps. "This isn't going to work, and it will send the wrong impression to the queens. They'll think that we don't trust them." Regarding the stern faces of those surrounding her, Renée amended her statement, saying, "Yes, we don't trust them, but we don't want it to appear as such. Now give me some room."

When her people grudgingly opened some small space, Renée said, "More." She was about to repeat herself, but the expressions on the twins' faces said they wouldn't hear of it. Renée meant to talk to them on the flight down, but she'd quickly fallen asleep as soon as her seat adjusted under her. Her concern was that the twins might feel responsible for failing to protect Alex, despite their incredibly swift responses.

The Harakens stopped 10 meters from the tents. Or better said, Étienne ordered a halt 10 meters from the queens' tents, and Renée was prevented from going any farther.

While the Dischnya made preparations for the judgments, Nyslara approached the Harakens. Pussiro wanted to accompany her, but she told him to stay back. Her decision appeared to be correct. The closer Nyslara got to Renée, the more the Harakens' hands twitched to grasp the weapons at their sides. Nyslara was careful to stop short of the group. "Ené, how fairs Dassata? Does he live?" she asked, after nodding gravely.

Willem provided a translation via implant, but Renée understood the question. "He lives, but he's unconscious."

Willem translated Renée's response as, "He lives, but he sleeps the deep sleep of the head injured."

This Nyslara understood, having seen many of her soma, who had been shot in the head, never join the living again. "Will he wake?" Nyslara asked with concern, glancing between Willem and Renée.

"This is unknown," Willem replied.

Nyslara watched Dassata's mate duck her head, sorrow etched in her face, but when she brought it back up, anger shone in her eyes, replacing the pain. Nyslara chuffed her understanding. "Judgment has been reached. Punishment will take place over there."

The Harakens followed Nyslara's arm, which pointed at a set of stakes pounded into the ground. Straps were tied to each set of four stakes.

Before Renée could ask a question, Nyslara strode back to the other queens. "We're too far away," Renée complained.

"Ser, what if the Dischnya use their slug-throwers to execute the perpetrators?" Alain asked.

"That's doubtful, Alain," Willem replied. The Dischnya appear to prefer to deliver their punishments up close and personal, such as what happened to poor Haffas.

Renée got her way, and the group edged over to stand about 5 meters from the sets of stakes. They didn't have long to wait before the warriors hauled over Chafwa's emissary warrior, the one who carried the blade. He was whimpering and unable to stand on his own, necessitating the emissaries drag him most of the way. The bonds of his hands were cut and he struggled to escape. It required four warriors to pin him down and bind his limbs to the stakes.

The Harakens expected some sort of ceremony, a pronouncement, or, at least, a reading of the charges and the judgment. But, no sooner had the traitor's last limb been tied with a strap than one of the emissaries, who tied him down, raked a clawed foot against his neck. Gouts of blood sprayed into the air, and the disgraced Dischnya keened in panic. Soon, his wail faded to a whimper, and he passed into unconsciousness, the rush of blood draining his life from him.

<Perhaps, we're too close,> Renée sent to Julien, <but too late to back up now,> she added, before Julien could reply. There was a cough behind her, and she sent an open comm, <Same rules apply as a Swei Swee greeting ceremony: If you can't handle the view, swallow, and make your way back to the ship. Under no circumstances do you dishonor the Dischnya's judgment ceremony.> Renée was wondering if she would need to follow her own instructions, especially with what she imagined was yet to come.

The wasats brought out Foomas next. Unlike the lowly emissary warrior, the commander walked unaided. When his hands were freed, he lay down and extended his arms and legs to the stakes. As the last strap was tied, Foomas uttered a deep, savage growl just before a wasat delivered the killing blow. His growl turned to a gurgle before he passed out.

The Harakens were rather sickened by the ceremony, but anger over what had been done to Alex kept them in place. However, the humans might have been even more disturbed by their SADEs, who were making good use of the proceedings. They calculated blood spray distance, blood volume loss, time elapsed until unconsciousness, time until breathing stopped, and time until the eyes indicated brain death, which they could witness via extended visual magnification.

When the queens brought Chafwa out, she wasn't struggling, but she was railing against the Fissla and Nyslara, in particular. Willem attempted to provide translations, but many of Chafwa's terms were deemed to be expletives, as they were references to animal organs and waste.

<I believe we get the gist, dear,> Miranda sent to Willem. <The queen's angry and about to die. We can fill in the blanks about what she's saying.>

Chafwa was still swearing, while she was strapped down. But unlike the first two executions, the queens formed a line, starting at Chafwa's side. One by one, each stepped up and raked a set of claws against a limb or chest, and they were none too gentle about it. Chafwa screeched with each blow, but the queens kept at it. While the young queens were more tentative in their punishment, the older queens sought to deliver harsh rakes with their claws.

For her part, Chafwa gained a brief moment's respite, as one queen stepped aside and another stepped up. Recognizing the new individual, Chafwa would cut loose with a fresh stream of invectives, but by the time the last queen stood at her side, Chafwa was blubbering in pain and torment. Blood spewed from deep gashes across her entire body. Yet, she was able to recognize her final punisher, Homsaff, her heir.

Unlike the first two judgments, which were decided by lots, Homsaff requested to be the one to deliver the judgment against her matriarch. Listening to Nyslara and other queens throughout the night, she came to understand what was at stake with regard to the aliens, and how damaging Chafwa's act of treachery was to the future of the Dischnya.

"If the Harakens come in the morning to witness our judgments," she told the assembled queens, "then they might place more faith in the Dischnya if they see the heir to the Mawas Soma takes the life of the perpetrator."

"Can you do this, Homsaff?" Posnossa had asked. While she managed to do the same thing, it was in a fit of anger over the mad queen's treatment of her and for the killing of her sibling. But this would be cold and calculating, a difficult feat for one so young.

"I must do this," Homsaff had replied determinedly.

Chafwa focused on her heir. She was drained of angry words. All she could do now was hiss at her young progeny, who poised for the killing stroke.

Homsaff tentatively lifted a leg, but set it back down. But when Chafwa barked in laughter at her, Homsaff raised her leg with determination and swept it hard across Chafwa's neck. For the old queen, there would be no lingering shock, no moments for her to contemplate her death, as blackness crept over her. Homsaff's strike had nearly cleaved Chafwa's neck in two.

The young queen's strike position was poor, and blood spewed up her legs and onto her belly. She howled in rage and terror over what she'd done, sinking to her knees in the blood-soaked dirt.

While the queens sympathized with Homsaff, none moved to comfort her.

Not so for Renée, whose heart was torn by the grief the young Dischnya was suffering. Before Renée could be stopped, she burst through her entourage and raced to Homsaff's side. Unsure of what to do, as she slid to her knees in the pooling blood, she heard Alex say, "Do what your heart knows is right, my love." Renée gripped Homsaff's shoulders, and it startled the youngster, who halted her cry.

Homsaff stared in confusion at Dassata's mate, never having been embraced in this manner and confused by what to do. She was desperate not to endanger the Fissla or an agreement with the Harakens by giving the wrong response. Much to her surprise, the Haraken female tilted her head back and gave a passing imitation of a Dischnya howl of pain, then regarded her. So Homsaff lifted her muzzle to the sky and sounded her own distress. She glanced at Renée, who repeated her pitch to the early light of Nessila. Then the two females joined in a duet of frustration, as they screamed their pain and anger in Dischnya fashion.

"Fitting," Nyslara remarked to those around her. "Whether alien or soma, females grieve the same."

The Harakens kept wary eyes on the Dischnya assembly, as well as Ser, who, in their minds, was too close to what appeared to them to be a distraught teenager — one capable of using the incredibly long claws on her feet to separate a head from a body.

When Homsaff quieted, Renée patted her shoulders and rose to rejoin her people. Her clothes were covered in Chafwa's blood. She didn't say a word to the Harakens or the Dischnya but simply trudged back to the traveler, her steps giving the impression she had aged a hundred years.

Turning to follow Renée, the Harakens missed an important clue about the makeup of the Dischnya society — the cleanup of the queens after Chafwa's execution. Wasats and the newly promoted Mawas Soma sub-commander ran for pails of water, prepared by the Tawas Soma to wash the feet of their queens.

Pussiro's warriors prepared additional water pails for Homsaff, and he fetched and placed them beside the young queen for her soma, who worked to remove the blood from her fur.

It wasn't that the queens were unsympathetic to Homsaff's agony for requesting to be the one to execute her mother; it was that the queens worked to prevent the mixing of their scents. They didn't share drinking water, waste pails, pillows, or robes. More important, they didn't touch one another. A queen wasn't an elected position. She was the psychological linchpin for her soma, who were physiologically dependent on her scent.

* * *

After the judgments were rendered to the Fissla traitors, Renée, Pia, and every Haraken returned to their vigilance of Alex, waiting and hoping for his revival. Rather than responding to every query for an update, which Renée received incessantly, she requested Miranda to post notices on the *Rêveur's* controller for the mission's crew to access. After reviewing Miranda's "no status change" hour after hour, most humans relented and decided to wait for a critical update, which they were sure would be broadcast shipwide. The SADEs simply linked an app to the controller to monitor every update.

But Julien detested the passive approach of waiting. He queried every SADE and every ship's database for medical treatment information, comparing the data to that stored aboard the *Rêveur*. To his great disappointment, he found enormous amounts of repetition. Terese had been thorough in ensuring her people's medical updates were widely circulated.

One particular SADE, Bartlett, a recent immigrant to Haraken, who had yet to touch foot on the planet, did have advice.

<Bartlett, your ID states that you were the SADE of a rescue ship,> Julien sent when he connected to the next SADE on his list, which enumerated those who had transferred from the *Allora* to the *Rêveur* at Haraken.

<Yes, Julien, and if I can anticipate your request, since your query is known, my medical databases were left aboard the rescue ship. I carry little of that information with me.>

As Julien restructured his line of questioning to prepare an alternate line of investigation, Bartlett checked for an update on Alex's condition and reviewed the operations' procedures.

<I can share this with you, Julien,> Bartlett sent. <While Méridien medical technology is adept at rendering injured humans unconscious for surgical operations or longer, if necessary, and reviving them, we've yet to conquer the process of waking those patients who fell into a coma due to a serious brain injury.>

<So you have nothing to add to the *Rêveur*'s medical database on this issue, Bartlett?>

<I reviewed your ship's database soon after we learned of Alex Racine's status, following his operations. There's nothing definitive that I can add.>

<You say nothing definitive. Why?>

<It's a well-known fact, in these cases, that humans in a coma receive sounds and comms via their implants, which is passed to the subconscious. Medical scans indicate that the more the subconscious is stimulated, on a continuous basis, the greater the probability that the conscious will be encouraged to come to the forefront, helping the patient wake.>

<My thanks for your information, Bartlett,> Julien sent.

Julien launched into an exhaustive search of his databases and that of the *Rêveur* for the appropriate material to entertain Alex's subconscious. Both ancient and modern vids and stories were enjoyed by many crew members, especially Renée and him, but they weren't Alex's preferences. In fact, Julien had noted that Alex only watched the vids in Renée's company.

Julien's frustration built, the more his investigation failed to produce results. Now, it seemed like a simple selection of stimulating material was proving to be a disaster. With his emotional applications overriding much of his analytical thought processes, Julien had no alternative but to halt many algorithms driving his anxiousness.

Calmly and logically, Julien reviewed his personal history with Alex from that fateful first day aboard the *Rêveur*. It wasn't that Julien saved every moment of contact time with Alex after the man jumped across vacuum to board the derelict liner. But Julien had a habit of keeping critical exchanges with Alex for future reference. However, over the years, as those conversations became irrelevant, he'd deleted most of them.

It was while reviewing their twenty years together that Julien realized he had faithfully stored something precious to both of them — their mock image battles. Not only had Julien backed them up in the Exchange's vault, but they were data that he carried with him, and their fanciful exchanges took up terabytes of his memory.

Walking from the bridge to the medical suite, Julien started whistling a tune, and his favorite fedora appeared on his head.

Crew, witnessing Julien's happy demeanor, quickly connected to the ship's controller, expecting to see good news about Alex's condition, only to be disappointed when they realized there was no change. Despite that, rumors circulated through the fleet that Julien appeared to be in fine spirits and hope revived among humans and SADEs.

Julien settled into an unoccupied corner of the medical suite, locked his avatar in place, signaled he was unavailable except for emergencies, and ordered his memories. For his first transmission to Alex's implant, Julien chose simple images, but before he could start, there was a little operation to be performed first.

Alex's implant was active since it was powered by his brain's heat. However, the comm app wasn't active. The only things that were recoverable from Alex's implant were his bio data. Those applications were purposely not security locked so that the data could be recovered in times of emergency.

However, Julien was one of the few individuals who had access to Alex's security applications, and he used that data to defeat Alex's implant security protocols and open the comm applications. Now the paths to Alex's applications and data storage were open. The access level was so complete that Julien could wipe the twin implants clean — not that the thought occurred to him.

Once Julien had access to Alex's implants, he sent a favorite image fight. It was simple, but one of their first, and Julien had enjoyed it immensely. He felt liberated that day, mentally sparing with a young captain, whom he admired.

But Julien wasn't satisfied with sending the image battles. He talked to Alex about their exchanges and how they made him feel. He commented on his favorites and why he prized them. He recalled the events that led to their creations, which were often moments of celebration for the two of them, for others, for the fleet, for the Swei Swee, or for the Harakens. And Julien engaged Alex nonstop.

People came and went from the suite — Pia, Renée, Teague, Ginny, medical specialists, and others. Some stayed for a little while to give comfort and check on Alex's conditions, and some sat with the unconscious man for hours. Everyone spared a glance for Julien, who seemed to be standing watch in the corner. Humans lamented that the SADE might be incapable of other actions until Alex woke, unaware of the extent of Julien's activities. There was nothing to tell humans or SADEs any different, Julien was offline to all entities and controllers. Even the medical controller couldn't detect Julien's one-way transfer of data to Alex's implants embedded in his cerebrum.

The hours passed for Julien, and his efforts were unflagging. Morning gave way to the afternoon. The afternoon gave way to the night. One day gave way to the next, then another, then another.

Midday meal signaled via code in Julien's kernel. He'd turned off the chime to prevent the sound from interrupting him. The next mock fight on his extensive list came up, and Julien sent it. He was about to comment on it when he heard these halting thoughts: <Last one … favorite … liked screams … you ran away … strange costume.>

<Welcome back, my friend,> Julien sent, while blasting the news out to the fleet. <Cordelia, you were right,> Julien sent to his partner. <We should have avatars who can cry tears of joy, especially at moments like this.>

The sounds of crew members yelling, clapping, stomping, and pounding on walls reached Julien, and immediately afterwards Renée, Teague, Ginny, Pia, and several medical specialists burst into the suite.

Pia released the table's cover and checked Alex's vitals via the controller. "How do you feel, Alex?" she asked.

"Tired … bored," Alex replied weakly.

"Bored? How could you be bored, my love?" Renée asked.

"You would be too if Julien was reliving your past and droning on and on and on," Alex said, coughing from a dry throat. Pia opened Alex's mouth and sprayed a mist to lubricate the passageway.

Those in the medical suite turned to regard Julien. Alex lifted a hand to wave his fingers at his friend and smiled. Renée grabbed Alex's hand and kissed it, as Teague, tears running down his face, laid his hands on his father's shoulder.

Alex discovered his implant security was wide open and quickly restored it. He sent a single message to Julien as the SADE quietly eased from the suite. <No human has a better friend.>

A smile lit Julien's face as he strolled down the ship's corridor. Sparkles of light cascaded from the top of his head in a half sphere down to his shoulders, partially obscuring his face. It was an amazing light show for the crew.

* * *

The queens, with their wasats and emissaries, waited out the days since Dassata was whisked away by his soma. Many queens urged an end to the Fissla. Their great concern was that they had been absent for too long from their nests. But Nyslara was adamant that they continue to wait. "If Dassata dies, then you needn't worry about returning to your nests," she told them. "The lives of you and your soma might be short lived."

"Queen Nyslara, you speak as if Dassata, who we saw receive two mortal wounds, might not be dead," Posnossa said. In the period since the shooting, the youngest queens, Posnossa, Sissya, and Homsaff, had emerged as the strongest supporters of Nyslara's opinions.

"I've been witness to many wonderful and strange things amid the company of the Harakens," Nyslara said. "I've been on their ships, which wait above this world. I've met ceena leaders and heard their whistles translated into words. I've written on a map that floated in the air and could look far and near at our planet through a strange device. I've slept on a bed that moved under to me to accommodate my body." Nyslara shook her head in amazement at the memories of those events. "There are many things these Harakens are capable of that will surprise and stun you. It's my hope that Dassata will be saved, and, if he lives, he'll expect to find us waiting for him.

Dassata's Return

The queens were fast approaching the maximum time that they could afford to be away from their nests. Nyslara was even losing the support of the young queens, who were getting anxious to leave. One evening, it was agreed that they would wait two more days, then declare the Fissla closed.

The following dawn, Pussiro woke Nyslara and whispered word of the descent of alien ships. Nyslara had slept with the other queens in the well-stocked tents, which were erected on the first day of the Fissla. Every accommodation had been made to keep the queens, wasats, and emissary warriors comfortable while they waited.

Nyslara hissed to wake the queens in her tent, while Pussiro passed the word to the wasats, who woke their queens. Sleepy eyed, the Dischnya leaders assembled in the early light, pulling robes and jackets close against the chill morning air.

To the Dischnya's eyes, the Harakens' routine mirrored the Fissla's first day. The same number of ships landed in the same exact formation. As before, myriad figures spilled forth onto the plains, but, to their amazement, so did Dassata, who descended from the central ship.

<People, I want the same calm approach we demonstrated on the first day,> Alex sent to his immediate entourage. <That means, Xavier, your people need to take their hands off their weapons.> Alex glanced to each side to ensure that his words were taken seriously. However, in deference to his security, Alex stopped about 10 meters short of the assembled queens and wasats, whose lips quivered in confusion.

Nyslara was the first to recover from her shock at the sight of Dassata, even though she'd stressed to the other queens that it was possible, but hoping wasn't always believing. When Dassata failed to approach the queens, it caused Nyslara to hesitate. *But then why should you trust us, Dassata?* Nyslara thought.

Instead of waiting for Dassata to make the first move, Nyslara walked slowly out to meet him. Her eyes glanced frequently to the two slender aliens, who had been so quick to fell Chafwa and Foomas. They watched her with calm regard, but she was relieved that she couldn't detect animosity in their faces. *As if you know the gestures and subtleties of their odd faces,* Nyslara thought, berating herself.

Alex watched Nyslara's tentative steps, as she approached, wondering what she was thinking and feeling. Her eyes showed concern, but whether for herself or him, he wasn't sure. Whatever Nyslara was feeling, she had the courage to close the distance until she was within arms' reach.

For Nyslara, it was difficult to believe that she was looking at Dassata, having witnessed the great wounds inflicted by Chafwa and Foomas. She sniffed delicately. It was the same individual — not a spirit. Nyslara tipped her head to the side to peer at Alex's scalp, and he turned his head so that she could examine the wound.

The twins and security stiffened as Nyslara leaned forward to eye and sniff at Alex's wound. Having witnessed the execution of the Fissla traitors, they were keenly aware of the deadliness of Dischnya in close quarters.

Nyslara regarded the shaved area of fur on Dassata's head. The wound lines appeared faded, something she would expect to see many days after the skin knitted together. She inhaled quickly, trying to detect a salve or ointment that would explain the quick healing, but her nose filled only with the scent of Dassata.

As Nyslara pulled away from him, Alex could see the amazement in the queen's eyes. True to the man he was, he shrugged and gave Nyslara a lopsided smile, teeth and all. To his surprise, Nyslara's lips curled up and away, revealing incredibly vicious-looking rows of teeth, and she held her arms wide.

Both sides, Dischnya and Harakens, were perplexed by Nyslara's gesture. But Alex wasn't. So much of life was about decisions made in the mind, but they held little value to those around you unless consideration was given to the needs of the heart. And, in this case, despite the absurdity of the idea, Alex knew what to do. He stepped forward and embraced Nyslara.

"Dassata lives," Nyslara hissed into Alex's ear, as her arms enfolded him. She'd been mentally prepared to accept the feel of a squishy body, reflecting the pale, alien skin. Instead, hard muscles of arms and chest encased her. *Like grasping a boulder,* Nyslara thought, relieved not to feel her hands sink into soft flesh.

<Your pardon, my love, for my earlier words,> Renée sent to Alex, < You still have a way with females. It just takes a little longer with the alien ones.>

Nyslara stepped back, and she worked to hide her embarrassment for her brash action, covering her teeth and returning to the amenities. She heard Dassata speak, and Willem translated his words.

"Dassata thanks Nyslara for her concern," Willem said, "and wishes to continue his discussion with the Fissla."

Nyslara stepped aside and gestured to Dassata. She held her head high and rose slightly on her long legs, enjoying the vindication of her faith in the Harakens' incredible technology. *And you, young ones, who believed, will reap the benefit of your support,* Nyslara thought, as she eyed the incredulity in many of the older queens' eyes. When she stopped in front of the assembly, she said, "As I foretold, the Harakens are capable of much that we don't understand. Despite the death wounds Dassata received at the hands of those who would desecrate the Fissla, he lives."

Homsaff, too young to have been taught the ways of the Fissla, could not contain her amazement. She tipped back her head and loosed a long, wavering howl at the sky. It was not an appropriate gesture for the council of queens, but it was an ancient call of celebration, born from the marrow of the Dischnya.

And Homsaff's call was infectious. Others tentatively joined her, but the noise emboldened the rest. Soon queens, wasats, and emissary warriors sounded off to the sky. The howls were deafening in volume and eerily beautiful in harmony.

Nyslara regarded Alex, the lips of her muzzle wrinkling in humor. She wanted to join with her Dischnya in celebration but held back, not knowing what Dassata would make of it. Instead, she replied in the manner of the Harakens and offered him a full display of her teeth.

Alex didn't know which was more disconcerting — a hundred howling aliens or one bearing savage rows of teeth at him in imitation of a human smile.

<Alex, you'll note that the number of queens still stands at thirty-four, despite the executions,> Julien sent to Alex when the calling ceased. He circled a youthful face in an image he sent, and Alex noted it was the one who began the celebratory call.

Nyslara saw Alex regard Homsaff, and she issued a request for the young queen to step forward. "This is Homsaff, who has inherited from the perpetrator, Chafwa. A queen of Chafwa's age should have had an older heir. We learned from Homsaff that many annuals ago Chafwa rid herself of Homsaff's elder sibling when the female pressed for a passing of the robe. Homsaff is not yet of mating age. However, she's the only heir the Mawas Soma nest possesses. We request your understanding of this chona replacement in the Fissla."

"Dassata," Homsaff said, by way of greeting and glanced at Nyslara. The Fissla remained a great mystery to her. Yet, she was expected to participate in it, as a queen, even after the traumatic event of dealing the death blow to her mother. If all this hadn't been enough to disturb a too-young queen, now she stood in front of a resurrected Dassata, at a loss as to why she was beckoned forward.

"Welcome to the Fissla, Queen Homsaff," Willem translated for Alex. "May your reign be long and bring peace and great honor to your soma."

Whatever Homsaff expected, it wasn't these words, and she dipped her head in acknowledgment. Emboldened by Dassata's statements, she took the opportunity to speak what was on her mind. "I'm pleased to see that Dassata was not slain by Chafwa's treachery."

"I'm pleased too," Alex said in his simple Dischnya, and both Nyslara and Homsaff chuffed in humor. "We must return to the purpose of the Fissla," Alex said to Nyslara, with Willem translating.

"We must hurry, Dassata," Nyslara said. "The time for returning is near."

Alex furrowed his brows at Willem, thinking that he misunderstood Nyslara's simple statement, but Willem wore a perturbed expression. So Alex and company waited while Willem and the queen launched into a protracted conversation. Other queens drifted over to add their thoughts into how Nyslara could explain the critical time that approached, and Willem linked the Haraken SADEs to support his analysis.

<What have you got so far, Willem?> Alex asked over the comm.

<First, the queens must return to their nests soon. This is an imperative and not to be challenged. It's the why of this, which is too complex for my understanding.>

<Best guess, Willem.>

<How did I know you were going to ask that?> Willem replied. < Hold one, Ser,> he quickly added.

<Julien, are you linked in?> Alex sent.

<Yes, Alex. I believe this is a sociological matter. What I intuit is that a nest's queen is not an elected or won position. The queen of a single nest comes from an unbroken line of succession, and this is critical to the nest. Apparently, too long an absence of the queen from the soma endangers the safety of the nest in some way.>

Willem, having heard Julien's explanation, sent his agreement to Alex.

<So how much time do we have?> Alex asked Willem.

<Today and tomorrow, Ser. The queens must leave on the morning of the third day. Even so, those farthest away believe harm might have already been done to their nest by the time they complete the long trek back.>

Alex cleared his throat loudly, and silence fell over the discussion. "First, by dawn on the second morning from today, our ships will return the queens, their commanders, and their emissaries to their nests via our ships, even if the Fissla hasn't reached consensus."

Alex's announcement was greeted with skepticism by the older queens, but the eyes of the younger ones glowed with excitement.

"Dassata, some of us have nests that are fairly close," Homsaff said, and everyone knew what the young queen attempted to wrest from Alex.

"Every queen, who wishes to ride, will be accommodated," Alex replied.

Homsaff, hearing Willem rephrase Dassata's answer, nodded politely, but Alex saw the young queen's claws repeatedly dig into the soil and relax.

<A teenager excited by the thought of riding an alien ship,> Julien sent to Alex, noticing the same thing he did.

<I hope her soma welcomes her,> Alex replied.

<From what the queens are trying to help us understand, Alex, I would say the nest is desperate for her return.>

<If that's true, we need to ensure Nyslara convinces every queen to ride. I don't want to be responsible for a single late return.>

Alex gestured the group toward the main tent. Space was made by rearranging pillows, and wasats hurried to bring the pillows from the smaller tents where their queens had slept. Alex and Willem were offered seats on small pillows of their own.

No queen or wasat missed the two slender, identical Harakens who stood closely behind Dassata and constantly scanned the Dischnya's faces.

Despite your swiftness, Dassata was severely injured, Nyslara thought, looking at the twins. *Are you now more protective or do you seek revenge?*

As the hours passed, the queens lounging on their body pillows and Alex and Willem sitting on theirs, the framework of an agreement slowly took shape. The greatest obstacle to progress was the lack of proficiency with each other's language. Repeatedly, Alex and Willem knew they were struggling to understand the point.

In contrast, the Dischnya queens easily comprehended Dassata's statements. His requests were simple — the ceena were to be left alone and the nests were to stop their fighting. They agreed to both.

It's what the queens wanted that the Harakens continually misunderstood. Alex offered to build a complex so that the queens might have a permanent location at which to facilitate their council, the Fissla. But when Willem reworded Alex's suggestion, it elicited growls, and Alex didn't need a translation for that.

The queens' reactions underscored the conjectures of Willem and Julien. The monarchs couldn't be separated from their soma for too long, much less permanently. What the Harakens became convinced of, over time, was that an entire nest must be moved, queen and soma. Forty-one structures would need to be built, one to accommodate each Dischnya nest.

"Speaking of nests, Willem," Alex said. "What about the seven queens who didn't attend?"

After Nyslara replied, Willem said, "According to Nyslara, their cooperation isn't expected to be a problem. The seven will accede to the will of the thirty-four or they will not live."

"Not exactly democratic," Alex murmured.

<Alex, I dislike being the naysayer in these seemingly progressive circumstances,> Julien sent. <But this mission isn't supplied with the equipment or material to fabricate the facilities that you're discussing. We don't even know what to construct ... doors or flyways ... refreshers or not? Do we build fire pits for cooking or supply them with food stock tanks and dispensers? Then what happens when the stocks are emptied?>

<Stop, you're giving me a headache.> Alex glanced over his shoulder at his friend, who wore a stricken expression. <Sorry, Julien ... wrong thing to say. I meant it as a figure of speech. I have no repercussions from the injury.>

Alex watched and waited for Julien to nod his acceptance of the explanation before he replied. <Look, Julien, I know we're in over our head here. I'll need time to think through the next steps, but, for now, the first goal is to get the queens to accept a peace agreement.>

Nyslara saw Dassata glance at one of his close companions, and he tentatively fingered the area of shaved fur on his head. So she called a break to the Fissla, allowing the Dischnya and Harakens to enjoy a midday meal. Strangely, as Dassata and his soma trooped back to the central ship, a vast number of the Harakens remained where they stood. Nessila's heat was fierce, but they seemed undisturbed by that.

"Why does Willem not have a scent?" Posnossa asked Nyslara, as the queens lay down to enjoy a small meal and sips of cool water.

"That's still an alien mystery," Nyslara replied. "The one who is the closest advisor to Dassata, the one who stood behind him this morning and is called Julien, doesn't have a scent either."

"And gaze on those who stand in the field," Sissya said. "They stand as if they're staked upright."

"And they endure Nessila's heat without a sip of water," Posnossa added.

"Are they a lesser soma to the Harakens?" Homsaff asked.

"When I was taken to the ship above," Nyslara replied, "Dassata treated each of his soma equally. I don't know who the ones are who have no scent, but they're valued by Dassata."

Nyslara kept to herself the odd discussion she had with Pussiro just before the Haraken captives were returned to their soma. Pussiro reported that although Willem had been careful to hide it, he neither ate nor drank nor eliminated waste during the entire time he was captive.

"How is that possible?" Nyslara had asked.

"This is what Simlan and Hessan report, and they're convinced of its truth."

"We won't speak of this to the other queens, Commander. The aliens are strange enough without the queens thinking that some things the aliens are capable of doing don't bear any resemblance to their soma's habits."

As the Fissla reconvened, Nyslara began with a question for Alex.

Willem looked at Alex and displayed a calm, relaxed smile, but he sent, <Uh-oh.>

<Rather an imprecise statement for a SADE,> Alex replied via implant.

<Your pardon, Alex, but Nyslara wishes to know when and where Dassata and his soma will build their nest structures.>

<Well, oh omniscient one, it appears the time that you thought you had to decide your next steps expired during midday meal. How fleeting time has become,> Julien quipped.

<This is getting to be more difficult than negotiating with the Confederation Council,> Alex shot back.

<Yes, peace is much more complicated. It's so much simpler to use our warships and win our way with military and technological power,> Julien remarked drily. The images he received from Alex, to which he didn't reply, made him smile — his friend was back.

<Willem, stall,> Alex sent.

"Dassata hasn't decided that," Willem replied diplomatically, and, much to his relief, the queens accepted that answer.

Nyslara made another statement and several queens chimed in.

Willem smiled cordially again at Alex. "The queens you heard speaking, Ser, each wish you to know that you're welcome to build your personal structure at their nest's site. Apparently, your presence near them will ensure their nest's protection."

"First, Willem stop smiling like that when the questions get tough," Alex said, turning his own strained grimace on Willem. "It's creepy. Second, time is running short. We have the queens' agreement to our requests. We need to conclude the Fissla with those things that temporarily satisfy the queens. Let's focus on those."

For the remainder of the day, the discussion went back and forth. Alex insisted on a greeting ceremony with the ceena. Nyslara thought the others would object, but since many queens had never met a live ceena, they were quick to agree.

Alex committed to building forty-one structures so that each nest could leave its tunnels and return to the light. In the minds of the queens, they saw their soma learning the ways of the Harakens and traveling between worlds, as the stories once said they'd done. While the subject of technology transfer was never specifically discussed, it was what the queens believed was going to happen.

As to where Dassata and his soma would live on Sawa Messa, the queens never asked the question again.

* * *

The following morning, one day earlier than the queens agreed the Fissla must end, Haraken travelers landed on the plains, and the crew and passengers waited inside for Nyslara's signal that the queens were ready for transport.

The Harakens, through the ships' controllers, observed a queen and her wasat separate from everyone else. Emissaries fetched pails of water from Nyslara's lookouts for their principals. The entire Dischnya assembly stripped and patiently wet brushed their clothing, laying them out in the morning rays to dry. Next, the wasat carefully washed his queen from head to toe, with a cloth and a fresh pail of water. Afterwards the wasat and his nest's warrior repeated the processes on each other.

"It would appear that a queen doesn't want her or her soma's scents to be contaminated by that of the other nests," Julien remarked.

"Perhaps that has something to do with what the queens were explaining about their concerns for returning to their nests sooner than later," Willem added.

"And it explains why they can't be housed together in facilities separate from their soma," Renée finished.

"The question is this: What happens to the soma of a nest if they're left too long without the scent of a queen?" Alex asked.

"I thought I was supposed to be the one asking the tough questions in Tatia's absence," Julien said, pretending disappointment.

"Do SADEs slow as they get older?" Alex asked innocently. He received an image of him walking. The figure slowed to a crawl, froze in midstep, and then morphed from young to middle-aged and on to elderly. Finally, the image cracked and crumbled to dust.

Alex returned Julien's last image. An enormous pitcher of water poured over the dust pile and the figure of Alex reconstituted itself, larger-than-life and quite heroic looking. Wind ruffled his longer-than-usual hair in a romantic fashion, and stars twinkled behind him.

<Must be special nanites in the water,> Julien remarked with a smile, and Alex patted his friend's shoulder.

Franz cued the Harakens that he'd spotted Nyslara's wave, and Alex and his compatriots headed for the hatch. The Dischnya were washed, dressed, and stood waiting.

"If Dassata will allow it, the queens wish to be carried one at a time," Nyslara requested of Alex.

<This unique characteristic of the Dischnya's dependence on the scent of a queen should be studied,> Willem sent enthusiastically to Alex.

<One step at a time, Willem,> Alex cautioned.

"We have the time and will be pleased to accommodate the queens' request," Alex replied to Nyslara. "There are seven ships. Have the first seven queens and their soma board separate ships."

Willem supplied a translation, and Nyslara chattered to the queens. She'd no sooner finished than Homsaff barked a command and loped across the open space, her soma eating up ground right behind her. The young queen's destination was the ship that she'd seen Dassata disembark. Nyslara's lips wrinkled in humor.

<Young or old, human or alien … it's amazing the similarities,> Renée sent to Alex, and her laughter followed.

"The ships will return shortly," Alex said to Nyslara, and Willem pointed at Nessila and indicated a slight position change to indicate the amount of time before the ships could accommodate a second trip.

Nyslara nodded, and Willem hurried to catch up with Alex and the others, who were headed for their ships.

* * *

Young Homsaff stood by the hatch, desperately hoping Dassata came her way. Her newly appointed wasat whispered his advice into her ear, but Homsaff found it irritating. She didn't care if her actions were not those of a queen. In her mind, the Dischnya were about to diverge from their historic path, and she was determined to lead her soma in an entirely new direction — and Dassata was the link to that future.

Homsaff's heart beat excitedly, as Dassata walked her way, and gestured for her to enter the ship. She clambered up the steps and stopped in her tracks, her wasat bumping into her from behind. The rows of chairs were a great disappointment. While she didn't know what to expect, she hoped for something more exciting than this. Her wasat whispered she must move, and Homsaff walked along the aisle to the front, passing into a small chamber. Two aliens with heads of metallic bubbles turned her way, and a single huge dark eye in each bubble stared back at her. Homsaff hissed in surprise and leapt backward into the arms of her wasat.

Homsaff's wasat pulled her backward and took a seat in one of the chairs. Their emissary warrior sat across from him, and the commander spread his legs so that Homsaff could sit on his thighs, allowing her tail to fall comfortably between them. The young queen had considered speaking with Dassata, but that desire had fled. Instead, her mind swirled with the images of the strange creatures who sat at the front of the ship.

Lights dimmed, nothing happened, and soon the lights brightened. Dassata walked to the small chamber's entrance, standing not far from her, and one of the bubble-headed creatures emerged to stand beside him. Homsaff would have jumped up, prepared to defend herself, but her wasat held her firmly. The strange entity grabbed his head with both hands and sought to pull it free of his body. Homsaff felt her head grow light, and the morning's meal churned in her belly. Suddenly, a Haraken stood before her, holding the shiny bubble in his hand.

Homsaff struggled to rise, and her wasat released her. The Haraken extended the object to Homsaff, who examined it, inside and out. It appeared to be a shell, like that of an empty gourd.

Dassata began speaking, and Willem explained in Dischnya.

What Homsaff understood was that Haraken ships could see. How this was possible since there were no views to the outside, couldn't have been more confusing for Homsaff, although Willem stressed it was the ship that saw for the pilot. And she did comprehend that somehow the ship spoke to the pilot through the bubble he wore over his head. But, in the end, Homsaff wasn't interested in the technical explanations. The Harakens possessed power that Homsaff wanted for her soma. A pledge formed in the mind of the young queen. Her nest would follow Dassata.

When the bubble was again in the hands of the one Willem called the pilot, Homsaff followed Dassata down the aisle to the ship's doorway and he and some of his soma exited before her. *A poor beginning for me and my soma*, Homsaff thought, *if Dassata refuses to carry a young queen for a foolish reaction.* Homsaff's muzzle hung low as the doorway opened and the light of Nessila flooded into the ship. She was still looking down, embarrassed to face the queens, when she heard the hiss of her wasat behind her, and her head jerked up.

A quick scan on the plains by Homsaff revealed there were no queens and no tents. A lookout's port opened and three warriors flooded out, clutching their weapons. Homsaff was pleased to see her soma and would have run to be welcomed by them, but her wasat's sharp barks of command checked her, as it did the warriors, who skidded to a stop and laid down their weapons.

Homsaff turned to Dassata and dipped her head, keeping it lowered in respect and apology. She heard Willem's words from the Haraken leader — "Long life to you and may you lead your soma well." Homsaff nodded and with her wasat and emissary warrior in tow, she walked in what she considered was a queen's dignified manner to meet her warriors, thinking that learning the aliens' ways would be more challenging than she could imagine. Yet, the prospect of the journey thrilled her to the marrow and made her feel more alive than she could remember.

Julien, Renée, and Willem started to board the traveler, but they hesitated because Alex remained fixed on Homsaff.

"A problem, my love?" Renée asked.

"Watch," Alex replied.

When Homsaff drew near to her warriors, the Harakens could hear their whimpers. The queen held out her hands to them, palms down, and muzzles drew deep breaths from the scent of her hands. The wasat barked a command, and the warriors grabbed their weapons, yipping in excitement, and escorted Homsaff below.

"This phenomenon must be studied," Willem commented again.

Alex turned around and gave Willem his own version of a Dischnya smile, a lupine grin.

"The only thing that would make that expression more fearsome would be sharp teeth," Julien commented.

"I don't know about Willem, but I can't wait to hear this one," Renée added.

"It's this, Willem. Suppose you study this interdependence between the soma and a queen with an eye to solving the challenges of Dischnya crewing Haraken ships in the future."

"Oh, that's a good one," Renée said, laughing and touching a momentarily stunned Willem, as Alex, Julien, and she climbed aboard.

Willem hastily reordered his research priorities to accommodate Alex's request. The process created numerous ancillary streams of thought, and he came out of his fugue to find he stood alone on the plains.

<You coming or staying, brother?> Julien sent, and Willem hurried to board.

-25-
Peace Negotiations

The delivery of the queens and soma to their nests went without incidence, and that freed Alex to plan the next step in the peacemaking process.

Alex recalled Teague and Ginny to the *Rêveur*, since Pia insisted on him spending a minimal amount of time away from a medical controller and her. As she phrased it, "I'm not about to have you die on me from some post-op complication just because you were too long out of my sight."

Resting in his cabin, Alex's app detected the approach of his two guests, and he signaled the door open. His own greeting was interrupted when Renée stepped from the sleeping quarters, uttered a cry of surprise, and ran to hug her son and Ginny. Belatedly, Alex managed to get a hug from each of them. He sat down and waited while the three of them chatted for a bit.

"I imagine you're here at Alex's invitation," Renée said, as the conversation wound down. "Then we better let him get a word in edgewise." She smiled at her partner when she delivered her last line and curled up next to him on the couch. Deliberately, she sat on Alex's injured side. In some respects, she sought to protect that area, although the red, raw lines from the surgery were disappearing, the medical nanites doing their job. But, in other ways, she wanted Alex to feel that she wasn't frightened by his injury — although that was far from the truth.

"Tomorrow morning, the two of you are taking a traveler with our Swei Swee and security planetside. Franz will set the mission shuttle down on the shore where our foursome hid out. Based on Wave Skimmer's word, a member of his hive should be offshore, waiting for your signal."

"What do we tell him, Dad?" Teague asked.

"That you want a meeting two days from that time."

"What's our purpose, Dassata?" Ginny asked. She held back her grin when Alex narrowed an eye at her. "What?" she piped up. "I like the word and what it means, and, besides, everybody's using it."

"Everybody isn't using it," Alex strenuously objected, but when he glanced at Renée, his partner deliberately looked away. "Everyone?" he asked dubiously.

"Well, maybe not everyone, Dad," Teague said, trying to mollify his father. "The Swei Swee still refer to you as Star Hunter First."

Teague's meager efforts might have had more effect, if Renée hadn't burst out laughing and Ginny giggled.

"Enough, back to business," Alex said. "We're inviting the Swei Swee Firsts to a greeting ceremony with the queens or land hunter leaders, as the local People call them."

"You can't be serious, Dad?" Teague vehemently objected. "Why should the Firsts participate in a greeting ceremony with the queens?"

In the quiet that followed Teague's outburst, Ginny said quietly, "Because Little Singer will ask, if not demand, it of them."

Teague stared in confusion at Ginny.

Alex could see the shifting emotions in his son's face and readied himself, as Teague's confusion turned to anger.

"So that's the reason why we're here. You don't even need me. You just need Ginny," Teague accused, standing and pointing a finger at his father.

Renée would have taken Teague to task, but Alex signaled her to wait.

"I think you have your priorities confused, Teague," Alex said quietly. "I require Ginny's help to secure peace for this planet's Swei Swee, and she's willing to help me do that. The question is this: Are you willing to support her?"

Teague was taken aback by his father's words. Since he'd first met Ginny, he'd led and she followed. It didn't occur to him that, in the past few days, their roles had reversed. "Are you okay with this?" Teague asked Ginny, hoping she'd support his indignation over his father's plan.

"I'm wondering why you're not," Ginny retorted.

"I think you two may have things that you need to discuss ... privately," Alex interrupted. "Right now, I wish to know if my request will be honored."

"I will deliver the message," Ginny said solemnly. "How do I phrase it to whichever individual meets with us?"

"The Celus-5 People wish peace ... an end to the hunting of their hives. This greeting ceremony is how the Little Singer says that must happen."

Ginny rose and addressed Alex in a formal fashion. "Understood, Dassata." When Teague turned toward the door with a sullen expression on his face, Ginny stood in his way. "Don't you have something to say?" she asked. When Teague stared at her, at a loss for what she meant, she sent, <I'll wait while you apologize to your father.>

That Ginny was right didn't make Teague feel any better about it. His mind was swirling with the strange transformation in their relationship that he'd just recognized was taking place, when in reality it had begun years ago. Teague did manage to mumble an apology of sorts.

"We'll have to work on that," Ginny said brightly to Alex and Renée and hooked Teague's arm to lead the way out of the cabin.

Renée waited for the door to close and the two young people to walk out of earshot before she burst out in laughter, clapping her hands. "Oh, I've been waiting for this day," she said, jumping up and dancing around the room.

Alex grinned, watching Renée enjoying herself immensely.

"And I'd hoped it would be Ginny," Renée said breathlessly, as she plopped back down beside Alex. "Finally, a young woman has grabbed our opinionated son by the ears and given that hard head a fierce shaking."

"Personally," Alex said, staring at the door Teague exited and working to keep a straight face, "I'm feeling a little sorry for the boy. Strong-willed women can be overbearing."

"You didn't just say that," Renée said, rising to her knees. She thought to strike Alex in the shoulder, but remembered his recent wound. "You're fortunate that you're hurt, my foolish partner. Otherwise, I'd give you a lesson you wouldn't soon forget."

Alex grinned at his love. He reached over, picked her up by her hips, and set her across his lap. "If you believe you have the skills to correct my wicked tongue, you should try," he said, and kissed her until she forgot about his injuries.

* * *

During the return trip to the *Sojourn*, all was quiet in the traveler's main salon. Franz had flown Teague and Ginny over to the *Rêveur*, picked up Svetlana for the trip planetside tomorrow, and was transporting the youngsters back to the mission ship.

Orly was none too pleased at being replaced again as the premier pilot of the mission shuttle for the meeting with the Celus-5 People, but, knowing who would be aboard tomorrow mollified his frustration. *Besides,* Orly thought, knowing the young people would be speaking with one of the formidable Swei Swee, *I don't want to be the one to bring Teague home injured, or worse, dead.*

<Real quiet back there,> Franz remarked privately to Svetlana over the comm.

<Lovers argument,> Svetlana replied laconically. When Franz rotated his helmet her way, even though he couldn't see her eyes, Svetlana added, <There can be love before there's sex.>

<Any idea what the argument is about and if it's going to affect our morning trip?> Franz asked.

<Hard to say. Eventually, it'll be over, and it'll end the same way.>

<And how will it end?>

<He'll be angry; she'll be upset. He'll make demands; she won't agree. He'll give in; she'll forgive him.>

Franz was quiet while he digested Svetlana's words. He thought about his last argument with Reiko, his partner, and was a little surprised to discover an eerie similarity. <But it's not always that way,> Franz finally objected.

<It usually is if the two people love each other,> Svetlana replied.

<How about you, Svetlana? Ever been in love?>

Franz waited, but he never received a reply. Svetlana kept her silence. No one Franz knew had discovered Svetlana's history prior to her landing on the Libran Independents colony.

* * *

Svetlana would eventually be proven correct about Teague and Ginny — just not for a while.

After exiting Franz's traveler, Ginny hurried to the Swei Swee's quarters. The foursome climbed out of the circulating tank to greet her. The medical specialists had pronounced them fully rejuvenated after their long period of deprivation.

"We're going planetside tomorrow," Ginny told them. "The Star Hunter First has a proposal for the People of Celus-5."

"Alex Racine will protect the hives," Bobs A Lot rejoiced, his whistles sounding off the walls of the chamber.

"But only if they accept the proposal," Teague commented, leaning back against a food dispensary.

Sixteen eyestalks turned to regard Teague's sullen manner.

"What must the hive Firsts do to achieve a peace?" Whistles Keenly asked.

"The Firsts must meet the land hunter leaders, who are called queens, in a greeting ceremony," Ginny replied. She'd tried to make it sound simple and positive, the way Alex stated it. But the immediate drooping of eyestalks told her that she wasn't successful.

"Why would the Firsts trust the land hunters?" Swift Claws whistled.

"That's what I asked," Teague replied defiantly. Ginny shot him a hostile look, which Teague returned.

"Haven't our brief encounters with the land hunters shown them to be dangerous and untrustworthy?" Sand Flipper asked.

"The four of you have missed a great many events while you were recuperating," Ginny whistled. She spent the next hour, bringing the Swei Swee up to date.

"I'm relieved that Wave Skimmer refused Nyslara's offer of sacrifice," Whistles Keenly said. "Otherwise, it would have shown that the People on this planet had deviated from the teachings of the past."

"I think every Haraken would have been shocked if Nyslara was sacrificed," Ginny whistled. "Tomorrow, it's our job to convince whoever is monitoring the shore to take a message of hope to the hives, and we must not fail." Ginny hoped to galvanize the Swei Swee or, at least, to impart a sense of the possibilities. Instead, she saw eyestalks retracted halfway, and most of them were pointed Teague's way. He'd said little, but his body language, which the Swei Swee could read as well as any, said too much.

* * *

After morning meal, Ginny grabbed a small pack and hurried to the *Sojourn*'s landing bay. She hustled through the airlock and clambered aboard the mission shuttle. Her implant count revealed the two pilots, the twins, security, and the four Swei Swee.

<We can liftoff and proceed planetside, Commander,> Ginny sent to Franz, dropping into a seat, a dejected expression on her face.

Franz picked up his helmet, but, before donning it, he eyed Svetlana.

"I didn't say if their tiff would be over by this morning," Svetlana shot back and pulled her helmet on.

Teague watched from the airlock, as the bay opened to vacuum and Franz lifted the traveler off the deck. Captain Azasdau informed him before morning meal that he wouldn't be accompanying Ginny planetside.

"This is my father's doing," Teague had replied hotly.

"I believe you meant to say, Is this my father's doing, Captain?" Asu replied, his eyes boring into those of his journey crew member.

It took a moment for Teague to rein in his temper. Ever since his father had arrived, he seemed to have lost his way. Nothing was going right. It wasn't that he could blame his father for the unfortunate circumstances of the mission. *But why did it require Dad to come here and untangle the mess?* Teague thought with frustration.

"To answer your question, Ser, not that, as captain, I'm required to respond to your poorly phrased request, but your father didn't have anything to do with you being removed from the planetside trip this morning. Journey crew member Ginny requested that you be left behind. As she stated it to me, you would prove disruptive to the mission that she was carrying out for Dassata.

So, Teague found himself staring through the airlock's plex-shield, as the traveler carrying his human and Swei Swee friends left him behind. Tears blurred his vision, but, after the bay doors closed, he was careful to wipe them away and dry his eyes before he left the airlock.

* * *

The survey shuttle's primary access was through the rear, and the narrow, steep beach placed restrictions on how the traveler could set down. Franz chose to place the ship 90 degrees to the shore. The bow was meters out in the waters, hopefully allowing sufficient room for the ramp to drop and clear the embankment.

"That was my first wet landing," Franz remarked with a grin.

Svetlana broke out in a hearty laugh but refused to take the bait. Instead, she exited the pilots' cabin, slapping Franz lightly on the shoulder, as she passed. Her job was to ensure the rear ramp would clear the steep cut behind the ship. She cracked the ramp about 15 degrees, looked through the opening, and determined the hatch had sufficient space to drop. Then she stood by the open sampling doors for the ready signal.

Security and the crew were eyeing Ginny, who announced firmly, "It'll just be the four Swei Swee and me out there. We don't want to scare off whoever is on lookout." She glanced at the twins to see how they were reacting. Unfortunately, the crèche-mates were gently shaking their heads in the negative.

"Then how about just one of you?" Ginny asked, gesturing at Étienne and Alain. Met with another dismissal, she eyed Captain Escobar for help.

"We'll all be out there," Xavier said.

"I'm supposed to be in charge of this mission," Ginny objected.

"Is that what Ser said?" Étienne asked.

"He made me responsible for delivering a critical message to the Celus-5 Swei Swee," Ginny pointed out.

"And that is your mission objective, Ser," Alain said politely. "Just as it's our duty to keep everyone, including you and our Swei Swee, safe."

"We'll try not to interfere with what you have to accomplish, Ginny," Bethany said, "but your safety comes first."

Svetlana eyed the group. "I take it that, despite the contention, an agreement has been reached?" she asked tartly. When she received assurances, especially Ginny's nod, she lowered the ramp.

Ginny whistled to the Swei Swee, and security stepped aside to let the foursome scuttle past. The moment the foursome hit the sand, they loosed tweets and whistles and raced toward the breaking waves. Ginny's signal to halt brought them up short.

With security spreading out behind her, Ginny decided to take a page from Dassata's playbook. Alex was a master at accomplishing things by making up the rules as he went along. While it frustrated many people, who sought to protect him, it also enabled him to succeed when events were considered to be unachievable.

As Ginny closed on the water's edge, she hurriedly stripped out of her uniform, whistled shrilly to her four companions, and dove naked into the first wave.

Sand Flipper and Swift Claws were closest to Little Singer and heeded her call for transport. They shot into the wave just behind her, striking out with their legs and powerful tails. Coming up under her, they felt Little Singer grasp the front of their carapaces, and they pushed up until her head cleared the waters.

As Ginny broke the surface, her next whistle sent the Swei Swee stroking for the shelf and deep water.

<Do you believe the madman's essence might be catching?> Alain sent to his twin, watching the flashing white form of their principal, whom they were supposed to be guarding, disappearing out to sea.

<Oh, yes, look at us,> Étienne replied. He glanced over at his crèche-mate, who was slowly nodding his head in agreement.

Dives Deep floated at the edge of the shelf where the shallows' blue green waters fell off into the deep's dark blue. He'd just consumed a small meal and was content to watch the shore for a while longer before he needed to search for more sustenance.

When the ship dropped into view, Dives Deep's curiosity was piqued. He watched with interest, as the vessel landed onshore and the visitors flooded onto the sand. But his eyestalks extended to their fullest when Little Singer and the four small Swei Swee raced toward the waters and she called for her companions to make for the deep. With a kick of his massive tail, Dives Deep launched toward the approaching figure of Little Singer.

Ginny didn't have to signal her Swei Swee to stop. The looming, dark carapace of the large male managed that all by itself. She whistled a greeting and recognized Dives Deep by his response. Using her Swei Swee's carapaces for support, Ginny levered herself up in an attempt to appear more impressive, but Dives Deep with his enormous claws dwarfed her.

"I bring a message from the Star Hunter First for Wave Skimmer," Ginny whistled.

"Dives Deep listens."

"When the day brightens twice more, the Star Hunter First wishes the People's Firsts to assemble here onshore. The hives will have the peace they've asked him to deliver."

"Wave Skimmer will want to know how the Star Hunter First will protect the People."

"This will be done by a greeting ceremony."

"With the Star Hunter First?"

"No … with the land hunter leaders."

Dives Deep lowered himself into the water so that his eyes could closely observe the Little Singer. An aspect of Singers was that they spoke the truth in all things. "Why should this be?" Dives Deep whistled.

"It is how the Star Hunter First will bring peace to the hives," Ginny replied. There was a pause before she added, "It's what I wish the Firsts to do, if the hives wish to hear me."

"Little Singer did not say this before she made her offer to us."

"I'm saying it now," Ginny whistled stubbornly. "Tell Wave Skimmer that this is important, and this is how truces are made."

"I will deliver the message, Little Singer" Dives Deep replied. "Now you must return to the shore. These endless waters aren't the same as on your world. The hunters, who roam these dark waters, will take the likes of you and your companions in jaws that would consume you in quick bites."

"We've seen one of the hunters, Little Singer," Bobs A Lot whistled. "Dives Deep tells the truth. Our People could never swim in this planet's endless waters."

Ginny whistled a farewell to Dives Deep and signaled her companions to return to shore. As they rode the breaking waves, Ginny eyed those waiting on the sand for her. *This is going to be fun,* she thought, unhappy at facing her minders and explaining why she deserted them. But what truly gave her concern was the discussion she would have with Alex.

To Meet or Not

At Ginny's request, Alex met alone with her. He'd already received the reports of her actions at the beach from the twins and Xavier. While he was none too pleased at Ginny leaving her protection standing on the shore, he understood her passionate commitment to the Celus-5 People.

"Dassata," Ginny said, taking a seat at the table in Alex's stateroom aboard the *Rêveur*.

Alex could see that Ginny, despite her youth and her obvious nervousness, wanted an air of formality to their meeting. "Report," he replied, noticing his terse command eased some of the tension in Ginny's shoulders.

"I met with Dives Deep and told him of the greeting ceremony with the land hunters. I stressed that both you and I wanted the meeting to take place."

"How did he take it?"

"Not well," Ginny said, and much of her body posture seemed to melt. "I think I failed."

"Well, Dives Deep seems the more pessimistic sort within Wave Skimmers' hive. There's still hope."

"What have I done?" Ginny said, tears welling in her eyes. "I promised I would sing for them every evening."

"It was a rash thing to do," Alex agreed quietly.

"But if the Swei Swee don't make peace with the Dischnya, our people can't stay here and protect them forever. Sooner or later, our ships will have to leave. Then how am I supposed to survive here by myself?"

"Those are things that we have to think of before we make promises. There's always the option of leaving with us."

"And break my promise?" Ginny declared, some of her fire returning.

Alex smiled a little, as he said, "It was just a suggestion, Ginny. Besides, you're presuming I'd leave the peace process unfinished. Just because the Firsts might not show up in two days, doesn't mean they won't eventually agree to a greeting ceremony."

"So you would stay until the Dischnya and Swei Swee agreed to a truce and then leave?" Ginny asked, her hands twisting nervously in her lap.

Alex considered that Ginny had suffered enough for her ill-considered promise. "There's no way we would leave Celus-5 without you, Ginny, and I would never ask you to go back on your word. We'll find a way to settle this. That I promise."

Ginny jumped up and threw her arms around Alex's chest, as he stood up to meet her. She sobbed quietly, the anxiety she'd harbored, flooding out of her. When she let go of Alex, she tentatively brushed at the tear stains that streaked his coat. "Thank you, Ser," she added and raced out of the cabin.

The door to the sleeping quarters opened, and Renée joined Alex. She'd been party to the conversation via Alex's implant. "I'm beginning to see Julien's point about the complexity of this planet's problems."

"And you think they'll be too great to solve?" Alex asked.

Renée gave Alex a noncommittal "hmm" as she settled on the couch.

Alex stared at the door through which Ginny exited and thought with a smile, *Easy enough ... the bigger the problem, the greater the solution required.*

* * *

<Alex, you're requested in the lab as soon as you're able,> Mickey sent with urgency.

<Trouble?> Alex sent, as he exited the bridge and hurried to the lab where Mickey, Claude, and Emile had set up their myriad projects.

<Negative ... this is enormous news.>

Alex's rapid stride downshifted to a stroll, a grin breaking across his face at the thought of some good news. When he entered the lab, everyone — Mickey, Claude, Edmas, Jodlyne, engineers, and techs — was beaming.

But no one looked happier than Emile Billings, who looked ready to jump out of his skin in ecstasy.

"I'm all eyes, ears, and implants," Alex said, basking in the room's celebratory energy and looking at Mickey.

"This is Emile's show," Mickey said, waving a hand toward the biochemist.

"Yes, well," Emile said, clapping his hands. "Edmas, if you will?"

Edmas hurried over to a small plex container, which held a Swei Swee shell fragment connected to sensors. Edmas activated a controller, and a harmonic issued from its speakers.

"That, my dear Sir, is the fundamental sound of a piece of Swei Swee spit, as Mickey calls it, which the matrons replicate to form a traveler shell." Emile held up his hands to interrupt Alex, who drew breath to respond. "Admittedly, none of this is news to you, Sir. I'm stating the obvious so that you understand that the piece of material Edmas just tested is a true piece of shell, which we're using as our control."

Emile hustled over to a large plex container, which housed several items. "If you would come close, Sir," Emile requested. "In here, we have a substrate layer of nanites. Above it is a sprayer, with our invented mixture. The harmonic that Edmas generated from our control piece was fed into this controller," Emile said, patting another device like it was his child. "Now, observe."

The sprayer moved quickly depositing a layer of gray substance over the nanites substrate. As it did, an ugly tone pulsed out of the controller, which Emile attenuated. The sprayer kept sweeping across the substrate, building a thicker and thicker layer. As it did, Mickey brought up the controller's output volume. Gone was the dissonant sound, replaced by a single tone.

The sprayer kept at it, and the tone shifted to a more complex harmonic. Alex, who had been leaning against a bench, straightened up and approached the plex container. He looked questioningly at Emile, whose grin was big enough to split his face. When Alex glanced at Mickey, the engineer nodded in agreement at his suspicions.

A final harmonic issued from the controller just as the sprayer halted. Alex compared the second sound to the control tone recorded that in his implant. His wave analysis app declared the two harmonics to be identical.

"Wait, Ser," Jodlyne said, hooking an arm in Alex's to prevent him from missing the final step. "It gets better. Watch."

Alex smiled briefly at Jodlyne, Edmas' rescued orphan girl, who appeared as far from that lost waif as you could possibly get. He focused his attention on the sprayed material, as its glossy sheen disappeared and then slowly changed from a flat gray to a smear of color. The single tone of color separated into blue, green, and cream streams, which wandered across the material until they were fixed in place.

When Alex started to speak, Emile held up a single finger, requesting more patience. It wasn't long to wait before a fine dust fell from the bottom of the sprayed material. "The original nanites substrate," Alex guessed, and Emile nodded enthusiastically. "So you and this team have reproduced the Swei Swee's method of layering up a shell?" Alex asked to confirm what he'd witnessed.

"Yes," Mickey shouted, and the room erupted in a chaos of cheers and celebration.

Alex was focused on Emile, who couldn't have been more content with the room's recognition.

"Congratulations, all of you! And, most of all, to you Emile," Alex said, shaking the biochemist's hand. "Do you see any challenges to scaling this up to provide a shell for a ship?"

Emile looked at Mickey, who nodded toward Edmas.

"With Mickey's help, I've already worked up the schematics for the construction process," Edmas replied. "We'll need complete isolation. So, it would be ideal to build this at an orbital platform, where we can use vacuum to keep the spray chamber clear."

"What's your time estimate for laying up a traveler?" Alex asked.

"Okay, who wins?" Jodlyne asked.

"I do," Mickey said, smiling at Alex. "Just won a nice bet, Ser, thanks to you jumping forward so quickly to the practicalities of our invention."

"Glad to be of help, Mickey. And the answer to my question?"

"Once we have the ship's girds assembled, the internal equipment installed, and the nanites substrate in place, we can lay up the shell in about three days," Edmas said, grinning.

"Three days," Alex repeated, shaking his head. Emile's invention was transforming. Only the Harakens with the help of their Swei Swee could produce grav-driven ships with the People's incredible shells. Now, anyone who possessed this technology could do it. Alex was aware that everyone in the room was ready to celebrate, but his mind was busy considering the opportunities.

<Take a breath, people,> Mickey sent to the room's occupants, except for Alex. <Judging by our leader's face, I think we just skipped past the celebratory stage and have entered the realm of possible new futures.>

Alex came out of his musing. This time, he regarded Emile with a serious expression. "You'll be an extremely wealthy man, Emile."

"That all depends," Emile said, returning Alex's determined look with one of his own.

"Whether you start a company on Haraken or license the tech, either way, you're going to make a fortune," Alex replied.

Billings grinned at Mickey, whose grin was even wider. "This is for whatever you want to do with it, Alex," Emile said, laughing at the secret the room held back.

Alex glanced around the room in confusion. The laughter was loud, and people were clapping their hands in glee at Alex's look of surprise.

"Sir, the Harakens rescued my family and me when my future on New Terra looked hopeless," Emile explained. "As far as we're concerned, you're owed everything, and there isn't a person in this lab who doesn't owe you for the new lives that you've given us, although Mickey might have only been saved from a life of boredom."

Mickey chuckled and nodded his head in agreement.

"This was a group discussion," Emile added. "We thought of gifting this invention to the Assembly, knowing it was a world changer. But, one of us suggested that we talk to others for some advice." Emile glanced toward Jodlyne, who had wandered next to Edmas and was leaning against his arm.

"The advice of Renée, Julien, Z, and many others was that this invention was best placed in your hands, Alex. You better than anyone would know what to do with it."

"Congratulations, Alex," Mickey said, slapping him on the shoulder with a resounding boom. "You're the proud possessor of the capability to construct artificial Swei Swee shells in mere days, without the involvement of a single matron."

Alex stood dumbfounded, as first Emile and then every individual in the room shook his hand and wished him success with the invention's future.

"Of course, Alex, you'll need the expertise of those here to scale up your new discovery into practical solutions, and we'll require some piece of the new enterprise," Mickey said, grinning, as Alex turned to leave.

"Of course, you will," Alex replied good-naturedly, his mind whirling with the incredibility of what had transpired.

Alex walked in a fog to his cabin. He did have the presence of mind to send a quick message to Mickey and Emile, requesting they and their teams keep the invention a secret for now, and they agreed.

Entering the salon, Alex sat heavily on the couch, lost in thought. Within moments, Renée flew through the cabin's door. "Did you get your present?" she asked gaily, but stopped in her tracks when she saw Alex's face. She snuggled next to him on the couch. "Didn't you like your present?" she asked.

"I'm not sure," Alex replied quietly. "The implications of this invention are enormous. Harakens have held the upper hand, economically and militarily, because only we could manufacture travelers and sting ships. It was our choice to sell the travelers as shuttles and limit the sale of fighters and warships. What happens if and when this tech ends up in the hands of societies that have no desire to live in peace with their neighbors?"

"Why do you think they handed their invention over to you, Alex?" Renée said, gently slapping his shoulder. "They know the incredible power of their creation, and it frightens them. That's why they asked for advice, and your people couldn't think of anyone better to shoulder the responsibility than you." Renée jumped off the couch, striding toward the sleeping quarters. "Didn't I tell you?"

"Tell me what?" Alex asked, with little attention for Renée's question.

"That the universe was waiting for you ... first this planet and now Emile's discovery. How loud does it have to shout before you listen?" Renée watched Alex return to his musings, and she took off a boot and threw it at him, the soft material striking him on the chest. When Alex looked up, she said, "If you're going to be inattentive, you can, at least, do so in the refresher, scrubbing my back." Renée gave him a bright smile and headed into the sleeping quarters.

As Alex climbed off the couch and followed Renée, Z commed Julien, <Does he know?>

<Yes,> Julien replied. <He's asked the inventors to keep it quiet.>

<I'll inform the SADEs to do so too,> Z replied. <How's he taking the announcement?>

<Not well, according to Renée,> Julien replied. <I wonder if it wouldn't have been better if Emile had been unsuccessful in his endeavors.>

<For the briefest tick of time, I considered the SADEs the better arbitrators to determine the use of this new technology,> Z sent. <We could envision many more potential futures than humans could ever imagine, but then I wondered what would we use for a guide to feel our way through the choices? In the end, I made a decision, which was illuminating at its core, and it was something I thought to never admit about humans ... better Alex carry this than us.>

<On that, my brother, we're in complete agreement,> Julien replied.

* * *

The day after Ginny's meeting with Dives Deep, Alex boarded a traveler for a trip planetside. He took a minimal entourage, intending to discuss with Nyslara how best to entice the queens to the Swei Swee greeting ceremony.

Franz floated the traveler 20 meters above the ground, while his passengers chatted. It gave the Tawas Soma lookouts time to notify Nyslara and for her to respond. When Alex picked up on two warriors emerging from a familiar tunnel location, he signaled Franz to land.

The twins and Xavier were happy to see that the lookouts weren't carrying any visible weapons, but disappointed that Alex was quick out of the hatch, leaving his SADEs and security to catch up.

<What part of caution does our madman not understand?> Alain sent to his crèche-mate, as he leapt lightly to the ground, forgoing the hatch steps, and ran after Alex.

<Possibly he believes only one misfortune will befall him per planet, and he's had his brush with death,> Étienne retorted, catching up to Alex at a sprint.

The lookouts propped the tunnel's hatch open for Nyslara and Pussiro, who bounded out and loped across the intervening distance with ease.

Much to security's concern, warriors from several other tunnels poured out onto the plains and came running with their ground-eating stride.

<Relax, people,> Alex sent to his company, as the crowd of aliens rushed at them.

<You'll have to instruct me later as to exactly how you expect us to accomplish that,> Xavier shot back, easing his hand away from his stun gun with a great deal of willpower.

Nyslara skidded to a stop in front of Alex and dipped her head. "Dassata, Fellum, Julien," she said, greeting the three primary Harakens.

"Nyslara, I wish to discuss how best to gather the queens and meet with the leaders of the ceena hives to declare a truce," Alex said.

The queen and her wasat listened patiently to the entire translation, having to ask Willem several questions of their own before they caught the gist of Dassata's message. When they did, both of them hissed, and Nyslara's warriors unconsciously bent their knees in a defensive crouch at their queen's reaction.

"Explain," said Alex, which Willem translated for Nyslara, as, "Dassata sees the queen's displeasure and asks the reason for it."

Nyslara responded through Willem with, "The queens took bold steps to meet in the Fissla, and judgment was rendered on a queen and her soma for their treachery. These events are unknown in the many annuals since the nests first broke apart after landing."

"The meeting with the ceena is important for this world," Alex replied.

Nyslara spent a good amount of time speaking with Willem, and Alex caught the names of several queens, but not much else.

"Nyslara understands the meeting is important to Dassata," Willem said. "She recently spoke with Sissya and Homsaff. Prior to their discussion, Sissya spoke with two other queens, who border her nest. Nyslara says that the mood of the queens is that they wait for Dassata."

"Wait for what, Willem?" Alex asked.

"They wait for proof of Dassata's words," Willem replied, "which I take to understand means our construction of buildings for the nests so they can live above ground. Nyslara also speaks of the Dischnya being elevated to their rightful place."

"The first part I get. What's the last part?" Alex asked.

"My guess is that the queens expect to share in our technology so they won't remain mired in their simplistic tech," Willem replied.

"Looks like the Dischnya half of the greeting ceremony is off," Alex said quietly.

Nyslara watched Dassata with expectation. She had great hopes for a liaison with the Harakens, but their leader seemed unsatisfied by her pronouncements. Yet, to see evidence of his words was, in her mind, a fair trade for the queens' willingness to end their strife.

<What now, Alex?> Julien sent.

<Good question, my friend. I'm not sure,> Alex replied.

As the silence continued, Nyslara glanced at Pussiro, who tapped his temple with a hard nail, indicating the Harakens were talking with their minds. This gave Nyslara cause for concern. Something was amiss, and that wasn't good for the Dischnya.

Nyslara huffed to attract the Haraken leader's attention and spoke rapidly to Willem.

"Nyslara offers to attend the greeting ceremony with the Swei Swee and apologize for the absence of the queens," Willem translated. "She intends to tell them that the queens wait for the fulfillment of Dassata's bargain before they can take this next step."

"Tell Nyslara that I accept her offer and will come for her tomorrow morning," Alex said. He waited for the queen to nod her acceptance of Willem's words, and then he pivoted and marched back to the traveler.

-27-
Busted Ceremony

Word circulated fast through the fleet that the truce process was crumbling. Ginny's estimation that the Swei Swee Firsts wouldn't show was now compounded by the Dischnya queens' refusal to attend. No one was happy with the circumstances.

Winston and the other SIF directors communicated privately with Confederation SADEs seeking their input. Captain Shimada talked to the other captains about possible exit plans.

On the other hand, Willem campaigned for extending the mission's time, citing the tremendous amount of data that could be gathered, but security constantly threw up blocks, reminding Willem of the traveler's netting, the capture of their people, the deaths of two mission scientists, and the attempt on Alex's life.

The only one who wasn't talking to anyone was Alex. He kept his own counsel, as he studied the predicament, looking for a way to achieve the goals required to create a lasting truce between the two resident species. Alex could envision the resources he required, but he just couldn't see a way to bring those disparate elements to bear on Celus-5.

In no time at all, Alex was back aboard a traveler and headed planetside to pick up Nyslara. She must have been waiting near the tunnel exit, because Franz had no sooner touched down than the queen and her wasat hustled out of the tunnel and ran for the ship. Franz signaled the hatch to drop, and the Dischnya clambered aboard.

Nyslara marched to the front where Dassata stood waiting for her, and Pussiro took up a position behind her.

During the short flight, the discussion between the major parties focused on trivial things. It seemed no time to bring up weighty matters.

When the lights brightened, the Dischnya swiveled around and headed for the exit, demonstrating they were becoming old hands at travel by Haraken ships. Nyslara was having daydreams of one day possessing alien vessels with her soma, who would be trained to fly them, although she hadn't yet made the leap to envisioning the Dischnya traveling between worlds and living in space. Dassata's soma exited the shuttle before her, but she found that appropriate — a queen shouldn't be first into a new space.

Alex and Ginny led the assembly to the edge of the calm waters, which gently lapped at the beach. Teague had been left behind again at Ginny's request. The two of them had yet to have a serious conversation, and Ginny didn't want to be distracted at this critical time.

Wave Skimmer's eyestalks and mouthparts were just above the surface. He watched the shallows-colored ship descend, and the Star Hunters walk the sands. All four eyes focused on the presence of two land hunters. This time, one of them was male. A quiet warble escaped his mouth, and Dives Deep, Long Eyes, and he launched toward the beach.

This was Pussiro's first view of the ceena in their environment. The creatures appeared large to him until they reached the shallow waters and levered themselves up. Then they appeared overwhelming. He involuntarily edged backward, but a hiss from Nyslara stopped him in his tracks.

When the three, Celus-5 Swei Swee reached the shore, they extended themselves fully on their walking legs and focused on the land hunters, not on Alex or Ginny.

<Say nothing,> Alex sent to Ginny. <Wave Skimmer is being rude.>

The moments dragged on. Nyslara stared at the giant ceena in front of her. She recognized intimidation when she saw it. Having met the ceena once before, this time she managed to contain her fears. Her concern was for her wasat, whose rapid breathing she could hear, and whose anxiety she could smell.

Wave Skimmer's eyestalks split. Two remained focused on the land hunters, and two swiveled to take in the Star Hunter First, who stared straight ahead toward the horizon. Little Singer was likewise ignoring them. Eventually, Wave Skimmer, who tired of elevating his walking legs to the fullest extent, lowered himself to the more comfortable bent-legged position. A quick warble to his companions caused the three of them to sidestep to the left to align in front of the Star Hunter First.

"The Star Hunter First greets Wave Skimmer," Alex whistled.

Wave Skimmer whistled his own greeting.

"Only one First chose to attend today?" Alex asked.

"We see only one female leader of the land hunters comes today," Wave Skimmer whistled in reply.

"Is it the decision of the Firsts that they will not offer a greeting ceremony to the land hunters?" Alex said, asking for confirmation.

"The Firsts don't trust the land hunters. The Star Hunter leader has promised protection for the People, and the Firsts wait to see how he will provide that."

Willem kept a running translation of the conversation between Alex and Wave Skimmer for Nyslara, and the queen recognized the same resistance from the ceena, as the chona offered Dassata. Faced with such reactions from both parties, she had visions of the Harakens loading into their ships and returning to their world.

"Your two species act as if they rule this planet," Alex said, switching to Haraken, and both Ginny and Willem translated. "The two of you should remind your peoples that you're all strangers to this planet. You didn't originate here."

When Wave Skimmer heard Ginny, he whistled indignantly. "The People were here first."

Willem had just finished the Swei Swee translation for Nyslara when the queen replied, "Perhaps not. Who inhabits the green?"

Alex glanced at Willem, who hadn't relayed Nyslara's reply. Willem's expression indicated he was in a fugue. Not again," Alex lamented. "What?"

Willem finished his review of the entirety of his Dischnya data before he replied. "Nyslara indicates that the Swei Swee might not be the first people on the planet," Willem replied. "She mentions the greens, which I take to mean the forests that border the plains to the north and south, and she indicates one or more species reside there."

"Do the People know of others who reside in the tall trees that border the shore?" Alex whistled.

Wave Skimmer warbled in confusion, asking Alex to clarify his request. In turn, Alex questioned the queen for more details, but it was her wasat who knew the old stories.

Pussiro related the events that took place soon after the Dischnya's first landings. On Sawa, their original home, the soma had preferred the open territories for their cities before the heat of Nessila forced them underground, where vast reservoirs of water provided support. As the first transports arrived on Sawa Messa, the nests dug deep wells in the plains searching for similar reserves of water. The wells were partially successful, but the soma never located the huge caverns filled with lakes of fresh water, as they had on Sawa.

Hoping to find abundant game in the tall greens of their new planet, hunters were dispatched by the first queens. As Nessila's light brightened and waned, the hunters, who had been sent out in pairs, never returned. Larger parties were sent to either recover the lost ones or discover what had happened to them, but they never returned. Fully a third of the first five nests to land were lost before a halt was called to sending hunters into the green, and the queens agreed that the space was to be placed off-limits to all soma. The nests would have to make do with the small animals that roamed the plains and the numerous ceena that inhabited the strip of land where the plains met the great waters.

"Are there any stories, Pussiro, told by the Dischnya of seeing the inhabitants of the forests coming out onto the plains?" Alex asked.

Nyslara and Pussiro both said they had heard of none.

"Could the hunters have been taken by a sickness?" Willem asked.

"Our warriors have great stamina," Pussiro replied. "If they had fallen prey to an illness, they would have struggled back into the open, but, according to the stories, none were ever seen again."

"A queen warns her heir that the green represents violent death to the Dischnya, and the soma are never to venture there," Nyslara added.

"Stories say the lookouts kept listening posts near the green and were to report any sounds of creatures, but I've never heard any tales that told of warriors hearing voices, speaking any sort of language," Pussiro continued. "The stories say that the warriors only heard the cries of animals and beasts that hunt them."

Alex looked up and down the seashore, trying to fit the pieces of information together. So much about this planet's recent history, as related to him, did not make sense.

"Wave Skimmer, where did the People build their dwellings?" he asked.

"Here where you stand, Star Hunter First," Wave Skimmer whistled in reply. "Many annuals ago, the shore extended several lengths farther into the waters. Soon after the hives were hunted and migrated into deep waters or caves, the sea bottom shook and cast a giant wave at the shore. The land and our dwellings were taken by the endless waters. Out where the shallows give way to the dark waters, you'll find the remains of our dwellings."

While Alex had been turning his head to regard the coastline, Long Eyes spotted the shaved portion of Alex's head and the faint red lines of his surgery. "Has the Star Hunter First been injured?" he warbled.

Alex's hand went to the site of the wound, but he shrugged in answer to Long Eyes' question.

"Dassata's injury was delivered by one of the queens and her wasat," Nyslara volunteered, after she heard the translation.

The Swei Swee rose high on their walking legs, alarmed by the news. "By whose claws?" Wave Skimmer demanded.

Alex sought to cut off this line of conversation, but his translators had their own thoughts on the subject and were busy supporting the exchange.

"Her name was Chafwa, and she broke the rules of the queens, bringing weapons to our meeting and attacking Dassata," Nyslara replied.

"Where's this leader now?" demanded Dives Deep, his whistle shrill and his hunting claws snapping.

"The queens passed judgment on her, her wasat, and her emissary warrior. They're dead," Pussiro replied.

When Willem provided the translation, the Swei Swee lowered their posture and regarded Nyslara with different eyes, tweeting their approval of the queens' decision.

Wave Skimmer's eyestalks bent to examine the shaved area on Alex's head, and he warbled humorously, "Hard like the shell of the People."

"It appears, Alex, people the worlds over have a common opinion about your skull," Julien remarked.

"If there's to be no ceremony, then we're leaving," Alex whistled.

A sharp whistle from Wave Skimmer halted Alex just as he turned around. "Little Singer promised the hives. We wish to know when she will sing."

Alex glanced at Ginny, who looked back at him before she faced Wave Skimmer. "If I sing to the hives tomorrow as the light fades, how will the People make it to safety in the dark of the night?"

Twelve eyestalks bent to stare at Alex, waiting for his response.

Boxed into a virtual corner, Alex relented and whistled his reply. "The Harakens will protect three coves of the shore … this one and one in each direction," he said, pointing up and down the coastline, "until such time as the People have a greeting ceremony with the land hunter leaders."

"That is not what Little Singer promised the Firsts," Dives Deep whistled angrily.

Alex walked over to stand directly in front of Dives Deep. His face was close to the Swei Swee's mouthparts, forcing the male to bend his eyestalks in a steep curve to keep Alex in sight.

"Little Singer is a youngling," Alex whistled so harshly that Dives Deep leaned away from him. "In the hives, do the younglings not make errors, and do the males and matrons not forgive them? She will sing for the hives, and I will protect three coves while she does."

Alex moved to stand close to Wave Skimmer, who, as a First, refused to be cowed by Alex's nearness. Whistling and warbling softly, Alex said, "Convince the Firsts that a greeting ceremony is in their best interest. One day, I'll forgive Little Singer her promise, as any First would forgive a youngling's mistake, and take our protection away."

Wave Skimmer's mind raced through the conundrum he faced. To enjoy the voice of Little Singer, the hives would need to relocate to the coasts where they once lived. They would be safe only as long as the Star Hunter First's people provided protection against the land hunters. But a sudden exit by Little Singer and her people would leave the hives defenseless. Many could die in the days it would take the People to move seaward again.

"Wave Skimmer forgives the promise of Little Singer. Younglings often whistle before they think," the First said. "The word will be passed to the other hives."

"Then the Harakens will protect the People until peace comes to this planet," Alex whistled softly.

Wave Skimmer warbled his humor. "A First always protects his younglings. Your message will be the more favorable one to send." The hives would lament the lost opportunity to hear a singer, but the promise of safety for one and all would be embraced.

When Wave Skimmer lowered himself until his belly was centimeters above the sand, Dives Deep and Long Eyes imitated him. The First extended his claws, the sharp points near Alex's midriff.

Nyslara watched Dassata deliver the same teeth-bearing expression to the massive male ceena that she had received when he was pleased with her. *A curious mannerism,* Nyslara thought.

Alex balled his fists and struck Wave Skimmer's claws with a loud thunk. Having been forewarned of the local Swei Swee's habit of returning the strike, Alex had the good sense to swing his hands down and aside as the Swei Swee's heavy claws smacked down on them.

Afterwards, the Swei Swee made for open waters, and Alex signaled his people to board.

* * *

The return flight for Nyslara and Pussiro was brief and quiet. When the interior lights brightened, Nyslara nodded to Dassata and led the way off the ship.

As the Haraken's vessel lifted, Pussiro watched it climb silently into the sky, his brow furrowed. "The more Dassata speaks, the more alien I believe him to be," he said to Nyslara. "He and his soma have simple choices. They could leave our planet or take it for themselves, but they do neither."

Nyslara too watched the ship disappear, lost in her own thoughts. "You and I are in agreement, Pussiro. I find Dassata's actions difficult to anticipate. In the beginning, I imagined him a powerful Dischnya so that I might determine his purposes. Now, I imagine him a pup, born without scent and grown to adulthood, who has no allegiance to queen or soma."

"But he has soma," Pussiro objected. "Willem tells of an entire world that follows him."

"He adopts soma, like our warriors shelter the mates and pups of those who fall in battle."

"So you believe Dassata to be a warrior?"

"The most terrible kind. He lives in here," Nyslara said, tapping her temple, "visiting you while you sleep and comes to you when you're awake if you've harmed his soma."

"What I find difficult to understand is how his soma are made of so many types."

"And soon to be many more."

"How so?"

"Do we and the ceena not already look to him for our future?" Nyslara asked. She turned and walked slowly toward the tunnel entrance where two lookouts stood by, and Pussiro kept pace with her. Both of them were alone with their thoughts of what might become of the Dischnya of Sawa Messa.

* * *

Alex and Julien faced each other aboard the traveler. Alex was lost in thought, and his unfocused eyes stared through Julien.

"I wonder if I understand our circumstances correctly," Julien said, breaking the silence. "The queens have temporarily halted their infighting, while they wait for a fulfillment of your promise to build structures to house forty-one nests ... an estimated 2,000 to 3,000 aliens, of whom we understand little of their needs."

When Julien saw Alex's eyes focus on him, he continued. "Three of our ships, explorer, warship, and liner, are overhead, and together they are ill-prepared to provide the labor or construction services the queens require. The Swei Swee hives have been promised protection, but unless we stay, again with our limited resources, we can't deliver on that promise."

Now that Julien had Alex's complete attention, Julien finished his list. "Now, we discover that someone or something, which probably originated on this planet, lives in the forest and is killing and possibly consuming the Dischnya. Have I forgotten anything?"

"Yes, one most important item," Alex said, appraising his friend with cool eyes. "Down below are three dark travelers. Since the Swei Swee are here, we can assume they and those ships came from the same Nua'll vessel that attacked the Confederation. Both species, Swei Swee and Dischnya, possess too little technology to inform us of the vector the sphere took on its approach into this system. But there might be someone who knows."

"So, does that explain why, under these most conflicting circumstances, we haven't packed up and left this world to its own problems?"

"It occurs to me that Nyslara's people on the next planet inward, Sawa, might have records of the sphere's approach. If we can bring peace to this planet and elevate the nests into the light, as Nyslara says, the queens might aid our communications with their home planet's people."

"You seem to have dwelt on the Nua'll's last signal, the one Cordelia picked up before the giant sphere detonated."

"And you haven't?"

"Admittedly, all Haraken SADEs frequently discuss new suppositions about the Nua'll sphere."

"I've worried for two decades about that message and its possible contents."

"Found formidable foe and extraordinarily rich worlds. Come quick," Julien intoned in a strange voice, surmising the words he would have sent.

"Exactly," Alex replied, "and myriad variations on that theme."

"And what if we were to discover from which direction the sphere originated?"

Alex uncrossed his arms and leaned forward. "Could be an opportunity for another expedition, a military one," he said, tapping Julien's knee to underline his words.

"I don't believe the Assembly would authorize that type of mission, Alex. They would be reticent to send their protective assets so far from home. And let's not forget that twenty years of relative peace and safety have done much to calm the people's minds and spirits."

"I quite agree. We'd have to form our own expedition."

"Our own expeditionary force? That would require an extraordinary amount of resources and time to develop."

"Hmm, yes. Yes, it would," Alex said quietly. He leaned back in his seat, and his attention drifted away.

Behind Alex and Julien, the twins regarded each other. <Stay or follow,> Étienne sent to Alain.

Alain knew what he was being asked. They were well-established and respected men on Haraken. But, despite that, administration of the plant's security forces was not what they were trained to do. <I believe the answer's obvious,> Alain sent back, and his crèche-mate grinned at him.

-28-
Realignment

Teague paced his cabin, still smarting from a conversation with his mother. Usually the more understanding and gentler parent, he'd been caught off guard by her forthrightness.

"You're acting less like my son and more like a stranger every day that passes, Teague, and your treatment of Ginny is abominable," his mother had said. "Quit your pacing, sit down, and offer me an explanation that I can understand."

"I don't understand Ginny anymore," he complained.

"Perhaps that's because you expect her to follow you around, as she used to do. But that's not what she wants. She wishes to be your companion, your equal."

"But how can she promise the People she would sing every evening without consulting me?"

"Why should she ask your opinion about what she wishes to do? And why can't you support her when she does make a decision on her own? As it is, Ginny won't have to sing every evening. Your father has seen to that."

"How do you know that?"

"How do you not know that, my son?"

Teague left his mother's cabin feeling as if he had tumbled off the crest of a tall wave to be pummeled into a rocky bottom. He tapped into the *Rêveur*'s controller to track Ginny's traveler, and when he saw it making for his ship, he decided to meet her in the corridor outside the bay.

Ginny exited the bay airlock beside Alex. When she saw Teague, she hugged Alex, whispered her thanks, and hung back to speak with Teague. It was the first time he had approached her since their argument began.

"I'm sorry," Teague said. "I've been told by everyone I know and some I didn't know that my behavior toward you has been extremely rude and foolishly stubborn."

"That's not true," Ginny said, the corners of her lips trembling, as she tried to hide a smile. "I haven't had the opportunity to add my voice to the list."

"Fine … tell me," Teague said with resignation.

"Not on your life," Ginny said, wrapping her arms tightly around Teague's neck and hugging him. "I'm just happy to have you talking to me again."

"I'm so sorry," Teague said into Ginny's pile of blonde curls.

* * *

Word circulated quickly across the fleet. The Swei Swee refused Alex's request for a truce. Those who crossed Alex's path were tapped by their fellow crew members and asked for a visual of their leader. Nearly everyone expected to witness dejection, mirrored in a strained face and weary steps. Instead, they were surprised, but pleased, to see an energetic Alex, who frequently disappeared into the *Rêveur*'s lab. The odd thing was that none of the humans were receiving any information or visuals from the lab or its goings-on. Unbeknownst to the crew, the SADEs ensured that.

It was two days after Alex's meeting with the Celus-5 Swei Swee when Reiko called for a conference of the entire fleet's principals. It was to be held in the *Sojourn*'s meeting amphitheater, the only place with enough seats to accommodate everyone.

Alex and the *Rêveur*'s people entered the amphitheater near the start time. Captain Lumley headed for the dais and the table where Reiko, Asu, and Willem sat. Alex scanned the front rows, but every seat was filled.

<My love,> Renée sent. <There appears to be a spare seat at the front table … the center one.>

Alex looked up at the table and caught Reiko's eye. The captain nodded her head toward the empty seat next to her, and Alex bussed Renée quickly before he strode toward the dais. He eschewed the steps on either side of the stage and leapt up the meter to the platform.

A group of Confederation SADEs, near the front, rose as one and proceeded to move to the amphitheater's rearward rows, and Julien guided Alex's people to take their places, sending his thanks to those who saved the seats.

Alex sat between Reiko and Asu, well aware that he was seated in the central position. "So who starts?" he asked, glancing left and right.

Willem nodded and stood up. "I'm speaking for Captain Azasdau and myself, as the original mission co-commanders. We believe the exploratory mission should continue, but we also believe this decision should be taken in concert with the many other ideas being circulated. This planet represents an incredible find of biodiversity and intelligent life. We would be remiss not to complete our original purpose for coming here."

Asu replaced Willem, standing to add a few words of his own, stating that the mission's crew, despite the loss of its two members, was in favor of continuing the research. In fact, it was because of the deaths of their friends that they didn't want to leave without completing the work they had traveled light-years to perform.

Reiko was next. "I find myself in a difficult position," she said. "I was given superior mission command to facilitate a rescue of the *Sojourn* and its crew, although some huge man and his compatriots seem to have taken care of that for me." Reiko's comments brought a ripple of laughter from the audience.

"The *Tanaka* is capable of the defense of the skies and nearby space," Reiko continued. "We're not outfitted to deploy a land-based force to maintain the peace between warring factions of Dischnya and prevent the hunting of Swei Swee. If the *Sojourn* votes to stay, then the *Tanaka* will remain to protect the ship, but only if the ground problems can be resolved to my satisfaction."

Alex's forearms rested on the table, and his face was stoic. The reminder of Reiko's eminent position was throwing hot plasma at his plans.

Winston rose from his audience seat. "If you don't know her, this is Trixie," he said, introducing the blue-faced SADE next to him. "She speaks for the Confederation SADEs, Ser Racine, except for the SIF directors, who are nonetheless sympathetic to their viewpoint."

Trixie rose and tipped her head to the front table. Her orange hair, pulled into a ponytail, swung forward, and she tossed her head to swing it over her shoulder. "We like this planet, Ser Racine. The SADEs who have recently immigrated to Haraken have shared their disappointment with the rest of us. They lament that they don't inhabit your sphere of influence, Ser, and haven't experienced the world-shaking events of your eight SADEs."

Alex was about to object to Trixie referring to the original Haraken SADEs as belonging to him, but she had already rolled on.

"Understandably, Ser, you don't view them in that manner, and we find that commendable, but they know they're unique and have earned a place in Haraken society. It's not the same for us. We're merely oddly appearing immigrants, and many of us now see our choice of avatars as an excess of celebration." Trixie raised her bare, blue arms, swung her orange ponytail, and smiled to accentuate her point.

"Our decision to follow you, Ser, and help with the rescue of the mission personnel has led to the discovery of a world full of opportunity. Here on Celus-5, all Harakens are aliens, no matter our appearances. In your role as Dassata, you've encountered intransigence with the Dischnya and the Swei Swee, who expect proof of your commitment before they will take further steps toward a peaceful coexistence. The Confederation SADEs stand ready to help you achieve your purposes."

"Are you aware that we've learned of a third dominant species on this planet?" Alex asked. It was a rhetorical question, but he wanted it out in the open.

"Yes, Ser," Trixie replied. "And we understand that it's not known the extent of this species' intelligence."

"And since we've barely explored a small percentage of the land mass and known waters, it's entirely possible that we might discover more intelligent life. There's a distinct possibility that the oldest of these might ask us to leave their world alone, and we would have no choice but to accede to their wish.

"This too is understood, Ser, but, if not this world, there's always an opportunity for another."

With that reply, another piece of Alex's puzzle clicked into place, and he smiled at the electric blue face.

Trixie beamed back at Alex, recognizing that what she had said resonated with the human, who was a significant asset in her and the other SADEs achieving freedom. She received a comm from every SADE, congratulating her on her choice of words. Trixie thought back to the vids she had reviewed in the *Rêveur*'s library. So much of her reasoning and phrasing originated from those stories, and she was determined to possess a copy of the entire collection, as soon as she had a sufficiently large enough data storage location.

"Let's return to your earlier statement, Trixie," Alex said. "How can the new SADEs help the peace progress?"

"It's obvious to us that you must leave, Ser." When Alex raised an eyebrow at her, Trixie explained by saying, "Analysis of the present situation reveals that you're without sufficient resources to accomplish your aims. Simple deductive reasoning indicates that you'll leave to gain those resources and return."

"Had you considered the possibility that I might leave and not return?"

"Yes, Ser. The probabilities were deemed too small to give it any consideration." When the audience laughed, Trixie looked around her, returning her bright smile. She hadn't meant to be humorous, and the audience's response to her words would require further attention, at a later time.

"It's our intention to remain here, Ser, and ensure, in your name, that the queens wait for your return without engaging in further conflict. We'll protect the Swei Swee and preserve the mission's safety." On the last note, Trixie directed her focus at Captain Shimada to underline the SADEs would provide the ground-based security the captain desired.

<Reiko, does the *Tanaka* carry enough stun guns to arm the new SADEs?> Alex sent.

<Negative, maybe one fifth of them,> Reiko replied.

"I'm informed by Captain Shimada that stun guns are in short supply. The majority of the SADEs would be vulnerable to the Dischnya's slug-throwing weapons," Alex said.

"If I may, Ser," Miranda said, rising from her seat. "If the mission and the new SADEs stay, Z and I will remain too. We've studied your style and know that our constant presence at the hives will do much to keep the queens patient. We're confident that we can manage the truce while you're gone, providing, of course, that you're not gone too long."

"You're aware, Ser, of our avatars' capabilities," Trixie said, alluding to the strength and speed that few humans were privy to. "Even unarmed, we can deter the initial instances when the Dischnya stray from the truce."

"Well, Captain Shimada, it would appear that you have the floor for the first response," Alex said.

"If our new SADEs, plus Z and Miranda, are willing to remain, protect the mission, and preserve the peace, then the *Sojourn*'s exploration can proceed, and the *Tanaka* will stay until relieved or recalled."

"I have one final question before we figure out who's staying and who's going," Alex said. "The question is for you, Trixie, and your companions. If we discover that Harakens can live on this planet, what do you intend to do here?" Alex watched Trixie enter a fugue, which suggested she was being inundated with comm exchanges between her fellow SADEs.

"Your pardon, Ser," Trixie said, apologizing for the delay. "The concepts are too numerous to enumerate, but the overarching request is to build a city."

"What type of city?" Alex asked, suspicious of seeing a reconstruction of the cubicle buildings the SADEs built on Haraken.

"A city that would welcome all intelligent beings," Trixie said. "Those who live on Haraken recognize the mistake of isolating themselves. On Celus-5, humans, Dischnya, Swei Swee, and SADEs would all be welcome."

"Is that the extent of your list?" asked Alex, a smile quirking one side of his mouth.

Trixie grinned in reply. "Ser Racine is, as usual, thinking of the future. Our new city would be open to any and all peaceful, intelligent species that Dassata discovers."

"Good to hear, Trixie," Alex said, leaning back in his chair, crossing his arms, and giving her a broad smile.

Winston stood, as Trixie sat. "It's the duty of the SIF directors to return to Méridien, despite our preference to join the others here. We'll be aboard the *Rêveur*."

<We'll be staying,> Ginny sent to Alex.

<And so you should, Ginny. Your work on the mission isn't complete,> Alex replied. He'd seen the pair aboard the traveler, talking and laughing, and was pleased with his partner's intervention with their son. Renée, who wasn't pleased to play the part of the heavy, had told him that it was an easier conversation to have than she thought. She had looked him square in the eye and said, "I just recalled my time with a younger Alex, and it all came back to me."

The remainder of the meeting dissolved into exchanges of who was staying and who was going. In the end, Alex was carrying a meager number back with him. Franz would stay with the *Tanaka*, but Alex would get Svetlana. Mickey, Emile, Edmas, Jodlyne, the engineers, and the techs working in the lab would remain aboard the *Rêveur*.

Z with Miranda and Claude's support transferred his collection of avatars to the *Sojourn*, where the two SADEs would stay. Claude was returning with Alex.

Julien, Cordelia, and the twins, of course, stayed with Alex.

* * *

The fleet took two days to reorganize, transferring people and equipment.

Immediately after the amphitheater meeting, Willem descended planetside with groups of SADEs, visiting each queen who had attended the Fissla and explaining Dassata was leaving to procure the resources he needed to fulfill his commitments. He told them that in the meantime Harakens would be stationed around the nests to ensure the truce. For the most part, the queens invited the Harakens to live inside and were surprised when Willem said they would remain outside. "Be aware, these Harakens can call our ships at any time," he told them, tapping his temple.

Four SADEs were left on the perimeter of each nest, requiring a full 164 of their number. The only queens who required some persuasion were those seven who refused to attend the Fissla. Z led the entourage for the visits to the seven recalcitrant queens and was often required to yank a lookout's locked tunnel hatch from its hinges.

In four cases, the soma immediately obeyed the Harakens' request to speak to the queen, who recognized when she was outmatched by the aliens. But, in three situations, the warriors fought with intensity, and the SADEs backed off. Extra SADEs were deployed at those three nests, and each one carried a stun gun, which, over the course of time, was used frequently to discourage warriors, who foolishly executed forays during the night against their minders, expecting the aliens to be unaware of them in the dark.

Z, Miranda, and Trixie kept in constant contact with the SADEs planetside to ensure the peace was being maintained. It was noted that not one group of hunters from Tawas Soma or Mawas Soma made for the shores. Nyslara and Homsaff were honoring their promises to Dassata.

It was the nest lookouts who were the most perplexed by the Harakens. Through their scopes, they watched the individuals stand their posts, never moving, except for their heads, which slowly and constantly swiveled from one side to the other. They stood there, silent and unmoving, enduring the day's heat, the night's cold, and the occasional rains and dust storms.

Since the SADEs were completely engaged with the nests, Reiko employed three travelers to guard the shores. The ships hovered above the shoreline at each of the three bays Alex proclaimed as protected, pointed bow first toward the plains and clearly visible to the lookouts of the six closest nests.

Reiko needn't have been concerned. There was no intention among the queens of the Fissla to hunt the ceena. As far as they were concerned, Dassata was more intimidating than the alien ships.

Haraken

When the *Rêveur* left the planet's orbit, Captain Lumley set a course inward toward Celus so that Alex could conduct the star services for Edward and Ullie. Julien broadcast the event to the fleet, as the crystal-canopied coffins were ejected from the bay, and the Harakens sent their first offerings to fuel the system's star.

Edward's services hit Alex particularly hard. The Harakens received only a few Earthers, a handful of elderly scientists and one ex-commodore, and it was unlikely that their society, in his lifetime, would benefit from other Sol emigrants. Now that precious number was one less.

Immediately after the services, Alex gathered some key individuals in the captain's cabin — Renée, Julien, Cordelia, Francis, Mickey, Emile, and the twins — and explained his plan on returning to Celus-5.

"I'm confused, Alex," Mickey said. "Are you saying you intend to live permanently on that planet?"

Alex glanced at his partner, who smiled warmly at him.

<I go where you go, my love … anytime and on any adventure,> Renée sent.

"I don't think I'll be living anywhere, permanently, for a long time, Mickey. I thought after my presidency ended that I could enjoy some retirement time, but that seems to have been a nice daydream."

"It's those dark travelers, isn't it?" Emile asked. "I've heard the stories from just about every ex-crew member that ever served with you. They're haunted by their memories of that massive sphere too."

When Alex agreed with Billings, Étienne asked, "Are we going hunting, Ser?"

"Eventually, I will. We have Cordelia's original vector from Libre, and we have a known point where the Nua'll sphere stopped, namely Celus-5.

If there remain records on Celus-4, kept by the Dischnya, we might get a vector toward their previous location, possibly their home world."

"The odds of that are quite improbable, Alex," Cordelia said.

"Yes, yes, they are," Alex admitted. "But consider this: What if the sphere's message home warned of a powerful enemy? What weapons do you think a second sphere would carry when it arrived in the Confederation, years from now? And remember that it's Haraken that lies on the Confederation's periphery and is the first in line with the sphere's previous approach vector. I would rather spend my life hunting the Nua'll than waiting for them to arrive in our home system, carrying even more incredible technological prowess."

There was no assailing Alex's argument, which silenced everyone. When Alex thought he'd given them enough time to absorb his plan, he interrupted the quiet. "There's one important point here. This is the path that I'm choosing. No one in this room, save for my lovely and delectable partner," to which Renée stood and delivered an impromptu curtsy, "should feel a need to follow me."

Alex's statements were met with soft laughter, which ignited others, and soon the entire room was roaring loudly, except for Julien and Cordelia, who merely wore wide grins and were incapable of the tears pouring from faces of those laughing hardest. The only exceptions to the demonstration were Renée and Emile.

When the room quieted, Alex said, "A simple affirmation of your intent would have sufficed," but his quiet grin showed his appreciation of their support. "I take it that you're out, Emile."

"Oh, no," the biochemist replied. "I just wasn't sure whether it was appropriate for me to laugh, but I'm definitely following you. Too much happens in your wake not to want to be part of it."

Emile's comment drew more laughter and smiles from the room full of friends.

"There's the small matter of a significantly sized labor force, materials, equipment, et cetera, the usual civilization-starter items, which would be required to construct and crew a powerful military expedition, which could take on the Nua'll home world. One can only imagine the forces that might surround their system," Julien said.

"Yes, I was thinking on that, my friend, and I'm glad you brought it up. Just how many credits do the Exchange directors have? I might need to borrow some."

Julien was sure that Alex's question was meant to elicit a conversation, but he wasn't sure what direction it would take. So, he waited.

"Furthermore, how much do you think the Assembly would charge me for a used city-ship?" Alex grinned at his friend and slapped his shoulder with such a resounding thwack that even the New Terrans shuddered, as the sound reverberated throughout the room. "Meeting's over, people, keep the news to yourselves," Alex said, as he exited the cabin.

While the attendees filed out of the captain's quarters, Julien took a moment to construct permutations of the future, having received an inkling of Alex's plan and knowing how the mind of his friend worked. He grinned at Cordelia and shared his hypotheses. He whistled, as the two of them left the salon, and reached out to the other two Exchange directors, who were either in Celus-5's orbit or planetside.

* * *

As the *Rêveur* entered Hellébore's system, Alex forwarded the reports of Reiko, Asu, and Willem to Tomas Monti. It would give the president time to read their summaries and brief the Assembly representatives before the liner made orbit around Haraken.

Alex sent Tomas a second message. He wished to make a presentation to the Assembly and discuss a matter of business.

The latter item in Alex's comm intrigued Tomas, and the president wondered exactly what type of business Alex wanted to conduct with the Haraken government. He asked Dane, an Assembly administrator to postulate on the subject, to which the SADE replied, "You wish me to speculate on what might be in the mind of Alex Racine? Why don't you ask me to count the grains of sand on our beaches? At least, that task would have a finite end."

"Well, at least I'm not the only one without a clue," Tomas murmured, as he prepared to leave his office for the day.

* * *

Alex and Renée exited the traveler, which had landed outside their home. It was late in the evening, raining hard, and visibility was poor. So, neither of them noticed Mutter waiting quietly on the front porch.

The pit of Alex's stomach sank when he saw the SADE. Only dire news would keep her waiting for him to deliver her message personally.

"It's my sad duty, Alex, to tell you that the First is dead."

Alex froze. The faces of those he lost flitted through his memory, and now an alien, as important to him as any of his close friends, was gone too. "How did it happen?" he asked.

"It's surmised, Ser, that a worm polyp rooted itself deep in a rocky crevice within the bay. It grew, feeding on small creatures. When the food source available to it no longer satisfied its hunger, the worm detached itself. By this time, it reached a length of 6 meters. The worm's quarry was one of several younglings that the First and other males guarded. The First spotted the worm's attack, which originated from below, and intercepted it. He killed the worm, but not before that mouth of horrendously sharp teeth devastated the First's carapace. He died before the males could carry him to shore and seek help from Terese."

Mutter paused before finishing her story. She wanted to say something that would ease Alex's pain, but the only words that she selected from her kernel's memory were, "I'm sorry, Alex. The hives sent him to travel the endless waters the day he died."

Alex turned from gazing across the waving grasses, lit by the moons' lights, and reached out to take Mutter's hands. The First was also a friend to her. "We'll both miss him, Mutter. Thank you for personally bringing me the news." Then Alex turned and walked out into the soft rain, headed for the family's gazebo that looked out over the bay.

Renée and Mutter shared a glance, and Renée briefly touched the SADE's shoulder in gratitude before she hurried inside for a coat and a blanket. When Renée returned to the porch, Mutter was already gone, her flyer a dim outline, disappearing into the night, and she wasted no time running after Alex. When Renée found him standing underneath the structure's canopy, she slipped the blanket over Alex's wet shoulders and closed her coat tightly against the wet chill.

Alex stared out at the bay's rolling waves. Only their white crests cast a reflection in the pale light. Memories of his time with the First danced through his memory. He smiled at the First's shrill whistles when the hive leader stopped the builders from constructing a house for him because the First wanted the People to have the honor. The image of the Swei Swee's four eyestalks peeking over the edge of the swim pool while he watched the females build the first traveler shell came to mind. But most of all, Alex remembered meeting the hive leader at the greeting ceremony before he became the Haraken hives' First. Few things Alex had done meant more to him than that moment. The realization that he'd freed a captive species, despite the protestations of his people, warmed his heart as few things had ever done.

The blanket's warmth sunk into Alex's consciousness, and he thought of his partner. Renée sat on her beloved swing, waiting patiently for him, and he took a seat beside her, opening the blanket so that she could snuggle next to him.

"Mutter told me a couple of days before we left for Celus-5 that the First was no longer able to hunt," Alex said quietly. "The only duty he could still perform was guarding the younglings."

"It's sad that the Swei Swee only live for fifty to fifty-five years," Renée replied.

"And I imagine many of our older Swei Swee will not reach the upper age limit due to their debilitating conditions during their incarceration in the sphere."

The two sat quietly, Alex gently pushing off the floor to keep the swing in motion. Renée had drifted off to sleep, when Alex murmured, "I'll miss him."

Renée woke in the early morning hours, as Hellébore slipped above the horizon and its rays slid under the gazebo's awning, warming her. She glanced at Alex, whose eyes were open, staring into the distance, and she crawled higher in his lap to throw her slender arms around his neck and hug him. She said nothing, just held him.

"The new First will be anxious," said Alex, his voice thick and choked. "We'll need to make arrangements."

Before Hellébore was high in the sky, Alex and Renée stood at the shoreline below his house. Swei Swee crowded the long beach, warbling their laments for their loss.

In quick order, Tomas, Terese, and a few key individuals, such as Bibi Haraken, worked their way down the cliff trail to stand beside Alex. Bibi was the matriarch of the Haraken clan and daughter of the much-loved Elder, Fiona Haraken, for whom the planet was named.

"We're here as you requested, Alex," Tomas said, breathing quickly from his exertion.

"In a moment, Tomas, I'll introduce you to the new First of the hives. His name is Bright Shell, but after this morning, he'll be addressed as First. Since I won't be around, the First needs a greeting ceremony with a Star Hunter, who leads the people. That's you, Tomas."

"No, Alex, I appreciate the honor, but I can't —"

"You can and you will, Tomas," Alex interrupted. "I'll help you through it," he added, coupling implant to implant with Tomas. Alex felt the president's revulsion at the thought of eating a live creature, which was a fundamental part of the greeting ceremony, and he flooded Tomas' mind with soothing images.

"What about later, Alex, when I have nightmares about this ceremony? You won't be there then," Tomas remarked.

"That's what Terese is for," Renée said. "I'm quite sure she's capable of distracting you until you can sleep." The two Méridien women and best friends shared wicked smiles.

"One more thing, Tomas, before we begin," Alex said. "The Assembly needs to enact a requirement that every new president is required to perform this ceremony and does it the day after he or she is elected. In my estimate, if the future presidents can't perform this duty, then they aren't worthy of the position, much less being called a Haraken. The Swei Swee were a critical part of the building of our economy and our warships. Without them, we'd be an agrarian society, scratching in the dirt.

"Fine, Alex," Tomas said, angry at being shamed into the ceremony. "Walk me through this, but, if I faint, you better catch me. I don't want to hit the sand face first."

Alex would have smiled at his friend's humorous statements, but his heart was too heavy. He whistled an introduction of Tomas to Bright Shell, and a young male scurried from the shallows with a small fish in his claw. Bright Shell accepted the offer, warbling his thanks, then proceeded to expertly strip the fish down to its fillets.

From the moment the young male raced out of the waves with the fish, Tomas' mind was overtaken by out-of-body sensations. Calm, relaxing thoughts swept through him. He felt at peace, with no concern for the ceremony's details. Instead, he thought of the event's honor, bonding with the First and the hives. Even when cool, wet flesh was in his hand and he was biting into it, he thought of the fight to get free of Libre and the pride and joy that echoed across the fleet when they cleared the system safely. On the heels of those images, he saw the events surrounding the founding of their new world.

The images for Tomas rolled on and on, and he participated in the ceremony in a dream state. Before Tomas knew it, the images were gone. He blinked and focused on the Swei Swee, then Alex, and then his empty hands. He'd eaten his ceremonial share.

Alex whistled to Bright Shell, who held out his claws toward him, and Alex thumped them. "Your turn, Tomas."

The newly titled First swiveled toward the new Star Hunter leader and held out his claws, and Tomas smacked them hard, happy to have made it through the ceremony without embarrassing himself.

With the ceremony concluded, the hives broke out in shrill whistles and tweets. Their previous First was lost, but Bright Shell was accepted as the new First by the Star Hunter leaders. The hives would continue to live in peace and prosperity.

As the humans left the shore and headed for the cliff trail, Alex said, "Tomas, I need that law in effect before I leave, and I need it binding on every new president."

"It might be a tough sell, Alex. It's against so many people's beliefs —" Tomas' words were cut off, because Alex stopped, blocked his path, and stared at him with burning eyes.

<Tomas, remember that Alex has just lost a good friend,> Terese sent urgently.

Bibi touched Alex's arm. "We're so sorry for the one you've lost, Alex," she said calmly. "Many of us know how that feels."

Reminded of Bibi's loss, Alex heard the enduring voice of Fiona Haraken, as she wished her people good fortune among the stars. He eased away from Tomas, and said forcefully, "I need you to make it happen, Tomas. I don't care what it takes." Then he spun around and strode toward the trail, climbing at a pace no one could match.

Renée touched Tomas' shoulder sympathetically and hurried after her partner.

"We've had tougher challenges, Tomas," Bibi said. "I wonder what our Assembly would think of the concept of the Swei Swee never laying up another shell because they believed there was no Star Hunter leader to protect them. Without a greeting ceremony, they might think they've been abandoned."

"I don't think the Swei Swee would stop building shells, just because —" Tomas' words died in his throat. Both Terese and Bibi were staring at him, as if he were a simpleton, and his mind raced to catch up. "Oh, yes, sorry," Tomas exclaimed. "The representatives only have to believe it might happen, but that's rather duplicitous on my part."

"As I see it, Tomas," Terese said sweetly, stepping close to her lover. "You have two choices. You can bluff the Assembly members into accepting something they should want to do if their heads were screwed on correctly, or you can wait until Alex returns one day and finds that you haven't honored his request."

Tomas shuddered at the latter thought. He glanced back at the hives, who were celebrating the acceptance of the First. Younglings scurried up and down the beach, sliding into the breaking waves. Young males handed off their catch to the matrons and young females, who warbled their thanks. And the new First stood in the middle of all it, bobbing in pleasure.

*   *   *

Alex entered Assembly Hall two days later. The representatives concluded the morning's business, and the gallery was packed with spectators. He caught sight of his sister, Christie, sitting next to Bibi Haraken.

Tomas briefly stated Alex's purpose before the representatives, and Alex took the lectern to address them. "You've received the reports of three mission leaders, and I won't bore you with the events, which they've covered in detail. I'm here to give you a summary of the conditions we've found, as I see them. I've already heard rumors that Haraken is about to adopt a second world. You might assume that to be true because you funded the expedition to Celus-5. But we've found two intelligent species there."

"But isn't it true, Ser," Jason Haraken called out, "that these species aren't indigenous to that world?"

"That's correct, Ser," Alex replied. "But you'll note that at least one more dominant species appears to inhabit the forests."

"Which might or might not be intelligent," Jason replied.

"All true, Ser, but you might want to ask yourself what right, as a society, do you have to displace intelligent species, who have called a planet their home for one or more centuries?"

"As I see it, we would have as much right as them to the planet's resources."

"On the other hand, I would prefer to be invited to join them rather than shove my society down their throats, but I think that's a matter of manners," Alex said. The entire audience felt a warming sensation in their implants.

Tomas sent an urgent message to Jason. <Ser Haraken, please tone down your questions and comments before the lot of us go home with massive headaches.>

Christie, who had felt this effect, many times before, when Alex and she were in heated arguments, grinned at Bibi. "I believe your son is irritating my brother," she whispered.

"I believe my son is annoying many more people than Alex," Bibi whispered back.

"Anyway, you have my opinion," Alex said, "and it's up to you, good people, to decide how you wish your society to operate. I believe the Dischnya and Swei Swee will request our permanent presence, provided we're willing to be good neighbors and share our technology. I've made commitments to both species that I intend to keep to help ensure intra-species and inter-species peace. As to those in the green, which is how the queens refer to the forests, it remains to be seen."

Bibi leaned over to Christie and whispered, "Anyone else sent to rescue a stranded party on an alien world would do so and return promptly. Not your brother. He goes to the rescue and discovers not one or two, but possibly three, intelligent species, who are fighting with one another."

Years ago, Christie might have been annoyed at the thought of more attention heaped on her already famous brother. But her mind was changed on that score when she was the one in trouble. It was her brother, who came running to her rescue when she was kidnapped. *The universe needs more Alex types to rescue those desperate for it,* she thought.

Alex fielded more questions and forced himself to control his temper.

At one point, Tomas stood and announced that since midday meal was quickly approaching, he wanted Alex to suggest his business proposal so the representatives could consider it over their food. "But before he does that," Tomas said, "I would like to thank Ser Racine for his time today and his continuing efforts on the part of our people."

Alex nodded his appreciation to Tomas and turned to the Assembly. "As the population's elected representatives, you have the authority to manage the disposal of any state assets, and I wish to buy the city-ship *Freedom*.

That created a buzz among the Assembly members.

"What would be your purpose in owning such a huge ship, Ser?" Jason asked.

"It would be better if you didn't know," Alex replied, which raised eyebrows and started comms flying.

"Ser Racine," Tomas said, interceding before Jason opened his mouth again. "While you aren't in a position of authority, your reputation as Haraken's preeminent citizen precedes you. It would be a legitimate concern of this Assembly if your actions were to reflect negatively on our world."

Alex sought some advice from Renée and Julien and received their support. "If this Assembly and I were to come to a reasonable business arrangement on the sale of the *Freedom*, you would have no reason for concern. I would no longer be a resident of Haraken, and I'd announce that to the worlds before I took any action involving the *Freedom*."

The uproar reminded Alex of the behavior of the New Terran Assembly. It was obvious that Librans were a minority in the audience, and most of the representatives had never served under Alex or Tatia.

<You have such a way of winning people to your side, oh sublime one,> Julien sent, but his thoughts tingled in anticipation of their future.

Tomas gained control of the session and allowed one more question before the Assembly adjourned for midday meal.

"Ser Racine," Eric Stroheim said, "if the present species acquiesce to you settling on Celus-5, will you make that world an extension of Haraken society?"

"You're asking the wrong person, Ser Stroheim," Alex replied. It always felt odd, using formality when speaking to his friends during Assembly sessions. "You'll have to wait and ask the residents and settlers of Celus-5 whether they wish to join Haraken."

"But as their leader, Ser Racine —" Tomas started to say, but halted when Alex raised a hand toward him.

"I won't be the leader of those who choose to call Celus-5 their home. I have other plans."

Amid shouts and questions from the floor, Tomas adjourned the session, and Alex cut off all comms except for a private few.

Word reached Bibi that Jason asked Tomas for a closed session after midday meal, citing too much interference from the gallery, and it was granted. The decision was a rarity for the Assembly, and one that rankled Bibi. *I raised you better than that,* Bibi thought, making a point to speak to her son, later, out of session.

<Christie, wait for this old woman,> Bibi sent. <You and I have business to discuss.>

* * *

"We'll enjoy a meal at my home," Bibi said, when she met Christie outside the Assembly building.

What amused Christie was that the old woman, as Bibi referred to herself, set a blistering pace to her nearby house.

"You're planning to conduct your interview broadcast in a half hour, aren't you?" Bibi asked.

"Yes."

"I wish to be the subject of your interview."

Christie started to question Bibi, but the elder held up a finger to forestall her.

"My beloved son is being an idiot," Bibi continued, "and before he makes a greater fool of himself, I wish to counter his actions. I'm an admirer of your early works with your brother on New Terra."

"I didn't know you were aware of those interviews."

"Elderly doesn't mean uninformed, young one."

"Why do you want to be interviewed?"

"Instead, let me ask you a question. What does your brother intend to do with the *Freedom*?"

"Haven't a clue."

"Aha, and that's the point. No one else I've spoken to does either. I'm probably one of the most well-informed individuals on Haraken, and I don't have a clue, as you say."

"So, no one knows, Bibi. That's not really news. Alex has always been enigmatic when it comes to his plans."

"Agreed. So should the Assembly sell him the *Freedom* at a reasonable price?"

"Of course."

"Why?"

"Because he's Alex."

"Yes, and who knows that better than you or me, child?" Bibi said, hooking her arm in Christie's, but she could see the confusion on Christie's face. "Are you aware that the Assembly is composed of less than 32 percent of people who founded this planet? Newcomers have voted in their own people as representatives. This isn't wrong, but the days of when Harakens would give Alex Racine anything he wanted are gone."

"So you intend to make your case for Alex via my show?"

"Precisely, child. People need to hear a valid argument for supporting him. If they do, they'll make up their own minds and comm their representatives with their opinions."

"This won't be an interview, Bibi, but a protracted sales pitch."

"Call it what you wish, Christie," Bibi replied, stopping outside her house and turning to face the young woman. "The question is whether you support your brother or not, and, if you do, are you prepared to do something about it?"

"I do want to support Alex, but we don't have any time to prepare."

"No, we don't. We'll have a quick meal, and then you'll have to trust this old woman."

There were few people whom Christie might have believed on hearing that type of comment, but Bibi had always been a huge supporter of Alex. While she didn't always agree with Alex's methods, Bibi's public criticisms disappeared the day Alex brought Eloise Haraken home, along with Christie and Amelia, following their kidnapping.

-30-
The Freedom

"This is the Racine Talk Time, and I'm your host, Christie Racine. Our scheduled guest has been preempted so that we might bring you an interview with our respected elder, Bibi Haraken. Bibi, you were adamant about wanting this interview time. Why is that?"

Bibi had to give it to Christie. She was no fool. She'd set it up with her audience so that they knew it was Bibi, who had pushed for the time slot. *So be it,* she thought.

"Time is of the essence, Christie. The Assembly members will soon finish their midday meals, and then they will reconvene to vote on a critical issue that will affect the future of Haraken."

"You make it sound dire, Bibi. What's the vote about?"

"Before I answer that, Christie, I wonder how many of your listeners are aware of the facts surrounding the founding of Haraken."

"I think all of them know that the Librans and a few New Terrans founded Haraken under Alex Racine."

"Yes, a simplistic enough summary. But, the often-forgotten part is that the Confederation was decimated by a giant sphere. The creatures that guided it were called the Nua'll."

Both Bibi and Christie skirted the point about the Swei Swee, who operated the dark travelers, unwittingly doing the Nua'll's dirty work.

"That sphere was destroyed," Christie said, now beginning to guess where Bibi was headed.

"Yes, it was, but not before it sent a message."

"Do we know the contents of that message?"

"Alien technology," Bibi remarked. "But what message would you send and to whom?"

"I see what you mean," Christie said. She drew out her words to underline the importance of Bibi's comment to her audience. "So what does this have to do with the vote in the Assembly today, Bibi?"

"Alex Racine has asked the Assembly to sell him the *Freedom*."

"What would Ser Racine want with a city-ship that's sat parked in orbit for more than twenty years?"

"I have no answer to that, Christie, but a critical clue is that Ser Racine said he would no longer be a Haraken resident."

"Do you think he intends to live on that newly explored planet, Celus-5?"

Bibi smiled at Christie. She was a clever interviewer, leading her subject right down the path that both of them wanted to walk.

"Alex Racine says that he won't be a leader of those who settle the planet, if the aliens even permit Harakens to live there."

"So, Bibi, let's get back to the subject at hand. You don't know what Ser Racine wants to do with the city-ship, and you don't know where he's going with it. Then, why is the Assembly's vote important to you?"

"Alex Racine has always protected the people. He traded tech to New Terra to return lost Méridiens home. He fought the Nua'll sphere when it would have been safer to run home. He and his people worked tirelessly to save the Librans, and, recently, he kept our worlds from being overrun by United Earth before the system changed its ways. I say this: If Alex Racine wants a city-ship, sell it to him, or, better yet, give it to him."

"How can you be so confident in what Ser Racine intends to do with that ship, even though he's not said one word about it?"

"My mother, Fiona Haraken, who remained purposefully on Libre with other elders, while younger Independents were evacuated, told us ... no, she warned us, to keep that wide-shouldered young man with the four stars on his collar close to us. She called him our protector. I see no reason to change my opinion about the man. Whatever Alex Racine intends to do with the *Freedom*, it will only serve to protect us."

"That's putting a great deal of belief in Ser Racine, Bibi. All humans make mistakes."

"Quite true, Christie. And I won't say that I've always agreed with the man's methods, but I dare you to argue with his results. Whatever Alex Racine's intention, my message would be the same. Let the man have the ship ... if not for the future, then for the past. No one deserves it more."

"Thank you for your time today, Bibi. I see that midday meal will soon end. To my listeners, I can only say that if anyone has a vested interest in the future of Haraken and its people, then it's Bibi Haraken, who you've heard expressing her opinion today on an important Assembly vote."

Christie signed off, and returned the broadcast to her media station. She stood up and was immediately embraced by Bibi.

"May the stars protect you," Bibi said, and rushed out the door of her home.

*   *   *

The representatives never got to enjoy their full meal time. Their comms were flooded with questions about Alex Racine's proposal. How did they intend to vote? For those Assembly members who expressed thoughts to deny the sale, Harakens wanted to know why. What were the representative's concerns? Were they founded or imagined? Could the first sphere have called home? Is a second Nua'll ship a possibility?

What the populace was reminded of by the broadcast was that Haraken was once the site of the first Confederation colony to be destroyed by the Nua'll sphere. That alone did more to wake up the people to the important role Alex Racine played in establishing Haraken, more than twenty years ago. Bibi had been right when she told Christie that people quickly forgot their own history.

The Assembly reconvened, and Jason was the first to state his opinion that the representatives should block the sale. He'd been bombarded with comms during his meal, as had the others, but he stood fast in the face of the Librans who had queried him as to why he was against the sale.

But, it quickly became evident to Jason that he was in the minority, and within an hour, the vote was taken, and the sale was approved.

* * *

<Alex, the Assembly has voted to sell you the *Freedom*,> Tomas sent.

<Their gift is much appreciated, Tomas.>

<Alex, please don't refer to the city-ship as a gift. That tends to make Haraken look complicit in whatever it is that you're about to do. >

<Still, you have my profound thanks, Tomas.>

<Oh, don't thank me, Alex. Save that for Bibi Haraken and your sister.>

<Why?>

<If you didn't hear their timely interview, conducted during midday meal, you should listen to a copy of the broadcast. That short show galvanized the populace, who besieged their representatives. Personally, as I listened to others during the start of the meal, I was sure the sale was doomed. Jason's anti-Alex rhetoric did much to convince the others to take a conservative approach to the issue.>

<I wonder what I ever did to him, except save his butt from becoming dust on Libre.>

<While you were on Celus-5, one of Mickey's companies was awarded a government contract instead of Jason's.>

<Ah, so this was payback.>

<Apparently,> Tomas sent in reply. <But the representatives were presented with other considerations, besides their constituents' opinions. The interview got people thinking and that included some representatives. Eric and I fielded their questions, which we passed to Dane for research. The SADE reported that maintenance crews and traveler support for the two city-ships are running the government about four million credits annually.>

<Black space ... and that's credits spent to just keep them parked in deep orbit,> Alex said, stunned by the enormous cost.

<The ongoing expense of a city-ship is one of the key reasons the Assembly is happy to get rid of one, and the representatives are now considering the fate of the *Our People*. A statement made during the

Assembly and pointed at the Librans, Jason in particular, was that Librans shouldn't be afraid to part with their lifeboats.>

<I bet that was painful for them to hear.>

<Yes, it was, especially after everything we went through to escape in those lifeboats. Nonetheless, it did have the ring of truth. Let's face it, Alex, the tech on those city-ships is outdated, and no one wants to travel in-system unless it's in a grav-driven ship, which these monsters aren't.>

<Just the same, I need a ship this size. In fact, I'd take a bigger one if you had it.>

Tomas took a moment to digest that last statement. *What would you want with a vessel larger than a city-ship,* Tomas wondered. <Well, Alex, last point, and I hope you're sitting down, because we must discuss the fee. I warn you … it will come as a shock. The representatives borrowed a contract element, which has become popular in the past few years.>

<I'm ready, Tomas. Let's hear it.>

<The Assembly will require the sum of one credit.> Tomas waited for a response but heard nothing. <Interesting, Alex, I've rarely heard you at a loss for words. I think I'm rather enjoying this moment. Well, I'll have the sale agreement forwarded to you later this afternoon. After you transfer the agreed amount, the sale will be final. By the way, to protect the Assembly and Haraken, the sale price will remain undisclosed.>

Alex could hear Tomas' chuckle when he referred to the single credit transfer.

<I've informed the maintenance crew aboard the *Freedom,*> Tomas continued. <They'll wait to update you on the ship's condition before they turn over any codes you might require.>

<Looks like I'll be busy for a while.>

<Alex, you know as well as I do that a city-ship was built to hold 250,000 people, and that ship has been minimally maintained for twenty years. It's going to need updating and restocking, and that's going to take labor and credits. You sure you want to do this?>

<I appreciate your concern, Tomas. One way or another, I'll work it out.>

<As you wish, Alex.>

After Tomas' comm ended, Alex sent the message out that the sale of the *Freedom* was approved. Everyone, who received Alex's comm, noticed he never said he owned the ship just that the Assembly agreed to the sale.

* * *

Alex's first stop, after receiving Tomas' news, was Sadesville. Winston wished to communicate the thoughts of the SADEs who chose to stay behind on Celus-5 to the SADEs resident on Haraken, and he'd asked Alex to accompany him.

For Alex's part, he stood idly by while Winston managed his exchange with the SADEs via comm. At one point, the entire assembly swiveled their heads to look at him, but then returned to staring at Winston.

When the SADEs' conversation finished, Winston turned to Alex with a pleasant smile on his face. "A consensus has been reached, Ser. The SADEs will help with the refurbishment efforts of the *Freedom* in exchange for passage to Celus-5."

"Winston, Harakens might not be welcome there. It's something we just don't know yet."

"This is understood, Ser. If the Harakens can't settle Celus-5, you'll still need individuals to maintain the ship. These individuals are willing to remain with you."

"Winston, you're talking about an annual stipend for nearly 140 SADEs, for the stars know how many years. That's an amount of compensation that I wouldn't be able to pay for more than three or four years."

"Leave that to me, Alex. I believe I have an idea that will further both your goals and ours, but I'll need to discuss this with others first."

* * *

Mickey, Claude, Julien, Cordelia, Winston, Hector, Esther, Didier, and most of the Confederation SADEs, who were free of their contracts, took two Exchange travelers to inspect the *Freedom*.

Cordelia organized the SADEs, detailing their assignments. As the original SADE who controlled the city-ship's construction and who flew it for nearly five years, Cordelia knew the vessel better than anyone. In her mind, she was sure that this was the reason Alex chose this ship over the other city-ship, *Our People*.

The SADEs and engineers crawled over the ship from bridge to bays, reviewed the maintenance crew's reports, and tested everything from engines to filtration systems. Every analysis was filed with the ship's controller, and Cordelia and Julien organized the lists and computed the costs for replacement equipment and labor.

The effort took several days. As the last inspection report was filed and every SADE acknowledged they were finished with their assignments, Cordelia sat in the captain's chair for several moments, summarizing the extensive lists. When she produced her final accounting report, Winston regarded Julien.

"Alex hasn't enough to cover the refit," Julien said, "much less afford to pay a significantly sized crew to maintain it.

"I'd hoped as much," Winston said with a smile. "I believe this is an opportune time for the SIF directors to speak privately with the Exchange directors."

Mickey glanced at Claude, and said, "I think that's our cue to exit, Claude. Why don't you and I go claim the spaces we want for our labs and manufacturing locations before they're gone!"

-31-
Alex's People

When the *Freedom*'s review was complete, Julien, Cordelia, and the SIF directors met with Alex and Renée at their home. As the guests were SADEs, Renée merely prepared thé for Alex and herself and invited the SADEs to be seated.

Even though the SIF directors were prepared to stand and lock their avatars, they followed the example of Julien and Cordelia, who not only took seats but adopted relaxed human poses.

Alex hid the beginnings of a smile behind his cup, noticing the SIF directors copied Julien and Cordelia's various positions exactly. *You learn by imitation,* Alex thought.

Cordelia waited until Alex had an opportunity to enjoy his thé before she sent him a summary of the *Freedom*'s refit costs.

Alex scrolled through the lengthy list, shocked at the number of items and their associated costs. He jumped to the end and set his tea down. Alex knew better than to question the report's accuracy, but it saddened him to see that the total was twice the credits he held in his Exchange account.

"Ironic, isn't it?" Alex said. "The *Freedom* was built and outfitted without a single credit changing hands. Now a simple refit is expected to cost more than sixty-eight million credits."

"We inhabit a capitalistic society, Alex," Julien commented.

"Well, I can afford half the refit," Alex said. "Can we accomplish half the work and still launch, Cordelia?"

"Alex, credits can be saved if we reduce the human accommodations," Julien replied instead, angling to get a hint from Alex of his plans for the ship.

"I want the ship refitted for humans, including food stocks, cabin furnishings … the works. I was hoping credits could be saved on the technical side."

"There's little that can be shaved off the refit from a technical aspect. Equipment must be upgraded, and it will take labor to do. I regret that our efforts there would result in minor cost savings," Cordelia replied.

<Where will the humans come from? Haraken?> Winston sent to Julien.

<Doubtful,> Julien sent in reply.

"Perhaps, you won't have to skimp on your refit, Alex," Winston said, leaning forward to place his forearms on his knees, as he had seen humans do innumerable times to emphasize their points. "The SIF directors, in concert with the Exchange directors, have proposals for you."

"I'm listening," Alex said cautiously.

Winston laid out the transitional phases of the Confederation SADEs, enumerating the challenges many of them were going through after liberation to adjust to life with Méridiens and Harakens. He summarized the complaints about Sadesville and the hopes of those on Celus-5. He would have continued to expound on the background for the proposals, but Hector cut him off.

"Your pardon, Winston, but I believe that Alex knows all this only too well. I believe the correct phrase, Ser, is that we want in."

"In on what?" Alex asked.

"In on whatever you're planning to do and wherever you're planning to go," Didier added.

"I'm not entirely sure I have the answers to those questions myself," Alex replied.

"That doesn't matter, Alex," Esther said. "The most important thing for us is that you and the people around you accept SADEs for who we are. That's a great comfort to us, in and of itself. We're quite adaptable, as you know, and wish to travel with you."

"But you have your duties as SIF directors," Alex objected.

"True, but not for all time and only for the four of us," Didier commented.

"Okay, what exactly is SIF's proposal?" Alex asked.

"First, Alex, the *Freedom* must accept up to 40,000 SADEs, for as long as it exists," Winston said.

"That's thinking far into the future," Alex commented drily, recognizing that it was 25 percent more SADEs than existed right now across the entire Confederation and the majority of those individuals were staying put.

"I think your first item is moot, Winston. Even if I was to agree to your point, I can't afford to pay them a stipend," Alex pointed out.

"But you won't have to, Alex," Esther said. "SIF will pay the stipend for any SADE who serves aboard your ship … or any ship in your fleet."

"Now, I have a fleet," Alex said, nodding agreeably to Julien, as if he had just received a wonderful gift.

"You jest with us," Hector said, "but the evidence of your past is there for all to examine."

"Now, that's true," Renée said, pointing a finger at Hector to underline his words.

"Whose side are you on?" Alex asked.

"On yours, my love, but I agree with them."

"Okay, if I were to accept this first point that the *Freedom* would accommodate up to 40,000 SADEs and any who serve will be paid by SIF, I want it clear that they have no sway over where I go or what I do with the ship … or ships, if I ever have more. Now, don't tell me that you or they can live with that," Alex challenged.

"It's agreed," Esther said, displaying a beatific smile.

Alex felt he was being maneuvered, and his mind raced ahead to comprehend the reasons for the SADEs' approach. Of particular interest to him was why the SIF directors were approaching him in concert with the Exchange directors, and he glanced Julien's way, but his friend wore his poker face.

"One final point, Alex," Winston said. "In recompense for SIF's payment of the SADEs' stipends, those who work on your fleet and who will participate in whatever assignments you give them, SIF requires a share of the profits."

"The contract will stipulate a rolling percentage of the gross profits, based on the ratio of SADEs to humans within the fleet," Didier noted.

Alex's hearty laugh rocketed around the room.

The SIF directors queried Julien, thinking that they had misstepped.

<Wait,> Julien sent them in reply.

"In case you haven't noticed, Sers, I'm not proficient at generating credits, save for the one thing I created while in New Terra, and, which after two years of generating revenue, I gave away to the government and the SADEs. My account balance is almost entirely due to the goodwill donations made by the Confederation SADEs."

"This is understood, Alex," Esther said, "but we've noted that the Haraken SADEs and many members of your original crew are the wealthiest individuals on this planet."

Alex glanced at Julien, who merely raised his eyebrows, as if it to indicate that, regrettably, it was true. "Good for you, my friend," Alex said, slapping Julien's knee.

"We're confident that your efforts, in pursuit of your goals, will generate credits, Alex," Winston said. "We know you'll do this to ensure the economic prosperity of the individuals you intend to load into your city-ship and future vessels."

"Okay," Alex said, holding out his hands in protestation. "Let's say I was to agree to your conditions ... SIF pays the way for the SADEs that come aboard and you get a percentage of credits generated. There are still the costs of the refit."

"And that's where we can help," Julien said.

"Let me guess. The Exchange directors want in as well ... profit sharing and all," Alex said with a groan. "I think I've freed a bunch of financial mercenaries." The fact that every SADE was smiling at him gave Alex an indication of a future that would be shaped by many players, of which he would be only one.

"Yes, we do wish a seat at the table, as you often phrase it, Alex," Cordelia replied. "The Exchange will cover the cost of the refit and will request a fair percentage of credits generated by your fleet's economic activities."

Alex knew that Cordelia and Julien were keenly aware of what Emile, Mickey, and the others had discovered. The invention was worth a world's fortune. More important to Alex than its economic value, it meant grav-built ships could be constructed independent of the hives, built quicker, and fabricated in space. If the Haraken SADEs wanted to play investors, Alex decided he'd better yank his negotiation hat down tight. It looked to be a bumpy night.

Julien watched Alex's eyes narrow, as his friend regarded him, and the SADE attempted to surmise the thoughts revolving in Alex's mind. His green-visored, poker cap appeared on his head, and he returned Alex's squint with one of his own.

The brothers were in protracted mental negotiations for the better part of a half hour. In the end, Alex reverted to verbal communication and said, "Done," as he extended his hand to Julien.

"Agreed," Julien replied, shaking Alex's hand.

"Winston, send me your agreement, and I'll review it," Alex said. But before he could finish what he intended to say, Esther's comm signaled a document waited for him.

"Pretty sure of yourselves," Alex commented.

"Pretty sure of you, Alex Racine," Hector replied. "You have a habit of single-mindedly pursuing those goals you believe to be critical."

Winston sent a message to Julien asking for the substance of the Exchange's agreement with Alex, but Julien replied that one of the conditions of the agreement, as stipulated by Alex, was that its details weren't to be revealed to anyone but the Exchange directors.

<Interesting,> Esther commented to her fellow directors. <To many humans, we are one thing, a group of similar beings, but, to Alex, we're individuals, and, in this case, he seeks to isolate the two banks from each other.>

<I believe he preserves competition,> Hector added.

<Just so,> Winston replied. <One of the many reasons we wish to follow Alex.>

* * *

News and rumors swept across Haraken, aided by the population's implants. Among the people's key concerns were how many and which people might be leaving with Alex. For the Assembly, it was the fact that the city-ship could accommodate 250,000 individuals, and those most loyal to Alex and, therefore, most likely to go, were many of Haraken's premier citizens.

To address these and other concerns head-on, Tatia sought a private meeting with Alex.

"Causing quite a stir, as usual, Alex," Tatia said, without preamble, as Renée placed a small repast and hot thé by the admiral's side.

"Is that how you see it, Tatia?" Alex asked.

Tatia held the hot mug in her hands to warm them from the chill that blew along the coast. She'd made the mistake of taking her flit since it was a short flight, but the open canopy provided little protection against the elements. "No, not really," Tatia admitted. "But, your actions are generating waves for me, professionally and personally."

Tatia waited for Alex to pick up the conversation, but he sat quietly observing her. Releasing a tense breath, Tatia leaned back in her chair, holding the mug to her chest. "Okay, Alex, let's talk plainly," which garnered a smile from him. "I've had submissions from people who wish to resign their commissions if they're accepted to travel with you. My question is this: Do you intend to accept them?"

"Things are happening a little faster than I expected, Tatia. I haven't gotten to that point yet."

"Word is that the Confederation SADEs will be paid by SIF to work for you."

"That's true. Who's on your list?"

"Ellie, Svetlana, and a good many pilots, but I expect to hear from Reiko and Franz, among others."

"And how about you?" Alex asked.

Renée could feel the heavy-bodied admiral's laughter, reverberating through the bones of her chest. "Have you spoken with Alain?" Renée asked quietly. Her question abruptly shut down Tatia's laughter.

"Yes, I have, Renée," Tatia retorted, none too happy to have Renée bring up the subject of her partner.

"And?" Renée pressed.

"It's obvious Étienne and Alain are bored, and Alex's new adventure calls to both of them. Étienne and Ellie wish to go, which represents a challenge for the twins. I don't believe the crèche-mates can ever be separated."

Alex and Renée watched Tatia drink her thé, lost in thought.

"There's a rumor circulating that you're going to hunt the Nua'll, Alex. If so, what about warships … sting ships and fighters? As far as I know, you only have the four travelers aboard the *Rêveur*."

"At this time," Alex said cryptically.

"I'm on the outside looking in, for now, aren't I?" Tatia asked.

"For now," Alex agreed.

"An odd sensation," Tatia replied, draining her mug. She stood up and said, "When you make up your mind about which humans you want aboard, comm me. I have until then to figure out my own future."

When Tatia departed, Renée cleaned up Tatia's food dish, which the admiral hadn't touched. She kept an eye on Alex, who hadn't touched his food either. "Listen to me," she said, when she stepped back into the main room. "You can't be responsible for the lives of those who wish to follow you any more than you were when we repaired the *Rêveur*. People must make their own decisions."

"Even if it means disrupting families?" Alex asked.

"That's for them to decide among themselves. It's not for you to worry over."

* * *

Alex affixed his approval, encapsulated with his implant's bio ID to the Exchange and SIF agreements. Anticipating Alex's affirmation of the proposals, the Exchange had pilots and travelers standing by outside Sadesville. The Confederation SADEs stood outside the ships with locked avatars, reviewing the enormous to-do list for the refit.

When the pilots and SADEs received Winston's go order, hatches were dropped, SADEs scrambled aboard, and ships lifted. Within a half hour of Alex approving the deals, the SADEs were swarming over the *Freedom*. Most carried heavy tool packs, worn over their backs. Others grabbed tools left aboard the city-ship. The first order of business was to pull the antiquated systems. It was of great help to the efficiency of their work that humans weren't aboard for several days, the maintenance crew having exited before they arrived, and they needn't worry about many of the support systems that humans required.

In short order, traveler transports, with their rear-loading ramps, arrived with the heavy equipment loads. The two director groups paid priority delivery fees to strip the local manufacturers of already-produced equipment destined for the manufacture of new ships. It would take a few days, but soon the ship builders would start screaming to their suppliers about the delivery delays. Traveler pilots, used to the loading and offloading timing of humans, even with grav-pallets, were shocked to find that they barely took a bite of a small repast when a SADE signaled a go launch.

SADE comms poured into Alex, asking for approval of strategic decisions about the use of certain spaces and bays onboard the *Freedom*. The callers addressed him as Captain Racine, but Alex deferred from accepting that title. Instead, the SADEs simply called him Ser.

Three major food stock manufacturers received orders to completely fill the *Freedom*'s food stock tanks and were astonished. Queries hit Tomas and Eric's comms. The rumors of a quarter-million citizens planning an exodus from Haraken were boosted. Both leaders reached out to Alex for assurances, and he told them that only a handful of humans would accompany him. At least, that's what Alex reasoned, not that Renée agreed with him.

Launch

The refit of the *Freedom* would have taken the same number of humans the better part of a year to complete. But a SADE, able to work around the thirty-hour clock, with unflagging energy and sophisticated coordination with others, was equivalent to ten humans. Truth was that they worked with fervor. The circumstances of Sadesville had been a great disappointment to every one of them. They had left the Confederation with hopes for new and exciting lives and found themselves relegated to second-class citizens. Alex Racine represented the type of future the SADEs craved and were anxious to begin.

As opposed to the Confederation SADEs, Alex was miserable. He desperately needed both humans and SADEs aboard to facilitate his plans, but he dearly wished all of them could remain on Haraken, where they would be safe from harm, at least, for the near future.

Julien and Cordelia tackled the *Freedom*'s bridge, controller and memory banks, automating many of the bridge positions that previously required Libran personnel to monitor and operate.

Huge shipments of memory crystals were diverted from their intended destinations to the city-ship. The controller's memory banks were duplicated to a backup position, and, at Renée's request, Julien copied the *Rêveur*'s library to the *Freedom*.

Two separate, secure sections of the ship received new memory banks and sophisticated controllers, which were tied directly into the comm systems, but without access from ship's personnel. Having Z and Rosette's prior approval, the only off-world Exchange directors, Julien and Cordelia proposed to the other Haraken SADEs that they expand the bank's territory to a base aboard the *Freedom* and wherever humans and SADEs established new colonies. It took mere ticks of time to reach unanimous approval. After the two new memory banks were installed, the Exchange directors' precious vault was copied and duplicated. It would be the controllers' duties to keep the massive memory banks in sync with the vault, where the Exchange records were kept, and where Alex protected his personal records.

It might be asked what the Harakens SADEs' ultimate purpose was in expanding their bank, since they were incredibly wealthy. But these were the original eight, who Alex freed from their starships, and they saw themselves as the financial bulwark that would ensure the expansion of humans in this corner of the galaxy, especially if the likes of the Nua'll were the more advanced entities out there in the deep dark.

* * *

Mickey and Pia, privy to Billing's invention, knew they would be aboard the *Freedom* without the formality of an invitation. The pair orbited Alex like planets swung around its star, and laws of gravity dictated that where the larger body went the satellites followed.

Mickey sold his ownership in every company, dividing it proportionately among the employees from the director down to the newest hire. The price of ownership began with a single credit for the smallest share portion, and the employees couldn't believe their good fortune. If it hadn't been for news of Alex's purchase and launch of the city-ship, they might have thought Mickey had lost his mind. But few people knew of Mickey's personal wealth. That's because, despite the amassing of a substantial amount of credits, he was the same good-natured engineer who many had always known.

Pia spent a few tearful evenings with Terese. Her good friend and Alex's first medical specialist would be staying on Haraken with her lover and partner, Tomas. Pia had requested that Cordelia copy Haraken's medical database to the *Freedom*, which Terese heartily approved.

"I believe we have the makings of the perfect surgeon for this expedition," Pia enthused, and Terese perked up.

"Who?" Terese asked, running through the survey mission's personnel list to see if she could guess who Pia meant.

"Miranda," Pia replied, struggling to keep her face from breaking into a grin.

"Miranda?" Terese repeated. "May the stars protect us."

"Seriously, Terese, you should have seen her operate on Alex's head injury. Bone fragments had to be pulled, positioned, and floated separately. One piece had to be fished out of his cranium. And Miranda was magnificent ... perfect control and positioning by linking into the scanner. She was optically blind but saw through the instrumentation. Her surgery was marvelous!"

While Pia enthused about the surgery, Terese grew quiet until tears formed in her eyes and threatened to spill over. Pia sank to her knees in front of her friend and grabbed her hands. "I'm sorry, Terese. I should have realized how details of the operation would distress you."

"You came close to losing him, didn't you?" Terese said, the pain of Alex's near demise, strangling her heart.

"Yes, yes, we did," Pia admitted.

"I fear for those close to Alex when they lose him, Pia, and I'll be one of them, even if it's a century from now and he dies of old age."

"Miranda and I will do our best to see if we can help him achieve the status of great elder," Pia said, giving her friend a hopeful smile.

Terese squeezed Pia's hands in return and said, "You have your work cut out for you. What does Alex think of your idea of Miranda, as the expedition's premier medical specialist?"

"When I told Alex of Miranda's efforts on his behalf and that I thought she would make a marvelous surgeon, he laughed and said, "And what better personality could there be to supplant our fiery redhead?"

Terese laughed quietly and shook her head. She could visualize Alex shaking off his brush with death in good humor, as he compared the personalities of Miranda and her. Truth was, the man had a good point.

"I have to admit, Pia, it's taken a long time for me to find happiness again after our awakening in New Terra, but I finally have it, and I covet the love and security Tomas and I have together."

"And you deserve it, Terese," Pia said, gently shaking her friend's hands. Mickey and I will accompany our enormous New Terran and work to keep you and this planet safe so that you can enjoy your lives. Pia hugged Terese one last time, wondering if she would ever see her again.

* * *

Emile Billings sat down with his wife, Janine, and daughter, Mincie, after the evening meal. Alex had given him permission to speak of his invention, in general terms, but not to expose the details.

Emile was overcome with excitement about the potential the new opportunity represented — the incredible discovery itself, his success as a biochemist, the future profit potential, and the thought of participating in an adventure beyond his wildest imagination. Only two problems he could foresee, his wife and his daughter. He considered the possibility that they might not share his enthusiasm, and he was right to be worried.

Mincie's adjustment to life on Haraken was challenging, the making of new friends and the adoption of her implant. As for Janine, she was torn, wanting to make both members of her family happy.

The break came for Emile's hopes when Mincie lamented that she missed her new best friends, who had helped her adopt her implant, Jodlyne and Ginny. As transplants to Haraken themselves, the pair understood the challenges Mincie faced and worked to smooth her entry into Haraken life.

"Edmas and Jodlyne will be aboard the *Freedom*," Emile said gently to his daughter.

"Jodlyne will?" Mincie asked, wanting confirmation. "And what about Ginny?"

"Edmas and Jodlyne will be working closely with Mickey Brandon and me on our new project. And the *Freedom* will be headed to Celus-5, probably before the survey mission is complete. You'll see Teague and Ginny there." Emile knew the *Sojourn* would remain in orbit around Celus-5 until Alex returned, but he kept that part of the situation to himself.

"Promise?" Mincie asked.

"Promise," Emile agreed.

While Emile wrestled with his family, Mickey made arrangements for procuring and shipping into orbit anything that could accommodate the spray construction of ships with Billings' methods. Claude was busy moving the remainder of Z's avatars and his manufacturing equipment for avatar construction. What delighted the Méridien tech specialist was that he managed to confiscate one of the *Freedom*'s gigantic bays for himself.

"I have a challenge for Z and you," Alex had said to him. "I'm wondering what sort of practical avatars can be designed and built that the SADEs might employ in some of our future challenges."

"What sorts of challenges?" Claude asked.

"Oh, you know, the usual and some of the unusual," Alex said and left Claude's office.

Claude commed Mickey to share Alex's request, and the engineer laughed until he ran out of breath.

"Looks like we're going to busier than ever, Claude," Mickey said, cutting the comm without ever contributing a single idea.

Between trips to the *Freedom*, Julien and Cordelia spoke to their children. They were hesitant to take them into an unknown future, but the SADEs underestimated them. They weren't typical Haraken children, but orphans, who had survived by their wits and handouts from the rebels, who fought the forces of United Earth for decades. In the children's minds, Julien and Cordelia came to their rescue and saved them from orphanages, and there was no way they were getting separated from their adopted parents, danger or no danger.

Julien and Cordelia spent moments in person with the other Haraken SADEs, who would remain on the home world. This included Mutter, whose delight remained composing and singing for the hives. "One day, the People will produce their own Singers, and my work will be done. I might join you then," Mutter told them.

Alex contacted Julien to set up the transfer of his house and land. For the price of one credit apiece, Alex's parents, sister, and son, received quarter shares in the wide swath of land along the coast that the Assembly had awarded Alex and Renée. Christie was staying on Haraken. Her media company was growing, and she couldn't be happier. Alex's parents, Duggan and Katie, were staying too, hoping Christie might give them grandchildren one day.

Julien checked database records across the planet and ensured that Alex and Renée's names were cleared of Haraken ownership titles. Even their Exchange account name was changed from Racine to Dassata. Every effort was made to support Alex's statement that he would no longer be a Haraken citizen.

At Alex's request, Julien contacted each human who was accepted to accompany Alex, making them aware their Exchange accounts would be accessible aboard ship. While most were initially surprised by that fortunate news, it reminded them that Alex and his associates were thinking far into the future and preparing for more than a simple expedition.

* * *

The Exchange and SIF directors did collude on one aspect of their arrangements with Alex. It was agreed that each group would make an annual contribution of a half of a percent of their income from the *Freedom*'s endeavors into Alex's personal accounts.

<Alex will notice this immediately after the first transfer,> Esther objected, when Winston and Julien sent their proposition for approval to the other directors. <We should communicate this to him now. Don't you

believe forthrightness to be the better option?> But Esther simultaneously received Julien and Winston's denials.

<This is one of those times, Esther, when it's better to execute and later apologize rather than ask for permission in advance and engage in a protracted and perhaps fruitless discussion,> Winston sent in reply.

<I can assure you, Esther,> Julien sent, <it will probably be years before Alex thinks to check his account balance. In the twenty years of his Exchange account history, he has queried the account's balance only sixteen times. Each time, it was to determine the amount that he could lend to a friend. Right now, he's aware that he possesses millions of credits and is content with that knowledge.>

* * *

Tatia and Alain were readying for bed, and she was replaying a conversation she had with a pilot, who graduated at the day's academy ceremony. Despite having just received his wings, he'd spoken to his training commander that he wished to resign his commission and apply to travel aboard the *Freedom*, and the commander thought it was worth involving her in the conversation.

Tatia had said to the new lieutenant, "You understand that Ser Racine has only four travelers, and he's got senior people seeking a place on his ship."

"Understood, Admiral," the lieutenant replied, "If Alex Racine doesn't have warships today, he'll have them tomorrow."

"And how do you think that will be possible, Lieutenant, if he's aboard a city-ship and away from the Haraken Swei Swee?" Tatia thought her question would have sobered the young man, but she was wrong.

"I have no idea, Admiral," he replied. "I don't doubt he'll find a way."

To that, Tatia had to agree, but she kept that thought to herself.

Alain watched Tatia shuck her uniform and enter the refresher. *So much woman to love,* he thought. He'd wrestled with how to approach Tatia on the burning subject of Alex's expedition, and he couldn't have been more conflicted. At present, he was bored with work. In contrast, he'd never felt more alive than when his twin and he guarded the madman. But he loved Tatia, who commanded the prestige position of Haraken's admiral, and he was desperate to find a way to have both.

To make Alain's decision more pressing, Étienne and Ellie announced they would be aboard when the *Freedom* launched. Alain knew Alex would never extend him an invitation. The man didn't want to come between Tatia and him, and he appreciated that. On the other hand, the job was his for the taking and he knew that too.

Crawling into bed, Alain waited for Tatia to join him, before he signaled the lights off. The Haraken moons shone brightly through the window. Snuggling in each other's arms, sleep failed to come for both of them. Instead, they lay awake, thoughts of their possible futures rolling through their minds.

"Would you go without me?" Tatia asked, breaking the silence.

"Direct as always, my heart," Alain replied, brushing a blonde curl from Tatia's face. "No," he replied, his voice thickening.

"Hmm," Tatia replied, snuggling closer. "Then it's a good thing I submitted my resignation today. I wouldn't want you to regret your decision to stay."

Alain pushed up on an elbow, anxious to see Tatia's face. She was grinning at him. "Then why did you ask me if I would leave you?" Alain challenged.

"Sometimes a woman wants to know where she stands," Tatia replied.

"But did you resign your commission for my sake or for your own?"

"Truth be told, I was getting tired of reviewing, signing, and sending documents, not to mention the endless meetings. I'm not cut out to be an armchair administrator."

"Neither am I," Alain admitted.

"But let's understand each other, Alain. While I've missed discovering new worlds and the universe's mysteries, I haven't missed the nearly dying part of Alex's adventures."

"So would you have gone without me?" Alain asked.

To Tatia, Alain's question sounded part tease and part earnest. In reply, she swept Alain's slender form over the top of her heavy-worlder body, and proceeded to demonstrate her answer.

— Alex and friends return in *Omnia*. —

Glossary

Celus-5 Swei Swee and Ocean Creature
Dives Deep – Member of Wave Skimmer's hive
Long Eyes – Member of Wave Skimmer's hive
Maga – Large predatory fish
Wave Skimmer – Hive First

Dischnya Soma and Nests
Chafwa – Queen of the Mawas Soma nest
Cysmana – Nyslara's personal attendant
Foomas – Chafwa's wasat
Fossem Soma – Nest that kills Haffas
Haffas – Emissary from the Tawas Soma nest
Hessan – Young warrior in Tawas Soma nest
Homsaff – Heir to the Mawas Soma nest
Mawas Soma – Chafwa and Homsaff's nest
Nyslara – Queen of the Tawas Soma nest
Posnossa – Heir to the Fossem Soma nest
Pussiro – Nyslara's wasat, a commander
Regents of Queens – Leaders on Sawa, home world of Dischnya
Sawa Messa – Celus-5, Dischnya second world
Simlan – Older warrior in Tawas Soma nest
Sissya – Queen of nest near Tawas Soma
Tawas Soma – Nyslara's nest

Dischnya Language
Bessach – Woven mats
Ceena – Dischnya term for a sea creature, the Celus-5 Swei Swee
Chona – Nest queen
Dassata – Peacemaker, name for Alex Racine
Dischnya – Dog-like species on Celus-5 and Celus-4
Diss – One

Emissary – Hunter or warrior, wearing a mask of peaceful intent
Ené – Pronunciation of Renée
Feedwa – Queen's dogs
Fellum – Pronunciation of Willem
Fissla – Council of queens
Fossar – Animal by-product used as a lubricant
Hira – Pronunciation of Keira
Mess – Two
Nessila – System's star, Celus
Sawa – Celus-4, Dischnya home world
Sheck – Unit of measurement, approximately 1.6 meters
Soma – People
Thile – Unit of time, approximately 0.14 Haraken hours
Wasat – Warrior commander
Zhinni – Pronunciation of Ginny

Harakens

Alain de Long – Director of security, twin and crèche-mate to Alain, partner to Tatia Tachenko
Alex Racine – Partner to Renée de Guirnon, Star Hunter First (Swei Swee name)
Amelia – Close friend of Christie Racine
Assembly Hall – Chamber where Assembly members meet in session
Asu Azasdau – Captain of the *Sojourn*
Bartlett – SADE, recent immigrant to Haraken
Bethany Latimer – Security escort, sergeant, New Terran, ex-TSF
Bibi Haraken – Matriarch of Haraken clan
Bobs A Lot – Swei Swee
Bright Shell – Swei Swee, First
Cedric Broussard – Z's New Terran avatar
Central Exchange – Haraken financial system
Christie Racine – Alex Racine's sister
Claude Dupuis – Engineering tech, program manager for SADE avatars
Cordelia – SADE, Julien's partner

Dane – SADE, Exchange director, Assembly SADE

Davi – Swei Swee medical specialist

Duggan Racine – Father of Alex Racine

Edmas – Young engineer, works with Emile Billings and Mickey Brandon

Edward Sardi – Earther physicist and mathematician, Willem's mission second

Ellie Thompson – Wing commander, partner to Étienne de Long

Eloise Haraken –Bibi Haraken's daughter, friend of Christie Racine

Emile Billings – Biochemist, emigrated from New Terra

Eric Stroheim – Assembly Speaker

Espero – Haraken capital city

Étienne de Long – Director of Security, twin and crèche-mate to Alain, partner to Ellie Thompson

First – Leader of the Swei Swee hives

Flit – Single person grav-drive flyer

Francis Lumley – Captain of the *Rêveur*

Franz Cohen – Wing commander, partner to Reiko Shimada

Giant sphere – Nua'll transport and former prison of the Swei Swee

Ginny – Little Singer to the Swei Swee, close friend of Teague

Hive Singer – Mutter, sings to the Swei Swee in their language

Janine – Wife of Emile Billings

Jason Haraken – Bibi Haraken's son, Assembly member

Jodlyne – Crew member, Teague's friend

Julien – SADE, Cordelia's partner

Katie Racine – Mother of Alex Racine

Keira Daubner – Security escort, corporal, Méridien

Linn – Confederation SADE

Little Singer – Ginny, sings to the Swei Swee in their language

Marie Soucis – Security escort, lieutenant, second in command, Méridien

Mickey Brandon – Senior engineer, partner to Pia Sabine

Mincie – Daughter of Emile Billings

Miranda – SADE

Mutter – SADE, Hive Singer to the Swei Swee

Nua'll – Aliens who imprisoned the Swei Swee

Oliver – Confederation SADE

Orly Saadner – Traveler pilot, New Terran

People – Manner in which the Swei Swee refer to their collective

Pia Sabine – Assembly member, medical specialist, partner to Mickey Brandon

Racine Talk Time – Media show created and hosted by Christie Racine

Reiko Shimada – Captain of the *Tanaka*, a sting ship, partner to Franz Cohen

Renée de Guirnon – Partner to Alex Racine

Rosette – SADE

Sadesville – Enclave of SADEs housing

Sand Flipper – Swei Swee

Security Directorate – Haraken security forces, twins are co-directors

Smitty Lange – Security escort, corporal

Star Hunter First – Swei Swee name for Alex Racine

Svetlana Valenko – Wing commander

Swei Swee – Six-legged friendly alien

Swift Claws – Swei Swee

Tatia Tachenko – Admiral, ex-TSF major, partner to Alain de Long

Teague – Sixteen-year-old son of Alex and Renée

Terese Lechaux – Medical expert, partner with Tomas Monti

Terran Security Forces – TSF

Tomas Monti – Haraken president, partner with Terese Lechaux

Trixie – Confederation SADE, original ID was Lenora

Ullie Tallen – Senior scientist, Méridien

Verlan – Expedition pilot

Whistles Keenly – Swei Swee

Willem – SADE, mission co-commander

Xavier Escobar – Security escort, captain, ex-TSF officer

Yaki – Medical specialist

Z – SADE

Méridiens

Confederation – Collection of Méridien worlds

Council – Organization of Méridien Leaders
Didier – SIF director, SADE
Esther – SIF director, SADE
Hector – SIF director, SADE
Independents – Confederation outcasts, originally exiled to Libre, rescued by Alex Racine
SADE – Self-aware digital entity, artificial intelligence being
SIF – Strategic Investment Fund of the Confederation SADEs
Winston – SIF director, SADE

Planets, Colonies, Moons, and Stars

Celus – Star the *Sojourn* visited
Celus-4 – Fourth planet outward from Celus
Celus-5 – Fifth planet outward from Celus
Haraken – New name of Cetus colony in Hellébore system, home of the Harakens
Hellébore – Star of the planet Cetus, which was renamed Haraken
Libre – Independents' ex-colony, now home to Swei Swee hives
Méridien – Home world of Confederation
New Terra – Home world of New Terrans
Sol – Star of solar system where Earth is located

Ships and Stations

Allora – SIF's liner, operated by Confederation SADEs
Freedom – Haraken city-ship
Our People – Haraken city-ship
Rêveur – Haraken passenger liner
Sojourn – Haraken explorer ship
Sternenvagabund (*Star Voyager*) – Passenger liner
Tanaka – Haraken sting ship
Travelers – Shuttles and fighters built by the Harakens based on the Swei Swee silver ships

My Books

The Silver Ships series is available in e-book, softcover print, and audiobook versions. Please visit my website, http://scottjucha.com, for publication locations. You may also register at my website to receive email notification about the publish dates of my novels.

If you've been enjoying this series, please consider posting a review on Amazon, even a short one. Reviews attract other readers and help indie authors, such as me.

Alex and friends will return in the upcoming novel *Omnia, A Silver Ships Novel.*

The Silver Ships Series
The Silver Ships
Libre
Méridien
Haraken
Sol
Espero
Allora
Celus-5
Omnia (forthcoming)

The Author

I've been enamored with fiction novels since the age of thirteen and long been a fan of great storytellers. I've lived in several countries overseas and in many of the US states, including Illinois, where I met my wonderful wife thirty-seven years ago. My careers have spanned a variety of industries in the visual and scientific fields of photography, biology, film/video, software, and information technology (IT).

My first attempt at a novel, titled The Lure, was a crime drama centered on the modern-day surfacing of a 110-carat yellow diamond lost during the French Revolution. In 1980, in preparation for the book, I spent two wonderful weeks researching the Brazilian people, their language, and the religious customs of Candomblé. The day I returned from Rio de Janeiro, I had my first date with my wife-to-be, Peggy Giels.

In the past, I've outlined dozens of novels, but a busy career limited my efforts to complete any of them. In the early 2014, I chose to devote my efforts to writing fulltime. My first novel, *The Silver Ships*, was released in February 2015. With the release of *Celus-5*, the series now numbers eight.

My deep appreciation goes out to the many readers who've embraced the series and its characters. Thank you!

41248569R00217

Made in the USA
Middletown, DE
08 March 2017

For Mam and Dad on

wedding annive

The Golden Anniversary

50 years of marriage, your love will last forever,

you met when you both were young and made a home together.

You brought your kids into the world and taught them right

from wrong,

You learnt them how to read and write and sing a happy song.

Family walks and picnics and rides out on a bike,

you both worked hard for family at work and home alike.

Days out all together, Helmsley, Whitby, Flamingo Land,

and when the kids got older you`d pay to see their favorite band.

You gave those kids everything, all that money could buy,

more importantly you gave them love and taught them
to aim high.

Many happy memories were made along the way,

and when the family grew with grandkids it really made
your day.

But it hasn`t all been so easy, you`ve had times of grief
and ill health,

but you got through it all together because your family
is your wealth.

So along with love and kisses,

we`re sending our best wishes.

And all your family would like to say,

congratulations from us all on your Golden wedding
anniversary day. xx

LOVE

I feel the grass on my bare feet,

as I walk across and take a seat.

I hear birds chirping in the trees,

and on my skin I feel a light breeze.

In the distance I hear bleating,

as I stretch to look, I see little lambs

leaping.

The laughter from children I hear as

they play,

Oh isn`t this a glorious day!

Bees are buzzing around all the flowers,

I really could sit watching for hours.

Butterflies flutter by,

as I watch I give a little sigh.

For all these gifts I`ve been given I

truly am blessed,

for I know there are many who have so

much less.

Now I feel like I`m floating in this beautiful

scene,

and wondering if it's all just a dream.

When a delicate feather floats down from

above,

I know it's my loved one sending he`s love. x

Life after death

My spirit gently lifts and prises away,
from the body below that peacefully lay.

I linger and watch my loved ones so dear,
In their tears, the love and the pain is
so clear.

I tell them I`m fine, I feel peace, I feel
light,
Oh boy they are hugging that body so tight!

That`s just a shell, I`m here I say,
They don`t seem to hear but the child looks
my way.

He gives me a nod and takes hold of my hand,
and tells me the next step is already planned.

Then comes a light to bright to ignore,

and I feel quite excited of new adventures

in store. X

Always be thankful

On a miserable day,

on the sofa I lay.

Watching the rain,

running down my windowpane.

I think of the homeless,

who I ask God to bless.

It's cold on the street,

when you have little to eat.

I look at my dogs with their toys

they have chewed,

and pray for the strays without

love warmth or food.

I look at my kids watching the tele,

I`m ever so grateful they have food

in their belly.

Then I say thanks to God for the roof

over my head,

and the fact that I sleep in a warm

comfy bed.

I don`t have much money,

but my hearts always sunny.

For I`ve always been thankful of

what I have got,

and try never to dwell on what I

have not. X

Just a shop worker

" I`m just a shop worker" I heard a girl say,

so, I asked her what she did in her day.

"Oh nothing special, the same every day,

serve on the till, put the order away."

As I carry on and get on with my shopping,

I see an old man with the basket he`s dropping.

She rushes past me to help the old guy,

and asks if there`s anything else he`d like

to buy.

Once served she offers to take he`s bags to

the car,

he says "thankyou dear. It`s not very far"

Then two ladies chatting come to ask her advice,

on a couple of products, they can`t decide which

is nice.

A child spills a drink and she`s there with a mop,
"Can you reach me those biscuits love? the ones at
the top"

The boss pops her head out from the office door,
says " why is that stock still sat on the floor"

"sorry " she says, "I will finish it now"
takes up half her lunchbreak but she doesn't row.

Then a girl with a pram says "you`re in my way",
as she pushes past and knocks over a display.

She smiles and says "don`t worry, its fine",
but you can see she`s glad it's nearly home time.

A teary guy tells her he just burnt he`s tea,
he just lost he`s wife who did all the cooking
you see.

"I`m finishing soon" she says, "I've got nothing planned",

"I`ll pop over yours and give you a hand".

Then a lad runs past with a bag full of cheese,

she grabs hold of the bag and says "I`ll have that back please."

To think that she thought her job was a bit dull,

personally I think her day was quite full. X

The gift of a pen

What is this object I hold in my hand?
its only small but its use big and grand.

Put it to paper and watch the ink flow,
and see just how much your knowledge will grow.

When you`re tiny you start with a line or a squiggle,
when you first learn to write you can get in a miggle.

The gift of a pen will bring endless joy,
so much more to a child than an expensive toy.

You`re setting them up with intention to learn,
then their knowledge they`ll pass to their children in
return.

Some people can sit and write the day long,
be it poetry, story, philosophy or song.

A handwritten letter delivered by post,

or a party invite sent by the host.

Can bring a smile or a little cheer,

to someone that you hold very dear.

A greetings card for whatever the reason,

or a piece of music wrote just for the season.

All of these things done with this object I hold,

with many more uses left untold .x

Happiness

I believe that we make our own happiness in life,

you may not agree if your in trouble and strife.

You may need to look deep within your own soul,

in search for happiness, your greatest goal.

It`s not really something that money can buy,

just listen to your heart, it won`t tell a lie.

You need to be able to dance in the rain,

and see the beauty in rainbows even when you`re in
pain.

Find it in the beauty given to us freely each day,

look out for the signs as you go on your way.

Take just for instance our years four seasons,

each one brings it with all different reasons.

Tulips and daffodils come in the spring,
along with the birds that wake us as they sing.

New baby animals are starting to be born,
and new little roots are shooting through the lawn.

Then comes the summer with the warm summer sun,
its festival season, the time to have fun.

Music and singing and dancing till dawn,
or even just chilling, laying out on the lawn.

Playing in the sand and long walks by the sea,
fish and chips for dinner and ice cream for tea.

In autumn when the leaves are covering the lawns,
go out and look for conkers and acorns.

You may catch a glimpse of the birds as they fly,
as they start to migrate, they make shapes in the sky.

Then comes the winter with dark nights ahead,
a cup of hot chocolate before going to bed.

Children excited playing in the snow,
up to hill with their sledges they go.

They are waiting for Santa and the reindeer to come,
but I know this is also a sad time for some.

It's a time that we shed many a tear,
wishing that our past loved ones were here.

But the excitement of kids on a Christmas morn,
brings happiness back to hearts that are torn.

So, smile and find your own happiness,
because my friends you deserve no less. X

Climate change

Our earth is in crisis and needs our help,
she`s crying out, she can`t do it herself.

There`s plastic polluting her beautiful seas,
and forest fires killing her trees.

The wildlife are gradually dying out,
it's time for us now to stand up and shout.

Us humans we think we`re the superior race,
but in years to come we`ll have vanished without trace.

The climate is changing, the signs are all there,
when we first heard of this no one listened to be fair.

Now we need to do more to make government's listen,
we really all should make it our mission.

A few little changes to our lives each day,

to show the children of tomorrow a better way.

There`s many small things that we can do,
right now we can start by doing a few.

Try taking a walk instead of the car,
if it`s nice outside and your journeys not far.

Peg out your clothes to blow in fresh air,
instead of using a dryer when the weather is fair.

Turn off the electrics, switch off all the plugs,
plant flowers in your garden to attract all the bugs.

Lets make plastic bags a thing of the past,
and invest in a good shopping bag that will last.

Let's show that we care, try to save our earth,
and her know that we value her worth .x

The rose garden

I went to a beautiful place today,

I passed through a meadow along the way.

I saw bunnies, squirrels, deer and birds,

such beauty that leaves me so lost for words.

I skipped and I danced through the abundance of
flowers and felt as if I had magical powers.

In the distance I saw a very big wall,

with a door that was locked and looked very tall.

I rifled about and found the key,

amongst the plants underneath a big tree.

Then excitedly I opened the door,

there before me more beauty, roses galore.

Red, white, pink and blue,

yellow, peach and violet too.

In the middle of the garden was a big wooden seat,
so I sat for a while wondering who I might meet.

Along came my nana who took hold of my hand,
she nodded to show me an image so grand.

The most beautiful sight in this magical place,
it was my little boy with a smile on he`s face.

He swung on the swing as he laughed and he played,
I`m not sure how long in this garden I stayed.

I didn`t want to go, I wished I could stay,
things on my mind I wanted to say.

But I was being called back so I said my goodbyes,
and I left the garden with tears in my eyes.

I`m ever so grateful for this garden I was shown,

and I go back there whenever I`m alone. X

The signs

What was that voice I heard whilst out walking?

I`m here alone, must be the wind! or are the trees
talking?

What was that shadow in the corner of my room?

maybe reflection from my lamp or the moon.

And those voices I heard when I was just small,

the imaginary friends that played in the hall.

The dreams I remember when passed relatives appear,

I better not tell folk, they`ll just think I`m queer.

I have visions of events from before I was around,

like my Dad as a child falling off a wall to the ground.

That familiar guy at the Albert Hall,

I still can`t believe I didn`t stumble and fall.

He was staring at me as he moved down the stairs,
He`s the guy from the band who`s been missing for
years.

All of a sudden things click into place,
especially when I saw little Nanas face.

I felt my old dog asleep at my feet,
the loveliest dog you ever could meet.

I`m wondering why he`s come to me now,
he passed years ago but he`s here somehow.

I feel him around whenever I`m down,
and that always turns my frown upside down.

And the Indian chief who lived years ago,
comes to give healing whenever I`m low.

All of these whispers and shadows and dreams,
I know who they are now or so it seems.

Proof that life is eternal and forever our souls will live on,

proof that spirit are with us long after their bodies have gone. X

Coronavirus 2020

I`m sure I`ve heard this pandemic was foretold,
they say it will kill off the sick and the old.

It doesn't care for religion or race,
and doesn't discriminate by the colour of your face.

Stay clear of anyone with a cough or a sneeze,
and for all our sakes wash your hands please.

The human race is in danger so what do we do?
mainly panic and stock up on rolls for the loo.

Stock up on food, handwash and gel,
which for a higher price the greedy will sell.

Buy enough cleaning products to last a whole year,
if others don`t have at least we can share.

We should self-isolate, stay home, close the schools,

but there`ll always be people who break all the rules.

They moan the can`t travel or go out for tea,
can`t go to the cinema or for a boat ride on the sea.

They complain about closures of venues and events,
whilst others are just worrying about paying their rents.

Some good folks will show kindness to others,
with offers of help to our sisters and brothers.

Think about times we`ve wished to stay home,
tired of work, wanting time on our own.

Then make the most of this time locked away,
leave the worries of the world for another day.

Play with the kids, tell stories, sing a song,
I`m sure before long this virus will be gone.

Make the most of the quiet if you have time

On your own,

Sit in the power, remember we're never

really alone.

And whilst we`re all home the air will get cleaner,

the earth will bloom, the sea will get clearer.

So I hope that my friends before very long,

With the power of prayer this virus will

be gone.

And when we are able to go out freely once more,

we`ll appreciate everything much more than before. X

Wanderlust

I`ve always been a wanderer, I like to freely roam.

I like to move around a lot, while others settle and

call it home.

Some people put down roots and live their whole life

where they were born,

but for me that would be boring and I'd feel a little

torn.

For there are so many places I`ve never been before,

I see that as new places for me to go explore.

Some people make a friend for life at the age of three,

but that is not the way I am, nor shall I ever be.

I like to meet new people, many of who come and go,

I just don`t cling to people, it`s who I am you know.

To me a house is a machine, a shell, a place to rest my head,

if I was alone with no family. a camper van would be my bed.

I`d drive around from town to town, meet new people along

the way,

In hope of new adventure each and every day.

Some people say it`s the gypsy blood or that I`m a free spirit,

maybe it`s true, I don`t know. Is it?

Or maybe it`s all just,

totally down to wanderlust .x

Hopes, dreams and aspirations

We all have high hopes, dreams and aspirations,
that seem to get higher with next generations.

Dreams of winning the lotto so we can sit on
great wealth,
and of course, we`d all like to live in good health.

University degrees with very big fees,
then take a year out and go overseas.

A dream job with good money to buy a flash car,
holidays abroad, we want to go far.

A big house with more rooms than we`ll ever need,
a pedigree dog to walk on a lead.

A million friends on Facebook or such like,
a brilliant singer when you take hold of the mic.

To be the best dancer, artist or writer,

some even aspire to be the best fighter.

To lose a bit weight and drop a dress size,

even though you are perfect in everyone's eyes.

To be beautiful and clever and know all the goss,

then people are jealous, oh well it's their loss.

Somewhere down the line I think we got lost,

and sometimes it comes at a very big cost.

To have hopes and dreams can be good, yes it`s true,

but it`s always best to be the real you.

Being honest and kind and a true friend,

appreciating all of the time that you spend.

With the people you hold dear in your heart,

being true to yourself is a good way to start.

Giving help where you can to others in need,

not being a prisoner to money or greed.

Finding happiness in the simpler things,

like watching a baby bird first flap it`s wings.

Speaking only nice words when you`ve got something

to say,

bringing some happiness to another's day.

I`m talking about aspiring to be good,

at being the best if ever you could.

The best thing you could aspire to be,

is the very best you, you ever could be. X

Happy Birthday Granda Ben

Happy 100th birthday to my Granda Ben,

I have such happy memories from all the

way back when.

We`d sit and watch TV together when I was just

a tot,

Trumpton, Mr Ben, Top Cat, you loved the cartoon

slot.

A proud, hardworking, honest man, labour

through and through,

Pebble Mill, the politics, you liked egg

sarnies too.

You liked to dance with Nana, a pint a game

of bingo,

but most of all I remember how you loved

your family so.

If you were here, we`d have a massive party

with celebrations lasting hours,

but instead I'll go to the cemetery,

visit your grave, bring flowers.

And once again I`ll wish you Happy 100th Birthday,

with all my love and kisses from your granddaughter

kay xx

Special thanks to my inspirers and those who helped make this book possible,

My amazing family, for always supporting everything I do.

Claire Graham for inviting me along to church, I'm forever grateful.

Everyone at church for making me welcome especially

Val and Gordon who are inspirational teachers and

everyone in the Monday class.

Claire Fahey, a brilliant friend, the laughs, the coffees & catchups.

my children who are always an absolute ray of sunshine and the biggest

inspiration in my life x

love and light to you all x

In memory of

Emile 30/12/2009

little nana Edna Tumilty 7/11/1924-13/1/2007

Granda Ben Tumilty 30/09/1920 - 16/10/1988

Granda Thomas Townsend 4/12/1921-4/8/1971

always in my thoughts x

Printed in Great Britain
by Amazon

42353761R00030

Manifesting Miracles

Short stories of manifestation magic

Creative Intelligence
Copyright © 2023 Wain Gordon-Seaton

Contents

Foreword

In the pursuit of a life well-lived, we often find ourselves navigating through a labyrinth of challenges, seeking a path that leads to fulfilment and happiness. Unfortunately, way too many never reach that destination.

I write this book with the hope that the stories it contains will serve as beacons of inspiration, guiding you toward the realisation of your inherent power to create a life of joy, peace and fulfilment, for I believe that is the life we all deserve.

It deeply saddens me to witness the unnecessary suffering of individuals when the keys to their liberation are within reach, and always have been.

Throughout my journey, I have encountered moments of both triumph and tribulation, each contributing to the fabric of my personal development. It is from these personal experiences that the stories within this book emerge.

If even one person can find peace, inspiration, or a glimmer of hope or guidance within these pages, then the purpose of this book will be fulfilled.

May these stories be a source of empowerment, reminding you that you hold the pen to your life's narrative.

With each turn of the page, I invite you to embark on a journey of self-discovery, understanding, and unwavering belief in your ability to create a happy and fulfilling life.

May the wisdom shared within these stories serve as companions on your personal development journey, illuminating the path toward the vibrant existence that awaits you.

Dedication

This book is dedicated to Oliver, Pilch, Shamps, and Mus, individuals whose significant contributions to my personal development have been invaluable. I extend heartfelt gratitude to my mother, Grace, and my beloved daughter, Ciarni, both of whom have played integral roles in shaping my journey. Their profound impact has not only influenced my growth, but has also served as a source of inspiration, making the creation of this book not only possible, but deeply meaningful.

The Magic of Storytelling

Introduction

Make yourself comfortable, you're in for an adventure. The pages you are about to read contain a collection of powerful, short stories waiting to transport you to places of wisdom, self-discovery and personal growth. Though fictional, these tales hold transformational potential. Their essence and themes traverse the boundaries of made-up worlds to take root in your day-to-day reality.

Storytelling has always been one of humanity's greatest gifts. Through vivid narratives, we experience life from new vantage points and uncover deeper truths. The range of stories curated in this book holds that same power, to entertain, engage and enlighten. You'll close these covers with a fresh perspective on how to work with the law of attraction.

Though short in length, these stories contain powerful pearls of wisdom, able to inspire and promote inner change. The messages spark self-discovery by resonating with the essential human experience inside each tale.

Each story contains seeds of insight, as well as keys that could open doors that may have previously appeared locked to you. Some stories uncover hard but necessary truths., whilst others offer hope in overcoming manifestation blocks.

This book is a vessel filled with knowledge gained from 'real world' living, condensed into bite-sized tales.

Rest assured, each story has something to offer you. Every character's journey may just mirror a piece of your own.

Enjoy!

Unleash the power within,
and watch the ordinary
transform into
the extraordinary."

Manifesting Her dream Partner

Kates Story

In a small town nestled between rolling hills and meadows, there lived a woman named Kate. Kate was a vibrant and independent woman, successful in her career and surrounded by a loving circle of friends. However, despite all her accomplishments, she couldn't escape the persistent yearning for a deep and meaningful romantic connection.

One day, Kate stumbled upon the concept of the Law of Attraction. Intrigued by the idea that she could manifest the love of her life by focusing on positive thoughts and energy, she eagerly delved into books and workshops on the subject. She created vision boards, recited affirmations, and visualised her ideal relationship down to the smallest details.

In her pursuit of love, Kate met several men who seemed promising. Each time, she felt a surge of excitement, convinced that the universe was finally responding to her desires. Yet, despite her efforts, the relationships would inevitably fizzle out, leaving Kate disheartened and questioning the efficacy of the Law of Attraction.

Frustrated and on the verge of giving up, Kate decided to seek guidance from a therapist. During their sessions, it became apparent that Kate was carrying deep-seated wounds from her childhood. Unresolved issues and unhealed scars were casting a shadow over her attempts to build a lasting connection.

Together with her therapist, Kate explored the roots of her emotional pain. She discovered that her parents' tumultuous relationship had left her with a fear of vulnerability and a belief that love was synonymous with pain. As a result, Kate unknowingly erected emotional walls, pushing away potential partners before they could get too close.

With newfound awareness, Kate embarked on a journey of self-discovery and healing. She confronted the painful memories of her past, allowing herself to feel the emotions she had long suppressed. As she faced these wounds head-on, Kate began to release the hold they had on her.

Slowly but surely, Kate's perspective on love shifted. Instead of seeing it as a source of potential pain, she started viewing it as an opportunity for growth and connection. The Law of Attraction, once a source of frustration, became a tool for self-improvement and self-love.

As Kate continued her healing journey, she found that her relationships took on a different hue. No longer driven by fear, she was able to connect with others on a deeper level. The walls she had built started crumbling, making way for genuine intimacy and understanding.

In time, Kate met a man who saw beyond her defences, embracing the authentic and healed version of herself. Their connection was different from anything she had experienced before – it was built on mutual respect, understanding, and a shared commitment to growth.

As Kate and her newfound love embarked on a journey together, they discovered that the Law of Attraction had indeed played a crucial role in bringing them together. However, it was the inner work that Kate had done, the healing of her childhood wounds, that allowed her to truly open her heart to love. In the end, Kate realised that the most powerful manifestation was the transformation that occurred within herself.

The Lesson

Kate's story offers a deeply personal journey we can all relate to in some way. As we follow her pursuit of love through the lens of the Law of Attraction, we witness the struggles that many of us face in our quest for meaningful connections. It becomes apparent that the lessons embedded in Kate's experiences hold a mirror to our own lives.

In Kate's journey, the therapist becomes a guide, and we can learn from this parallel. Seeking professional guidance in our own lives when faced with challenges, especially matters of the heart, may provide the necessary insights we need to navigate complex emotions and barriers.

The crux of Kate's narrative lies in the profound lesson about childhood wounds and unresolved issues. We are prompted to reflect on our emotional baggage, recognising how past experiences might influence our present relationships. The story encourages us to embark on our healing journey, understanding that it is this inner work that can pave the way to true connection.

As Kate shifts her perspective on love, we too can adopt a similar transformation. Fear, often an obstacle to meaningful connections, can be replaced with a view of love as a catalyst for personal growth and profound connections. The narrative nudges us to examine our beliefs about love and consider how they might be shaping our personal experiences.

Kate's journey of self-discovery serves as an inspiration. We are reminded of the power of confronting suppressed emotions and painful memories, acknowledging that true healing requires us to face our innermost vulnerabilities. The story encourages us to break down our emotional walls, allowing for authentic connections to blossom.

Ultimately, as Kate opens her heart to love, we are invited to consider our own readiness for connection. The tale concludes with the realisation that the Law of Attraction while playing a role, is most potent when coupled with our inner work. Kate's story becomes a shared narrative, teaching us that the most profound manifestation occurs within ourselves.

"Healing within is the first step to becoming a magnet for the love that you seek

Finding Abundance Through Surrender

Amy's Story

Amy sighed as she sat down on the couch after another long day at work. She was exhausted, both physically and mentally. For months now, Amy had been trying every trick in the book to manifest more money into her life. She had visualised giant checks coming in the post, said affirmations of abundance each morning, and even tried to physically emulate the feeling of having more money by going on shopping sprees with credit cards. But her bank account remained disappointingly low.

Amy had always been a go-getter, working hard and hustling to try to get ahead. Manifesting money felt like just another project she could will into existence through sheer determination. But lately, all her efforts were leaving her burnt out, frustrated, and feeling like a failure.

"I just don't get it," Amy said aloud to her empty apartment. "I'm doing everything the books and videos say. Why isn't this working?"

She thought back to the latest failed attempt, the vision board full of luxury holidays and fancy cars that she had spent hours creating and decorating. She had read that surrounding yourself with images of your desires would help align your vibration to attract them. But the vision board above her bed seemed to mock her every morning, showing extravagances as far out of reach as ever.

Amy could feel herself sliding into desperation and anger. She picked up one of the manifestation books on the coffee table and launched it across the room.

"This is all nonsense!" she yelled. "What's the point of trying so hard when the universe ignores me at every single turn?"

But as her words hung in the air, Amy realised how tightly she had been gripping onto the outcome she wanted. Her whole body was tense with frustration and exertion. She knew then that all her efforts had come from a place of lack, the belief that she didn't already have abundance.

Amy took a deep breath and softened. She realised that money would not come by forcing it, but by relaxing into the understanding that she already had it. The universe was not ignoring her, but waiting for her to align with what she wanted by feeling like it was already here.

So Amy made a decision, she would now choose to release the struggle. She took her vision board down, cancelled her daily affirmations, and decided to let go of trying to make anything happen. Instead of looking for money, she looked for joy, in her friends, her hobbies and in her work. She focused on appreciating what was already good.

Slowly, without her noticing at first, things began to change. A close friend asked Amy to help out with a big project that came with a sizeable payment. The woman who lived next door hired Amy to care for her pets while she was away and paid her generously for it. A long-forgotten relative passed away and left Amy a small inheritance too.

Over time, money began to flow to Amy in all sorts of surprising and effortless ways. Soon her bank account was fuller than it had ever been before. Her manifestations had happened, but only once she stopped trying so hard to force them.

Amy saw now that it wasn't always about vision boards or affirmations. It was about choosing feelings of abundance, and then allowing the universe to deliver the opportunities. Just like magic, as she let go of trying to control the hows or the whens, the money came, because she found and tapped into the peace and plenty already within her.

The lesson

Amy's journey teaches valuable lessons about the art of manifestation and the mindset necessary for attracting abundance. One of the primary takeaways is the importance of shifting one's perspective from a mindset of lack to a mindset of abundance. Amy's initial approach, driven by determination and effort, left her feeling burnt out and frustrated. The story encourages readers to reflect on their own efforts and consider whether they are coming from a place of scarcity or abundance.

The narrative highlights the pitfalls of attachment and desperation in the manifestation process. Amy's frustration and anger stemmed from her tightly gripping onto the outcome she desired. From this we can learn that true manifestation involves letting go of the need to control every detail and instead embracing a sense of trust in the universe's timing.

The story emphasises the significance of feeling abundance in the present moment rather than constantly seeking it in the future. Amy's decision to release the struggle and focus on joy and appreciation in her current life showcases the transformative power of gratitude. We can apply this lesson by acknowledging the positive aspects of our lives, cultivating a sense of contentment, and allowing abundance to flow from a place of fulfilment.

Furthermore, Amy's experience underscores the idea that manifestation is not solely about external tools like vision boards or affirmations; it's about the internal shift in one's beliefs and emotions. Her story encourages us to explore our own beliefs about abundance and to recognise the impact of our emotional state on the manifestation process. Amy's decision to let go of external practices and focus on inner peace illustrates that the true magic of manifestation lies in the alignment of thoughts and feelings.

In conclusion, Amy's journey offers us valuable insights into the principles of manifestation. By shifting from a mindset of lack to abundance, releasing attachment to outcomes, embracing gratitude in the present, and understanding the internal nature of manifestation, we can apply these lessons to invite positive changes into our own lives. Amy's story inspires a reevaluation of approaches to manifestation, encouraging a more relaxed and trusting relationship with the universe.

Surrendering is not a sign of weakness; it's a declaration of trust in the divine timing of the universe.

Lessons Of Appreciation

Paul's Story

Completely satisfied with his life, Paul glanced around his tidy apartment. He had a great job, close friends, and was financially comfortable. When he learned about the Law of Attraction, he got excited to use it to gain even more. Just think of the wealth, relationships and success he could manifest!

Paul started big. He made extravagant vision boards with photos of expensive clothes, six-figure sports cars, and multi-million-pound mansions. He repeated positive affirmations and visualised each morning and night to attract these things, imagining how much better his already good life would be.

Initially, Paul felt energised by the possibilities. But after a few weeks, he felt frustrated that none of the items on his vision board had materialised yet. Around the same time, things he had always appreciated about his life started to irritate him. His apartment felt too small, his car too old, and his job too boring.

Paul doubled down on his manifestation efforts. He used the Law of Attraction techniques for hours each day, fixated on picturing his perfect life. But the more he focused on what he wanted but didn't have, the more dissatisfied he felt with what he did have.

Soon Paul was unhappy and anxious all the time. When he hung out with friends, he was distracted by the haunting thought that all the new things he wanted, just weren't coming. All he could think about was using the Law of Attraction to get the life he wanted.

One day, an old friend named Sam invited Paul to get coffee. Though distracted, Paul agreed. As they caught up, Sam asked Paul what was new.

"I've been trying to use the Law of Attraction to get more of what I want; A bigger home, luxury car, travel and financial freedom," Paul explained, embarrassed to admit nothing had happened yet.

Sam nodded. "I tried that too, wishing for more and more. But it made me less happy."

"What do you mean?" Paul asked, confused yet intrigued.

"When I was focused on what I didn't have, I lost appreciation for what I did have," Sam said. "My life was already good, just not as 'perfect' as what I imagined."

Paul's eyes widened with realisation. In his quest for an ideal life, he had stopped counting his current blessings, therefore taking his health, job and loved ones for granted.

"You're right, I got so fixated on what I wanted that I forgot to be grateful for what I already have," Paul reluctantly admitted.

They talked more about the dangers of seeking unattainable perfection, versus nurturing existing joys. When Paul got home, he took down his vision boards and the affirmations he had scattered around his home. He vowed to stop endlessly chasing more and focus on appreciating the great life he already had now.

Paul started writing daily gratitude lists, noting things down like his comfy bed, reliable car, and friendships. During meals, he savoured each bite, thanking the food for nourishing his body. On walks, he noticed details like singing birds and cool breezes that had always been there, but he had stopped paying attention to.

Gradually, the anxiety Paul had been feeling seemed to fade away. He realised that by fixating on what he didn't have, he was missing out on all the goodness he already did have.

The Law of Attraction didn't bring Paul all the specific things he had envisioned. But he did attract more happiness, fulfilment and peace back into his life, simply by being grateful for what he had in this moment, rather than wishing for something else in the next. This allowed him to enjoy his life as it was now, and realise he already had what he needed to be content.

The lesson

In Paul's journey with the Law of Attraction, we find valuable lessons about the delicate balance between manifestation and gratitude, and how it shapes our overall sense of well-being.

The story mirrors the initial excitement and allure many of us feel when we stumble upon the Law of Attraction. Paul's eagerness to use the principles to enhance his already satisfying life resonates with anyone seeking self-improvement and personal growth. However, his experience serves as a cautionary tale, prompting us to reflect on our pursuits and consider whether our desire for more might be overshadowing our appreciation for what we currently have.

Paul's journey emphasises the risk of attachment to external outcomes. As he fixated on manifesting grandiose visions, he began to overlook the blessings he already enjoyed, leading to dissatisfaction and restlessness. It's a gentle reminder to balance our aspirations with an appreciation for the present, understanding that the journey is as significant as the destination.

The pivotal conversation with Sam introduces the concept of happiness being linked to gratitude rather than material acquisition. Sam's revelation about losing happiness when fixated on what was lacking serves as a turning point for Paul. It urges us to contemplate the true nature of contentment and how it relates to acknowledging and appreciating what is already present in our lives.

The story culminates with Paul's shift toward gratitude, illustrating the transformative power of appreciating the present moment. His decision to dismantle the vision boards and replace them with daily gratitude practices becomes a practical lesson for each of us. It encourages us to integrate gratitude into our daily lives, focusing on the simple joys and blessings that might be overlooked in the pursuit of larger goals.

Ultimately, the story suggests that while the Law of Attraction may not always bring about the specific external manifestations we desire, it can certainly attract a sense of happiness, fulfilment, and peace when combined with genuine gratitude. It invites us to reassess our pursuits, appreciating the abundance that already exists in our lives and understanding that happiness often lies not in acquiring more but in recognising the richness of the present moment.

The more you count your blessings, the more blessings there will be to count.

Master Manipulator

Tony's Story

Tony had always been an adept manipulator. He knew how to charm people to get them on his side. He leveraged and twisted situations to his advantage. Tony was so skilled at scheming manoeuvrers to benefit himself that manipulating people and circumstances became second nature to him.

When Tony heard about the Law of Attraction, the idea that you manifest your desires through thoughts and energy, he saw it as the ultimate life hack. Now he could sit back and just let the universe do the manipulating for him!

Tony started using the Law of Attraction techniques right away. He made vision boards of wealth, fame and luxury. He repeated affirmations daily, watched manifestation videos on YouTube and continually tried all sorts of creative ways to coerce the universe to bend situations to serve him.

At first, Tony revelled in this new form of passive manipulation. It felt effortless! He praised the Law of Attraction for delivering him parking spots close to building entrances and conveniently timed green lights. But Tony grew impatient when it came to manifesting his bigger desires of career success, romance, luxury and financial abundance. He couldn't understand why the universe wasn't handing him everything immediately.

One day, an old friend named Beth invited Tony to catch up over lunch. Though in a low mood from lack of manifestation success, Tony agreed.

"How have you been?" Beth asked. "What's been happening?"

Tony shared how he had been trying to use the Law of Attraction to get the universe to give him the job title, relationship and money he wanted.

Beth looked concerned. "The Law of Attraction isn't about manipulating external things. It's about manifesting internal changes."

Tony was sceptical. Beth explained that while visualising desired outcomes can help, the real goal should be aligning one's consciousness with positive energy.

"If you try to use the Law of Attraction to control people and events, you'll stay stuck in that manipulation mindset," she said. "But if you focus on raising your own vibration, you'll attract joy organically."

Tony left lunch feeling confused but open-minded. He realised he had been treating the Law of Attraction as another strategy for scheming to get his way. But Beth was right, the external things he manifested were just surface level. For deeper change, he needed to work on himself.

Tony decided to stop demanding the universe to deliver him certain outcomes. Instead, he started meditating, reflecting and doing whatever felt good and natural for him to raise his own energy. He focused less on controlling situations, and more on cultivating inner peace.

Over time, Tony's drive to manipulate faded. He no longer kept score of how much he could get from others or the universe. When good things happened, he saw them as natural blessings rather than rewards he was entitled to. Tony's work became fuelled by passion, not self-gain. His relationships grew based on mutual care, not advantage.

Tony saw that he had been chasing after specific externals when what he truly needed was internal growth. As he focused on being his best self, he attracted more of what he had been seeking all along...happiness, purpose and fulfilment.

Tony realised the Law of Attraction wasn't about manifesting shallow desires from a place of lack or entitlement. It was about doing the inner work to align with higher energy and truth. This allowed him to let go of manipulation as his automatic approach. Instead of trying to control people and situations, Tony tuned into controlling his own thoughts and actions.

When Tony focused on improving himself, he found what he had been seeking externally started to blossom naturally. By watering the seeds within, Tony grew into the happiest version of himself. And he discovered lasting joy comes not from chasing circumstances, but from nurturing inner peace.

The Lesson

In Tony's transformative journey with the Law of Attraction, there are profound lessons about the shift from external manipulation to internal alignment, showcasing the true essence of personal growth and fulfilment.

As we delve into Tony's story, it's hard not to see reflections of our own journeys. Here is someone, much like many of us, eager to unlock the secrets of the Law of Attraction for a shortcut to success. Tony's initial excitement mirrors our own when discovering a new method for improving our lives.

However, as Tony's impatience and frustration unfold, we find ourselves nodding along, recognising the familiar human tendency we all share, the desire for instant gratification and the questioning of why our efforts don't yield immediate results. This story prompts us to reflect on our own experiences and consider the importance of patience and understanding the Law of Attraction as a process.

The turning point during Tony's lunch with Beth hits close to home. Beth's wisdom about the Law of Attraction not being about manipulating external circumstances but manifesting internal changes makes us pause. How often have we focused solely on external gains, neglecting the internal shifts that are at the heart of true transformation?

Tony's decision to shift focus from external demands to internal growth becomes a call to action for us. The story encourages us to recognise that true transformation originates from within, urging us to embark on our personal development journey rather than relying on external circumstances for fulfilment.

As Tony's mindset shifts, we see an opportunity for personal introspection. The story prompts us to consider whether we approach personal development from a place of entitlement or a genuine desire for growth. It resonates with the idea that the Law of Attraction isn't just about manifesting shallow desires but doing the inner work to align with higher energy and truth.

In conclusion, Tony's story isn't just his story; it's a narrative that invites us all to reflect on our own journey with the Law of Attraction. It reminds us that true fulfilment arises when we tune into controlling our thoughts and actions rather than attempting to control external factors. The lessons from Tony's experience become a personal guide for navigating the nuanced path of manifestation and personal growth.

The more you try to
control something, the
more it controls you.

The Importance Of Gratitude

Rachel's Story

Rachel frowned as she sat in the driver's seat of her brand-new luxury car. She had finally managed to manifest the vehicle of her dreams after months of trying. But instead of feeling excited and grateful, Rachel felt... let down. This was supposed to make her happy, but the thrill had worn off after just a few days.

"I can't believe I wasted so much time and energy trying to get this car," Rachel complained to her friend Zoe. "Now that I have it, it just feels like another thing."

"Maybe you'd feel more grateful if you didn't manifest stuff so easily," Zoe suggested. "You're always seeking the next best thing."

Rachel brushed off Zoe's comment, but inside she wondered if it contained some truth. As far back as she could remember, she had always been restless. As soon as she attained something, she moved quickly on to wanting something else without pausing to fully appreciate it.

Over the next few weeks, Rachel amped up her manifestation efforts, visualising and asking the universe for more luxury items, exotic trips away and financial gains. Rachel had become obsessed with manifesting the life she wanted.

But each time she acquired something new, that familiar feeling of disappointment always crept in.

Meanwhile, other areas of Rachel's life seemed to stagnate. Her job stopped offering promotions. Friendships felt superficial and romantic relationships fizzled out quickly.

One day, Zoe invited Rachel out for coffee. Rachel spent the entire time complaining about her unhappiness and how manifestation wasn't working.

Finally, Zoe spoke up. "Rachel, don't you see you're manifesting from a place of lack? You think the next thing will make you happy, but it never does."

Rachel fell silent. She realised that Zoe was right, her mindset had become entangled in dissatisfaction. By constantly seeking the next thing without gratitude, she was emitting an energy of scarcity to the universe. In response, the universe kept reflecting experiences that left her unfulfilled.

Zoe encouraged Rachel to take a 30-day gratitude challenge. This entailed writing down three things she was thankful for each day. Rachel agreed, wanting to break her cycle of ingratitude and discontentment.

The first week was admittedly difficult. After so much focus on what she lacked, it felt foreign to acknowledge the blessings already present. But slowly, Rachel's outlook began to shift. She felt warmth writing "I am grateful for my cosy bed" and "I am grateful for my health." Tiny joys she had overlooked started standing out.

Halfway through, Rachel was feeling more optimism and peace. By the end, gratitude had become a natural reflex, she felt it washing over her as she sipped coffee, hugged friends, and watched the sunset. For the first time, Rachel felt true fulfilment welling up from within.

Rachel realised the mistake she had been making. No external manifestation could make her happy if she didn't already feel gratitude inside. When she appreciated what she had, abundance seemed to flow effortlessly.

Rachel stopped obsessively chasing manifestations. Instead, she tuned into the blessings already around her. Miraculously, she got everything she had been trying so hard to manifest before because now she could receive it from a place of gratitude. She was now able to fully appreciate them too.

The Lesson

Rachel's journey with manifestation holds powerful lessons for us all, urging us to reevaluate our approach to desires and fulfilment.

As we step into Rachel's world, it's a familiar scenario, the excitement of attaining a dream, only to find it lacking in the expected joy.

Many of us can relate to the initial thrill of achieving something we worked hard for, only to have it fade away quickly. Rachel's experience prompts us to ponder whether our pursuits are driven by genuine fulfilment or a constant need for the next best thing.

Zoe's insightful suggestion to Rachel becomes a mirror for us to look into. How often do we find ourselves relentlessly seeking the next goal without pausing to appreciate the present achievement? Rachel's restlessness echoes our own tendencies to move swiftly from one desire to the next, never fully embracing the joy of the moment.

As Rachel intensifies her manifestation efforts, the narrative becomes a cautionary tale. The pursuit of external desires grows into an obsession, leaving other crucial aspects of life stagnating. It's a reminder for us to evaluate the holistic impact of our pursuits. Are they enhancing various aspects of our lives, or are they causing imbalance?

The pivotal coffee outing with Zoe becomes a moment of truth. Rachel realises the profound impact of her mindset on the outcomes she attracts. The idea of manifesting from a place of lack strikes a chord, prompting us to assess our own mindset when setting intentions. Are we emitting an energy of scarcity, or are we manifesting from a place of abundance and gratitude?

Zoe's 30-day gratitude challenge becomes a personal invitation for us to break the cycle of ingratitude and discontentment. Rachel's initial struggle resonates with our own experiences, where acknowledging existing blessings may feel foreign after a period of focusing on lack. Yet, as Rachel's outlook begins to shift, we are reminded of the transformative power of gratitude.

By the end of the challenge, Rachel's journey takes a remarkable turn. Gratitude becomes a natural reflex, and she discovers that external manifestations lose their grip when she cultivates fulfilment from within. This becomes a profound lesson for us all. True happiness arises when we appreciate what we already have. It prompts us to ask ourselves: Are we chasing external validations, or are we embracing the richness of the present moment?

Rachel's realisation becomes our invitation to stop obsessively chasing manifestations. Instead, let's tune into the blessings already around us. Through Rachel's story, we learn that abundance flows effortlessly when we feel gratitude inside. It becomes a call to open our eyes to appreciate what has been there all along.

Appreciation is the currency of the universe.

Power Of Attention

Michael's Story

Michael sighed as he looked around his messy apartment, bills piling up on the table. His career was stagnant, relationships rocky. He felt like life kept dumping more problems in his lap. Why did he have such bad luck?

"Everything always goes wrong for me," Michael complained to his friend James. "I must have manifested a curse that makes my life crappy."

"Maybe you manifested it in a different way," James said cryptically. Michael gave him a puzzled look.

James continued, "Your thoughts and focus have a lot of power, even if you don't realise it. What do you spend your mental energy on each day?"

Michael thought about it. He realised he did tend to obsess over everything that wasn't working… financial struggles, work stress, relationship issues. He vented about these problems constantly.

James nodded, seeing the lightbulb go off in Michael's mind. "Exactly. You manifested but through unconscious negative focus."

Michael reeled as he recognised the truth in this. He had indeed manifested his own reality, but by perpetually fixating on everything he didn't want. Like attracts like, so this energy had boomeranged back problems into his life.

Michael knew he had to change his focus. He began watching his thoughts vigilantly, redirecting away from complaints. When negativity arose, he shifted intentionally to what he was grateful for, like his health and close friends. He also visualised how he wanted life to be, focusing on these positive visions.

The change was challenging at first. Michael's habitual mental patterns resisted the switch. But over time, he trained his mind to focus on the good. It wasn't too long before Michael began to see tangible shifts start to occur.

Creative ideas flowed for fulfilling work projects he was passionate about. Fun social connections drew new kindred spirits into his life. Michael felt more empowered navigating challenges with a solutions-oriented mindset too.

Within a few months, Michael's whole reality had transformed. He felt happier and so much more excited about his life. He realised this was the true power of manifestation. It wasn't some magical force outside himself, it was his own consciousness creating through where he placed attention.

Michael saw that he had never been a victim of circumstance. He had unconsciously manifested exactly what he focused on, which always seemed to be, problems and lack. But by being mindful of his thoughts, he was able to intentionally manifest the life he wanted.

Whilst on a relaxing holiday, Michael met a spiritual teacher named Silvia. He told her all about his recent realisations.

"You're exactly right," Silvia said. "Most people believe they see the world as it is. But in fact, we see the world as we are! Our inner state creates our outer reality."

Michael shuddered as he grasped the full significance of this truth. He had created his own suffering by dwelling on the negatives. But he also had the power to create joy by choosing where to direct his energy.

The Lesson

In Michael's introspective journey, we discover profound insights into the transformative power of thought and conscious focus, prompting us to reconsider our own mental habits and the impact they have on our lives.

As we enter Michael's cluttered apartment and feel the weight of his stagnating career and rocky relationships, it becomes a familiar scene. Many of us have experienced moments of feeling overwhelmed by life's challenges, questioning why things seem to go wrong. Michael's sentiment of bad luck becomes a shared emotion, resonating with our struggles.

James, the insightful friend, becomes a symbolic figure challenging us to examine the energy of our thoughts. The cryptic suggestion that Michael may have manifested his challenges through unconscious negative focus becomes a mirror for us to hold up to our own mental landscapes. What are we fixating on daily? Where is our mental energy directed?

As Michael contemplates his thought patterns, we are prompted to do the same. The realisation that he had manifested his reality through unconscious negativity becomes a wake-up call for us. Like Michael, have we been unintentionally creating our challenges by obsessing over what's not working? James' wisdom becomes a catalyst for us to question the nature of our manifestations.

Michael's intentional shift in focus becomes an actionable lesson for us all to learn. The struggle to break free from habitual negative thinking resonates with our own experiences. How often do we find ourselves dwelling on problems rather than solutions? Michael's journey becomes a guide, urging us to redirect our thoughts consciously, focusing on gratitude and positive visualisations.

The tangible shifts in Michael's life become a beacon of hope. His career gains momentum, new connections enrich his social life, and a solutions-oriented mindset empowers him to navigate challenges. It inspires us to consider the potential transformations within our own lives if we shift our focus from problems to possibilities.

Silvia, the spiritual teacher, becomes a voice of universal truth. The revelation that we see the world as we are, not as it is, strikes a chord. Michael's realisation that he had created suffering by dwelling on negatives becomes a reflective moment for us. How often have we allowed our inner state to shape our outer reality, unconsciously attracting what we focus on?

In Michael's meeting with Silvia, the profound wisdom becomes a universal message. We, too, have the power to create joy by consciously choosing where to direct our energy. It becomes an invitation for us to take control of our thoughts, recognising the immense influence they have on our reality.

In conclusion, Michael's journey becomes a shared exploration of the profound connection between thought, focus, and reality. It prompts us to introspect, redirect our mental energy, and embrace the transformative power of conscious manifestation. Through his story, we learn that we hold the key to shaping our own experiences by where we choose to place our attention and focus.

Where attention goes,

energy flows.

The Importance of clarity

Matt's Story

Matt stared at the blank vision board in front of him, overwhelmed by indecision. He had just learned about manifesting through vision boards. But what exactly did he want to manifest? A new job, relationship, car? His desires felt like a jumbled mess. Matt had always struggled with choosing what he wanted in life.

Sighing, Matt started half-heartedly cutting out photos to represent vague goals...travel, money, and friends. But he felt doubtful this vision board would work without clarity.

Over the next few weeks, Matt tried other manifestation techniques too, like writing desires on paper and doing elaborate visualisation he had learned from TikTok videos. But his efforts felt empty, as he seemed to just be going through the motions without conviction.

"I don't get why manifestation isn't working for me," Matt complained to his friend Kendra. "Is the universe broken or something?"

"Maybe the problem isn't the universe, but your lack of clarity," Kendra suggested. "How can you manifest anything when you don't know what you want?"

Matt nodded slowly. Kendra had a point. He had sleep-walked through life drifting from one thing to the next without strong preferences. Expecting manifestation to work without deciding what he desired was unrealistic.

Kendra encouraged Matt to take some time for serious self-reflection. Matt realised he needed to gain insight into his goals and values so he could tap into his true vision.

Over the next few weeks, Matt journaled, meditated and observed his thoughts and feelings more closely. Gradually, he uncovered genuine desires that resonated at his core, like wanting to help people through social work, travel to Iceland, and have deeper connections.

Armed with this newfound self-knowledge, Matt re-approached manifestation. This time, he felt a strong pull behind his vision boards and affirmations. Before acting, he considered whether something aligned with his values and genuine desires. His energy shifted from apathetic to inspired.

Amazingly, Matt's unclear life also started coming into focus. He discovered work which gave him the perfect opportunity to help underserved communities. He planned an adventurous trip to Iceland, and meaningful relationships blossomed. The universe delivered because Matt finally knew what he truly wanted from life.

Matt realised he had been stumbling through life blindly, never pausing to get perspective. But once he gained clarity, he could act decisively instead of drifting. Things seamlessly fell into place, guided by his inner compass.

Kendra was right, manifestation relies on knowing what lights you up. Without clarity, any goals will just be hollow. Deciding what you want lets energy and intent flow into making it a reality.

The Lesson

In Matt's exploration of manifestation, we encounter a relatable journey of discovering the vital role that clarity plays in the process, prompting us to reflect on our own goals and desires.

As we join Matt in front of his blank vision board, we sense the familiar overwhelm of indecision. Matt's struggle to pinpoint what he truly wants resonates with our own experiences. How often do we find ourselves faced with a multitude of desires, unsure of where to direct our energy?

Matt's half-hearted attempt at a vision board becomes a metaphor for the challenges of manifestation without clarity. The vague representation of goals feels empty, echoing the emptiness we may feel when our intentions lack precision. It becomes a shared realisation that manifestation requires a clear and focused vision.

The various techniques Matt tries, from writing desires on paper to elaborate visualisations, highlight the common tendency to go through the motions without genuine conviction. Matt's frustration mirrors our own when manifestation seems elusive, prompting us to question whether the issue lies with the universe itself.

Kendra's insightful suggestion becomes a pivotal moment in Matt's journey and a profound lesson for us all. The idea that manifestation may falter due to a lack of clarity strikes a chord. Kendra's wisdom becomes a catalyst for self-reflection, urging us to ponder how well we truly know our goals and desires.

Matt's commitment to serious self-reflection becomes an invitation for us to do the same. The journey of journaling, meditating, and closely observing thoughts and feelings mirrors our own potential path to uncovering genuine desires at our core. Matt's self-discovery becomes a guide, encouraging us to tap into our true vision.

Armed with newfound self-knowledge, Matt's re-approach to manifestation becomes a beacon of inspiration. The shift from apathy to inspiration reflects the transformative power of clarity. It prompts us to consider whether our actions align with our values and genuine desires, inviting us to shift our energy from hollow efforts to inspired intentions.

The ripple effect of Matt's newfound clarity becomes evident as his life comes into focus. His career aligns with his desire to help underserved communities, he plans an adventurous trip to Iceland, and meaningful relationships blossom all around him. Matt's story becomes a testament to the idea that the universe responds when we finally know what we truly want from life.

In conclusion, Matt's journey becomes a shared exploration of the profound connection between clarity and manifestation. It urges us to pause and reflect on our own goals, emphasising that without a clear vision, our efforts may be hollow. The lesson from Matt's experience resonates: manifestation relies on knowing what lights us up, and with clarity, our goals can seamlessly fall into place, guided by our inner compass.

Clarity precedes success.
You have to be clear on
what you want before you
can obtain it.

Self-Sabotage again

Louise's Story

Louise sighed as she looked at her manifestation journal on the table. In it, she had printed beautiful photos of amazing holidays, beachside mansions and a selection of hot men. She had created it weeks ago, believing it would magically manifest her desires. But her bank account was still empty, her social life was lacklustre, her career was going nowhere, and no hot men were knocking on her door.

"I don't get why this manifestation stuff isn't working," Louise complained to her friend Danielle. "Has the universe got a problem with me or something?"

"Maybe the problem isn't the universe," Danielle said gently. "How do you talk about your desires day-to-day?"

Louise thought about it. Though she visualised luxury on her vision board, in life she constantly moaned about her money problems, and she forever joked about being single and lonely, despite longing for a partner.

Seeing Louise's eyes widen in realisation, Danielle said, "Our words have power too. Constant negative talk counters the energy behind your visions."

Louise knew Danielle was right, she had been unconsciously sabotaging herself without even realising it. That night, she vowed to monitor her speech going forward.

The next day, Louise caught herself mid-complaint about bills. She pivoted to saying, "Money always comes through for me somehow." When joking to a colleague about being known as the lonely cat lady, she turned it positive, "I know my soulmate is on the way!"

These small shifts felt awkward at first. But over weeks of consciously transforming her inner and outer voice, Louise's energy changed. Her vibes lifted from hopeless to optimistic.

One day, Louise received a surprise check refunding an old overpayment, helping her financial struggles. She also met a kind man named Ethan and felt an instant soul connection. A whole host of positive things started to flow into her reality. It seemed the universe was mirroring her new positive speech.

In the past, Louise had viewed manifestation as a visual exercise. But now she understood words carried equal weight too. We speak our realities into being. Even with vision boards, undermining self-talk would sabotage the energy behind them.

Louise realised she had drawn in negativity by habitually vocalising it, even if she did think she did so in a joking way. But by becoming mindful of her words, she could manifest blessings instead. Talk of lack only created more lack, while talk of abundance invited abundance in.

Through her journey, Louise learned a very empowering lesson...our words shape our worlds. When we speak negatively, we curate negative lives. But by speaking affirmatively, we call in what we desire. The tongue manifests.

The Lesson

Louise's journey through the realm of manifestation unfolds as a compelling narrative that prompts us to examine the power of our words and the impact they have on the reality we create.

As we join Louise in her sigh of frustration, we resonate with the familiar scene of unfulfilled desires despite the visual beauty of her manifestation journal. Louise's bewilderment becomes a shared sentiment, questioning why the manifestation process seems ineffective. It prompts us to reflect on our own experiences when our envisioned reality doesn't align with our day-to-day existence.

Danielle's gentle guidance becomes a pivotal moment in Louise's realisation and a profound lesson for us all. The suggestion that the issue may lie in Louise's daily expressions and language strikes a chord. Danielle's wisdom becomes a mirror for us to hold up to our own speech patterns, urging us to consider the energy behind our words.

Louise's acknowledgement of her unconscious self-sabotage becomes a moment of self-awareness. It becomes an invitation for us to examine our own habitual expressions and how they may be counteracting the energy behind our visions. Louise's realisation becomes a catalyst for us to monitor our speech and its alignment with our desires.

The conscious shifts in Louise's language become a transformative journey. The initial awkwardness of changing her expressions mirrors our potential discomfort when altering deep-seated speech patterns. Louise's commitment to transforming her inner and outer voice becomes an inspiration for us to embark on a similar journey of positive self-talk.

The tangible results that follow Louise's shifts in speech become a testament to the profound impact of words on reality. The surprise financial refund and the meaningful connection with Ethan underscore the idea that the universe mirrors the energy behind our speech. It becomes a powerful reminder that our words are not mere expressions but potent tools in shaping our experiences.

Louise's evolving perspective on manifestation becomes a universal lesson. The understanding that words carry equal weight to visual exercises challenges the conventional view of manifestation. Louise's journey prompts us to recognise that even with vision boards, undermining self-talk can sabotage the energy behind them.

In Louise's final realisation, a profound truth emerges: words create our realities. The shift from vocalising lack to affirming abundance becomes a fundamental lesson for us all. It becomes an invitation to choose our words consciously, understanding that talk of lack only begets more lack, while talk of abundance invites abundance.

In conclusion, Louise's journey becomes a shared exploration of the intricate interplay between words and manifestation. It encourages us to be mindful of our daily expressions, recognising that our words shape the reality we experience.

Through Louise's story, we learn that a shift in language can be a powerful catalyst for manifesting blessings, inviting us to speak our desired realities into being with intention and positivity.

Our words are the
paintbrush of your life.
Use them wisely.

His Dog Was His Teacher

David's Story

David bounced his leg anxiously as he sat staring at his vision board. It had been several weeks since he started using the law of attraction to manifest his desires, but nothing had come through yet.

"I've been visualising and believing, so where is my new car, big bank account and dream girl?" David complained to his friend Chris. "This manifestation stuff must not work, I knew it was all rubbish."

"Manifestation doesn't happen instantly," Chris replied. "You need patience."

But David struggled with patience. He wanted the life he envisioned now. David amped up his efforts, spending hours a day visualising and believing in his manifestations. Still, after a few more weeks, he was disheartened nothing had appeared yet.

One afternoon, David was venting his frustration to his dog Max about the failed manifestations. Max just gazed at David with calm, loving eyes.

"At least you don't have to wait for anything boy," David said as he pet Max. "You're such a patient pup."

Just then, David had an idea. He grabbed Max's leash and a bag of dog treats. He held up a treat, showed it to Max, and then put it in his pocket. Max stared longingly but didn't make a move.

David was impressed. "Good waiting, Max! You didn't just jump and snatch the treat." He patted Max, then finally gave him the treat.

Trying this game a few more times, David was struck by Max's patience and trust. He never tried grabbing; he waited until the treat was offered.

David realised he needed to have more of Max's zen-like faith. He had been attempting to aggressively seize his desires through impatient manifestation. But the real magic came not from forcing but from trusting in divine timing.

So David let go of constantly obsessing over his vision board. Instead of demanding the universe deliver, he took inspired action when he felt guided, while releasing attachment to outcomes. He focused less on what he wanted, and more on enjoying life's gifts in the present.

Remarkably, David soon started noticing new opportunities and blessings flow in. A few months later, to his delight, all the major manifestations on his vision board had come to fruition, even better than he imagined. But they only came once he adopted Max's patience and inner calm.

David saw that manifestation was not about waving a magic wand. It required gracefully allowing things to unfold in their right timing. When he stopped demanding the universe deliver on his timeframe, the universe could actually deliver.

He realised impatience came from a place of lack, needing something because nothing was enough now. But when he approached life with Max's patience, he tapped into the understanding that he was always provided for.

David learned an important lesson that day. He realised that we can't force things to happen before their time. We need to let go of the timeline and find fulfilment in the present. When we trust in the perfection of how our desires unfold, they can materialise even better than we imagined.

The Lesson

David's journey into the world of manifestation unfolds as a relatable exploration of impatience, trust, and the profound lesson he learns from an unexpected source...his loyal dog Max.

As we accompany David in his anxious contemplation of his vision board, we recognise the universal impatience that often accompanies the practice of manifestation. David's frustration becomes a shared sentiment, questioning the effectiveness of the law of attraction and seeking immediate results. It prompts us to reflect on our own experiences when the timeline between envisioning and manifesting feels prolonged.

Chris's wisdom becomes a guiding light for David, introducing the essential element of patience in the manifestation process. The notion that manifestation doesn't happen instantly becomes a crucial lesson for us all. It challenges the impulsive desire for immediate results and emphasises the need to trust the timing of the universe.

David's struggle with patience becomes a relatable aspect of the human experience. The desire for instant gratification prompts him to intensify his manifestation efforts, spending hours each day visualising and believing in his desires. His disheartenment when results don't appear mirrors our own when faced with delays in our manifested outcomes.

The pivotal moment in David's journey occurs during a candid conversation with his dog Max. The observation of Max's patience and trust becomes an epiphany for David. The simple act of teaching Max to wait for a treat reveals a profound lesson about the essence of manifestation. Max becomes a symbol of zen-like faith, embodying the idea that real magic comes from trusting in divine timing.

David's shift in approach becomes an inspiration for us all. Instead of aggressively seizing his desires through impatient manifestation, he decides to adopt Max's patience and inner calm. The realisation that manifestation is not about forcing but gracefully allowing unfolds as a transformative lesson. David's decision to release attachment to outcomes and focus on enjoying life's gifts in the present becomes a paradigm shift in his manifestation journey.

The subsequent positive changes in David's life become a testament to the power of patience and trust. New opportunities and blessings flow in, and eventually, all the major manifestations on his vision board come to fruition, exceeding his expectations.

David's story becomes a profound illustration of the understanding that manifestation is not about demanding the universe to deliver on a specific timeframe but allowing things to unfold naturally.

David's realisation about impatience originating from a sense of lack strikes a chord. The understanding that approaching life with Max's patience connects him to the understanding that he is always provided for becomes a universal truth. His journey becomes a lesson in finding fulfilment in the present, trusting in the perfection of how desires unfold, and acknowledging that manifestation goes beyond waving a magic wand.

In conclusion, David's story becomes a shared exploration of the intricate dynamics of patience, trust, and the unfolding of desires in the manifestation process. It inspires us to let go of the timeline, embrace the present, and trust that our desires can materialise even better than we imagined when we align ourselves with the wisdom of divine timing.

With love and patience,
nothing is impossible

The Power of Storytelling

As we reach the final pages of this book, we find ourselves richer than when we started. The collection of stories we've explored together, while fictional, contains truth and wisdom that will stay with us long after the covers are closed. Now is a chance to reflect on the lessons learned, and how we can carry the light these stories present.

Storytelling is one of our oldest human traditions, yet its power has not diminished. We've seen how impactful these parables can be, teaching timeless life lessons through simple narratives.

Stories speak to us differently than bare facts. They awaken our imagination, touch our hearts, and open our minds. We put ourselves in the shoes of the characters, feeling their struggles, revelations and triumphs first-hand.

Beyond being entertaining, stories instruct us. They can convey meaning not easily captured through straight explanation.

Like parables passed down for generations, these tales become imprinted in our memory when tied to the trials and breakthroughs of their protagonists. Their messages filter into our consciousness, shaping how we see the world. An impactful story can be referenced years later to provide guidance when we need it most. This is why stories have always been essential for transmitting ideas, morals, and insights across time and culture. They teach while uniting us through shared experiences. We learn best through narrative. Tales that stir our emotions and imagination leave more indelible marks than any textbook lesson could.

Now you hold these stories in your hands to carry with you. They are yours to revisit whenever you need a spark of hope or a dose of wisdom Let their messages take root and bear fruit through how you choose to live.

As we draw close to the end of this book, we are filled with gratitude. For the opportunity to learn together through storytelling, and for the gift of those who came before us passing down their truths. May the words written here echo through the lives they touch.

If you would like to listen to the audio versions of these stories, please visit

www.creative-intel.co.uk

Conclusion

In the enchanting realm of the Law of Attraction, what initially appears as a straightforward and easily graspable concept unfolds into a nuanced journey, as echoed in the stories we've explored.

The allure of manifesting one's desires through positive thoughts and energy often draws us in with promises of simplicity, yet the tales reveal the intricacies and depth that underlie this practice.

Kate's story, for instance, illuminates the hidden complexities of childhood wounds. Here, the Law of Attraction encounters a formidable adversary—unresolved emotional scars. This narrative beckons us to consider our own past traumas, acknowledging that these unhealed wounds can become unforeseen barriers on our path to manifestation.

Amy's journey, marked by the pursuit of wealth, mirrors the pitfalls of striving from a place of lack. Despite fervent attempts to attract abundance, her story unfolds as a cautionary tale about the importance of cultivating feelings of abundance within oneself before expecting external manifestations. Amy's struggle offers a valuable lesson on the significance of aligning one's vibration with the desired outcome.

Paul's experience sheds light on the consequences of fixating on external achievements. His relentless pursuit of material gains, highlighted in the Law of Attraction framework, ultimately left him feeling unfulfilled. Paul's story nudges us to reflect on our motivations and directs attention to the importance of inner growth over external validations.

Tony's narrative, with its exploration of manipulation and control, serves as a poignant reminder that the Law of Attraction is not a tool for bending circumstances to our will. Tony's misguided attempts to wield the law for personal gain underscore the essence of manifesting from a place of authenticity and positive energy rather than attempting to manipulate external forces.

As we weave through these stories, the overarching lesson emerges: the Law of Attraction is a journey that extends far beyond the initial allure of wish fulfilment. Each narrative offers a unique perspective on potential blocks and hidden pitfalls, encouraging us to delve into the intricacies of our own beliefs, emotions, and motivations. It invites introspection, urging us to navigate the path of manifestation with a keen awareness of the complexities that lie beneath the surface. In this collective exploration, we discover that the magic of the Law of Attraction lies not just in the external manifestations but, more profoundly, in the transformative journey within ourselves.

Personal message from the author

I hope you go forwards with the understanding that your ability to shape reality is not just a personal endeavour but a collective responsibility. As you engage with the Law of Attraction, may your intentions be woven with threads of kindness, compassion, and a genuine desire to contribute to the well-being of the world.

Choose to manifest a reality that transcends personal boundaries, one that not only brings happiness, health, and wealth to your doorstep but extends these blessings to touch the lives of others. In creating a life that inspires and uplifts, you become a beacon of positivity, contributing to the collective vibration of the planet.

Remember, as we individually create better worlds for ourselves, we collectively contribute to the transformation of the entire planet. Your thoughts, energies, and manifestations are not confined to the realm of personal desire; they echo in the universal symphony, resonating with the interconnectedness of all things.

As we each take conscious steps towards creating a reality steeped in love, compassion, and abundance, we become co-creators of a world that reflects the beauty within our hearts. May your journey be adorned with miracles, and may the life you manifest be a testament to the limitless potential that resides within you.

With boundless optimism and a heart full of hope,

Wain

Printed in Great Britain
by Amazon

35041636R00046

A Brief History
of Stoke-on-Trent

Arthur John Gater

Edited by Andrew Philip Davies

Published 2019

Photographs under Copyright © 2019 Andrew Philip Davies

ISBN: 9781691286263

On behalf of my grandfather, this book is dedicated to those who value knowledge, education, and heritage.

Contents

Preface

Arthur John Gater

My grandfather, Arthur John Gater, was born in Orme Street, Burslem, in 1920. His parents, Evelyn and Frank, rented a small, working-class property there.

Arthur wrote a short autobiography towards the end of his life, in which he describes, *inter alia*, the living conditions of his childhood home. He states that the residence had little more than two large rooms; and, until 1930, the only toilet facility was two outdoor closets, which served four houses and were not connected to the sewers. Instead, these closets were emptied by men who patrolled the streets at night with their soil carts. When the closets were finally connected to the sewerage system, Arthur still had to use several buckets of water to flush away his excrement!

His most vivid childhood memory, however, was when he was diagnosed with rickets – a disorder characterised by bowed legs in infants. In those days, the condition was treated by breaking the child's legs, setting them straight, and then wrapping them in casts to heal. This treatment was available at the hospital in Hartshill.

On the day of his operation, Evelyn took Arthur to

Hartshill on a tram, for he could not walk far on his bowed legs. He played with the hospital's toys in the waiting room until his name was called by a nurse, who carried him with due diligence to the room where the procedure was to take place. There, he sat on his mother's knee whilst he was put to sleep.

When Arthur woke, he was outside the hospital with his mother, who was waiting for the next tram to take them home. It took only a moment for him to realise that he was strapped to a board, with both of his legs in plaster. With this realisation, the pain in his legs suddenly came to the forefront of his mind, and he vocalised the pain with continuous yelling. He screamed so much on the return journey that passengers proffered money in an attempt to pacify him. He wrote, 'I was absolutely rolling in it.'

After the three-month healing process, which was rife with excruciating pain, Arthur returned to the hospital to have his casts removed. As he walked across the room like a newly ambulant toddler, Arthur and his mother were overjoyed to find that his legs were perfectly straight. The experience made him 'scared stiff' of hospitals, but he came to appreciate and admire their miraculous nature in his later years.

Arthur's education was typical of a working-class family at that time. It was short-lived and elementary when compared with the education of more affluent children; but, nonetheless, Arthur discovered the beauty of music, which developed into a life-long passion. He went on to play many instruments throughout his life, such as the mouth organ, the accordion, and the piano, which can be seen in *Figure 1*.

Figure 1. Arthur playing the piano.

He also wrote briefly of his experiences during the Second World War. He was initially trained in London by the King's Royal Rifle Corps, before being given the opportunity to join the Royal Artillery. The Royal Artillery trained him as a gunner for the QF 25-pounder howitzer, which he used in North Africa and Italy. He was awarded, among other medals, both the Africa Star and the Italy Star. He spoke lovingly of Italy, especially of the Amalfi coast, which had 'amazing scenery'. He describes the Italian people as 'friendly', and he made many of them his friends.

Arthur described the war as horrific, of course, but it is also clear from his reflections that being in the army was one of the best experiences of his life. During his time with the King's Royal Rifle Corps, for instance, he was trained as a bugler, and he quickly became the most proficient, for he was made the official bugler for his company. In this honourable

3

position, his bugle services were often called upon for Royal Air Force funerals. He also played the accordion at army dances, where his musical talent was well-received.

After the war, Arthur worked predominately in the pottery industry. During this period, he married my grandmother, Violet, who also worked in the pottery industry – a capture of this can be seen in *Figure 2*. My grandparents had four children: Ronnie, Bernard, Gloria, and Shirley.

Figure 2. Violet working in the pottery industry.

Most unfortunately, Arthur's health began to deteriorate in 1967. A range of medical conditions meant that he had to register as disabled; but, despite this, he continued to seek employment in a less laborious environment.

It was, perhaps, about this time that the advice of one of Arthur's school teachers, Mr Redfern, came to the forefront of his mind, for Arthur started to acquire many books and read more. Mr Redfern's advice was, 'The best way to learn is to read plenty of books.' It would seem that Arthur had reflected on his own short-lived education, too, and wished it had been prolonged and richer. He concluded that learning should be a life-long process. Perhaps these very thoughts were the reason he embarked on an admirable attempt to write and publish a book of his own, unbeknownst to the family until recently.

The Manuscript

My grandfather died in 1984, but my grandmother lived until 2018. Her passing meant that the emotionally difficult task of 'sorting' her belongings was at hand. It was during this task that my grandfather's manuscript was found, which had been typed on a typewriter.

After inspecting the manuscript, it seemed to be, for the most part, a complete first draft about the history of Stoke-on-Trent. The thought that my grandfather had not managed to finish his book was met with a great sadness. In response, I have done what I think to be the most honourable thing: I have, in the form of this book, edited and published his manuscript.

It is not possible to say with certainty when my grandfather created the manuscript, for it is not dated. An approximate date for the manuscript is somewhat important, however, because my grandfather frequently makes comparisons with, and references to, 'today', and so the correct contemporary context would aid a reader with such comparisons. There are clues in my grandfather's autobiography, in addition to the memories voiced by my mother, who recalls occasions during the 1970s when Arthur spent long periods of time in his study. The publication dates of some of the authors he used have provided further clues, too. For instance, he makes many references to Ernest Warrillow's *A Sociological History of the City of Stoke-on-Trent*, which was published in 1977, and has greatly contributed to this book. This does not mean that the year 1977 is the *terminus post quem* because he cites works of an earlier publication date, but it does show that he was working on his manuscript in the late 1970s. Furthermore, in the years close to his passing, Arthur was indisposed to such an extent that concentrating on writing would have been quite difficult; therefore, it is unlikely that he was writing in the 1980s. With these clues, and other contextual clues in his work, it seems reasonable to concluded that when Arthur refers to 'today', he must be referring to the 1970s.

Editing the text has been somewhat problematic, because, as aforementioned, my grandfather, in all his wisdom, did not have the benefits of a higher education, which has led to unidentified referencing when using the work of other authors, who he highly respected. That is, in the spirit of academia, he seems to have used a variety of credible sources to support his work, but he did not reference those sources in any accepted academic manner. For instance, an intext citation is absent from some quotations. In such circumstances I have omitted the quotation to avoid plagiarism. In other instances, where I've been able to identify the ideas of a particular author, but their work has not been cited, I have introduced the author and their work in the most appropriate place. A bibliography has also been included at the back of this book.

To that end, because of my grandfather's respect for education, and his inclination towards life-long learning, I thought it apt to replace his final chapter on education with an excerpt from his autobiography, which describes his own childhood education. The new chapter greatly contrasts with the factual tone presented in the former chapters of this book, but I think there is great value in reading a first-hand account of education in the 1920s and 1930s too.

With all these points considered, then, this book should not be used as a reference tool for academic research; instead, it should be explored by a general audience, especially those who reside in Stoke-on-Trent, as a pleasant pastime or as a gateway to seek out more detailed discourse on the broader themes, certain subjects, or even specific buildings – some of which still survive. If just one person heads out to see any extant remains of our city's heritage, then my grandfather and his well-respected authors will have been rewarded for their efforts.

With regard to the copyright, some of the publishers in this book's bibliography, such as The Ironmarket Press, are no longer in business, and so I cannot request copyright permission. With this in mind, I do not believe there is an infringement of copyright.

Finally, this book could not have been edited and published without the unwavering support of my wife, Katie, and the patience of my son, Julius. For that, I'll be eternally grateful.

Andrew Philip Davies

I

Long before *Vis Unita Fortior*

Millions of years ago, where the City of Stoke-on-Trent now stands, the land was situated on the equator, and so the landscape was a scorching, arid desert. Later, however, about 310 million years ago, during the Upper Carboniferous period, the landscape was a stark contrast to the arid desert. The district was carpeted with lush, verdant vegetation. As the foliage from these plants fell to the ground, they formed layers, also known as *strata*. The organic material then slowly decomposed, and, over time, gradually compressed to form peat. Over millions of years, a combination of heat and pressure changed the peat into coal. The coal formed in seams, also known as coal measures, between deposits of clay, silt, and sand, which varied according to fluctuating sea levels. Fossil plants were found in one of these clay deposits when the foundations for the North Staffordshire Railway were being dug at Fenton Low. The coalfield, too, which covers approximately 100 sq mi, has been recognised as an unrivalled deposit for the study of carboniferous marine fossils.

The emergence of the pottery industry depended

almost entirely on these rich coal and clay deposits. Ernest Warrillow writes in his *A Sociological History of the City of Stoke-on-Trent* that the coal deposits were of the 'long flame' type, which is the best type for firing ovens; however, it is not the *best* fuel, for gas-oil and electricity are now used for the same purpose. The clay deposits were suitable for the manufacturing of 'saggars', and construction products, such as drainpipes, chimney pots, sanitary pipes, roofing tiles, and bricks.

The topography of the district was sculpted by climate changes, and the extreme climatic conditions of the ice ages made these periods significant contributors. Large glaciers formed, and they were so heavy that they moved great distances, and, as they did, they etched at the softer rocks which exposed ridges of hard sandstone. Warrillow records that one of these ridges can be found between Milton and Norton-in-the-Moors, which is colloquially known as Ten Feet Rock. The upper part is gritstone, which is over 15ft thick. Some of these ridges are much larger than Ten Feet Rock, and became known in common parlance as 'edges'. Settlements that formed on, or in the proximity of, an edge adopted epithets to distinguish between them, such as Brown Edge, Baddeley Edge, and Congleton Edge.

The end of the last ice age was about 10,000 years ago, and when the glaciers of that period receded, they left some souvenirs. Boulders, for example, also known as glacial erratics – derived from the Latin *errare*, which means 'to wander' - were transported from other regions of the United Kingdom, such as the Lake District, and even as far as Scotland. One of these erratics, which is made of granite, can be found by Adam's Clock Tower in Tunstall Park.

The glaciers also created and transported yellow boulder clay, which is typically a mixture of fine clay and boulders of irregular size that also tend to be sharp and angular. The clay from these deposits, however, is too fine to be of any commercial value, unlike the clay-bed that formed at Etruria - known to geologists as the Etruria Marl formation. Here, the clay was perfect for the brick and tile industries. Some of the clay was red, which was predominately used for roofing tiles; some of the clay was blue, which was used for the well-known Staffordshire blue brick. Throughout the nineteenth century, the Staffordshire blue brick was sought after all over the country.

The ending of the last ice age loosely coincided with the end of the Palaeolithic period, which is also known as the Old Stone Age. The frozen land gave way to pastures; therefore, humans were able to start developing new tools for cultivating the thawed land. Movement across the continents became possible too, and by the Neolithic period, also known as the New Stone Age, which was about 5,000 BCE, large numbers of people were gathering at places they had marked out as significant – Stonehenge is a good example.

Thousands of years later, by about 100 BCE, which historians now consider to be part of the Iron Age, our island was not yet ruled by a monarch or a democracy, but, instead, the land was divided into large territories, which, to some extent, might be likened to the counties of today. Each territory was inhabited by a tribe and governed by a tribal leader. Druids, who might have been considered religious leaders in those days, also had a great authoritarian influence on the tribes. It is thought that the druids predominately resided in Anglesey.

In the mid-first century BCE, the Roman general Gaius Julius Caesar was engaged in a military campaign against the Gauls, who resided in what is known today as France. During his campaign, which lasted about seven years, he also made a small expedition to the south-east coast of *Britannia* - the Latin name for our land - with part of his army in 55 BCE. Caesar left *Britannia* for the winter, and returned the following year, but, after leaving *Britannia* for the winter again, Caesar never returned.

It was from 43 CE when *Britannia* gradually started to be incorporated into the Roman Empire. In that year, the emperor Tiberius Claudius Caesar Augustus Germanicus, more commonly known as 'Claudius', sent four legions, headed by his general Aulus Platius to establish a presence there. At this time, the district where the City of Stoke-on-Trent is now, the *Cornovii* tribe controlled the area, but their main stronghold is thought to have been situated on the well-known Wrekin in Shropshire, near Wroxeter. Their territory expanded as far as Flintshire and Cheshire, too.

As the Roman occupation spread north, Roman military structures were erected, but the Romans introduced the idea of towns, too, which were also being gradually constructed across the country. Evidence for such things in the City of Stoke-on-Trent can be dated to *c.* 70 CE. A Roman kiln, for example, has been excavated at Trent Vale, with two V-shaped ditches nearby, which might be part of a Roman fort. It is indeed novel to think that the Romans could be considered to be the earliest potters of the Potteries.

The Romans differed slightly from the industrialised potters of the nineteenth century, however, for they imported pottery, too, such as Samian ware, which was often decorated with mythical reliefs, and used for middle to upper-class dining. Samian ware has also been found in Trent Vale.

There is evidence for Roman roads, too. To give you an example, a Roman road passed through Trent Vale into Newcastle-under-Lyme – specifically through Wolstanton and into Chesterton, where an excavation has revealed what appears to be another Roman fort. There is thought to be a Roman temporary camp in the Chesterton area, too, and a substantial civilian settlement at nearby Holditch, which was perhaps a Romano-British town. It is not certain how long these Roman sites were occupied, but it can be said with some certainty, until new evidence is discovered, that the sites were not occupied in the Anglo-Saxon period.

The Saxons had kings, and so the country was divided into large kingdoms, with the Potteries district situated within the large, centralised kingdom of Mercia.

At about the time of the Norman Conquest in 1066, it is thought that most of the district was covered in woodland, especially as half of Staffordshire was recorded as being woodland, and sparsely populated. There was some agriculture in the area, especially in Burslem, and although there was some potential to farm the land in Fenton, it was not being cultivated. Farming was normally carried out by villeins to produce provisions, primarily for the local lord of the manor. Villeins legally straddled somewhere between a slave and freeman. Certainties about the population of the district, their occupations, and their land ownership was recorded as part of a census in the Doomsday Book in 1086, at the behest of William the Conqueror. Burslem is referenced as 'Barcadeslim' in the Doomsday Book.

By the mid-fourteenth century, it must have been realised that an abundance of clay and coal lay in the area, for licences were introduced to dig for these raw materials. In 1368, for instance, a man called Robert le Potter is said to have paid twelve pence to the lord of the manor for a licence to gather raw materials for pottery crafting. This might have been the origin of our now industrialised pottery craft.

The pottery company William Adams & Sons has its roots in the fifteenth century. History records William Adams and Richard Adams working in Tunstall's coal mines in this period. One of their descendants, also called William Adams, was described as a 'master potter' in the early seventeenth century. The pottery craft stayed within the family throughout subsequent generations, some of whom established and administered two of the earliest factories in the district: William Adams & Sons in Tunstall, and the Brick-House Works in Burslem.

II

Vis Unita Fortior

In the early seventeenth century, the representatives of the parish governed the district, but not in an official, authoritative capacity like the local councils of today; instead, these representatives were volunteers who fulfilled important and necessary municipal positions, such as surveyors, overseers of the poor, and church wardens.

By the late eighteenth century, the quantity of volunteers, perhaps relative to the rapid population increase, vastly increased, and many new positions were available to them, such as councillors and alderman. Those considered dignitaries were also offered important positions. This group of volunteers established themselves as the Ancient Corporation of Hanley; yet, this title still did not provide them with any official powers of authority; that is, they were still merely considered as guides. The corporation introduced an initiation ceremony, part of which was to drink a yard-length glass of ale.

But as the Industrial Revolution continued to have a profound impact on the district, there was a major need for a governmental body that had the power to make developmental decisions for the district, such as implementing or improving the district's infrastructure. The government fulfilled this need by instating improvement commissioners, who had the power to levy rates for town projects and hire full-time officials, amongst many other duties. Any subsequent commissioners were appointed by election, though only a small percentage of the district's population voted, because the qualifying requirement was to have a property with the minimum set rateable value. In 1833, for example, there were only 1,349 registered voters.

The electoral process was cemented in the district by the introduction of the Great Reform Act of 1832, which also established the district as a borough. The borough typically had two dignitaries for parliamentary representation, and the first two were Mr Josiah Wedgwood I and Mr William Davenport. The recognition of the district as a borough suggests unity, but many people still considered the six towns to be separate, so a meeting was called in 1834 to debate this matter. The meeting did not conclude with a united Potteries, but not all was lost, for it was decided that two alderman and several councillors should be allocated to each town to relay each town's affairs and concerns to the borough leaders. The towns were one step closer to cooperating and working as one.

However, for many years, no further meeting took place, and any serious talk of amalgamation subsided. Instead, the towns continued to develop their own institutions, which, in some cases, led to some towns enveloping a proximate district. Hanley, for example, extended its influence over Shelton, and the two areas became the Borough of Hanley in 1857. In the same way, by the 1870s, Longton had encompassed Lane End. Longton's boundaries, perhaps unexpectedly, continued to grow, both in influence and in physical territory. By the mid-1880s, for instance, its urban area encompassed East Vale, Dresden, and Florence.

As for Longton's influence, this could largely be attributed to the Duke of Sutherland, who, by 1895, was the profoundly respected Mayor of Longton. To him the towns of the Potteries were often thought as one anyway, so it seemed logical to officially unite them. With this, he campaigned to unify the Potteries, but there was still resistance from some chief officials in Hanley, who did not want advice from the 'neck-end' of the district. Therefore, this opportunity proved to be fruitless, and another opportunity would not come for a few years, for important national events would occupy the district's leaders into the next century.

Warrillow explains in *A Sociological History of the City of Stoke-on-Trent* that just a few years later, on 23 June 1897, the excitement and focus of the Potteries' populace - and indeed the country's - was on Queen Victoria's Diamond Jubilee. The mayors of the six towns were invited to Buckingham Palace to meet Queen Victoria, who conferred upon each of them a diamond-shaped medal.

There was also the outbreak of the Second Boer War, which took place in South Africa from 1899 to 1902, and many men from the Potteries participated. Queen Victoria also died during this period, in 1901. Her eldest son, Edward VII, and his wife Alexandra, succeeded the throne, and their coronation took place on 9 August 1902.

During these events, however, not all of the

district's occupants were preoccupied with national events. Warrillow explains that in 1902, Sir Hugh Owen, a municipal and financial expert, engaged in many meetings with a joint committee to discuss the prospect of a federation, not just between the six main towns of Tunstall, Burslem, Hanley, Fenton, Stoke, and Longton, but also surrounding districts, such as Newcastle-under-Lyme, Audley, Smallthorne, and Kidsgrove, for it was considered to be of North Staffordshire's best interest to unite as many local authorities as possible. Owen secured the approval he needed to form a plan for the House of Commons, but, in unbelievable contrast to the township feuds and jealousies of the recent years, Hanley and Longton put their differences aside, and were the only two towns who agreed to sign the federation proposal. This time, it was the other towns who squabbled over the details, and so Owen's scheme was abandoned in 1903.

Nevertheless, the notion of federation was revived again in 1906, which was primarily advocated by Longton, with the unwavering support of Hanley. A careful analysis was made at the time of the last failed federation attempt which revealed that the main opposition to unity was financial caution – that is, whether or not the new, united city's funds would be invested proportionately and properly amongst the Potteries' towns. With this, Alderman Geen put a new federation plan together, which proposed that each town should have a separate rating for 20 years; thus, accommodating and protecting the financial interests of the individual towns. Geen's plan was well-received, but Hanley, as the most wealthy and progressive town, suggested some amendments to the details which would further protect its financial dominance. The reformulated scheme was then sent to the Local Government Board, who approved it, and then, finally, issued a Provisional Order for federation in the spring of 1908.

By the summer of that year, the Potteries Federation Bill was before the House of Commons. The bill was not approved quickly, however, and it was, instead, discussed extensively over many months, with many adjustments being implemented. Some of the towns disagreed with such adjustments, but for the sake of pushing the bill, they acquiesced. With this, the bill was approved by the House of Lords, and given Royal Assent in the winter of 1908. The Potteries was finally united by the Federation Act on 31 March 1910, and hence was known from that date as the City of Stoke-on-Trent.

Stoke's Town Hall became the headquarters for the city's affairs - a building certainly worthy of this honour. According to Neville Malkin in his *A Grand Tour*, the magnificent building was constructed in 1834, and it was designed in the Classical style by Henry Ward. The building's frontage still proudly displays its massive Ionic columns, which support a projecting portico. The portico is surmounted by a decorative, stone capital.

A new coat of arms was designed for the city, too, which are still used today. A good example of this crest can be seen adorning the semi-circular pediment of the Magistrates' Clerk's Court in Fenton, which was built in 1914. A photograph of this stone relief can be seen in *Figure 3*.

Figure 3. The stone relief of the crest of the City of Stoke-on-Trent, which adorns the Magistrates' Clerk's Court, Fenton.

This new crest illustrated both the unity of the City of Stoke-on-Trent and some of the notable contributors to the city's success by incorporating a symbol from the coat of arms of each of the six towns on the prominent shield. The shield is divided into quadrant panels, with a symbol in each panel. The upper-left quadrant contains the Portland Vase, which represents the Wedgwood family; the upper-right quadrant contains the Ridgway family's camel, which represents Hanley; the lower-left quadrant contains the black, spread eagle of James Glover, which represents Longton; and the lower-right quadrant contains the scythe of the Sneyd family, which represents Burslem. The panels are divided by a broad, fretty cross border, which represents Fenton. The red chief, which caps the shield, bears a gold boar's head in the centre to represent Stoke and the Minton family. The boar's head is flanked each side by Staffordshire Knotts, which represent Tunstall. Surmounting the shield is an Egyptian potter, who, working a primitive potter's wheel, symbolises the city's pottery heritage. The thematic symbolism of the crest is expressed underneath the shield with the Latin dictum '*vis unita fortior*', which translates to 'united strength is stronger'. Warrillow provides a more detailed description of the crest, but, in addition, he researched the history of the coats of arms for each of the pottery towns, which adds further depth and meaning to our city's badge.

III

The Unsanitary Potteries

In 1738, the Potteries was nothing more than a few villages on the edge of the local moorlands, with a squire's mansion here and there. The population was estimated to be just 4,000 - the majority of whom worked leisurely on farms, others used kilns for firing pottery and bricks. The summers must have been idyllic. Barely 100 years later, however, the population had increased exponentially to approximately 52,000, and by 1851 to approximately 84,000. Providing provisions for such a large population - and one that was still swelling – was becoming of major importance. Typically, the staple diet for those who worked in factories, iron works, and collieries was beef and bread. The demand for meat was more than equal to the supply, even though it was expensive.

One only has to look back to Ancient Rome to find one's answers – a civilisation that was not just able to provide provisions for a large populace, but also sanitary conditions throughout an urbanised area. Baths, latrines, drains, and a sewerage system were typical in a Roman town. In the Potteries, however, sewage conditions were no better than the Elizabethan era (1558-1603), according to Warrillow's research in his *A Sociological History of the City of Stoke-on-Trent*.

The main consequence of poor sewage treatment is disease, of which a good example was the Black Death (bubonic plague), which arrived in Britain in 1348. The deadly epidemic was transmitted by fleas that jumped from rats to humans. The disease struck Burslem and Hot Lane in 1647. The countless dead had to be buried in a huge communal pit, near Rushton Grange - now known as Cobridge.

This tragedy was blamed on the lack of cleanliness in the streets. There were no standpipes to wash the streets, for instance, because the water supply was so limited. As a result, refuse and filth clogged the gutters; detritus and slops covered the streets. It would have been most unpleasant in the heat of summer, when this filth and these cesspools befouled the air. Human excretions were removed by night carts, but there was no sewerage works to process it: instead, the faeces were put to use on farmland as fertiliser, even though it was hazardous and of poor quality. A lack of paved streets made the situation even more difficult in winter, because the mollified soil became pocketed with pools of stagnant water.

When Highway Act 1835 was introduced, there was some improvement. Burslem's streets, culverts, and sewers were cleared by an appointed parish surveyor, whose duty was to maintain all of the highways in a given area. Bins were also emptied on the outskirts of the town, and the refuse was transferred to a dump at Velvet Croft.

Around this time, however, cholera was rife, but typhus and scarlatina were common too. Some of these diseases were thought to have originated from an open brook, near the Blue Bell Inn on Waterloo Road. All of the neighbourhood filth drained into that brook. In an attempt to eradicate cholera, the Board of Health decided to establish a hospital just for dealing with cases of cholera, where one guinea was charged, per diem, for medical attention. Many quibbled at the cost.

Burslem was inspected by a representative from the Health of Towns Association, who attempted to convince the townsfolk of the advantages of the 1848 Public Health Act, but not all were so easily persuaded. Warrillow says that Mr Povey, the Police Superintendent, accompanied the inspector to the worst areas of the town, especially the lodge houses and brothels. The curator of St. John's Church also spoke to the inspector with regard to profligates in the town.

Privies were still an issue in 1849. In Market Square, Burslem, one privy served six shops, which was just an open sump near a kitchen. Despite the lack of adequate facilities for these commercial buildings, the rental cost was £255 per annum. Privies in the backyards of squalid houses had the night soil removed, but it was carried through the living-rooms. Open drains made houses damp too. Despite the unsanitary privies, the mortality rate from the subsequent disease was surprisingly low.

In 1854, the unsanitary condition of the city had been criticised by the Board of Health in London. The board was trying to help, but the people of Hanley were so angry that they rejected any aid. With this, the government withdrew its proposed plans of assistance.

It was not until the introduction of the Public Health Act 1858 that Hanley finally had its own Board of Health. These boards were typically established where the mortality rate in each of the previous seven years had exceeded 23 for every 1,000 people.

It is evident, then, that some of these fatal diseases were certainly caused by the inadequate treatment of human waste, but the blanket of smoke in the Potteries, no doubt, inundated funeral directors with plenty of business, too. This may seem exaggerated, but satirical postcards of the Potteries depict a grim picture of the urban landscape, which is almost obscured by a pall of black smoke. These postcards are often emblazoned with captions, too, such as 'this place 'soots' me nicely' and 'a whiff from the Potteries'. But these jocular captions bore a serious message about the health implications for the people of the Potteries, which were not unknown in the nineteenth century. In fact, as early as 1820, factory owners pondered how they might prevent the emission of smoke from their factories. Mr Spode, for example, at his factory in Stoke, carried out various experimental solutions on his factory's chimneys, but without success.

In addition to the air pollution, infectious diseases, such as smallpox and scarlet fever were relentless and merciless. In June 1871, for instance, there were 200 cases of smallpox in Longton and Stoke alone. It seemed that those born into the lower classes amidst the Industrial Revolution were ensnared by poverty and squalor. Many parents, in their ignorance, had large families, and their habitations were too small to accommodate. With these conditions came evils such as child neglect, drunkenness, vice, sordid houses, cesspools, and violent attacks in ill-lit streets.

In Hanley, for example, there lived three families at 24 Princess Street, and not all the parents were lawfully married. It was a small house that only had three rooms and a scullery. Two of the bedrooms measured just 8ft x 8ft. In one of these small bedrooms, a husband, a wife, their grown-up son, and their 12-year-old daughter all slept in one bed. Likewise, in the other small bedroom, a man, a woman, and four children under 16 years of age slept in one bed. The mattresses and flock beds were infested with vermin, and the children had lousy hair. Sometimes, one of the boys slept outside and, as a consequence, he had frequent parasitic skin eruptions. One child from each family had been in court for theft, too. Yet, when an inspector from the National Society for the Prevention of Cruelty to Children inquired, he was met with contempt and laughter.

The unsanitary conditions persisted into 1900. In Hanley, this was largely due to a lack of adequate facilities to deal with inordinate human faeces being produced. It was estimated that there were only 1,600 water closets with flushing cisterns, 4,000 chamber pots, and 1,606 privy cesspools. The night soil was taken to mass dumps at Hartshill, Oakhill, and Basford, with no regard for what effect the stench might have on the local inhabitants. Fenton was lucky enough to have a sewerage works, but, through ignorance, some of the night soil was taken to Fenton Park for agricultural purposes, instead.

Longton endured a diphtheria epidemic, with 36 cases recorded in one particular week. In response, there was some attempt to upgrade water closets, but there were still parts of the town where one privy had to serve a row of houses.

The conditions in Tunstall were somewhat better than the rest of the Potteries. There, only eight houses had night soil carried through the parlour to the horse-drawn cart outside.

Some of the Potteries' sewage did make its way into the sewers, but most of that eventually found its way into the river Trent, and it seemed to accumulate at Trentham where most of the city's tributaries met, such as the Fowlea Brook and the Longton Brook. Local inhabitants, and all who visited the place complained of the stench from the pestilential sewage. By 1867, the Duke of Sutherland's Trentham Estate was becoming the cesspool of the Potteries. The duke could have brought charges against local authorities, but he was tolerant, because a representative from each town of the Potteries made some effort to resolve the issue, especially during a meeting at the North Stafford Hotel in January 1870. By the end of the meeting, there was a consensus that all sewage should be prohibited from streams.

However, sewage from the towns kept increasing, and the only solution was to construct more sewerage works. Hanley constructed its sewerage works at Trent Hay Farm, not far from Leek Road. There, 1,000,000 gallons of sewage was processed. The sewage was initially treated in four precipitation tanks, which was followed by intermittent downward filtration, before it was discharged into the Trent. In 1880, mine water was piped to the sewers too. The people, however, still complained. Therefore, in 1897, an agreement was made with Leicester Bacillite Purification Syndicate Limited to adopt their patented sewage treatment process, which completely sterilised sewage. The integration of this process into the existing works cost £62,000.

In the same year, Burslem opened its sewerage

works, which cost £30,000. It had screened chambers and storage tanks. A set volume of sewage was pumped from here to a sewerage facility situated on Bradwell Hall Farm. However, it was found that the wells at Longbridge Hays and Longport were being polluted, so the treatment of sewage at the farm ceased in 1908.

Sewage in Tunstall was chemically treated in circular precipitation tanks, which housed polarite filters. The effluent was pumped to Peacock's Hay Farm, where it underwent irrigation.

Warrillow's research shows that in Longton, in addition to its sewerage works, a dust destructor was built, which was the first in the Potteries. Here, 220 tons of waste material was being consumed per week. The process also produced clinker, which was used in mortar mixtures.

Despite all these improvements to the Potteries' sewerage system, complaints were still made. Therefore, according to Warrillow, in 1902, George Granville, the Third Duke of Sutherland, was forced to take action by issuing a series of injunctions to the Potteries district. It was not enough, however, and, by 1910, when the County Borough of Stoke-on-Trent was officially formed, the duke decided to leave, and the furnishings of his estate were sold in September 1911.

IV

The Water Supply

Wells had always been the main source of water in the Potteries, as elsewhere, but, because of the exponential population increase in the nineteenth century, wells could not meet the demand; therefore, other sources were explored. In 1820, John Smith established a waterworks by Ivy House paper mill in Hanley. A 48hp engine at the waterworks pumped water from a deep well to a reservoir on Windmill Hill, Hanley, where it was filtered before being distributed through pipes to Hanley, Shelton, and Burslem. During summer, however, it was common to have a water shortage, so, instead, people had to collect their water from wells. Warrillow, in his *A Sociological History of the City of Stoke-on-Trent*, explains where these wells were situated: in Hanley, there was a well at Well Street; in Burslem, the wells were at St John the Baptist's Church and Rushton Grange; and the people of Tunstall had Lady's Well, Sugar Well, and Round Well. The Local Board of Health decided to ensure the preservation of these wells so that the Potteries would not be dependent on the supply from Leek. There was concern in 1844, however, for according to the Buccleuch Health of Towns Commission, rain water was found to be contaminated with carbon and sulphur from the smoke of industry; thus, the water was of poor quality to say the least.

It was decided that a waterworks company should be formed to address this issue, and to provide the Potteries with a constant supply of clean water. Therefore, on 23 October 1845, the first meeting of the Staffordshire Potteries Waterworks Company took place, and it was agreed that one of the first actions was to appoint a competent engineer to conduct a survey of the area so that the infrastructure of the water provision could be planned.

The plan was presented to the Chief Bailiffs of Hanley, Burslem, Shelton, and Fenton, who gave their approval on the 26 November 1846. However, before commencement, the company had to wait for a bill to be granted Royal Assent on 9 July 1847. Samuel Alcock then joined the company, and, with a capital of £60,000, work began.

Water from springs that discharged into the river Churnet at Wall Grange was collected and pumped to a newly constructed reservoir at Ladderedge, which was 20ft deep and covered an area of 2 acres. The elevation of Ladderedge meant that the water could be moved by gravity to another reservoir near Birches Head, where it could then be distributed to Hanley, Stoke, Shelton, Burslem, Tunstall, Fenton, Trentham, and Newcastle-under-Lyme. By October 1849, water was flowing into the Potteries. The bells sounded in Burslem from the church tower of St John the Baptist, as water was allowed to run freely from the tap that was installed in St John's Square. With this achievement, the people were promised that pipes would be laid directly to their homes.

The following month, a dinner was held at the North Stafford Hotel, Stoke, to celebrate the opening of a new waterworks at Wall Grange. The intention was to install a steam-beam engine at Wall Grange, but it was lost when the vessel transporting it sunk into the river Mersey. Therefore, instead, the works had the latest pumping engine installed called 'The Stafford'. Various other issues were discussed during this dinner, too, such as the adverse effects mining had on the supply of water from the springs, and the woeful quality of the water in the wells.

An Act of Parliament in 1861 meant that the company's capital increased to £140,000. An option to borrow up to £38,750 was also available, but on the condition that an additional reservoir was to be constructed to store more water. Strict management came with the shortage of water, so periods where the water was turned off became more frequent. Conversely, this was welcomed by mill owners, but fire became a destructive force in the towns once more. The Duke of Sutherland's reservoir was presenting an issue for the water supply, too, because it had caved in and become overgrown with vegetation. Despite this, the Staffordshire Water Works Company still managed to supply key public buildings at no cost, such as the North Staffordshire Royal Infirmary and schools.

The company's attempts to pipe water directly to people's homes was challenging, and the relentless increase in demand coincided with the relentless rapid increase in the local population. The first attempt to directly supply homes with water was made with wooden pipes, which were later upgraded to lead or other metals. By 1884, over 2,000 houses in Longton had an unlimited water supply, which was charged from seven to ten shillings per annum - according to the size of the property.

In Tunstall, Burslem, Hanley, and Stoke water was collected from wells at Woodwall, Botteslow, Bryan's Well, Washerwall Lane, and Werrington, which was sold from watercarts at halfpence per bucket. The water was not as pure as today's water, of course, but it was clean enough to drink. However, the supply from the watercarts was not enough to meet the demand, so people rushed eagerly out of their homes upon the sight of such watercarts.

In Hanley, these conditions started to change *c.* 1850, when the affluent people of the district finally had a direct supply of water to their homes, which was available three times per week. The water came from an old colliery in the adjoining valley where a reservoir had formed. However, the water's proximity to the colliery meant that it contained a significant amount of calcium sulphate, so, where possible, filters were used for the most opulent residents. According to Warrillow, the working class still used the water supplied by the watercarts, but for drinking only - all other tasks, such as washing dishes, washing clothing, and boiling vegetables were conducted using water from stagnant ponds, or even from the canals. The Staffordshire Waterworks Company continued to make progress, however, by establishing a new site at Stockton Brook. Here, a test hole was bored into the millstone grit formation, and a new water supply was discovered that could be pumped to Goldenhill.

As the supply of fresh, clean water to the Potteries increased, it started to affect the habits of people. For instance, water closets were introduced and large baths became available. However, such things used a large volume of water; ergo, the demand increased further. In response, an Act of Parliament in 1912 provided waterworks companies with the power to construct more pumping stations. Two were built in the Potteries: at Mill Meece and Creswell. The construction at Mill Meece was not completed until 1928, however, due to the First World War. By this time, the local authority had taken over its management.

The interest of the local authority to oversee the water services of the Potteries began as early as 1899, but negotiations could not commence until the government was satisfied that the Staffordshire Potteries Waterworks Company had fulfilled its obligations, which happened by the passing of a bill in 1925. Then the local authority purchased the property from the company for £840,000, and appointed Mr Paddock as the chairman of the Staffordshire Potteries Water Board. The board finished the construction of Cresswell Pumping Station in 1932, complete with dual steam-driven pumps. It also started to upgrade all the main pumping stations in the 1930s. The steam engines at Wall Grange, for instance, were replaced by three electrical pumps in 1933. Any Devonport engines, along with their boiler houses, were demolished. At the Stockton Brook works, electrical-driven pumps replaced the Davey steam engines in 1936. Additional bore holes had to be created at the site, too, due to the slipping of local shale beds, which drastically reduced the quantity of water reaching the well.

Due to mining, extracting water had also become an issue at the northern-end of the Potteries. Therefore, in 1938, work started on two new sites at Peckforton and Tower Wood, but progress was impeded by the Second World War. The project continued at full speed from 1947, which aimed to lay 16 miles of main pipes to Cooper Green reservoir for storage. This could then be repumped to Bignall Hill reservoir for service. This meant that the high demand from Staffordshire University could be met, and a new service created for Keele Village. By November 1953, the project had cost £1,000,000. Further developments, and the meticulous chemical and bacteriological testing of the water, meant that supply cost for the domestic service increased in 1957.

V

Hospitals

Little is known about the early history of hospitals in the Potteries, but it was clear by the end of the eighteenth century that a designated medical centre was much needed to aid the poorer areas of the district where epidemical fevers were rife. Warrillow, in his *A Sociological History of the City of Stoke-on-Trent*, talks of a meeting that was held at the old Swan Inn, Hanley, between local surgeons and prominent manufacturers. At this meeting, it was proposed that a medical dispensary with a ward should be constructed as soon as possible. The initial subscriptions provided £580 for the construction of the building and £187 for the annual support of the institution. The land for the medical dispensary was purchased from Josiah Wedgwood II at a cost of £370. The construction of the medical dispensary, which had a three-storey centre and one wing, was completed on 1 May 1804. The first surgeons appointed to the practice were MD F H Northern, MD John Robinson, MD Richard Bent, MD Bernard Coombe, MD W H Smallwood, and MD George Wood. MD Isaac Wilde was the first resident apothecary and secretary, who had a salary of £40 per annum. Mrs Mary Birch of Cobridge was the first resident matron, who had a salary of £10 per annum. Between 1804 and 1813, well over 10,000 patients were treated for fever or vaccinated.

However, it became clear that the entire building was not needed as a house of recovery for fever victims, so it was thought that a section of the building ought to be a general infirmary. Therefore, on 18 November 1814, another meeting was held at the old Swan Inn to consider this idea, but it was decided that the site was not suitable for a general infirmary because the encroaching industrial buildings were starting to isolate it. This meant that access to the site was poor, with only one road leading to the site over rough terrain.

A different site and building were therefore proposed. To fund the project, appeals were made to colliers and potters to contribute at least one penny per week, if they earned at least eighteen shillings per week; or halfpenny, if they earned up to seven shillings per week. The new site was on the turnpike road leading from Etruria Wharf towards Rushton Grange. On this elevated ground, the Potteries Motor Traction garage at Tinkersclough had been recently demolished, so the new infirmary was constructed in its place. The building's foundation stone was laid by Mr John Heathcote on 3 July 1816, who was the Chairman of the Committee, and the building's opening was marked by a grand celebratory gathering at the Etruria Inn.

The North Staffordshire Infirmary was another major hospital that opened in the area on 05 May 1819. The buildings of the institution were coated in Roman cement, and were therefore somewhat plain, but the portico was ornamental, and supported by columns in the Classical style. The words 'North Staffordshire Infirmary' were emblazoned across the pediment. It many aspects, the layout was quite typical of the period, but, unlike other buildings of its type, there were some functionality issues when it was being applied to its purpose. For instance, there were only two baths available for patients; there was not enough beds to meet the demand; and the lavatories were ill-placed for convenient use. However, the space in the operating room, which measured 16ft x 9ft 6in, was deemed adequate. Fever wards were added, too, which were opened in April 1829. Additional wards for burns and scalds opened in 1852 – no doubt, as Warrillow says, due to the proximity of Shelton Iron and Steel Works, known colloquially as 'Shelton Bar', which had its furnaces first 'blown-in' in January 1841.

It is interesting to note that during this early period of the hospital, it was not unusual to receive one's body parts which had been amputated during an operation. For example, in 1862, eight-year-old Mr Rupert Simms, of Newcastle-under-Lyme, had been involved in a terrible accident. His right arm got caught in the cogs of a brick-perforating machine at the local brickworks. His arm was so mutilated that the surgeons had no choice but to amputate it. Once the operation was successfully completed, Warrillow says that Simms was handed the gruesome remains in a bag, which he and his mother took to the clergyman at their church in Longton to be buried near the circuiting wall. The two partners of the brickworks compensated Simms with a sixpenny piece, and a threepence.

The district obviously needed a decent infirmary, then, so it was considered most unfortunate to learn that the building was suffering structural problems, which Warrillow's research shows to be a direct consequence of the encroaching subsidence from the coal mining industry, as noted in an inspection conducted by the architect company Messrs Ward & Sons, based in Hanley. There were few rooms that did not have cracking walls, and, in some places, there was a 5in difference between the floor levels. The main sewer pipe had cracked, too, from which foul smells escaped into the cellar. At least 12lbs of chloride of lime was used each day to contain the smell. In addition to the failing structural integrity of the building, the air and noise pollution, such as the sulphurous smoke from the surrounding chimneys of industry, were negatively influencing the recovery of the patients. By 1860, slag and refuse were also being deposited in Tinkersclough valley. The noxious fumes from this waste was so deadly that children playing in there were overcome by the fumes, and often taken to the infirmary. These adverse industrial conditions meant that the infirmary had to be relocated to Hartshill. In its final year, between October 1868 and October 1869, the infirmary treated 1,232 in-patients and 5,449 out-patients.

The relocation to Hartshill, however, was not without difficulties. Warrillow states that on 3 January 1861, a committee was appointed to look for a new site on which to build the new infirmary, and 11 sites were considered. A site at King's Field, Basford Bank, was discussed as having good potential, but Dr Garner opposed the idea, because the site might become surrounded by lower-class buildings. Following this, the majority of the committee was in favour of a site on the Mount Estate, because it lay beyond the boundary of the North Staffordshire coalfields, and, therefore, the building was unlikely to encounter any ill-effects from the mining industry. To some extent, this was guaranteed, too, because the landowner, Mr Bishop, had purchased the minerals beneath his land from the Duchess of Lancaster. In addition to good elevation and quietness, it had a spring and good soil, with excellent drainage. With this, the proposal for the new site to be on the Mount Estate was carried with a vote of 18 against 5; however, progress could not be made because of an argument with Bishop, who refused to have a road constructed from Cliffe Lodge to Hartshill as part of the purchase agreement. Warrillow writes about the 'wrangle' in great depth, and confirms that the disagreement was not settled until early in 1865, when the plans were finally drawn-up and put to the committee. It was proposed that the infirmary's water would be supplied from a well via a pumping engine, in addition to soft water collected from the roof. The soft water would be used for baths, lavatories, and wash-houses; the infirmary would be heated by open fireplaces. Miss Florence Nightingale was consulted about the layout and style. It was decided that the main building should accommodate 160 beds, and there should be a fever ward with 20 beds.

Once the plans were sanctioned, Mr Barlow's company, based in Longton, was contracted for the entire project. The land cost £3,000; the building cost £26,964, and the adjoining new roads cost £34,000. There were some generous donations for the project. For instance, Mr William Yates of Eastwood, Hanley, former Chief Traveller for Mr Ridgeway of Cauldon Place Works, said he would leave £5,000 to the infirmary on his deathbed; although, to expedite matters, he was prepared to hand over this sum before his final hour. The foundation stone was laid on 25 June 1866, by His Royal Highness, Albert Edward, Prince of Wales. Warrillow describes the occasion: at 12.45pm, the Prince and Princess of Wales arrived in Stoke. They were seated an open carriage, with a large body of cavalry flanking it. On ascending to Hartshill Bank, Albert and his entourage were warmly greeted by ten-thousand children, who had assembled in a field on the left-hand side of the road. Before laying the stone, two sealed glass bottles were deposited in the cavity, which, between them, contained a document inscribed with the details of the ceremony; a collection of current coins; and newspapers, such as *The Times*, *The Staffordshire Advertiser*, and *The Sentinel*. On one side of the stone, there was a carved depiction of a women attending to a sick man. The building was officially opened by the Duchess of Sutherland on 16 December 1869.

The new infirmary at Hartshill brought greatly improved medical facilities and medical treatment, but it was still burdened by the vast amount of sickness and accidents in the Potteries. For instance, Warrillow indicates that 20% of in-patients were accidents, which were transported to the infirmary on open carts. The governor of the infirmary suggested that each town should have its own horse-drawn cart to serve as an ambulance, and that collieries and ironworks should have their own, too. In 1869, there was also a small peak in victims of fever, which were usually those in poverty, evident by their sordid, tattered rags that hardly covered them. They had to be placed in an isolated area, usually an outhouse, until they had recovered.

Eventually, more land was purchased from Bishop in 1888, which extended the estate to over 24 acres. With this, major upgrades to the infirmary began. In the following year, for instance, the Victoria Wards were added, as Warrillow confirms, at a cost of £961, and then an eye hospital in 1890. The heating system was also replaced by low-pressure, hot-water pipes and radiators. The next major upgrade was an electrical installation, which meant that the latest treatment for lead poisoning – an electrical bath – could be implemented. The Duchess of Sutherland pioneered this technology, so she opened the new department to accommodate this treatment in June 1902. The electrics also replaced all the gas lighting. The construction of a new out-patients building was completed in 1911, at a cost of £12,000; and, in 1914, a well-timed surgical theatre was incorporated just as the First World War started. Huts were also erected in the grounds to receive war causalities. A total of 2,562 wounded soldiers passed through the infirmary during the war.

On 5 June 1925, King George V laid the foundation stone for the new medical block, under which he placed a sealed casket containing a commemorative copy of the *The Sentinel* newspaper and a history of the infirmary. The King also acceded the request that the infirmary should be known hence forth as The North Staffordshire Royal Infirmary. The new medical block had an X-ray department, an orthopaedic department, known as the Twyford Memorial, a general medical ward, known as the H R Johnson Ward, and a female ward, known as the Matilda Burgess Ward.

During the early part of the Second World War,

the hospital was evacuated because of air raids. This was sage, for Warrillow records that a high-explosive bomb struck the hospital, which extensively damaged the nurse's quarters, and destroyed the eye theatre. The cost of the damage was estimated to be £10,000. After the danger of frequent air raids had passed, the hospital resumed service and treated over 3,000 wounded soldiers.

Other hospitals in the Potteries started out as Poor Law institutions, also known as workhouses. These hospitals are now known as the City General Hospital in Newcastle-under-Lyme and the Westcliffe Hospital in Chell. In the nineteenth century, when both of these were workhouses, the conditions were sometimes less than humane, often resembling a prison. Of the two workhouses, though, Westcliffe, which was known loquaciously as 'Bastille', was the most notorious for this. Upon entry, as Warrillow describes, the inmates had their clothes taken away to be disinfected; the garments were replaced with a clean nightgown. A hot bath was provided, along with a good bed for the night. Tramps who wished to use the workhouses had to obtain a ticket of admission from a police station, and, even then, they were only allowed to enter after 6.00pm. Supper for any new arrivals was 8ozs of bread, with water. All rooms were lit with batswing burners, but the governing taps were always outside the rooms. The tramps were usually locked in a room for the night; therefore, from *c.* 1900, electrical bells were installed, so that the knights-of-the-road could ring if anything was of immediate importance. Breakfast was 6ozs of bread, and one pint of gruel, or 8ozs of bread, with water, after which a tramp was usually required to break 10cwt of stone. This task was carried out in a cell adjoining the room they had slept in. The stone had to be broken into pieces that were small enough to pass through a grated window in the cell's door. Tramps were permitted to stay two nights, after which they would have to search for admittance to another workhouse.

These conditions drastically improved, however, with the amalgamation of the Wolstanton and Burslem Unions on 1 April 1922. Warrillow explains that under the new scheme Bastille remained a workhouse, but the City General Hospital, in addition to being a workhouse, became the official destination for all medical cases. For this to work, the building known as 'A' Block had to be converted into the official hospital for the site. Inspectors from the Ministry of Health objected - instead suggesting that a new building should be constructed to form the nucleus of a new, modern hospital. This advice was well-received, and so proposals for a new hospital were submitted to Dr F W Ellis, who was the Chief Medical Officer of the Birmingham Union. He suggested that the hospital should be on a suitable site along London Road, and that the hospital should accommodate acute cases of illness, as well as provisions for maternity cases, which would then also require an extensive nurses' home. Dr Ellis' revisions were accepted, and Warrillow's research shows that the purchase of the land completed on 1 April 1926, at a cost of £2,400. The construction of the hospital cost £185,000. The hospital was able to accommodate 180 acute medical cases, with extensive provisions for those that required surgical procedures. In addition to the original plan, a children's block was built, which accommodated 44 beds. The hospital went on to be a success, and today the hospital has about 946 beds. An out-patients department was established in 1948, which incorporated an operating theatre, a mortuary, and areas for orthodontics and X-rays. The hospital today, however, is most well-known as medical school for training nurses.

Another hospital steeped in history is Longton Cottage Hospital, which is rooted in the work of The Reverend Adam Clarke and the skilled nurses that helped him tend to the sick between 1864 and 1868. Warrillow says that these nurses took provisions of cooked food, wine, spirits, linen, and bedding to the homes of the sick. The visits were appreciated the most in homes where the parents and children were indisposed at the same time, which, due to unhygienic conditions and overcrowding, was common in those days. These visits were risky, however, for the nurses could become sick, too.

Warrillow has thoroughly researched this hospital. He confirms that the Longton Cottage Hospital received its inauguration on 30 July 1868. It was built at Mount Pleasant, at a cost of about £700, of which £130 was contributed by the working class. The land was owned by Clarke, but on 15 November 1872, by a Deed and Settlement, Clarke vested the property into the care of a group of trustees representing the town's people. The ground floor housed the sick wards, a surgery, bathrooms, and an ice-house. The first and second floors housed bedrooms. The hospital's first staff were Dr John Thomas Arlidge, a consultant physician; Nurse Short, who supervised a small team of nurses; and a house-keeper. Small weekly payments were made by the patients, but this was an appeal to their dignity rather than a demand, which prevented the feeling of charity. Convalescents were transferred to other sites so that the hospital could continue to admit cases of serious illness. A converted farmhouse at Farley, near Alton, was frequently used for this purpose.

On 1 May 1871, 120 cases of smallpox were recorded in Longton, of which 14 resulted in death. The odds were against the hospital, not just because of how prevalent the disease was, but also due to the ignorance of some people, which, in some cases, aided the disease. Some people, for example, refused vaccinations because they did not trust them; others did not recognise the disease - instead, concluding that the smallpox eruptions were measles. As a consequence, parents allowed their infected children to play with non-infected children. Warrillow says that some cases were so serious that arms were amputated. Also, Hansom cabs, a nimbler version of traditional horse-drawn carts, were used to transport smallpox patients to the Longton Cottage Hospital, which, though essential for the sick, risked infecting more people. Therefore, the cabs had to be disinfected, or the owners risked a fine of £5.

Warrillow says that by 1887 the site of the hospital, unfortunately, had become almost obscured by factories and the pall of smoke emitted from them. These conditions made the relocation of the hospital urgent. The land for the new site was on high ground at Normacot, which was given as an act of benefaction by the Duke of Sutherland. Architects from Ford & Slater of Burslem planned the building, and the construction was carried out by Messrs H & C Inskip of Longton, which cost approximately £3,360. In 1906, a new operating theatre was added at a cost of

£1,220, which was lit by electricity. Florence Coal and Iron Company Limited supplied the electricity free of charge. Further upgrades took place in 1914, such as new wards, which were highly-valued during the First World War.

The erection of a new out-patients building on adjacent land started in 1921, which was also given as an act of benefaction by the Duke of Sutherland. This building had a casualty dressing room; a minor operating theatre; a dental operating room; an eye, ear, and throat consulting room; a sterilising room, and a dispensary. The building was officially opened by Sir Francis Joseph on 1 October 1923. The hospital greatly aided the fight against smallpox, and, in 1958, there were no cases of smallpox recorded.

One of the most well-known hospitals in the City of Stoke-on-Trent is Haywood Hospital, which would not be standing if it were not for the generosity of the Haywood brothers – Howard and Richard – who, in the nineteenth century, as Warrillow's research shows, left £30,000 in their wills for the construction of a hospital. They were fervent helpers of the poor and sick, and evidence of this can be found behind Tunstall's old police station on Westley Street, where a building bears a stone with the inscription 'Ambulance House, erected by Howard Haywood 1871'.

The funds from the brothers' wills were available in 1880, so a group of governors were formed to oversee the project. Their first meeting took place at Burslem Town Hall on 21 February 1881, with Mr John Maddock, the Mayor of Burslem, in the chair. The terms of the wills were stated: to establish a cottage hospital that included a dispensary scheme, and provisions for convalescent patients, which would service Burslem and the surrounding neighbourhood.

By 1882, a suitable plot for the hospital was found on Moorland Road at a cost of £425. Warrillow's impeccable research shows that a hospital committee was formed who announced a competition for architects, in the usual way, to design the building. Mr William Cooke won the competition. His design meant that the hospital could accommodate 14 beds, at an approximated cost of £2,400. The foundation stone for the building was laid on 27 July of that year, by Mr W S Shoolridge. Later that evening, to celebrate, Mr William Woodhall provided dinner and entertainment for the project members at his residence, which was Bleak House, Cobridge.

The construction of the hospital was finished in 1887, and it was officially opened by the Mayor of Burslem on 20 June that year. Warrillow points out that the crest of the Haywood family was embossed in a large terracotta tile and affixed to the central pediment of the red-brick building. He also describes the interior: the ground floor had two wards, with four beds in each; a mortuary with a bathroom; a surgery; and offices. On the first floor were five rooms to be used as wards, if necessary. The construction of an additional storey to house 12 new wards began in 1889, following a gift of £1,000 made to the hospital by the Dobson family. The new storey was opened on 18 February 1891.

The hospital was used during the First World War for wounded soldiers. Warrillow says that the service provided by the hospital was thought so commendable that a new hospital should be built as a commemoration to both the hospital service and those who had fallen during the war. A committee for the project was formed, who wanted to raise £6,000 to purchase Greengates House, Tunstall, which was situated near the top of Furlong Road, opposite Christ Church. The house was built by the illustrious potter William Adams in the eighteenth century, and it was well-known for its elegant interior and exterior. The funds were gathered, the house was purchased, and a plan was drawn-up, which included some necessary modifications to the building to make it suitable as a medical facility.

However, before implementing the plan, the project committee learned that the governors of the Haywood Hospital wished to build a large extension on another site. The Greengates House project was suspended, and friendly negotiations with the Haywood Hospital governors followed, who agreed to amalgamate the two schemes.

Suitable land for the new project was found on High Lane, where the hospital stands today, and it was purchased for £43,000. The foundation stone for the building was laid on 1 October 1927 by Prince Henry, the Duke of Gloucester. The hospital was called the Burslem, Tunstall, and Haywood Memorial Hospital.

In the first few months, the cost of running the hospital was between £800 and £900 per month. This was more than expected, so many schemes were introduced to increase the income of the hospital. Frequent contributions were made by the local colliers, for example.

The Burslem Ladies' Linen Guild made it possible for the hospital to train nurses. In 1939, as Warrillow says, a home was built on the site for the nurses, which was funded by Mrs A J Tellwright. The construction of a maternity block followed, too, in 1940, which accommodated eight beds. The block was extended in 1944 to provide a further 22 beds.

When the hospital was originally built, the surrounding area was predominately rural, but, shortly after the Second World War, the construction of many houses on High Lane and Chell Heath made the area predominately urban. In some ways, this has ensured the success of the hospital, which was treating as many as 2,000 patients a year shortly after the war, and this figure has increased year upon year. In recent years, the number of beds available has risen to 96, of which 30 are for maternity cases.

VI

Cemeteries

Some of the earliest burial records are marked by seventeenth-century headstones, for cremation was preferred before this period. In those rare instances of a burial before the seventeenth century, it is unlikely that any headstone's epitaph would be legible following centuries of erosion. However, some burials are still known without headstones, for they have been documented in written records. Warrillow provides a good example in his *A Sociological History of the City of Stoke-on-Trent*. His research shows that eight victims of the bubonic plague were buried in a shallow, communal grave, known as 'Singing Kate's Hole', near Rushton Grange. This can be found in the parish records of St. John the Baptist's Church, Burslem, which began recording burials in 1636. Such hastily burying of the deceased was not uncommon during outbreaks of infectious diseases.

Fatal disease was not just conspicuous during outbreaks, however – it was ubiquitous - and this was no less true in the nineteenth century. Burial practices varied considerably between the social classes in this period. At a pauper's funeral, one could expect the coffin to be made of rough-cut wood and crudely nailed together. The ceremony was short so that the body could be buried quickly. The rich, by contrast, experienced the polar opposite, and their final resting place was usually a family vault or mausoleum. Although these stone tombs were a status symbol to some extent, they, when constructed correctly, provided the means for the deceased to be laid to rest with dignity and without posing any dangerous risks to the living. The same cannot be said of the abhorrent post-burial treatment of the poor, which was not only shocking, but it negatively impacted the local sanitation too. This was, in part, due to the unlimited burials permitted in churchyards. The dead may only have been laid to rest for a few months before being piecemealed by a spade, or secretly removed to make room for others. Exposure to the putrescent remains resulted in many diseases, so it was hazardous to the graveyard worker. Sometimes, the effluvia emitted from the bodies was toxic and lethal. In addition, Warrillow points out that precipitation also washed some of the putrid remains into streams and wells which contaminated them.

Warrillow says that this was brought to the attention of the Burial Board in December 1857, who took measures to improve local conditions. The principal aim was to establish a new, large cemetery, and a suitable site was found at the Chatterley Hall estate, also known as Shelton Hall. The purchase of the land was approved in August 1858, and a competition quickly followed for the best design of the cemetery. Messrs Ward & Sons of Hanley won first prize. They had paid special attention to the workings of the drainage system in order to safeguard the proximate environment from the toxins of putrefaction.

In April 1860, the cemetery was consecrated by the Bishop of Lichfield, and then opened shortly after. Warrillow describes how the cemetery road was made private, however, so the gates were only opened for funerals and for the residents of a few large properties situated there. As time passed, though, the lodge-keepers neglected their duties more and more, until, from about 1926, the gates remained open, and the road became a semi-public through-fare. The gates did close one more time during the air-raids of the Second World War, when bombs struck the houses opposite them. After the war, the gates were removed, and the road entrance was widened.

The design of this cemetery, then, to some extent, demonstrated that the danger decaying corpses posed to sanitation could now be averted, but this innovative cemetery stood alone in the nineteenth century, which meant that abhorrent burials still ensued throughout the Potteries. For instance, foul matter from shallow graves had been washed in to the cellar of a house, near the old churchyard in Hanley. In some places, burials were done at such speed that only 6in of sod covered them; in others, inspectors were opening vaults containing horrendous smells. In short, any measures the Burial Board took did nothing to ameliorate the burial malpractices. Therefore, in 1864, a notice was issued from the Home Office to all those responsible for the churches and cemeteries in the Potteries. The notice advised that, for the time being, burials were prohibited.

On 31 December 1866, it was proclaimed that interment would be permitted only if a body was embedded with powered charcoal and enclosed in well-cemented brickwork. With this new rule, new cemeteries were laid out. Tunstall Cemetery, for example, was laid on 7 acres of sloping ground, which was on the clay hills, situated on the western part of the town. It was then consecrated in July 1886, by the Bishop of Gibraltar.

Other towns followed, too, such as Longton in 1878, Burslem in 1879, and Fenton in 1887. However, in some cases, the new mandatory burial regulations were ignored. In April 1882, for instance, The Reverend Topham of St. Matthew's Church, Etruria, violated this order. Warrillow describes how Topham had been discovered overseeing the burials of still-born babies in shallow graves, for which he charged a fee of three shillings, and of that the sexton received one shilling. An investigation at the time revealed the full extent of his abhorrent malpractice: over a period of 5 years, he had buried the bodies of 50 children in little boxes, but the ground depressions were hardly deep enough to be described as 'shallow', so the sod barely covered them. The Reverend Topham was fined the full penalty of £10.

VII

Housing

Warrillow's *A Sociological History of the City of Stoke-on-Trent* is a rich and comprehensive guide to the history of the city's housing. Within said guide, he mentions the lodging houses of the Victorian period and compares them with The Salvation Army's lodging houses of today. He says that the majority of today's lodging houses are clean and respectable, but the smell still might be considered something of a nostalgia. There was more to the nineteenth-century lodging houses than a distinctive bad smell, though, for most were considered quite scandalous in their nature. Colloquially, they were known as 'dosshouses', and they often attracted tramps and the destitute who were looking for a place to stay. For one night, a single bed cost sixpence, and a half-double bed was fourpence. Once a bed had been 'booked' for the night, the 'guests' could also make use of a communal room for cooking, and a living-room for leisure. Imagine the smells: cooking; wet clothes drying on the line; paraffin lamps feebly trying to illuminate the living-room through a haze of smoke emitted from clay pipes; and unwashed people. Warrillow's research indicates that at about 11.00pm, the lodging-house proprietor urged the guests to retire for the evening, and it was usually about this time, too, that a policeman would stop-by to check for any 'wanted' characters in there. Despite the grimness of the dosshouses, the accommodation was often envied by those living in some of working-class houses of the Potteries.

Very little is recorded of the early working-class dwellings in the district. One thing that Warrillow claims, however, is that the humble poor lived with fresh air about them, which had swept across the nearby moorlands. This, of course, was certainly true before the Industrial Revolution, which drastically changed the topography and living conditions in the area. The fresh, clean air blowing in from the nearby moorlands was exchanged for the smoke emitted from the rapidly growing industries, and it filled the lungs of the humble poor. Rows of houses were thrown-up haphazardly for the potters, coal miners, and steel workers, but even this mass of buildings was completely inadequate to meet the needs of the rapidly expanding population, which, according to Warrillow, was 4,000 in 1738; 23,706 in 1801; 31,000 in 1811; 63,000 in 1838, and 208,875 in 1901.

In the mid-nineteenth century, the areas with this type of housing developed into slums. Burslem was one of the worst towns, which was sometimes referred to as 'the hell hole'. Here, half-starved and half-dressed women and children could be seen; drunken men stumbled along the broken pavements; open drains brought disease; immorality and obscenity were around every corner.

Pottery workers were about the main streets, too, going to and from work. These workers usually rented houses which, according to Warrillow's research, cost approximately three to four shillings and sixpence per week. However, paying rent did not guarantee adequate accommodation, for landlords were not obliged to maintain their properties. Therefore, many houses were in some severe states of disrepair. Yet, less than a quarter of a mile away, the urban landscape suddenly gave way to the rural – there, the windmill at the Jenkins received the pure breezes coming in from the moorlands. Yet Burslem was, and still is, often affectionately called 'The Mother Town'. Burslem was not alone in its run-down state, and one often wonders, both then and now, what visitors to the City of Stoke-on-Trent would expect to find in our Classically named towns, such as Etruria, Dresden, and Florence. I don't think their expectations would be actualised!

In Longton, some of the worst slums were in the Edensor Road district; lower John Street; and Lockett's Lane. The area stank, and it was said that half an inch of filth could be scrapped off the walls. The area was overcrowded, too. For example, in a block of 30 houses, there were 140 residents. The lavatory for these residents was a communal outhouse which was divided into six privies, but without individual doors. The rent for such properties was three shillings and ten pence each per week. Similar blocks of houses still stood at the junction of Normacot Road and Chelson Street, opposite The American Inn, until shortly after the Second World War. There were 13 houses to this block, but it was only serviced by one communal lavatory – a water closet. There was also only one water tap. Despite the limited utilities, the community was said to be educated and very happy. The houses were clean and swept, too.

The same could not be said of the slums in Hanley, but at least Hanley's landlords were not as negligent as those in Burslem: the landlords in Hanley tried to improve the living conditions by maintaining their properties. To achieve this, though, the rent had to be increased to pay for repairs. However, some tenants could not afford the extra rent, so they would take in a lodger or two, which, of course, led to further overcrowding and awful living conditions. In 1890, for instance, Warrillow's research shows that the population density was 34.8 persons to the acre. The density figure was likely to be much larger than this, however, because not every acre of land was used for housing. Warrillow continues to say that some of the houses were in such a bad state of disrepair that opening a window would see the whole frame fall out onto the street.

Action was taken in the early twentieth century, however, which would eventually lead to the fine estates we know today. It took the best of part 60 years, though, and no real progress was made between 1900 and 1918, partly due to the First World War. The Housing and Town Planning Act of 1919 (The Addison Act) started any real transition from slums to estates. The act provided the government, and therefore the local authorities, with generous subsidies to start postbellum housing programmes. In the City of Stoke-on-Trent, the first housing programmes were implemented at Basford, Abbey Hulton, Trent Vale, and Meir; other long-term housing programmes started in 1924. It was an ambitious scheme, but it was still not meeting the needs of the city's inhabitants, neither in slum clearance or erection of new properties.

Warrillow provides Massey Square, Burslem, as an example, which, still having about 92 tumble-down houses, was still in urgent need of attention. In addition, it was also estimated that there was a shortage of 10,000 to 12,000 houses across the City of Stoke-on-Trent.

The Housing Act of 1930 made extensive provisions for the demolition of slums. With this, the Corporation of Stoke-on-Trent felt it was able to take action, and therefore put forth a five-year plan, which was submitted to the Ministry of Health. With the Ministry's approval, work started in 1936. Warrillow says that the Corporation was able to construct about 1,000 houses per year until war was declared in 1939, which, consequently, meant that the work was suspended.

After the Second World War, the council was determined to bring their housing plans to completion; thus, the slum clearance continued in 1952. Meakin's Row, Fenton, was demolished, for example, along with Smith Square and Star Bank, which was a total of 98 houses. These were replaced by 600 new houses at Fenton Park. A report from the Ministry of Health in 1955, however, still showed that about 12,000 houses were unfit for purpose, so Stoke-on-Trent Council proposed to deal with at least 6,000 of these over the next five years.

The clearance of houses in some areas, however, could not be accomplished without compulsory orders of demolition, which the council had the powers to enact using recent legislation. This meant, in some instances, uprooting aged people, which mentally hurt them and often reduced them to tears. The inhabitants quickly learned that any appeal against such orders was a forlorn hope. Financial compensation was not considered proportional to the loss, either, which caused much hardship. People were, however, rehoused in new housing estates, but sometimes these were miles away, and had a much higher rent.

Despite these problems, the scheme was finally eradicating an impoverished way of life that had existed for over 100 years. Plenty of new, adequate houses had been constructed by 1958, which was said to be about 15,750. There were also dignitaries who were excited about the city's development and wanted to contribute. Warrillow says that Mr W G Barratt of Burslem, for instance, gave £20,000 to the city for the construction of bungalows for aged people. These bungalows were built at Carmountside, and they were collectively called Barratt Gardens. Barratt laid the foundation stone on 30 November 1954.

VIII

The Police and Fire Service

Hanley's 'lock-up' was in the old Market Hall, which was built in 1790. Warrillow's research, in his *A Sociological History of the City of Stoke-on-Trent*, describes how the north-east corner of the prison had two secured dungeons - each suitable for just one person. Due to this limited capacity, Warrillow explains that criminals were usually incarcerated here for a short period until their punishment could be undertaken, which did not always take place within the dungeons. For instance, women, who were suspected of witchcraft or deviated from the expected female social decorum, were often subject to the ducking-stool. Such stools typically took the form of a wooden chair that was suspended on a long, wooden pole. This meant that the accused could be restrained in the chair, and then immersed in a pond or river to 'test' for their innocence. In the case of testing for witchcraft, it was thought that women should float if they were guilty. This, of course, presented a predicament to the suspected witch, who, to declare herself innocent, must sink and remain submerged, and, therefore, guaranteed her death by asphyxiation; the alternative was to 'float', which assured a guilty verdict, followed by the death penalty.

Other barbaric punishments, with medieval roots, were still commonplace in the early nineteenth century. In Newcastle-under-Lyme, for example, branks were used on women who 'exercised' their tongue. The device took the form of an iron mask which, when secured to the culprit's head, inserted an iron tongue in the throat. Wooden and iron stocks, which clamped the culprit's neck and appendages, were used in busy public places. Tunstall's stocks were in front of the clock tower in Tower Square, which was last used in 1852. The stocks were mainly used for those caught being offhandedly inebriated, which usually carried a fine of five shillings, with six hours in a stock. This might seem quite lenient, however, when one considers Warrillow's finding: in 1800, a boy in Etruria was hung via a gibbet for stealing a sixpence.

There were, of course, real criminals to deal with too. Street gangs, for instance, were commonplace menaces. Many local historians have mentioned the leader of the Rough Fleet gang, Jack Wilson, who operated in Hanley. His gang was, perhaps, the most notorious in the Potteries. The majority of their crimes are said to have taken place during the night, when it was easy to rob people under the veil of darkness, for, unlike today, there was no large, organised police force to oppose them. There were a few constables and watchmen on duty during the night, but Wilson and his gang did not fear them. Instead, according to Warrillow, it was not uncommon for Wilson's gang, on wet nights, to overturn the heavy, sheltered sentry-boxes and trap the constables inside. Wilson's gang were no strangers to firearms, either – Wilson was reported to have accidently shot his brother, who died shortly after from shock. The Potteries was no haven of virtue.

In a way, though, because crime was so prolific and, to some extent, a serious and professional affair where gangs were concerned, it provided the catalyst needed for the Potteries to respond with an official police force. The government recognised similar problems prevalent throughout the country and responded by introducing and endorsing the County Police Act 1839, which empowered the Justices of Peace to assemble a police force in their county. At the head of the new police force was the Staffordshire County Constable, Mr Rose, who had a reputation for being somewhat strict. He declared that he would make the people fear breaking the law so much that he would be able to hang his watch up in the Market Square overnight without it being pilfered.

By 1842, however, it was clear that the new police force was perceived to have no authority over rioters. It was in July that year that the colliers went on strike to oppose a reduction in their wages. This strike coincided with the unrest and protests of the Chartists too, who sought to reform the voting system so that all men could vote. A conflated riot ensued, with an abundance of fuel provided by these concurrent movements. In Hanley, the mob destroyed the Magistrates' House, and took the wine from its cellar. The mob then made for the police station, where it assaulted the clerk, destroyed police records, and released prisoners. After this ransacking, the police station was ignited and left to burn down. Stoke Police Station was their next target, and, after dealing with that, they carried on to Lane End, Longton. Here, an open-air meeting was in progress, but, still, the mob ransacked all the shops there. Eventually, soldiers from Fenton arrived and arrested them.

However, riots arose in Burslem, too, which were supported by farmworkers from Leek, and Congleton, who had arrived via Hamil Road. The George Hotel was ransacked. Pandemonium ensued, and so the military representative, Captain Powis, rode into Burslem on horseback with a detachment of dragoons to read the Riot Act to the people. His actions were in vain, though, and the crowd had to be fired upon. The brains of those fatally struck lay on the footpath. With the sight of these horrors, the crowd dispersed. It is estimated that 20,000 people took part in these riots, of which 700 were arrested, and then taken to the Stafford County Gaol and House of Correction at Stafford. According to Neville Malkin, in his book *A Grand Tour*, 54 of those arrested had prison sentences ranging from 7 years to life, and 146 were sentenced to hard labour.

In 1847, Warrillow explains that the Potteries' police force was made tripartite between Stoke, Hanley, and Burslem, with some of these stations having responsibilities beyond their district appellation. Stoke, for example, also encompassed Longton under its remit. They all used the same prison, though, which was still the Stafford County Gaol and House of Correction, but there was only one horse-and-cart to transport convicts. With this knowledge, it is remarkable to note the efforts of this cart, which shipped approximately 342 prisoners to the Stafford County Gaol and House of Correction in six months.

On a less serious note, in 1903, the police were

called to Hanley's indoor market to investigate a strange, new food on sale. When the police arrived, they found that Mr Charles Mellor was selling bananas, and he claimed to be the only person selling them in the whole district. The police were not impressed, however, and, because they had not seen bananas before, they decided to temporarily prohibit the sale of them until it could be determined they were not a danger to the public's health!

As for firefighting, in the mid-eighteenth century, it was carried out with buckets of water, which, of course, was not effective to extinguish large conflagrations. The advent of the fire engine, then, was welcomed with open arms. Warrillow says that one of the first fire engines in the Potteries was constructed in 1783 for Josiah Wedgwood I's factory at Etruria. Though primitive by today's standards, it could, impressively, throw a jet of water over the roof of the work's highest building. The fire engines were so effective that brigades naturally followed, and two of the earliest were based in Etruria and Hanley; however, the brigades frequently fought over the local water supplies. For this reason, some conflagrations ensued unchallenged. Eventually, a public meeting managed to resolve the contentious issue.

Other brigades sprung up across the towns of the Potteries, and, in 1854, Burslem had a fire brigade to take pride in. According to Warrillow's research, it was headed by Superintendent Povey, who had 36 firemen and 3 fire engines at his disposal. Burslem upgraded one of their fire engines to the latest model in 1869, which was sold by Messrs Merryweather & Sons of London. This new model replaced the fire engine called Niagaro, which was moved to Cobridge.

The new fire engine was named Lord of the Manor. It was a double-acting manual that required 24 firemen to operate. As for its appearance, it had large, brass lamps; a desirable high-seat for the driver; one pole for two horses; canvass buckets; and a leather-webbed hose. This engine was something Burslem boasted about, but, in reality, operating the manual engine over a long period of time exhausted the firemen, and therefore a water jet could not be sustained for severe conflagrations.

By 1864, Hanley's fire brigade had become quite efficient, too. Warrillow provides a good example of their efficiency which came in that very year, when the fire brigade, led by Superintendent Cole, saved Chatterley House from a blaze that had started early one morning – before 8.00am. Once the brigade had received the emergency call, a bell was rung, and, in a short time, two horse-drawn fire engines, firemen, and policemen arrived at Chatterley House. An insurance company paid out £500 for the fire damage.

The technology of the fire engine developed quickly, and, by August 1870, a fire engine that was powered by a light steam engine was being paraded around Market Square, Burslem. It discharged an enormous volume of water via two jets. To operate and repair the engine, the fire brigade had to employ an engineer and stoker. But, due to the infrequent nature of fires, these positions were not permanent, which had devasting consequences. For example, a few years later, a building was completely ravaged by a fire because the engineer assigned to the fire engine was working at Whitfield Colliery, and was therefore unable to reach the site of the fire in time. The firemen could not operate the engine, so they were left helpless. Problems of this nature were not just limited to personnel: engines that were still horse-drawn responded slowly too, because the horses were usually stabled elsewhere. These issues were compounded by the problematic system of the emergency call, which was raised with the police first who then contacted the fire brigade.

All these problems, *inter alia*, reached a point of crisis in 1913, so the officials of the City of Stoke-on-Trent decided to discuss the restructure of the six towns' fire brigades - aiming to improve the service and unite the brigades. The officials decided to sever the brigades from the police, and then appoint an overseer for all the brigades. The first overseer was Fire Chief Officer Mr Fred Bettany, who was based at the city's new fire-brigade headquarters in Hanley. All emergency calls were initially transmitted to these headquarters. The new fire service received benefits and upgrades too, such providing an insurance policy for firefighters, which compensated them in cases of injury or death during service; a new petrol-driven engine was also purchased. The new petrol-driven engine's speed made the horse-drawn engines redundant, so the last horse-drawn engine was used in 1926. This increased speed also meant that the petrol-driven engine could operate over a larger area, and thus increased the reach of the fire service from Hanley's station. Consequently, this made the fire stations of Tunstall, Stoke, and Fenton redundant, which also led to their closure. Warrillow says that after these closures, Hanley was equipped with two more petrol-driven engines; several 50ft laddered fire-escape devices; several hook ladders; and other life-saving apparatuses. Burslem and Longton stations remained in service, and they were given one petrol-driven engine each.

With the fire service adequately equipped to carry out its duties, in 1928, there was a focus on decreasing the response time of the fire service. This was achieved by providing living accommodation above the fire station so that firemen could be permantly stationed there. When an emergency arose, they were alerted by an electric bell in their residence. This greatly improved the response time by itself, but this was, for some companies, further improved by the installation of an automatic fire alarm in their factories, which was connected to their local fire station.

By the outbreak of the Second World War, the fire services across the country were experts in their profession, and they had the best tools. For these reasons, they were united under the National Fire Service, and therefore fell under the control of the government to assist the populace during the German aerial bombardments of the Blitz. The National Fire Service was open to both men and women, although women usually applied for administrative roles. After the war, the government gave the power of the fire service back to the local authorities through the Fire Services Act 1947.

IX

Road Transport and Maintenance

In the mid-seventeenth century, it was not uncommon to hear the sound of a stagecoach's post-horn echoing in the distance. But this was not to be in the Potteries, for stagecoaches, especially mail coaches, demanded first-class roads, and the roads of the Potteries fell short of this expectation. Instead, stagecoaches would pass through Newcastle-under-Lyme.

Eliza Meteyard, in her *The Life of Josiah Wedgwood*, notes that Josiah Wedgwood also condemned the roads of the Potteries, stating that some of the ruts in the roads were simply impassable. He recognised that, unless the district's roads started to resemble something more civilised than muddy lanes, his improvements to the pottery industry would be worthless, because trade communications were too difficult for his clients. Meteyard points out that the Romans opened up most of the country's resources with a network of magnificent roads, and so they were well-advanced in this respect.

It was clear, then, that the roads of the Potteries desperately needed to be improved, repaired, and maintained; and it was this realisation that brought about toll charges. The idea of the toll-charge scheme was to charge road users a fee to pass through a gate at fixed points along a given road - the fees would then be used to maintain the roads. A gated point was called either a tollgate, tollbar, turnpike, or tollhouse.

Tollgate keepers had to man a gate for long periods of time; therefore, tollhouses were often erected in proximity to a gate so that the tollgate keeper and his family could live there. Some of the tollhouses were placed between the forking points in a road, with a gate each side. One of these tollhouses was on a junction in Burslem, which took the toll from both the road going to Newcastle-under-Lyme via Brownhills, and the road from Burslem to Tunstall.

Warrillow says, in his *A Sociological History of the City of Stoke-on-Trent*, that towards the end of the eighteenth century, trustees would sell or let turnpikes by auction. Those who won such auctions, saw the opportunity as a lucrative business. Tariffs were set for all forms of traffic passing through the gates – including animals. For example, for one horse, one mule, or an ass the owner was charged one penny. It was eight pence per twenty cows, and four pence per twenty sheep. Some local, industrial traffic had a discount, however, and the military and mail coaches were exempt from the charge.

Once the system had been established for a few years, it was realised that narrow-wheeled vehicles were causing the most damage to road surfaces, so laws were put in place to abate such damage. In some areas, narrow wheels were even made illegal; in others, fines were given if a vehicle had wheels that were less than 6in wide, according to Warrillow.

Despite the charges, and the efforts to abate the wearing-down of road surfaces, travellers in the early nineteenth century still condemned the roads of the Potteries – stating that they were the worst in all of England! In addition, the frequency of toll gates in the district made travelling through the Potteries expensive. For instance, the road from Tunstall to Stoke had three tollgates, and they all charged a farthing for a two-wheeled light carriage. This, perhaps inevitably, led to assaults on tollgate keepers, and attempts to circumvent the turnpikes, which often meant crossing private land. Some people were willing to wander up to a mile away from the road. In September 1852, for example, the police fined a man for wandering across farmland in an attempt to avoid the tollgate at Cobridge. Other people tried to forgo the toll charge by changing the date on an old tollgate ticket – Warrillow provides a vivid example of this in his work. The discontent with the tollgates led to a decline in profits for the tollgate keepers; subsequently, without tollgate keepers renting the tollgates, some trustees were finding it difficult to pay their bills.

Long before these problems, however, by the end of the eighteenth century, the toll gate system had improved the quality of the roads enough for stagecoaches and mail coaches to enter the Potteries. A newspaper cutting, dated 20 March 1813, shows that coaches travelling to Liverpool from London would stop at the King's Head Inn, Shelton, both on the way to Liverpool and on the way back. According to Warrillow and an article dated 12 May 1824 in *The Potteries Mercury* newspaper, there were many stagecoaches offering transport services at that time, and many of them ran from places in Burslem, such as St. John's Square and The Leopard.

However, these coaches also became targets for thieves. Warrillow describes how, in 1840, a box owned by thc Manchester and Liverpool Bank, which contained £5,000 in gold and banknotes, was stolen from a stagecoach called 'The Potter'. It was not long before mail coaches had to be accompanied by an armed escort. The scarlet-coated guards were armed with blunderbusses, pistols, and cutlasses, and they were willing to sacrifice their lives for their duty. It has been recorded, for example, that, during one particularly bad winter, a mail coach got stuck in the snow, but, rather than delay the post, one of the guards tried to carry the mail to the nearest village – unfortunately, he froze to death.

In the latter part of the eighteenth century, stagecoaches were popular as 'cabs' too – the service was quite similar to the 'taxi' service of today. By 1870, for instance, the service was regulated in this way: the cabs and horses had to be kept in an immaculate condition; the cab driver had to produce a table which displayed the fare; a ticket had to be given to the passenger once a destination and price had been agreed; and the cab driver had to produce a licence when requested by an authority.

However, the life of a cab driver was much different from those of today. They worked long hours, and often found themselves waiting outside for long periods of time in adverse weather conditions. It was not uncommon, for instance, for coachmen as young as 11 years of age to be working from 6.00am to 7.00pm.

Accidents were frequent, and who could say if it was due to some of the young, inexperienced, and exhausted drivers, or due to the unpredictable nature of the animals – either way, horses extemporaneously taking flight were dangerous. In 1860, for example, a gentleman called Mr Tennent was driving his carriage from Hanley to Stoke when his horse suddenly took flight. It narrowly missed a small boy as it smashed through a wheelbarrow. It continued along a pavement where it struck a little girl, but, even then, the horse would not stop. Opposite Cauldon Road, it violently collided with a tollgate post, which smashed the cab and released the horse from its yoke. The emancipated horse galloped on into Fenton. Fortunately, all of those involved only suffered minor injuries. Another example can be recalled from June 1866, when a horse had taken flight with its cart, and trampled over a gentleman called Mr Williamson. He was quickly taken to the home of a surgeon called Mr Davies, but Williamson died four hours later. Despite the fatalities, no official authority intervened, so accidents continued till at least 1906. In that year, Warrillow says that a horse smashed the windows of a jewellery shop in Market Square, Hanley, which was owned by Pidduck & Sons.

By the early twentieth century, however, motor vehicles were starting to replace horse-drawn transport. In 1903, for instance, Mr Hales owned a motor-vehicle shop in Market Place, Burslem, and sold some of the earliest motor vehicles, such as the Velox, De Dion, Rex, Lagonda, Singer, Swift, and the Royal Enfield. The power of these engines varied from 8.5hp to 10hp. Hales owned his first motor vehicle in 1887, which was a 2hp Benz.

By this time, too, most of the major roads we know today had been built. Waterloo Road, for example, which takes its name in commemoration to the famous

Battle of Waterloo, had been upgraded from a hollow way *c*. 1815. Leek Road, which connects Leek and Hanley via Holden Lane bridge, was constructed in 1839. Holden Lane bridge had to be upgraded at a cost of £20,000 in 1930, however, because it was too narrow. Victoria Road in Fenton was laid in 1843.

As for repairing these roads, in the early nineteenth century, this was accomplished with the aid of a horse-drawn roller. In many instances, though, using a horse was counterproductive, because its feet damaged the road surface during repairs. New road surfaces were created by filling rut cavities with broken stones and sand. With the advent of the much more effective steam roller, the broken stones and sand were slurred with mud and water to form a cement. Then, a fine, top layer of flint was pressed with a steam roller to form a metallic sheen. Steam-roller drivers were paid between twenty-seven and thirty shillings per week.

X

Other Modes of Transport

In the eighteenth century, pottery was being sent to Ireland, Europe, North America, Africa, and the West Indies, but road transport was slow, limited, and perilous for the ware, which often sustained irrecoverable damage by the time it reached British ports, such as those at Liverpool, Bristol, and Hull. According to Eliza Meteyard, in her *The Life of Josiah Wedgwood*, some earthenware-laden waggons were swept away whilst fording the river Trent, and, due to the notorious dishonesty of those employed in the conveyance of goods, some of pottery was untraceably purloined. Poorly maintained roads, however, meant that the majority of the loss of ware was due to breakage, and it was known that pottery could be transported much more safely by water, but most of the rivers in the vicinity of the Potteries were too small to be navigable; therefore, a solution was needed so that the people of the Potteries could access seaports via a waterway – the solution was a canal system.

Meteyard records that, in 1760, the area surveyed by Mr James Brindley, an esteemed engineer, at the sole expense of Earl Gower, to determine if a canal system was viable. Brindley decided that the construction of a canal system was possible, if they could somehow negotiate Harecastle Hill, which rose to 700ft. Brindley proposed to overcome this obstacle by cutting a large tunnel through the hill. This was considered a novel and appropriate solution, but it required the permission of Parliament. Following a successful meeting with major landowners, local dignitaries, and the Duke of Bridgewater, Brindley submitted an application to Parliament, which was supported by Mr Josiah Wedgwood I, who, according to Warrillow's *A Sociological History of Stoke-on-Trent*, contributed £1,000 to the project. The project was approved by Parliament in 1766.

The project took 11 years to complete, and it was overseen by the Duke of Bridgewater. He appointed Brindley as the operation's chief engineer, and Brindley's brother-in-law, Mr Hugh Henshall, as the chief clerk. The plan was to cut a canal 93 miles long that would connect the river Trent and the river Mersey with navigable points. For this reason, the waterway was called the Trent and Mersey Canal, or, as Brindley called it, the Grand Trunk Canal.

Warrillow's research shows that in 1766, Wedgwood officially began the canal's construction by cutting the first sod near today's canal bridge number 129, which is in Brownhills. Shortly after, a celebration ensued in Burslem, where a sheep was roasted near the marketplace, accompanied by ceremonial gunfire in front of Wedgwood's house.

At least 600 men worked tirelessly to cut the canal, and during this process they discovered new coal seams. Typically, the canal was cut to a depression of 16ft at the base, tapering to 29ft at its margins, with a depth of 4ft 6in. The huge depression was then lined with clay.

Locks were used to traverse any gradients. Etruria is 408ft above sea-level, for instance, so the descend to the Mersey was made possible by incremental drops over 40 locks. Some of these locks are 14ft wide.

Brindley died in 1772, so, unfortunately, he never saw the completion of his arched tunnel in 1777. Warrillow confirms that the tunnel was 2,897 yards in length and 8ft 6in in width, and lined with brick throughout. However, there was no towing path; so, to traverse the tunnel, bargemen - colloquially known as 'boaties' – lay supine on top of the barge and pushed their feet against the tunnel's roof to propel the barge. Propelling a barge in this manner was known as 'legging' in common parlance. Meanwhile, the horses were taken via a road over the hill. The road still exists today, and is aptly called Boat Horse Road.

Typically, it took about two-and-a-half hours for a fully-laden barge, which was about 25 tons, to navigate the tunnel. During this process, the fire in the cabin had to be extinguished. Only a few candles and oil lamps made some attempt to illuminate the confined space. Indeed, there was so little room, that barges devoid of cargo had to be filled with soil before entering the tunnel to submerge them enough for legging. The soil was then removed at the end of the tunnel.

By the early nineteenth century, technological advances meant that the quantity and frequency of boats passing through the tunnel greatly increased; however, because the width of the tunnel could only accommodate a single vessel, it became heavily congested. Therefore, Mr Thomas Telford, a civil engineer, proposed to build another, much larger tunnel parallel to Brindley's. Telford's plans were approved, so construction began in 1824. Remarkably, it took just three years to finish the tunnel, which was almost perfectly straight – so much so, that points of light could be seen from either end of the 2,926-yard stretch. The generously-spaced towpaths were made 5ft wide and below the water level; however, as Warrillow's research shows, some fearful horses still refused to enter the pitch-black tunnel, while larger horses bumped their heads on the, still, relatively-low roof. The canal itself was wide enough for two barges to pass each other, and, along the roof, ventilation shafts were incorporated at regular intervals.

Telford's tunnel was a feat of engineering, and it successfully improved the transport of raw materials and goods, both in and out of the Potteries. However, by the 1840s, the railway infrastructure of the Potteries was well-developed, and therefore greatly expedited the safe transportation of goods. The speed of the service was particularly noticeable in mid-winter when the canal service would be impeded by frozen water, even with the specially designed barges that went ahead to break the ice.

However, for a short period at least, these modes of transport became fraternal rather than competitive when the North Staffordshire Railway incorporated the Trent and Mersey Canal into its business. According to Warrillow, the newly unified company had its first meeting on 23 September 1846, with Mr Ricardo in the chair. A public holiday was also granted for the occasion. The company built its new headquarters and main station at Stoke, on the area known then as Winston's Wood. The construction cost £30,000. The proximate North Stafford Hotel was also built as part of the project.

It was not long before the new company saw an opportunity in the market for the transportation of passengers, not just raw materials and goods. So, in 1854, a number of meetings were held to discuss the construction of a loop line to link the towns of the Potteries. However, there were many unforeseen objections to the project. Warrillow explains that some thought the use of a drawbridge to cross the Trent and Mersey Canal was dangerous. The people of Burslem strongly opposed, too, preferring to have just a single line to link Burslem and Tunstall. In 1863, the company engaged in public meetings to discuss the objections, but little progress was made.

Despite this, the company continued to expand its lines. A spur line, for example, from Etruria to Hanley was opened on 13 July 1864. To accommodate the line, the course of the Fowlea Brook was shifted; the bridge near the station at Etruria was enlarged; and the foot of Basford Bank was filled and levelled. Sadly, these rail developments, along with the nearby ironworks, eroded yet more of Etruria's idyllic and silvan beauty. As you will recall from Chapter V, the North Staffordshire Infirmary fled the industrious plague of Etruria. The timing of this escape was just before the spur line was laid.

The company considered the spur line a success, so a meeting was arranged in the same year to discuss a loop line project that would connect Burslem, Tunstall, and Kidsgrove to the main station at Stoke. It was noted that because most of the Potteries' towns were on hills, there were some engineering difficulties to resolve.

However, in the following year, the company faced more pressing problems from the rippling, financial issues caused by the end of the American Civil War. The depression in the United States slowed trade, which had a profoundly negative impact on railway companies. For this reason, although plans for the loop line had been approved by both the company and legislation, the North Staffordshire Railway company cautiously postponed the loop line project, which caused much bitterness in Burslem again, with people claiming the company's financial woes were due to bad management.

Warrillow, however, records that, in 1870, an agreement had been reached with Messrs John and William Pickering of London to commence the construction of the Potteries Loop Line. In July that year, the Chief Bailiff of Burslem cut the first sod in a near Moorland Road, and everyone in attendance cheered. A celebration party then ensued that evening in The Leopard.

The North Staffordshire Railway continued to struggle financially, though, not unlike North Staffordshire Tramways Company operating in the Potteries at the same time. By 1871, the North Staffordshire Tramways Company was still executing the necessary repairs to its tramlines, but, in the following year, financial figures continued to decline, and the company's accounts started to show negative balances. The directors had considered expanding the service to acquire more revenue, but the opening of the Potteries Loop Line spur between Etruria and Hanley made expansion impossible, so the directors were losing interest. Before explaining how the two companies resolved this difficult situation, a necessary divergence into the history of trams in the Potteries will provide the necessary addition context.

Warrillow's research shows that, in 1842, the main form of public transport for the working class in the Potteries were horse-drawn omnibuses, which operated back and forth between Longton and Burslem. This might have been an adequate service for a few rural villages, but the Potteries was quickly expanding into a large urban landscape, so a more substantial service was required.

According to Warrillow, the solution came in October 1859, when Mr George Francis Train, an American from Boston who pioneered the horse-drawn railway, came to Birkenhead, England, and laid the first tramway for public transport, which was officially opened in August 1860. With this success, Train approached other towns and cities to propose the implementation of horse-drawn tramways into their infrastructure. Hanley was one of those towns, and his discussion with the town's council took place in June 1861.

Train, Lord Mayor J Dimmock, and the borough surveyor, with the blessing of the town's council, produced a plan showing where the new tramlines should be set. Once the plan was approved, Train obtained the necessary permission needed to lay the tramlines. These tramlines were administered by the North Staffordshire Tramways Company.

Along Waterloo Road, Burslem, tramlines were laid on wooden sleepers to provide a service between Burslem and Hanley. There was some opposition, however - especially, and understandably, from the Hansom cab drivers. A farmer also protested by placing his cart-load of hay across the tracks, but the police quickly intervened.

Despite objections such as these, the section opened on 13 January 1862. From 8.00am, the tramcars left their stations at one-hour intervals. Warrillow says at 11.00am that day, a tramcar left Hanley with the company directors on board and, just nine minutes later, they arrived safely in Burslem. Many people were overjoyed with this success – they considered the new mode of transport a step in the right direction, so to speak, because there were about 900 people from Burslem who were employed in Hanley. The tollgate at Cobridge was still operational, so the company paid the tollgate's proprietor £15, and then equated for this fee in the passengers' fare.

Despite the optimism, it was quickly realised that the horses were under a lot of strain by the constant stopping and starting. You see, each tramcar was equipped with a brake that was activated when the driver turned a wheel twice, but it was not always adequate, so some horses had to absorb some of the tramcar's momentum with their buttocks. The distressed horses would then skid across the road.

On 30 January 1862 the high-ranking employees of the company and its shareholders had their first meeting. During the meeting, they celebrated the company's recent achievements, such as expediting journey times, which meant that some of their customers could travel further in a shorter time, and therefore discover areas of the Potteries that were previously out of reach. Furthermore, the quantity of people that could be transported vastly increased, too, which provided better employment opportunities. For example, before the Potteries' tramway, approximately 200 people travelled between Hanley and Burslem each week, which increased to about 5,300 each week, *per tramcar*.

About 40,000 passengers had used this service without any serious accidents, but the tragic and fatal accident of a child brought this record to an abrupt end. Warrillow says the child was a 16-year-old boy called George Gater. He was travelling on a tramcar along Waterloo Road when he decided to leap from the tramcar with the intention of continuing on foot down Pitt Street. However, his foot somehow got caught, and he tumbled under the tramcar's wheels. The entire weight of the tramcar passed over his stomach, and he was pronounced dead within 15 minutes.

Improvements and upgrades had to be made; therefore, the company formulated an upgrade plan, which it protected by submitting a protection bill to Parliament. However, the proposition to upgrade the service was met with objection and protests. This was surprising to the company's representatives, who considered that the influx of passengers was evidence that the service was popular. The planned improvements were still carried out regardless. Consequently, by November 1864, tramcars were running simultaneously in both directions at the improved rate of half-hour intervals.

This now brings us back to 1871, when the company fell into financial difficulty. The steam-power of the railways continued to gradually supersede horsepower; therefore, by 1881, the company had to concede, and the last horse-drawn service took place in that year.

In spite of this, a solution also came in the same year for both companies. The North Staffordshire

Tramways Company took over the North Staffordshire Railway, and introduced steam-trams to the Potteries in accordance with the Tramways Orders Confirmation Act 1881. The company's new steam engines pulled both single and double-decker tramcars, though rather more ungainly than their horse-drawn predecessors. Warrillow also points out that they produced a lot of smoke and noise, which was not welcome by the inhabitants of the Potteries. The drivers and fireman did not welcome the working conditions, either, for the tram engine at the head of the column did not have weather protection, which resulted in hardships during stormy weather.

The new company's headquarters remained at Stoke, where it upgraded the depot with tramcar sheds, workshops, new stores, and new offices. However, some local people made complaints about the pollution produced by this site, and the service in general. The company was therefore ordered to integrate a drainage system into the depot for greasy water; to ensure tramcars do not exceed a speed of 8mph, nor should they have smoke bellowing from them. Shortly after this order, however, a steam tram was reported for contravening these conditions in Longton. In response, the leaders of Hanley held a meeting in January 1882 to discuss the complaint. Conversely, it became clear that many of the constituents supported the company, because they easily overcame any objections presented to them, whether those objections pertained to the complaint or not. One participant, for instance, objected to steam trams passing by his place of employment because the road was too narrow. Another participant counted, however, by asserting that the new tramcars were not as wide as the previous horse-drawn version. Warrillow says that a similar meeting took place at Fenton, and its leaders offered the company a capital investment of £125,000.

However, it was not long before the other towns of the Potteries called meetings to raise their grievances with the company. The leaders of Burslem, for example, accused the company of not keeping its pledge to lay tramlines along Newcastle Street and Davenport Street, which would link Burslem to Brownhills, Tunstall, and Goldenhill. The company explained that, instead, they wanted to link Burslem and Tunstall via Scotia Road. Burslem's leaders accepted this notion, and, at once, contacted the Chatterley Iron and Coal Company to request the erection of a gate where its railway crossed Scotia Road to make it safe for a tramway. With regard to the proposed tramline along Newcastle Street, the company explained that they were concerned about how safely its tramcars could handle the steep decline of the road.

Dignitaries at Stoke complained about the fume emissions and fatal accidents, such as children being runover and collisions with horses. The company continued to advance, however, by implementing the new Wilkinson steam engine, which, weighing 8 tons, was a featherweight when compared with the previous engines. It was also hoped that the reduced weight would reduce the wearing of the road surfaces.

Throughout the Potteries, however, it was clear that the stream trams were not free from practical problems, and that they were major contributors to accidents. For example, in Burslem, horse-drawn carts would often stray across the tramlines which, of course, compelled tramcars to stop. If this occurred on

Swan Bank, though, the tramcars would not start again, and they would be forced to return to the bottom of the hill to try again. The gradient of Swan Bank was much steeper than it is today. Dignitaries did not want to tolerate such a service, so they and the North Staffordshire Tramways Company agreed to remove the Stoke service. At this point, the pollution, complaints, and accidents were becoming too much for the directors. Moreover, the maintenance cost of the service was becoming too expensive and non-profitable for both the directors and shareholders. The era of steam trams quietened.

Before moving on to discuss the advent of electric trams, a remarkable act of heroism should be noted here. On 13 April 1884, a conductor called Timothy Trow was riding a tramcar along London Road. Glancing out a window, he noticed a child fall into the nearby canal. Without hesitation, he leapt from the tramcar, vaulted the adjacent railings, and jumped into the canal. Trow saved the child, but he drowned in the act. It was thought that a terrible cramp prevented him from swimming. The child was four-year-old Jane Ridgway, who lived nearby, and had been playing on the towpath. An obelisk memorial was erected for Trow on London Road, opposite James Street, which was thought to be the approximate area where the tragedy took place - it is still there today. Trow was just 21 years of age.

By the end of the nineteenth century, much of the tramway system had been disused for a number of years, particularly in Longton. British Electric Traction, which was founded in 1895, saw an opportunity for the disused lines, so the company secured an agreement to use electric trams in the

Potteries by 1896. This agreement stipulated that the purchase of the tramway system was for 21 years. This figure was not random: it was taking into consideration new legislation that empowered property owners to veto proposed tramway routes near their land, which was valid for 21 years.

With this agreement, British Electric Traction inspected the current tramway routes, then proposed some routes of expansion with the Board of Trade. Goldenhill, Smallthorne, and Longport were considered. The condition of the tramway routes was discussed in a company meeting. It was mentioned that some of the streets were quite narrow with sharp, right-angled turns; but, worse than that, there were miles of tramlines with compromised structural integrity, which was caused by honey-combed mines. A plan of improvement was agreed, and, by June 1898, with a workforce of 200 men, heavier and stronger rails were being laid. Each rail weighed 87lbs per yard.

The generating station was constructed at the former steam-tram depot in Stoke, on the bank of the river Trent. The engine room contained three Lancashire boilers, which measured 7ft by 30ft, with a working pressure of 120lbs per square inch. There were also two steam-compound engines, with a power capacity of up to 330hp, to drive the general electric generators. These were coupled directly to two 200kW dynamos. The electric trams were conducted by overhead wires, also known as trolley wires, which powered the electric motors beneath the tramcars.

The tramcars were procured from the Electric Railway and Tramway Carriage Works based at Preston. They had motors capable of delivering up to

25hp, which were controlled by nine gears. The tramcars were also fitted with slipper brakes. When activated, these brakes were pushed onto the track by compressed air, and then held in position by magnetism, which was created by a current passing through the electromagnetic coils in the brake shoes. Each tramcar could seat up to 24 persons, which would later increase to 52 persons, made possible by the procurement of larger, bogie trams.

By the completion of the project, which cost about £80,000, British Electric Traction had amalgamated with several tram companies, such as the North Staffordshire Tramways Company, Longton Corporation Tramways, and the Potteries Electric Traction Company Limited. The new company used 'Potteries Electric Traction Company Limited' as their unified name. Approximately 170 drivers, conductors, and inspectors who worked on the steam trams were re-employed. They were contracted to work ten hours per diem, at five-and-a-halfpence per hour. A successful trial of the new tramlines was conducted on 19 April 1899, which was followed by an inauguration ceremony in the following month. Warrillow states that on the day of the ceremony, a demonstration took place in Burslem, near Messrs Boote's pottery factory. During the ceremony, five-year-old Albert Hawley broke from the crowd and inadvertently ran in front of a tramcar which fatally struck him.

In 1900, a second generating station was built at May Bank that was capable of producing 1,280kW of power. Then, over the next five years, depots were erected at Goldenhill, Chesterton, and Fenton. This power network meant that the overhead trolley wires could be connected to nodal substations every half a mile so that, in the event of a breakdown, the power could be disconnected from a small section, rather than turning off the entire network. The Potteries' inhabitants could find very little to complain about. The new tramcars were well-managed, economical, and generated very little noise or pollution.

The tramway system, however, like the people of the Potteries, was a victim of the industrial pollution and destruction. Warrillow says that mining subsidence damaged tramlines, for example, even though these were laid on concrete foundations and paved with granite sets on the outside of the track. Also, a bridge crossing the canal in Etruria had to be raised several feet to overcome mining subsidence. Moreover, the chemicals in the atmosphere corroded the overhead cables.

During the First World War, motorcars, which ran on gas obtained from Etruria Gas Works, were appearing in the city. Warrillow says that the motorcars performed well using this fuel, but it could not provide the same power output as petrol. This was evident when some vehicles, especially heavy-laden lorries, failed to ascend Basford Bank. Some vehicles had the momentum to make it halfway, but they were soon rolling dangerously backwards, out of control.

After the First World War, there was a surge in the adoption of the motorcar. These vehicles competed with tramcars for space on the road, which resulted in congestion, and, consequently, many accidents. This situation was exacerbated by the advent of Brown's buses in 1921, because a multitude of war veterans were buying these buses, which was facilitated by hire-purchase agreements. The ownership of Brown's buses grew to such an extent that the City of Stoke-on-

Trent had to seek parliamentary powers to restrict the quantity of buses permitted in the city. These powers were successfully obtained in 1923, which also gave tram companies the right to appeal against any unfair competition.

However! Potteries Electric Traction was not completely innocent in this affair, for, in 1900, knowing that the advent of a motorbus was near, the company purchased several prototype models and implemented experimental public services, but these services were not popular or successful. With this failure, the company decided to buy three double-decker buses, which they put to public service in 1904. That said, these vehicles frequently malfunctioned, too, so they were replaced with open-sided, single-decker buses in 1910, and they proved to be more reliable.

Between 1913 and 1925, Warrillow's research shows that the company acquired a fleet of about 86, 40hp Daimler buses, which cost about £127,000. The War Office appropriated some of these buses for the war effort, by deploying them in France during the First World War.

Between 1922 and 1928, new bus models were appearing in the city, such as the Tilling-Stevens' buses, and motorised charabancs - both had single decks.

In 1925, 113 buses were licenced to run over the city's tramway routes, of which 27 were owned by Potteries Electric Traction.

By 1926, it was clear that the popularity of the city's tram service was in decline, so representatives from the City of Stoke-on-Trent and Potteries Electric Traction had a meeting to consider the cessation of the city's tram service. The cessation of the service was agreed and implemented quickly, but, as Warrillow says, the removal of the tramway infrastructure was a slow and gradual process.

In 1933, Potteries Electric Traction was renamed to the Potteries Motor Traction Company Limited (PMT); however, the company had not removed all of the remaining tram lines, and, by 1941, Warrillow says that 18 miles of tramlines were still embedded in the city's roads, which was thought to weigh approximately 2.3 tons. This figure was reduced to 13 miles in 1952, and then, in the following year, when the tramlines were removed from Glebe Street, Stoke; King Street, Fenton; Stoke Road, Hanley; and Waterloo Road, Burslem, it was reduced to 11 miles. Finally, in 1955, the city's last remaining tramlines were removed from Hope Street, Hanley.

XI

Trade Unionism

Mr John Ward, in his book the *The Borough of Stoke-upon-Trent*, attributes the inception of a potters' union to the agitations of political reform between 1817 and 1820; however, Mr Harold Owen, in his book *The Staffordshire Potter* argues that it was due to the improvements and innovation in the methods of manufacture. Either way, the pottery workers felt that their rights were starting to be violated. In opposition, the Potters' Union was formed in 1824.

In the following year, the pottery workers demanded better wages, and they enacted this demand with a strike, but this was opposed and forbade by the government through the Combinations of Workman Act 1825. Warrillow, in his *A Sociological History of the City of Stoke-on-Trent*, says that after this unexpected failure, the new and inexperienced workers returned to work on worse terms than before. Leaders of the strikes had difficulty acquiring employment elsewhere, especially when such employers were strict, top-hatted, and swallow-coated men – a new rich breed that dominated many of the management positions.

Despite this initial failure, renewed hope came in

1833, when the Combinations of Workman Act 1825 was repealed. A new union was formed, and the committee met with employers each week to discuss the rights of the workers. Many employers detested such meetings, and stubbornly refused to increase the remuneration of their workers. They claimed it was impossible, because the competition between manufacturers had driven down prices, and, consequently, profits. This explanation was rejected by the pottery workers which resulted in another strike in 1834, lasting for four months. According to Warrillow, the union was victorious - it secured a 25% pay increase for their clients. The union, however, was not satisfied, and it made further demands to address two other ill-treatments of the workmen: annual hiring and the good-from-oven policy. The former was the contractual hiring, or renewal, of a factory's workforce on the Martinmas (11 November), every year. The issue was not with the annual hiring *per se*, but with some of the contractual terms. For example, the employer could terminate the contract at their discretion, but the employee was tied to the employer until the next Martinmas or face prosecution. The good-from-oven policy stipulated that employees firing ware, especially the oven-men, would only be paid for fired articles that were flawless. The unfairness of this policy was further acerbated because the oven-men were not permitted to check the ware post-firing, and were therefore at the mercy of their employer's subjective notion of flawlessness. The employers had the upmost conviction in these policies, so, in 1836, they came together to form their own union to represent their rights: The Potteries Chamber of Commerce. After much deliberation between the unions, failure to reach a compromise resulted in the pottery workers striking again, just before Martinmas in that year. This is often referred to as 'The Great Strike'.

Owen speaks extensively of this period of unrest in his discourse, and he reveals the extent of the financial and operational disruption to the pottery industry, in addition to the financial hardships of the pottery workers on strike. Owen states that 3,500 workers across 14 factories breached their contracts through striking, but, safe in numbers, it was determined too impractical to prosecute all of them. The number of strikers increased further at the passing of Martinmas, when the annual contracts had expired. The strike persisted for 20 weeks across 64 of the largest pottery works, and approximately 78% of the workforce participated. David Colclough, who was the governor of a workhouse in the Potteries, insisted that those who were unemployed should seek work at their local workhouse, but 'local' is subjective, of course. For instance, it was not uncommon for families to walk up to *six* miles to reach a workhouse. Once there, work commenced from 8.00am until dusk. Typically, men were assigned work in the fields; women were assigned domestic duties; and children were schooled, but certainly not to the standards we have today.

Despite these challenges, Warrillow says that the pottery workers remained firm and devoted to their cause. Some of the most devoted sold pieces of their household property, valuables, and family heirlooms to prolong the strike. The Potters' Union also provided financial support, which was five to six shillings per week, but only men with families were eligible. There was some extra financial assistance from unions outside the district, too, but only as one-off donations. It became clear that, financially, the strike was not sustainable, and the cause fell into a state of attrition. Many potters had to return to work, which left a small number to fight the losing battle; however, most fortunately for the remaining activists, the employers wanted peace; therefore, eventually, a conciliation meeting was called at Betley, which was chaired by Mr Twemlow - an impartial county magistrate. Some satisfaction was achieved by both parties: the potters got 16 days of guaranteed work per month, and they were permitted to end their contract with one month's notice, but the employers still insisted on the good-from-oven policy of payment. With this, work resumed on 20 January 1837, and the Potters' Union disbanded.

Employers soon capitalised on the defeated workers, though, by reverting to the old terms. This was tolerated until the Martinmas of 1843, when, once again, employers wanted to reduce the workers' remuneration, which the potters had to oppose. The potters formed another union called the Committee of Management.

According to Warrillow's research, the union started its own periodical called *The Potters' Examiner*, which was published in Longton. It was also published under the appellation *The Potter* between 1854 and 1863, and it made its final publication as *The Potteries Examiner* in 1892. Despite being created as the mouthpiece of the potters, the newspaper came to be impartial, but also reporting with a religious-moral lens. This meant the stories it published attacked both employer and employee alike for contravening religious principles. A caricature of the idle, drunken worker, for example, came to the fore.

Early in 1844, however, the advent of innovative pottery machinery threatened to mechanise some of the workers' skills, and therefore make skilled workers redundant. Instead, unskilled operator positions were now available to unskilled workers for lower wages, such as women and children. Men formed the majority of the workforce, so this news flooded the workers with much consternation.

Mr Ridgway was one of the innovators creating the mechanised workers. One of his machines could make toilet-paste boxes. This was quickly followed by another machine which displaced flat-pressers. These inventions stirred the Committee of Management to action, which was strengthened by the new influx of fearful potters. However, the union was not intent on opposing the new technology; instead, the committee proposed a radical scheme that empowered the indignant potters to acquire land in an American colony.

In May 1844, the Potters' Joint Stock Emigration Society was formed and registered to oversee the scheme. Warrillow explains that the members raised £5,000 for the scheme, and, subsequently, 1,200 acres of land was purchased using a deposit, with instalments to follow over a ten-year period. The land was in Wisconsin, and it was divided into 20-acre plots. The new settlement was called Pottersville. Mr William Evans, a member of the Potters' Joint Stock Emigration Society and editor of *The Potteries Examiner*, was the impetus behind the idea, and he wrote about it obsessively and energetically as though this was a golden age for the impecunious, and soon to be redundant, workmen.

In February 1846 the estate steward, a deputy, and other officials of the Potters' Joint Stock Emigration Society embarked on a ship headed to New York to prepare the colony – a journey that took almost six weeks. An account of the officials' journey to America, and, indeed, the first erections of the colony, were published in England, and this seemed to actualise the scheme for the workmen, and thus stimulated funding. During that year, however, the Potters' Joint Stock Emigration Society was experiencing difficulties. Disputes between the society representatives ensued - generally over principles and finances - which led to many members leaving and a subsequent breakdown of the society. Later that year, the remaining personnel renamed the union to The Potters' General Union.

Over the next two years, the officials at Pottersville continued to work on the emigration scheme, but their funds depleted, so they contacted the union to request more money. Warrillow's work shows that the union sent a further £600, which was enough to complete the scheme. Therefore, in 1847, a committee and about 40 families, who had stayed true to the scheme, were transported via a canal barge to the port at Liverpool, so they could set sail for Wisconsin. As they departed from the Potteries, thousands of people stood on the canal-side to watch and wave goodbye. Barges that had other pottery workers onboard followed for part of the journey to cheer the success of the families. Some of these barges had bands, who played music suited to the occasion.

In the following year, although many skilled pottery jobs remained, the pottery workers' wages were reduced, but The Potters' General Union, chiefly concerned with the emigration scheme, had now disbanded, leaving sectional unions representing specific skills and jobs to continue any opposition. One of these sectional unions was the Union of Oven-men, for example. The impartial Board of Arbitration tried to help in the union's place, but it was not successful. Without a union, the employers implemented whatever terms they pleased for the next 20 years. In 1865, for example, Owen recalls how another strike had taken place to challenge the evil system of hiring on a year's contract, which, once again, could not be terminated by a month's notice. This time, the Union of Oven-men was successful in legally securing a new, and fair, contractual agreement.

For Pottersville, the cessation of The Potters' General Union meant that the funding for the emigration scheme also ceased, which led to quarrels. Therefore, by 1849, some families had returned home. Those who stayed had to quickly learn new skills and, as Warrillow says, fend for themselves.

In 1882, the workers formed the National Order of Potters to oppose the employers' The Staffordshire Chamber of Commerce. Owen tried to expand the potters' union to included all the pottery unions and those of other industries, too, which he proposed to the National Society of Pottery Workers, but this unification attempt was not successful. It was the unions that represented some of the distinctive pottery skills that would not unite, such as hollow-ware pressers, flat-pressers, handlers, turners, printers, transferrers, decorators, engravers, dippers, packers, and oven-men etc.

However, Owen's idea, and his effort to actualise it, was not in vain. In 1906, all the pottery craft skills, except dippers, packers, and oven-men, amalgamated under the National Society of Pottery Workers, which was for both men and *women*. Until 1906, despite 20 years' campaigning by Miss Bennett, previous unions and societies had taken little interest in the affairs and rights of women workers. This inclusion was most welcome, however, for it meant that the new union had *many* members! Warrillow records that a new building was constructed for the union in Old Hall Street, Hanley, on the site of the Old Hall Pottery Factory. The foundation stone was laid in 1907.

By 1920, the small unions representing dippers, packers, and oven-men had amalgamated into the National Society of Pottery Workers, and, so, finally, it represented the whole pottery industry.

XII

Industry and Commerce

The mining of coal took place in the Potteries from at least the mid-seventeenth century. Warrillow, in his *A Sociological History of the City of Stoke-on-Trent*, refers to Dr Robert Plot's 1686 publication *The Natural History of Stafford-shire* when writing about this early period. Plot says there was an abundance of coal to be found on the surface at that time; therefore, it did not require mining, as such. By the nineteenth century, however, coal and ironstone mining had become extensive throughout the Potteries, especially in Tunstall, Burslem, Cobridge, Fenton, and Longton. Many of the mines, and therefore raw materials, were owned by proprietors of pottery factories, which eliminated supply costs.

Warrillow states that a coalpit in those days was considered to be *very* deep if it reached a depth of 300 yards or more. The coal and ironstone were extracted by hand with a pickaxe, then placed into tubs which were pulled to the surface by pit ponies, who spent most of their lives underground. Not all of the material could be extracted fast enough by hand, however, so explosive charges were used to blast the coal apart. Typically, to do this, the miners would undercut a coal seam by a few feet, then drill a hole large enough to place an explosive charge. Such holes were known as shot-holes. Once the explosives were set in position, a train of gunpowder was traced back from the explosives for a considerable distance, where it could be safely ignited. In theory, this practice kept the miners away from the subsequent explosion, but, in practice, as Warrillow's research shows, this method of extraction was the cause of many tragic fatalities. For example, at Leycett Colliery, on 21 January 1889, 62 men were killed from a shot-fired explosion. Today, a mechanical cutter undercuts coal seams, and then the shot-holes are bored with an electric drill. Then, at a safe distance, the explosives are triggered by an electric current, which is delivered through a wire connected to a battery. Pneumatic picks then break up the coal. In this way, though the mines are still worked today, Warrillow says the toil cannot be compared with that of the early miners, whose clogs could be heard on the pavements in the early hours, heading for another day full of sweat, hazards, and perilous situations.

In the early nineteenth century, Warrillow's research shows that there were about 4,000 collieries in North Staffordshire. These were worked by men, women, and children until the Mine and Collieries Act 1842 forbade the inclusion of women, and children under ten years of age in the workforce. This legislation also forbade payment of the miners' remuneration in public houses – much to the annoyance of the 'butty' men, who were often contracted by the proprietors of collieries to hire and administer labour. To them, this administrative role did not encompass the safety of the site, nor the welfare of its workforce. For a butty, the primary focus was the evil formula of minimum expenditure and high productivity to maximise profit. This ideology often meant forgoing urgent repairs on some sites, which greatly vexed uninformed firemen who had a legal obligation to carry out the necessary repairs. Despite legislation, butty men took advantage of cheap, child labour. Perhaps, then, it was for site safety reasons and the safeguarding of children that the government introduced legislation to eradicate butty men.

However, it was not uncommon for employers to turn a blind eye to the legislation, so the butty men continued their duties, but somewhat more furtively. Warrillow discovered, for instance, that butty men stopped paying the miners inside their usual public house - instead arranging their meetings in an adjoining building or even an outhouse. This was popular with the miners too, for they could quickly get to spending their wages in the public house, as usual. The miners were also still accompanied by their children, because many fathers had chosen to forgo the prohibition of child labour in the mines. Many miners thought this was necessary to earn extra shillings for their household. Some of these children were as young as eight years of age.

However, some sources, including Warrillow, confirm that the coal trade was thriving in the mid-nineteenth century, so a miner could expect to earn a comfortable twenty to thirty shillings per week. This was even higher for iron workers, who earned about fifty shillings per week. With such earnings, miners lived on luxurious food, such as poultry, geese, and ducks. They even had the first choice of vegetables;

they drank beer and spirits in inordinate quantities, and they could, occasionally, acquire port wine. This was not always perceived with envy, though, for the upper class thought miners had low intelligence – it is claimed only half of them could write – and therefore were prone to wasting money on vice, proclivities, and mindless self-indulgence, especially when alcohol was involved.

The generous remuneration was, of course, to somewhat compensate for the perilous working conditions, where accidents were frequent and life-threatening. Some dangers were common throughout the shift, such as coal and stone becoming unstable and falling upon the workers. If this were to happen during the night, the severely injured or incapacitated miners would have to wait until the morning for a rescue, because there was no nocturnal workforce on the surface. Some of the injured workers probably attempted to gain attention by shaking their safety chain, which was affixed to the surface, but passers-by would have been seldom.

Once injured, Warrillow says the miners and their families were at the mercy, or 'generosity', as one might have said in those days, of the pit owner to substitute the household income. Although accidents were frequent, compensation was not standardised. It varied between pit owners, depending both on the owner's assessment of the injury and on the miner's contribution to the firm's sickness fund. If, for instance, a miner was injured but would probably recover, a pit owner might pay the convalescent sixpence a week. In the case of a fatality, the pit owner would probably cover all the funeral expenses and support the miner's family for a set period thereafter.

One's mortality was something a miner had to come to terms with quickly in his occupation, for it was not uncommon for a single accident to claim many lives. When one thinks of such accidents, the Talk-o'-th'-Hill disaster at Kidsgrove comes to mind, which claimed 90 lives on 13 December 1866, but there were many other accidents that were equally devasting, such as the explosion at Mossfield Colliery, Longton, on 16 October 1889, which resulted in 59 deaths.

Warrillow also records a flood in Diglake Colliery, Audley, where at least 77 men and boys drowned on Monday, 14 January 1895. The miners had literally dug themselves a lake of death, as water rushed like a river down the mine shafts, carrying in its current many helpless boys to their subterranean grave. A pump was brought to extract water from the mine at a rate of 180 gallons per minute, but by the end of the first day the water level had only been reduced by 6in. It was estimated that the remaining depth at the bottom of the pit was 4ft 6in.

Warrillow goes on to say that the scene that night was eerie. The colliery's gas-jets had been extinguished, but flames from small lamps still punctured the pervading darkness, which looked like will o' the wisps. Grief-stricken family members wandered the grounds like dark-shrouded figures, whose features were only distinguishable when the moonlight was cast upon them. The air was freezing, and some had braved snow drifts as high as 8ft to try and rescue their loved ones, but it was a forlorn hope.

When the rescue operation continued, men worked relentlessly to get access to the bowels of the pit. It was not uncommon to hear eerie tapping sounds from the air pipes, which were, no doubt, from those that needed rescuing, but the origin of the sound was difficult to determine.

By Wednesday, it was calculated that approximately 70 people remained trapped in the pit, and when this remained the case by Thursday afternoon, all hope of them being alive had been abandoned. Bizarrely, according to Warrillow, a 30-year-old horse called King, who had worked at the site for 20 years, was found alive, and he was rescued from a deep pool of water where he was stranded. An analysis of the disaster showed that old plans were being used on the site, which resulted in the erroneous digging into a thin wall that divided the old water-logged pit from the new one.

When Queen Victoria learned of the disaster, she expressed deep sorrow, but also admiration for the gallant rescue workers.

Mining was so extensive across the Potteries that mine shafts were ubiquitous, and, because they were prone to collapsing without warning, they were dangerous. The best-known example happened in St John's Street, Hanley, in December 1903: 56-year-old Mr Thomas Holland was walking to work when a huge hole opened in the pavement, right under his feet. Holland fell about 120ft, and he was presumed to have died either from the fall or from the noxious gases that filled the old mine shaft. Either way, it was considered too dangerous to make a rescue attempt.

Ironstone was an important raw material in the nineteenth century, too, and it was mined from Holditch Colliery and Wolstanton Colliery. Both these collieries were sunk in the 1920s; however, they were deepened so they could be put to use as coal mines.

The deposit of ironstone in North Staffordshire is quite large when geologically compared with other deposits in the country, save central Scotland, where a rich deposit also exists. It is thought that the North Staffordshire deposit has 13 seams of blackband ironstone, which is interlaced with the uppermost coal seams.

The ironstone was made into pig-iron, and Mr Walter Sneyd of Silverdale was the first to achieve this feat in the district, closely followed by Apedale Iron Works, Chesterton, in the late eighteenth century. Other furnaces followed across the district, which gradually started to sculpt the natural topography with mountainous slag mounds.

Many of these mounds sprung up around the iron works in Etruria, which was known loquaciously as 'Shelton Bar'. The work's first furnaces were constructed in 1839, on the north-east side of Cobridge Road, by the company's first chairman, Lord Granville. On 4 January 1841, the furnaces were 'blown in'. The site was then extended onto the west-side of Cobridge Road, into the Etruria Estate. Here, in 1850, on the banks of the canal, Granville started the construction of more blast furnaces, which were completed in 1852. Then, in 1864, puddling furnaces and rolling mills were constructed. The furnaces were later upgraded to open-heath steel furnaces, and the mills were augmented with the capacity to roll large steel sections in the latter part of the nineteenth century.

Warrillow, in his book *History of Etruria*, extensively covers the early industrialisation of this site in fascinating detail. Warrillow explains that Granville owned Shelton Colliery, too, and he amalgamated the two companies to form the Shelton Iron, Steel, and Coal Company Limited in 1891. Unfortunately, Granville had no influence beyond this amalgamation, because he became serious ill and died 31 March 1891, at 76 years of age. He was buried in his family's vault at Stone Parish Church. Granville was a public benefactor, so he was sorely missed in the district. He was also an advocate of education, for example, and he expressed this through the founding of Granville School, Cobridge, and Hanley's library in Pall Mall.

However, although Granville's works had grown as successfully as his reputation in the latter part of the nineteenth century, employment in the ironwork industry was problematic for the working class. Fluctuations in trade meant that in the early months of 1865 a general strike was called to challenge a proposed reduction in the workers' remuneration. Many ironworks across the Potteries were affected, such as Shelton Bar, Kidsgrove's puddling furnaces, and Ford Green's forges. But it was not long before many of the men wished to return to work, for they were only paid an unemployed rate of ten shillings per week.

Warrillow's *A Sociological History of the City of Stoke-on-Trent* explains that in the same year, in Longton, distressed colliers, forge workers, and potters, who were demanding financial assistance, had the Poor Law Amendment Act of 1834 clarified for them by the town's dignitaries. It was explained that the only relief for their situation was to appeal for public funding. Appeals were made, and the result was the implementation of soup kitchens across the six towns. These soup kitchens provided free meals for the workers and their families at public cost. Conditions were imposed, however, which meant that an adult's portion would be twice the size of a child's portion. In addition, a family would not be entitled to free meals if the household earnings amounted to two shillings per head, per week. Those in receipt of parish relief were also incrementally penalised.

Poverty for the forge workers and their families continued for many years. By 1895, Warrillow says that the poor of Hanley were relying not just on soup kitchens, but also the generosity of philanthropists, such as business owners, who often handed out free loaves of bread.

Men still worked on the forges, of course, but it was said that a man was struggling to make twenty shillings a week on average. This was, perhaps, due to the infrequency of work, for some forge hands were only required a few days per week; others, who were even more unfortunate, had not worked more than one week in ten. In many cases, this meant that families could not pay the rent and were being evicted. It was not uncommon for families with eight to ten children to have a household income of just ten shillings per week!

There was some attempt to provide other forms of work for the forge men and other working-class trades that were suffering. A labour yard, for instance, was setup on Trinity Street, Hanley, where men could work for about two shillings per diem. Warrillow says the work was typically cutting wood for the 'gentlemen' of the district. One gentleman, for example, had purchased 7 tons of railway sleepers from a railway company at a modest price, and then preceded to hire local workers to cut the wood into manageable bundles. The bundles could then be sold on by door-to-door salesman.

The difficulties between the working class and the stability of industry continued into the twentieth century, which resulted in another general strike in 1926. Warrillow explains that the strike was of such magnitude that *The Sentinel* was forced to cease publication for five days. Approximately 19,000 pottery workers ceased work. The strike for the pottery workers was short-lived, however, for they wished to return to work, but this proved difficult because the miners continued to strike which cut the vital supply of coal for the kilns. Such things had always been true in the Potteries, though, where the various industries were inextricably linked to, and relied on, each other.

Commerce was indirectly linked to the iron, coal, and pottery industries too. The opening hours of shops in the early nineteenth century, for instance, were set to accommodate the long-working hours of the industry workmen, which meant that some shops were open as late as 10.00pm. For this reason, many of the shops' proprietors 'lived in' – that is, their residence was often on the floor above the shop, so they could go downstairs to serve the odd customer in the quieter periods.

In most cases, however, the proprietor would hire a shop assistant to oversee the shop's business from open until close, which was often between 6.00am and 9.00pm, or even later, if necessary. In addition to serving customers, the shop assistant would thoroughly clean the shop, trim the lamps, and then, when necessary, fill them with oil. Warrillow's research shows that for younger assistants, it was considered good character-building to attend Sunday school, every Sunday; read good literature; and to donate one guinea a year to the church.

The employment of children in shops was, from a proprietor's perspective, adversely affected in 1903, when the Employment of Children Act 1903 set restrictions on the age and working times of children. In some trades, the employment of children was forbidden, such as in barber shops, where barbers used the inexpensive labour of young boys to lather the face of a customer, which would soften the coarse, facial hair in preparation for the tensorial proficiency of the barber. These boys were, rather uninspiringly, called 'lather boys'. Local barbers protested against the new legalisation.

One of the largest stores of the early twentieth century, according to Warrillow, was owned by Mr Michael Huntbach. It was a draper's shop, situated on Lamb Street, Hanley. The floors above the shop formed an extremely large resistance so that Huntbach's 20 to 30 assistants could 'live in'. In exchange, Huntbach insisted on the 'correctness' of his assistants' attire, which was typically pinned-striped trousers, a shirt and tie, and a luxurious black jacket. Huntbach, as the treasurer of the Bethesda Town Mission church, on Jasper Street, also impressed upon his assistants that they should accompany him to the church every Sunday morning for worship. It was said that the procession of Huntbach and his assistants on such mornings was impressive. The ostentatious nature of Huntbach's store, unfortunately, died with him; however, he and his firm are immortalised in Arnold Bennett's short story - *The Feud.*

Huntbach's shop assistants, like other shop assistants across the Potteries, toiled through long-working hours too. The unreasonable working hours were challenged as early as about 1842, when the Early Closing Association was formed. However, the association's attempts to reduce the opening hours of shops was met with much opposition throughout the latter part of the nineteenth century. By 1892, though, with the association's contributions, the Shop Hours Act 1892 gave powers to the local authorities to regulate the employment of shop assistants. This meant that, finally, the opening times of shops were curtailed. In the Potteries, as Warrillow says, the recommended closing times were 9.00pm on Mondays and Fridays; 8.00pm on Tuesdays and Wednesdays; 1.00pm on Thursdays; Saturdays were left to the proprietor's discretion; and on Sundays, trade should not take place, which was in accordance with the Lord's Day Observance Act. In addition, a shop assistant was permitted to work a maximum of 52 hours per week, with a one-hour lunchbreak, and a half-hour tea break per diem. In 1898, however, the adoption of this practice had somewhat waned, but it once again, steadily improved through additional legislative acts that have provided us with the comparatively ideal conditions that shop workers experience today.

XIII

Childhood

Both women and children assisted men in the pottery industry, but, in particular, the working conditions for children were appalling. In 1816, these conditions were somewhat better under Josiah Wedgwood II, who, in his factory in Etruria, tried to ameliorate the exploitation of employed children. Of course, Wedgwood probably had a humanitarian agenda, but it was also important for his business, for children made up about a third of his workforce, some as young as ten years old.

Typically, according to Warrillow's *A Sociological History of the City of Stoke-on-Trent*, children worked from 8.00am to 5.00pm, with a half-hour break for breakfast, and a one-hour break for lunch. Due to the lack of light, these hours were shortened during autumn and winter, except during the busy period from 11 November to 2 February. During this period, the working day was from 6.30am to 9.00pm, and it was conducted under candlelight in the darker hours. Candles typically cost half-a-pence each.

Josiah Wedgwood I recognised that children were not being properly educated because they started work so young and worked such long hours. To rectify this, he built a school next to his factory in Etruria, and made provisions for the children employed at his factory to attend. Wedgwood considered this to be so important that the incorporation of a school was a fundamental aspect of his plan for a new factory at Barlaston. When Josiah Wedgwood II inherited his father's estate, the benefits of educating the workforce were apparent to both parties.

Employed children elsewhere in the Potteries were at the mercy of men. Charles Shaw, from his own childhood experience, recalls such hardships in his book *When I was a Child*. In those days, Shaw says that factory owners paid men to conduct the main work, such as 'dipping' and 'piece work', and the children were paid by such men to be their assistants. There were no rules on how to manage young assistants, nor was the welfare of the children overseen by factory owners, so men were free to exploit children as they wished. Not all men exploited children, of course, but accounts of this evil were common.

The jobs of children were quite varied, with some employers not considering any child too young to turn a jigger, but the most common jobs were those that involved moving ware, such as mould-running. Mould-running was risky work, though, because children were often beaten for accidentally breaking the ware, which often left them with bruised backs.

Warrillow refers to a report in his research, which shows the statistics of children in employment and education in the year 1840-41, and he concludes that there had been little improvement since the first concerns were raised by the Wedgwood family. Children as young as five and six years of age were being employed in the pottery factories of Tunstall, Burslem, and Cobridge. On average, according to Warrillow, children formed one-eighth of the pottery factories' workforce. Typically, the children's working hours were 6.00am to 9.00pm. The children had to arrive early to light the fires in the hothouses for the men, and, all too often, the little workers would burn themselves. During the day, it was not uncommon for plate-makers to spend at least few hours in a public house, because their bosses would let them make up the hours later. This was a problem for children, however, who saw no use at that age to visit a public house, and therefore wasted many hours, waiting.

The long hours that children worked were not just exhausting and cruel, but they had serious health complications too. Warrillow refers to a study conducted by Dr John Thomas Arlidge of the North Staffordshire Royal Infirmary, who found many children to have scrofula, which he believed was linked to being overworked. Statistics from the time show that the death rate for those under 21 years of age was 65.5%. Of that figure, 52% were under five years of age. Of course, not all of these deaths could be attributed directly to a work-related disease, but it was believed that a significant proportion was. What can be sombrely deduced, however, is that the life expectancy at this time was certainly low.

The government did introduce legislation under the 1833 Factory Act to abolish such evils being inflicted on children, but many factories were slow to adhere to its new regulations, such as the prohibition of employing children under nine years of age. Therefore, in 1861, Parliament and Lord Shaftsbury, backed by public opinion, set about enforcing the act by appointing employment commissioners to investigate industries which were not regulating its labour in accordance with the law. This proved to be effective, especially in the chimney sweeping industry, where it was still commonplace for a child, petrified by fear, to get stuck in a chimney flue. In such instances, some employers committed the worst of evils. For example, rather than be caught employing a child, amoral employers would start a fire to 'encourage' the child to exit the flue. If an employer was caught engaging in such atrocious behaviour, they were handed a £5 fine.

Not all children worked in the pottery factories or swept chimneys. As you know from the former chapters of this book, some were employed in other industries and shops, but the very unfortunate, as some might say, were taken in by workhouses. This was typically because they were orphaned or deserted, for example, but whilst this saved them from a cruel life on the streets, it did not save them from all the cruelty in the world. In the mid-nineteenth century, for instance, the aforementioned Bastille workhouse treated children like prisoners. Warrillow says that new entries to the workhouse were taken to its large, bare cellar, before being washed in cold water, and then dressed in workhouse attire, which was usually a rough linen pinafore.

Warrillow does say that the children were offered an education, which was presided over by a schoolmaster. At meal times, the schoolmaster would sit with the children, but he would only partake by saying grace, for the children's food was awful. Some might have described it simply as a few lumps in greasy water. Supper was a hunk of bread, and a jug of skilly, which was meat and water without any seasoning, such as salt or sugar.

The bedrooms were long and narrow, with a row of beds along each of the longest walls. A communal bathtub was placed at the far end, but many children were too shy to use it.

Children, both then and now, are not infallible, but the punishments acted upon them in those days may be considered barbaric now. A child could be flogged with a salt-seasoned rod, for instance. Warrillow brings this grim vision to the fore: the flogger was usually assisted by older children who held the culprit prostrate across a table. The victim's clothes were stripped or torn to expose defenceless flesh. The flogger would then read out the child's misbehaviour before striking. The victim would struggle and scream as the salt-seasoned rod fell again and again, leaving red stripes in its wake. Blood often flowed, too.

Children were also victims to the illicit alcohol trade that pervaded the Potteries. In addition to public houses that never closed, it was not uncommon for men to acquire a barrel of beer to sell to children from their own cellars at home. This type of 'trade' was further exacerbated by the popularity of distilling whiskey at home. The alcohol distributed to children by these amateurs was so potent that imbibing just a small amount would ensure a child was dangerously intoxicated. In some instances, the potency of the whiskey was fatal to children. Warrillow names a perpetrator living in 1850 - John Shields, from Hanley - who was fined £30 for selling such a dangerous product.

Warrillow also goes on to state that these makeshift distilleries posed a danger to their operators, too, for, in February 1851, Robert Dunn's illicit distillery exploded in his home near The Black Horse, Hanley. Dunn sustained serious injuries from the explosion, and he painfully walked to the infirmary in Etruria, where he died.

In the late nineteenth century, finally, the welfare of children began to receive some serious and urgent attention. The introduction of the 1870 Education Act, for example, made it mandatory for children to attend school until the age of 11. Warrillow provides an interesting account of this change in attitude: from 1898, Miss Jermimah Lord, of Hanley, presented lectures which generated money to buy spectacles and shoes for poor children. Dr R Read was the initiator, who was the chairman of Hanley School Board at that time. It became known as the 'Hanley Boot and Spectacles Fund'. With this, by about 1913, a barefooted child was a seldom sight.

XIV

My Education

My brother Frank started school at the age of three-and-a-half. However, when I started school, in 1924, I was four years old. My school was St Paul's Church of England Junior School, which was situated on Shirley Street, Dalehall.

My first teacher was Miss Cotton. She was a medium-build, thirty-five-year-old lady, with auburn hair. I always remember learning to count in her class. When it was time to move into the next class, I remember Miss Cotton saying, 'When you children go into your next class under Miss Brown, I shall cry.'

I felt quite comfortable in Miss Brown's class, because she spoke to us in a very kind voice. I still remember her face and her silvery hair, which she had combed up. She was slightly taller than most, and not too thin. One day, Miss Brown said, 'Those who can sing a song, come forward.' Eager, I was out immediately. She smiled, then said, 'All right, sing.' I sang, 'Knees up, Mother Brown', twice through, although I replaced the word 'mother' with 'Mrs'. She laughed her head off at that. She then asked, 'Where did you hear that song?' I told her my father sometimes sang it to me. This might sound like odd behaviour; that is, for a student and teacher to get on, but there were no ruffians at school in those days - we all used to obey the teacher.

At six years of age, it was time for me to move into First Class, which was taken by Miss Lindop. She lived near the church at the bottom of Hall Street, Burslem. She was nice to speak to, so I did well in her class, and I was well-liked.

The last class I entered in that school was Standard I. The teacher was very young. She had a small face and dark hair. Her name was Miss Copland, and she could play the piano. In this class we had to stay at least half-hour longer than the infants, which meant that school was between 9.30am and 4.30pm. I did have a month off, though, because I got a pen stuck in my finger which went septic. During this year, our class also put on a Christmas concert for our parents. I remember a little girl called Miss Alcock, who was always chosen for the leading part in plays. Once, in a small play, she acted as a fairy, and, to be fair, in my imagination at least, she was every bit a fairy.

The headteacher was called Miss Brammer, who was about 35 years of age. She was of ordinary build, had light-brown hair, and wore rimless glasses that had no arms.

There were two girls that always stuck out in my mind, for throughout their school life they always sat and played together. They were Millicent James and Irene Beech, and they lived in St Paul's Street, Burslem. They were always clean and wore pretty frocks. I managed to persuade Irene to be my girlfriend, but this didn't last very long. Unfortunately, she had a very serious illness when she was about nine to ten years of age, and I didn't hear from her after that.

It was in Standard I that I discovered I was musical. It was about this time that my father taught me to play the mouth organ, too. One day, Standard I's music teacher gave us a lesson in tonic sol-fa which opened up my ears to music. I found I could play a tune on any instrument, as long as I found a scale on it.

In 1928, at eight years of age, I left Standard I, and I was marched along Ellgreave Street to St Paul's Middle School, near St Paul's Church, and into my first class called Standard II. My brother was already in attendance there, so I'd heard all about the canes that the teachers used, and I was already scared of them. In this way, I was, at first, learning under fear.

My first teacher was called Miss Clarkson. She was tall, with frizzy hair. She lived in Lindop Street. She taught us our times tables, and we had to recite them each afternoon. It used to tire me out, but I managed to learn all right, and it did stand me in good stead in the future. The headmaster was named Mr H Jennings. He succeeded Mr Cross, who died at 90 years of age in Ellgrave Street. Once, when I was very young, I remember seeing Mr Cross when he paid a visit to my infant school. He looked very old.

In 1929, I moved into Standard III. The teacher was Miss Copestick, who was rather corpulent, with dark hair that was always combed straight. She lived at the far end of Newport Lane, on the left-hand side of the road, about 200 yards past Middleport Park. During the twelve months I was in Miss Copestick's class, I had the cane about three times, which really did hurt. Despite this, Miss Copestick grew quite fond of me. She made me her monitor, and she bought me a suit for my new role. She gave it to me in private, and asked me not tell anyone in the school about it.

At nine years of age, I had a strong faith. I always believed God was by my side, so nothing could harm me. During a scripture lesson with Miss Copestick, for instance, she said that no one has seen Jesus. I immediately put my hand up and said, 'Please, Miss, I have.' She was astonished and called me out to explain myself. I then tried to explain my psychic happenings to her. You see, I used to go out in the dark at night, and, with having a religious background, I tried to see God whilst I prayed. In a dark street near my house, a gas streetlight cast some of its light on a wall, and, in this dim light, I could see a man in a white Eastern cloak. After this experience, I tried to go out in the dark every night to see this man. At the time, I thought the man was Jesus. In later years, however, I discovered I had been seeing a spirit guide of Eastern or Egyptian origin. After I told Miss Copestick about the vision on the wall, I told her I was a Salvationist, too, and so she began to have great faith in me.

One afternoon, when all the children had gone out to play, Miss Copestick invited me to have a cup of tea and a biscuit with all the teachers, so I could tell them all about The Salvation Army. She would call me to the front of the class to sing hymns. I knew a lot of hymns then.

In 1930, when I moved up to Standard IV, Miss Copestick took me to my new teacher, Miss Huntbach, who was noticeably younger than the other teachers. Her dark hair was styled into frizzy curls. She always sat with her back straight and recommended it. Miss Copestick told Miss Huntbach about my nice character. Following this, she made me her monitor, along with Frank Alcock, who became my friend. He was always at the top of the class in examinations, and I always came second. I could never beat him. He was very intelligent and a fast reader. He always dressed smart and clean, too.

During this school term, I also took a tin whistle to school, which Miss Huntbach allowed me to play. For our music and singing lessons, we used to go into Mr Griffiths' class for one afternoon per week. He was on the short side, a bit fat, and wore horn-rimmed glasses. Many times, he played the big organ in St Paul's Church. He was a Doctor of Music, and he had composed music many times. I liked his playing. He was also strict, however, but he still allowed me to play my tin whistle, because he knew I had a good ear for music.

Standard V was taught by Miss Clark, who was quite an elderly person. She lived in Vale View, Porthill. She made me her monitor for about half of the term, then she stripped me of the title, saying, 'Never mind what other teachers say. I don't think you are what they say you are. I'm picking who I want as my monitor.' She chose Charles Hewitt, who lived on Reid Street. I soon forgot about it. She didn't seem to be as merry as the other teachers, so we used to call her fatty Clarke. She taught us fractions and arithmetic, but she also used to take the girls for needlework every Tuesday afternoon. On those afternoons, Mr Miller, a tall man, took us for geometry but he often spoke to us about his experiences in the Great War instead. He lived in Hall Street, and we called him Daddie Miller outside school, because his son also attended our school. I wasn't much for Daddie Miller's lessons at the time, so I began to dodge Tuesday afternoons. The school got wise to this, so Mr Grocott, the School Board man, questioned me about it. I told him that I had a cold in my bladder, so my mother had to put warm fomentations on the lower part of my stomach. He was so confused that he let it go. I did see the light, however, and attended regularly after that.

One day, however, when Miss Clark had been trying to teach the girls how to make a woollen rug, she found that there wasn't a single girl who could get the hang of it. Miss Clarke gave up, and said, 'Is there a boy who would like to try?' Two or three boys did volunteer, but they also failed. She called every student who failed a 'jackass'. I decided to try, so I got up. She was relieved to discover that I could do needlework very well. This solved the Daddie Miller problem for me, because, every time Miss Clark took the girls for needle work and Mr Miller took the boys for geometry, I was permitted to remain with the girls, week after week, till I'd finished making a rug.

When I was almost 12 years of age, I should have moved into Standard VI, but a new law came out which prevented it. My school was now for children aged 8 to 11 years of age. From age 12, pupils had to attend Middleport Senior School until, at 14 years of age, it was time for them find a job. So, under these revisions, I was sent to Middleport Senior School. There, girls and boys were no longer mixed. Instead, all the girls were downstairs with female teachers and all the boys were upstairs with male teachers. I learned in later years that this policy of keeping boys away from girls was a load of tripe and harmful to certain growing adults in years to come. It created bad sex relations in later life. It certainly felt as though it did me harm. By not mixing with girls, I became shy, and

I never did any proper courting till I went in the army, and, even then, I had difficulty getting along with the opposite sex.

I was very anxious about going to Middleport Senior School. It was that blasted cane that was the big scare. If you couldn't get something right, you were probably for it. One lad had the cane just because he didn't know what league Stoke City Football Club was in. It was nothing to do with the lesson at all. However, I managed to go through all the classes in this school with only two strokes of the cane.

I started Middleport Senior School in Mr Cooper's class, which was AII. There were three classes at this stage: AII, BII, and CII, and you were assigned in accordance with your progress and intelligence. BII was the equivalent to Standard V, and CII was for, as I was told in those days, backwards children. I found AII rather advanced, and, because I didn't like this school, I did my best to fail the examination, so I would be moved down into an easier class. My plan worked, so I went down to BII class, which was taught by Mr Brown - a fat man, who wore horn-rimmed glasses.

Mr Brown was all right with me. He used to emphasise that I shouldn't stay away from school, especially to nurse the baby, because it was a mother's place to be at home for that job. Due to this, I went to school ill one day, but I had to be taken home, and I remained indisposed for a fortnight. Of course, Mr Brown and the headteacher, who was a real nice and considerate man, asked me why I came to school in such a condition. I explained that Mr Brown was always saying what would happen if I was absent. After I said this, Mr Brown and the headteacher went to my parents, and told them that their strict rules did not apply to sickness. Mr Brown said to me, 'For God's sake, Arthur, don't come school like that again.'

Mr Brown was always teaching about Africa. I learned from it, but it used to tire me out. He also taught me how to find the areas of circles and cones; about diameter, radius, and circumference. However, I wasn't keen on this at the time. I felt all my schooling there was merely a waste of time. I would have been happy to have moved up the steps of education at St Paul's, and I would have left school a very educated youth. I was eager to learn all I could there, and I was always near the top of the class.

At 13 years of age, I moved into my penultimate class which was BI. This class was taught by Mr Redfern. He was young, tall, and dark. He was also a very strong and a fast swimmer, so he took us to Burslem Baths on Moorland Road, one morning each week, to give us a swimming demonstration. In this way, because Mr Redfern didn't teach us to swim, I didn't learn that skill until I joined the army.

As part of BI, we also went to a woodwork class, which was held at Central School, on Moorland Road. The class started at 10.00am, so on those days schooling was half an hour shorter. In the afternoon, of course, we had to turn up at Middleport Senior School, as usual. Mr Redfern was always pretty easy with us, although he did use a cane.

One day, many students in my class began to shout and make a tumultuous racket until Mr Redfern gave up. When he did, he left us alone for about half an hour. The headmaster looked in, too, but walked out again. The noise eventually died away. I felt so sorry for him. I always remember him saying, 'The best way to learn is to read plenty of books.' After some years, I put this advice into practice. I now have a book on every subject under the sun, and I learn many interesting things from them. I feel no matter how old we get learning goes on and on till we leave this world and finally cease to think. Others, however, think that because all we learn in this world is taken away at death, learning is a waste of time. As my children say, for instance, 'Why do you keep on learning at your age? All that knowledge is no good to you at old age - after all, you will just finish up in a wooden box to be forgotten about.' But that is what they say. I have better ways, and my thoughts are totally different.

My final class, then, was AI, which was for all the students who were 14 years of age. Mr Chadwick taught this class, and he taught all of that age alike, whether they were good, bad, backward or intelligent. He moved me up into the section for intelligent boys, claiming that I should never have gone down into the lower groups. He tried to teach me algebra, but I could never take to it. I preferred sums with ordinary figures, so I asked him if he would let me forgo algebra, and he fulfilled my request.

Later on, he found out that I was a competent gardener, so he took me to his new house in Wolstanton, along with another boy named Leonard Wain, who lived in Reid Street. At Mr Chadwick's house, we did his gardening, and he gave us one shilling and sixpence each for doing so, which made me feel rich.

Mr Chadwick seemed to like me, but I didn't care too much for him, and I was also made a little bit nervous by the threat of his cane. He was very strict, and the hardest caning teacher of all. He always boasted how hard he could cane a fellow, and it wasn't long before we learned this lesson. It was about two months before we left school, early in 1934. A boy kept leaving the classroom to have his inkwell filled, which, as it was later discovered, was because he kept putting a chemical in the inkwell to rapidly evaporate the ink. Mr Chadwick wrote something in a book, and then called the boy to the front of the classroom. Mr Chadwick took his cane, and said, 'Right, Fuller, you know I cane the hardest in the school, which you will experience now. Get your hand up!' He took one big swipe down, and we heard the whistle of his cane. My heart missed a beat as the cane struck his hand. Fuller folded over in pain. His face suddenly changed to a red colour, then a bluish red. Mr Chadwick then said, 'Right! Now the other.' It was many a while before he could get him put his other hand out, for, at first, Fuller refused. So, Mr Chadwick got hold of him and began cracking him across the buttocks. The boy screamed out, 'No! All right! I'll hold my hand out.' And, so, Fuller finished having two strokes on each hand. I fainted for him. Everyone in the class was shocked at the results, so I never liked Mr Chadwick after that. I always held at the back of my mind, *that boy, who Mr. Chadwick unfairly caned.* Mr Chadwick sensed my thoughts on this when I became cold in conversation with him. He once asked me about The Salvation Army, but I only told him enough to be polite. I said, 'They have two brass bands, a junior one for boys, and a senior one for men, but most of the musicians had left, so there was only a small band of about six players.' The remark was hardly enough to make any real impression.

Anyway, Fuller's punishment had upset him so

much that he told Mr Chadwick he wouldn't come to school any more. In response, Mr Chadwick threatened to summon Fuller's parents, and followed-up by saying, 'When you go home for dinner, be back! or else.' If it had been me, I'm sure my father would have murdered him, for I had seen my father fight many times after a drink of beer. Fuller did return from his home in Trubshaw Cross, near Longport, after his lunchbreak, but he never looked at Chadders, as we called him in secret. So Chadders went to him and asked if he had eaten any dinner. The boy replied, 'No,' in a low voice. Chadders then offered him a bun. Of course, Fuller was a bit reluctant to take it at first, but finally he decided to eat it. All this then blew over, as though it were an afterthought, but I met Fuller in the army when war broke out. I asked him, 'Do you remember that day when Chadders caned you.' He said, 'Yes.' So, I said, 'It wasn't fair to cane you that much, although you had done wrong. It was only a childish trick.' I also explained how sorrowful I was that Chadders would always be a hated man with me. I told my parents how unfair the caning was.

There was one good memory from my final year. Mr Griffiths of St Paul's was transferred to Middleport Senior School to teach the music classes. One day, I was sent to his class to fetch something for another teacher. As I approached, I overheard him saying to the students, 'Do not put your head in the music, put the music in your head.' They repeated this several times as I entered the class, for I was after the headteacher to get my free dinner tickets. That moment was more important than free dinner tickets, however, for it had sparked the musical side of my life. I remembered Mr Griffiths' expression for years and years - all throughout my manhood. I always tried to implement the rule. I made it my business to find out everything I could about music. I taught myself everything I possibly could. I never had a music lesson in my life, save for the musical knowledge I picked up at school and in The Salvation Army. I now know all the scales, all the cords, tonic Sol-fa etc. I can read music, too, but my reading is not fast enough to play a sheet of unfamiliar music on the piano. I have always been congratulated on my musical ability.

As for the free school dinners, it was a recently introduced experiment. I was one of the first boys to ever get them, which shortly became two. We collected our dinners from Mrs Bews, who was a very good and kind cook. She was related to Mr Bews of the wireless shop in the main part of the town. After some time, more students joined the two of us, and it became quite a crowd.

It was soon 12.30pm, on 29 March 1934. We were called out, in turn, to receive our learning certificates. On mine, Mr Chadwick wrote, 'A good, steady worker.' I left school that dinner time happy as it were. It was a load of worry off my shoulders. *No more sitting and learning in fear*, I thought. But was it a load off my shoulders? I walked straight to Ellgreave Pottery, Dalehall, which was something I've always regretted. I was told getting a job was being a 'good boy', but now I know it was foolish, but other opportunities weren't available in those days, I guess. Work was either found on pot-banks or digging for coal in the pits. This was my fate in life: plenty of hard work, with very little wages to show for it, and a major risk of developing an industrial illness. Like an idiot, I gave my learning certificate in at the office, thinking they'd take notice of it. But what did they care? They were just waiting for anyone, dunce or clever, to work themselves to a standstill. Whether you were a dunce or held GCEs, you all got the same job, which was mould-running. Once I took this job, my parents wouldn't let me get out of it, even though they knew it was killing me. I begged my mother to get me off the job, but she said there were no other jobs. I never felt like eating my meals while I worked there, so I soon lost weight. I saw Mrs Bews again, after I had been working a few months, and she said, 'I can see that you've lost a lot of weight. I feel so sorry for you.' She was nearly crying, then asked, 'What have they done to you?' I didn't reply, so she said, 'Do you like your job?' I told her, 'Like hell I did - I haven't got a minute to breath.'

Bibliography

Caesar, *The Conquest of Gaul*, trans. S. A. Handford (1951), London, Penguin Group.

Malkin, N. (1976) *A Grand Tour: A Personal View of the Potteries*, Madeley Heath, Ironmarket Press.

Meteyard, E. (1865) *The Life of Josiah Wedgwood, Vol. I*, London, Hurst and Blackett.

Meteyard, E. (1865) *The Life of Josiah Wedgwood, Vol. II*, London, Hurst and Blackett.

Owen, H. (1970) *The Staffordshire Potter*, Trowbridge & London, Redwood Press Limited.

Shaw, C. (1977) *When I Was a Child*, Hampstead, London, Caliban Books.

Ward, J (1843) *The Borough of Stoke-upon-Trent*, London, W. Lewis and Son.

Warrillow, E. J. D. (1977) *A Sociological History of the City of Stoke-on-Trent*, Newcastle-under-Lyme, The Ironmarket Press.

Warrillow, E. J. D. (1953) *History of Etruria, Staffordshire, England, 1760-1951*, Stoke-on-Trent, Etruscan Publication

Printed in Great Britain
by Amazon

40204066R00079